Joseph Irving

Supplement to The Annals of our Time

A Diurnal of Events, Social and Political, Home and Foreign - from February 28,

1871 to March 19, 1874

Joseph Irving

Supplement to The Annals of our Time
A Diurnal of Events, Social and Political, Home and Foreign - from February 28, 1871 to March 19, 1874

ISBN/EAN: 9783337129118

Printed in Europe, USA, Canada, Australia, Japan

Cover: Foto ©Andreas Hilbeck / pixelio.de

More available books at **www.hansebooks.com**

SUPPLEMENT

TO THE

ANNALS OF OUR TIME:

A DIURNAL OF EVENTS,

SOCIAL AND POLITICAL, HOME AND FOREIGN,

FROM FEBRUARY 28, 1871 to MARCH 19, 1874.

BY

JOSEPH IRVING.

London:

MACMILLAN AND CO.

1875.

TABLE OF ADMINISTRATIONS.

	Gladstone Ministry, 1868.	Feb. 1874.
First Lord of Treasury	W. E. GLADSTONE, Esq.	B. DISRAELI, ESQ.
Lord Chancellor	Lord Hatherley / Lord Selborne	Lord Cairns
Lord President of Council	Earl De Grey / Lord Aberdare	Duke of Richmond
Lord Privy Seal	Earl of Kimberley / Viscount Halifax	Earl of Malmesbury
Chancellor of the Exchequer	Robert Lowe, Esq. / W. E. Gladstone, Esq.	Sir S. Northcote
Home Secretary	H. A. Bruce, Esq. / Robert Lowe, Esq.	R. A. Cross, Esq.
Foreign Secretary	Earl of Clarendon / Earl Granville	Earl Derby
Colonial Secretary	Earl Granville / Earl of Kimberley	Earl Carnarvon
Secretary-at-War	—	
War Secretary	Edward Cardwell, Esq.	Gathorne Hardy, Esq.
Board of Control (India)		
Indian Secretary	Duke of Argyll	Marquis of Salisbury
Board of Trade	John Bright, Esq. (res.) / Ch. Fortescue, Esq.	Sir C. Adderley
Duchy of Lancaster	Lord Dufferin / John Bright, Esq.	Colonel Taylor
Postmaster-General	Marquis of Hartington / W. Monsell, Esq.	Lord John Manners
First Lord of Admiralty	H. C. E. Childers, Esq. / G. J. Göschen, Esq.	G. Ward Hunt, Esq.
Lord-Lieutenant of Ireland	Earl Spencer	Duke of Abercorn
Chief Secretary of Ireland	C. H. Fortescue, Esq, / Marquis of Hartington	Sir M. H. Beach
Woods and Forests (Public Works)	A. H. Layard, Esq. / A. S. Ayrton, Esq.	Lord H. Lennox
Vice-President of Board of Trade	W. H. Gladstone, Esq.	G. C. Bentinck, Esq.
Attorney-General	Sir R. P. Collier / Sir H. James	Sir R. Baggallay
Solicitor-General	Sir J. D. Coleridge / Sir James Jessell / Sir W. V. Harcourt	Sir J. Holker
Lord Advocate of Scotland	J. Moncreiff, Esq, / Geo. Young, Esq.	E. S. Gordon, Esq.
Majorities determining the fate of above Ministries.	Ministerial Majority. Irish Church Bill (third reading). For . . . . . . 361 Against . . . . . 247 Majority . . . . . 114 (See May 31, 1869, p. 872.) Resigned Feb. 1874.	

ANNALS OF OUR TIME.

Feb. 24.—Earl Granville, on the part of her Majesty's Government, endeavours to obtain some modification in favour of France of the war indemnity of six milliards of francs said to be demanded by Prussia. Government, he wrote, felt the difficulties which arise from their ignorance of the offers made on the side of France, and they bear in mind that this country is one only among the neutral powers, all bound by the obligations of friendship to both parties. "But her Majesty's Government are willing, in consideration of the extreme pressure of time, to make representations to Germany on the amount of this indemnity, and to tender their good offices in the spirit of friendship to both parties, under the conviction that it is the interest of Germany, as well as of France, that the amount of the indemnity should not be greater than that which it is reasonable to expect could be paid."   .

— Invasions of Looshai tribes into the tea districts of Cachar and Sylhet, North-east India, leading to the despatch of a combined party of British and native troops to recover a young girl named Winchester, who had been carried off after the murder of her father.

26.—Some remarks in the way of censure having been made in Parliament regarding the manner of the withdrawal of the British ambassador from Paris in September last, Lord Lyons writes to-day from Bordeaux :—"I conceived at the time that it was my duty neither to reject the advice of the French Minister for Foreign Affairs, nor to separate myself from my principal colleagues, and I thought it would be on all accounts inexpedient for me to allow myself to be shut up in Paris and to be deprived of all speedy and satisfactory means of communicating with your lordship. My subsequent experience has, I confess, confirmed me in these opinions. On the day after I left Paris, all communication by road with that place was intercepted, and on the following day the last telegraphic wire was cut. The diplomatists who were left in the besieged city were refused by the German authorities positively all facilities for corresponding with their Governments otherwise than by letters left open for the inspection of those authorities. My having resided at the seat of the Delegation of the Government at Tours, and having followed them to Bordeaux, have been accepted by the French as manifest proofs of the desire of her Majesty's Government to maintain intimate and friendly relations with them, while my doing so has afforded her Majesty's Government the readiest and most effectual means of maintaining such relations in fact."

26.—A person understood to be a police spy, engaged in watching the National Guards defiling in front of the Column of July, seized by a mob of infuriated Republicans, and, after being subjected for hours to a series of gross outrages, is at last bound hand and foot and thrown into the Seine.

27.—Proclamation signed by Thiers and Picard posted in Paris, urging the inhabitants to accept even the hard terms of peace imposed by the Germans as the only means of saving France. During six days, it was said, the negotiators fought foot by foot, and did what was humanly possible to obtain the most favourable conditions. "If the Convention be not respected the armistice will be broken, and the enemy, already masters of the forts, will occupy in strong force the entire city. Private property, the works of art, and the public monuments are guaranteed to-day ; but should the Convention cease to be in force misfortune will await the whole of France. The fearful ravages of war, which hitherto have not extended beyond the Loire, will then extend to the Pyrenees. It is absolutely true to say that the safety of Paris affects the whole of France. Do not imitate the fault of those who did not wish us to believe, eight months ago, that the war would be so fatal. The French army, which defended Paris with so much courage, will occupy the left of the Seine and ensure the loyal execution of the new armistice. The National Guard will undertake to maintain order in the rest of the city, as good and honoured citizens, who have shown themselves to be brave in the face of the enemy, and this cruel situation will end in peace and the return of public prosperity."

28.—Treaty of Commerce between Spain and Sweden and Norway signed.

— The American House of Representatives pass a bill repealing the duty on coal.

— News from Paris indicate great uneasiness regarding the entry of the German troops and some necessary precautions were taken for avoiding a street conflict. In the afternoon the statues in the Place de la Concorde were veiled with thick crape, though "Strasburg" was still permitted to retain the flags and immortelles with which it had been bedizened for months past. By midnight the streets were reported to be unusually clear, a result partially accomplished by the closing of the theatres and *cafés*.

— The first Act of the Session, authorising an annuity of 6,000*l.* to her Royal Highness the Princess Louise, receives the Royal assent.

1

B

March 1.—This (Wednesday) torenoon the German army, to the number of 30,000, commence to enter Paris. The first Uhlan made his appearance at the Arc de Triomphe about nine o'clock. He was soon followed by other Uhlans, and then by the main body of the occupying troops, the 6th and 11th Prussian Corps, with about 11,000 Bavarians, which had previously been reviewed by the Emperor at Longchamps. Not being able to pass under the arch, they turned down the Avenue des Champs Elysées, and proceeded in the direction of the Place de la Concorde, their bands meanwhile sounding out the ever-popular "Wacht am Rhein." The Duke of Coburg, General Blumenthal, and their respective staffs, rode in at the head of the troops, followed by a squadron of Bavarian Hussars, with bright pennons of blue and white silk. Following these, and evidently in honour of Bavaria, came two batteries of Bavarian artillery, and then rifles and infantry. There (writes the *Times* correspondent) was the "Leib Regiment," with its shattered companies only a quarter of their original strength, and their flag hanging in ribbons from the stump of a broken staff. As they marched past the closed arch an officer's horse slipped and fell, and a crowd pressed round the dismounted rider. Instantly a comrade rode to his assistance amid the hisses of on-lookers ; one man was ridden over, and two or three horsemen charged along the pavement. This had the effect of scattering the mob, and from that moment they looked on in profound and respectful silence. For an hour and a half did the incessant stream of Bavarians continue, with here and there an interval occupied by some general and his staff. Then came the Grand Duke of Mecklenburg. Bismarck himself, smoking a cigar, rode suddenly up, looked on the scene for a few minutes without going beyond the crest of the hill, and then turned away in the direction of Versailles, whither the Emperor and Crown Prince had retired after the review in the morning.

— Lord Lurgan's famous greyhound, Master M'Grath, shown to the Queen at Windsor, and afterwards to various members of the Court circle.

— Came on at the Central Criminal Court before the Recorder, the trial of Martha Torney, aged 28, described as a married woman, charged as an accomplice in the robbery of jewels belonging to W. H. Ryder (see Jan. 12, 1871, p. 973). The shopman, Parkes, detailed his experience within the house in Upper Berkeley Street, into which he was admitted by a man describing himself as Tyrell, but now known to be Torpey. He took, he said, some of the jewellery out of a bag, and stated the prices of the different articles. He there saw the prisoner sitting at the fire. Witness stood at one side of the table, and the man on the other. When some of the articles were exa-

mined, the man suggested that the prisoner should go and call her sister. She went out of the room. When she returned she placed a handkerchief over his face, and the man immediately rushed at him and held his arms. He struggled, but the man continued holding him, and the prisoner pressing the handkerchief over his face. This lasted some minutes. He was then forced backwards on to a sofa. When he came to himself he found himself tightly strapped. The man Tyrell was standing over him, and said, "If you move I will murder you." Witness asked him to loosen the strap over his breast, and he did so. Witness attempted to get up to a sitting position and look at the table, but Tyrell forced him down, and put a handkerchief over his eyes. He afterwards heard the front door slam. He succeeded in loosening the straps on his wrist, and broke a pane of glass in the window, and gave an alarm. All the jewellery on the table was gone, with the exception of a small gold chain. The jury acquitted the prisoner on the charge of robbery with violence, and also on a second charge for assault, on the ground that she had acted under her husband's coercion.

1.—Died at Edinburgh, John Carmichael, M.A., Senior Classical Master in the High School.

— The Burials Bill, permitting Dissenters to bury in parish churchyards with their own rites, or no rites, read a second time in the Commons by 211 to 149 votes.

— The London School Board, by a majority of 41 to 3, reject a proposal for teaching the Bible without religious note or comment in schools under their management. Lord Sandon protested against the startling notions and new religion Professor Huxley had formerly brought before the Board, to which the Professor replied by reminding his lordship that as Keats was reported to have been justly killed by an article, so "any faith which can be killed by human effort ought to be so killed."

— Died at Bordeaux, M. Kuss, Mayor of Strasburg and Deputy for the Bas-Rhin.

2.—Bank of England rate of discount raised from 2½ to 3 per cent. The comparative quiet prevailing at Paris combined with the acceptance by the Assembly of the preliminaries of peace, caused the Stock Market to maintain a firm appearance, and even before business hours the French loan had been run up over 1 per cent.

— Describing the desolate condition of Paris, the *Journal Officiel* records: "The Bourse and all the shops are closed. Paris has voluntarily suspended her life, and feels the responsibility weighing upon her in such a painful moment, that it becomes her not to add to the misfortunes she has already to bear others more terrible that might be irreparable. After having heroically endured famine and miseries, Paris is capable of a still greater courage." Other journals appeared with black borders. To-day the German soldiers, in large numbers, visited the Louvre, Carrousel and other places of public resort, the populace, as a rule, looking on with sorrow and resignation. The "Red" leaders still maintained their cannon and barricades in the Belleville, St. Martin, and Temple districts.

2.—Writing to Cardinal Patrizi, Dean of the College of Jesuits and Vicar-General of the Holy See, the Pope explains the nature of his connection with the Jesuits, and defends the order against attacks made on it by "the invaders of our secular dominions." "We often apply to the Fathers of the Company of Jesus and entrust them with various interests, more especially those appertaining to the holy ministry ; and they have continually shown more and more of that laudable affection and zeal in their fulfilment, for which our predecessors often had occasion to praise them largely. But this most just attachment and esteem which we entertain for this order—so well-merited from the Church of Christ, the Holy See, and the Christian community in general—is far from the abject servility attributed to us by the scoffers, whose calumny we disdainfully reject from us, as well as from the humble devotion of the Fathers."

— Explosion in the Victoria Pit, Ebbw Vale, Monmouthshire, causing the death of 19 out of 30 persons in the works at the time.

— In the Commons to-day the sitting was chiefly occupied with a debate on the Government proposal for a Select Committee to inquire into the present disturbed condition of Westmeath, Sir Robert Peel, Mr. Osborne, and others, taunting ministers for seeking to obstruct free inquiry. On a division the Committee was carried by 256 to 175 votes.

— Explosion of the powder arsenal at Morges, causing the death of twenty soldiers engaged at the time in withdrawing bullets from the French cartridges.

3.—The German soldiers begin to leave Paris on their march homeward, Count Bismarck having obtained from Jules Favre, in the forenoon, official intimation of the Treaty being ratified by the Bordeaux Assembly. The Emperor telegraphed from Versailles to Berlin :—" I have just ratified the conclusion of peace, it having been accepted yesterday by the National Assembly in Bordeaux. Thus far is the great work complete, which by seven months' victorious battles has been achieved, thanks to the valour, devotion, and endurance of our incomparable army in all its parts, and the willing sacrifices of the whole Fatherland. The Lord of Hosts has everywhere visibly blessed our enterprises, and therefore by His mercy has permitted this honourable peace to be achieved. To Him be the honour ; to the army and the Fatherland I render thanks from a heart deeply moved." This telegram was publicly read at Berlin amid salvoes of artillery

and peals from the church bells. The city was illuminated and an enthusiastic reception given to the Empress and Princesses.

3.—Acting under the advice of his medical adviser, Mr. Childers retires from the Admiralty and is succeeded by Mr. Goschen. Mr. Stansfeld afterwards succeeded to the Poor Law Board, and Mr. Baxter became Secretary to the Treasury.

— Destructive earthquake at Tanglandang Island, one of the Sanguir group in the Malay Archipelago, the sea rising to a great height and sweeping hundreds of the inhabitants off the streets and plantations on the coast.

4.—Commenced in the Commons, a debate on the proposal for a second reading of the Army Regulation Bill, Col. Lindsay moving that the expenditure necessary for the National Defences did not at present justify any vote of public money for the extinction of purchase.

— Died at Haverstock Hill, aged 98, Lewis Doxat, connected with the *Morning Chronicle* in the early part of this century, and for fifty years editor of the *Observer*.

6.—The Pope congratulates the Emperor of Germany on the assumption of the Imperial dignity as an event likely to be beneficial to all Europe. "We return your Majesty, however, special thanks for the expression of your friendship for us, as we may hope that it will not inconsiderably contribute to the protection of the liberty and the rights of the Catholic religion. On the other hand, we request your Majesty to be convinced that we shall neglect nothing by which, when the opportunity presents itself, we may be useful to your Majesty."

— The ex-Emperor writes from Wilhelmshöhe, protesting against the deposition of his dynasty as unjust and illegal—"Unjust, because, when war was declared, the feeling of the nation, roused by causes independent of my wish, produced a general and irresistible enthusiasm ; illegal, because the Assembly, elected for the sole object of concluding a peace, has exceeded its powers in dealing with questions beyond its competence, and because, even were it a Constituent Assembly, it would have no power to substitute its own will for that of the nation. The example of the past confirms this. The opposition of the Constituent Assembly, in 1848, yielded to the elections of the 10th of December, and in 1851 the nation, by upwards of seven millions of votes, supported me against the Legislative Assembly. Political feeling cannot overcome right, and in France the basis of all legitimate government is the plébiscite. Beyond it there is only usurpation by some for the oppression of the rest. I am ready, therefore, to submit to the free expression of the national will, but to it only. In the presence of lamentable events, which impose on everyone self-denial and disinterestedness, I could have desired to remain silent, but the declarations of the Assembly compel me to protest in the name of truth disregarded and national rights despised."

6.—First bankruptcy trial by jury under the new Act—Emanuel, jewellers, *v.* Talbot. Verdict for plaintiff by consent.

— The Marquis of Salisbury introduces, but withdraws, after debate, a motion regarding the foreign guarantees of the British Government, and the deficiency of the naval and military forces of the country. What other people thought of us, he said, was shown by the conduct of Russia, Prussia, and the United States, the first of whom tore up a treaty in our face, the second concluded a peace on indefensible terms and in contempt of our views, while the third openly received and honoured those whom we had cast out as rebels. To maintain guarantees extending over Europe and even into other hemispheres, we had only a small army and a fleet, which, since the Declaration of Paris, was valueless except for the defence of our own shores.—Earl Granville maintained that our armaments were sufficient to support our policy, and that at no time had the influence of this country in Continental politics been greater.

— Public intimation given of the sale to Government, for 70,000*l.*, of Sir Robert Peel's fine collection of paintings by old masters, including the well-known "Chapeau de Paille," and the finest Holbein in existence. They were soon afterwards arranged and hung upon the walls of the National Gallery.

—Died, aged 45, Henry Blackett, head of the publishing firm of Hurst and Blackett.

7.—In reply to Mr. Disraeli, Mr. Gladstone states that Government had not been informed of any treaty negotiated last year between Prussia and Russia regarding the late war, and consequently Mr. Odo Russell had received no instructions on the point when sent to Versailles. Replying in similar terms to Lord Carnarvon on the 9th, Earl Granville ventured to ask, in return, if her Majesty's Opposition had any knowledge of the treaty in question.

— The freehold of White's Club House, St. James's Street, sold at the Auction Mart for 46,000*l.*

8.—The condition of Paris reported to be uneasy and threatening, the streets crowded with men in uniform, and the heights of Montmartre still in possession of the disaffected portion of the National Guard, with guns disposed so that they commanded the whole city. "The insurgents may at any moment drop a shell in the Tuileries, the Hôtel de Ville, the Palais Royal, or any of the crowded boulevards. The respectable portion of the press and the people begin to cry aloud for the subversion of the Government of Montmartre. Troops of the line are pouring into Paris ; but the party of order does not trust them—the party of disorder does not fear them. Some soldiers are already to be seen at Montmartre fraternizing."

8.—A report on the elections in Algeria submitted to the National Assembly. Gambetta, Andrien, and Colas were declared duly elected ; but with respect to the fourth, General Garibaldi, the reporter proposed that, as he had already given in his resignation, a fresh election should take place. Suddenly a member rose and exclaimed that Garibaldi had no right to sit in a French Assembly, a declaration which brought M. Victor Hugo to his feet, exclaiming "that when all Europe had abandoned France, one man came forward ; but he was a power in himself. He came and fought, and was the only general who was not conquered." This speech encountered the loudest interruptions, and the tumult was such that Victor Hugo in vain endeavoured to obtain a further hearing. At length he exclaimed : " Three weeks ago you refused to listen to Garibaldi ; you now refuse to listen to me. I give in my resignation." Frantic applause on the Left followed this declaration, and Victor Hugo proceeded to confirm his words in writing.

— The monitor ship *Glatton,* commenced in 1868, from designs by Mr. Reed, undocked at Chatham, Miss Scott, daughter of the Dean of Rochester, performing the christening.

9.—Russian Five per Cent. Loan of 12,000,000*l.* issued at about 80¾ net. It was attempted to raise a popular feeling against this loan, but much more than the amount required was subscribed. A protest circulated on the Stock Exchange gave the following reasons for objecting to the loan :—1. The Conference is now sitting in London to consider the conduct of Russia in the matter of the Treaty of 1856. 2. The question raised by Prince Gortschakoff was, in the opinion of her Majesty's envoy, Mr. Odo Russell, of a nature in its present state to compel us, with or without allies, to go to war with Russia. 3. Under these circumstances, as good citizens and loyal subjects of our Queen, we consider that to supply Russia with means which might be used for aggressive purposes is most unpatriotic, and until the Conference has concluded its sittings in every way to be condemned.

— A party of French sailors excite a disturbance at the Column of July by fastening a tri-coloured flag round the statue of Liberty on the top.

— Riotous proceedings at Zurich, originating in a meeting held by Germans in the Town-hall to celebrate the restoration of peace.

10.—The National Assembly, by a majority of 461 to 104 votes, resolve to remove from Bordeaux to Versailles. Speaking of the situation of Paris in the debate which preceded the division, M. Thiers said the action of a certain part of the population did not originally amount to anything culpable, because it was directed against the Prussians. It had, how-

4

ever, degenerated into a culpable and factious attitude, but the Government hoped to be able to bring back the deluded people, and to avoid civil war. " As regards myself and my colleagues," said M. Thiers, "we are all of one mind. If the peace should be disturbed, you may count on our patriotism to repress disturbances with the utmost energy. We shall never fail in this, but let us hope that this extremity, which has been momentarily feared in France, will be finally avoided. If we can avoid the shedding of blood, we shall consider it an honour to have done so."

10.—Gustave Flourens and M. Duvorne sentenced to death by a council of war for taking part in the riots of Oct. 31.

11.—The *Sun* newspaper, established in 1792, discontinued.

— Holker Hall, near Ulverstone, a seat of the Duke of Devonshire, nearly destroyed by fire.

—The American Senate confirms the removal of Mr. Sumner from the chairmanship of the Foreign Affairs Committee.

— Fire at Tooting, causing the death of an aged couple, Mr. and Mrs. Binfield, who were found suffocated in their room.

13.—Died, aged 70, Madame Bonaparte-Wyse, widow of Sir Thomas Wyse, and daughter of Lucien Bonaparte.

— The Black Sea Conference terminates its labours by agreeing to a treaty abrogating the restrictions imposed in 1856, and permitting the Porte to receive ships of war of friendly and allied Powers, in case the Porte should deem it necessary to do so in order to ensure the execution of the stipulation of the Treaty of Paris. The treaty also provided for the prolongation of the European Commission of the Danube for twelve years, for the continual neutrality of the works already created or to be created by the Commission, and reserved the right of the Porte as a territorial Power to send ships of war into the Danube.

14.—Trades Union Bill read a second time.

16.—Died, at St. Andrew's, aged 38, Dr. M'Gill, Professor of Hebrew in the University of St. Andrew's, and a member of the Bible Revision Committee.

17.—After a debate extending over five nights, the Army Regulation Bill is read a second time.

— The Emperor William arrives at Berlin, and is received with great rejoicings.

— Mr. J. A. Froude, the new Rector of St. Andrew's University, addresses the students on the subject of " Calvinism."

— Died, at St. Andrew's, aged 69, Robert Chambers, LL. D., author and publisher.

17.—Earthquake shocks experienced in Yorkshire, Lancashire, and Durham.

18.—Revolutionary outbreak in Paris. Early this morning a Government proclamation was issued, announcing that, after having given to the disturbers of public tranquillity time to return to duty and obedience, seeing that no attention was paid to counsels and injunctions, they were now determined to act in the interests of the city and of France. " Those culpable individuals who have pretended to institute a Government of their own are about to be given up to justice. Your cannons are about to be returned to the arsenals, and to execute this urgent act of justice and reason the Government counts on your assistance." To carry out this determination strong detachments of troops, under the command of Generals Vinoy and Lecomte, were marched in the direction of Montmartre. The artillerymen of the troops mounted the hill, armed with their muskets, and engaged in parley with the officers in command, who made no opposition to the cannon being taken away. Meantime, the *rappel* sounded through the neighbourhood, and brought out great numbers of disaffected National Guards. Rushing upon the cannon, they were received with shots, when some of the Guards and a woman and child fell. After this words were exchanged between the National Guards and the soldiers, the ranks broke up, and they went off to fraternise and drink together. The 88th regiment joining the insurgents, seduced other troops of the line, and all together made an attack on the *gendarmerie* posted on the Place Pigal. The officer in command here drew his sword, and ordered his men to fire, but he was shot down, and his detachment thereupon withdrew. In a state of wild agitation the insurgents, now complete masters of the *butte* Montmartre, rushed upon General Lecomte, whom Vinoy, Military Governor of Paris, had placed in command of the faithless 88th regiment. He was led, amid circumstances of gross indignity, to the Rue des Rosiers, where he was joined, later in the day, by General Clément Thomas, who had ventured there, in plain clothes, to look after his comrade. These two generals were shot in a small garden adjoining the place of detention without trial, not, so far as could be learned, by the National Guard, but by infuriated soldiers, aided by some Mobiles who bore a grudge against General Thomas on account of the severity of his discipline during the siege. It was afterwards said that at the last moment General Lecomte, till then dignified and resolute, felt his courage fail. He tried to struggle, to fly, he ran several steps in the garden; then, instantly retaken, shaken, dragged, hustled, he fell on his knees and spoke of his children. " I have five !" said he, sobbing. The father's heart burst through the soldier's tunic. There were fathers in that crowd, and some voices replied with emotion to this heart-stirring appeal; but the implacable linesmen would not hear a word.

"If we do not shoot him to-day, he will have us shot to-morrow." He was pushed against the wall. A sergeant of the line almost immediately advanced towards him. "General," said he, "if you will promise——" Suddenly changing his mind, he stepped two paces back and discharged his Chassepôt full in the General's chest. The others had only to finish the deed. Clément Thomas never showed a moment's weakness. His back against the same wall as Lecomte, but two paces from his corpse, he made head against death to the end, and spoke very harshly. When the guns were lowered, he by an instinctive gesture placed his left arm before his face; and this old Republican died in the attitude of Cæsar. Later in the day the insurgents took possession of the Hôtel de Ville, the Ministère de Justice, and the military head-quarters in the Place Vendôme. Barricades also began to appear in all directions. A proclamation signed by "The Central Committee of the National Guards" was posted up in the afternoon:—"Citizens, The French people, until the attempt was made to impose upon it by force an impossible calm, has awaited without fear and without provocation the shameful fools who desired to touch the Republic. This time our brothers of the army would not raise their hands against the arch of our liberties. Thanks to all, and that you and France have proclaimed the Republic, with all its consequences, the only Government which can close for ever the era of invasions and civil wars. The state of siege is raised. The people of Paris are convoked in their comitia for the communal elections. The security of all citizens is assured by the co-operation of the National Guard." At ten o'clock at night an eye-witness writes:—"The rebels are gaining upon the town point by point. They have come down from Montmartre and taken possession of the Prince Eugène barracks; they have planted the red flag on the column of the Bastille; we are expecting them on the boulevards every hour; half Paris is in their hands; and when we wake in the morning we expect that the town will be under the Government of the Red Republic. Private persons are in consternation, and the Government offices are in the greatest anxiety. On the exterior boulevards hardly any civilians are to be seen—none but armed men; and those few civilians who venture out in this quarter are immediately followed and suspected of being police spies. With the help of lanterns, the insurgents (it is now ten o'clock at night) are busily engaged in erecting barricades. The barricade at the top of the Rue Rochechouart is becoming quite formidable. The makers of the barricades encourage themselves with solemn oaths that they will die rather than surrender."

18.—Dr. Payne Smith installed as Dean of Canterbury, in succession to Dr. Alford.

— The Paris elections were to have taken place to-day, but the Mayors put aside the action of the Committee till the consent of the National Assembly could be obtained. The Paris press also published a joint declaration counselling the electors not to vote. The Committee thereupon deferred their election scheme till the 22nd, seizing in the interim such of the *mairies* as were not already in their power.

18.—Died, aged 64, Professor Augustus De Morgan, an eminent authority in mathematical science.

— The *Queen of the Thames* steamer lost near Cape Agulhas, on her homeward voyage, after making a trip of only 58 days to Sydney, the shortest known.

20.—The "Central Committee" issue an official organ, with a manifesto declaring that it is the offspring of the free expression of the suffrage on the part of 215 battalions of the National Guard. It repels the accusation brought against the Committee of being the promoter of disorder, for it says the National Guard which directs it has shown itself imposing and strong by the wisdom and moderation of its conduct. The manifesto further accuses the Government of having calumniated Paris, and of having incited the provinces against the capital. It adds:—"The Government has endeavoured to impose a commander-in-chief upon you, it has sought by nocturnal attempts to deprive us of our cannon, and has finally intended to take from Paris her crown of capital of France." A second proclamation fixed the election to "The Communal Council of Paris" for the 22nd (afterwards deferred to the 26th), and a third intimated that the Committee would, after the elections, lay down its provisional power in the hands of the people.

— The Emperor Napoleon arrives at Dover from Ostend, and receives a hearty reception as he passed up the quay with the Empress to the Lord Warden Hotel. They proceeded to Chislehurst in the afternoon.

— The French Assembly meets at Versailles for the first time.

— M. Rouher, ex-Minister of the Empire, mobbed at Boulogne, and afterwards placed in arrest at the Hôtel de Ville.

— Died, at Heidelberg, aged 66, Professor George Gottfried Gervinus, historian, and Liberal politician.

21.—The German Reichstag opened by the Emperor in person. He described its first duty to be the healing as much as possible of the wounds inflicted by war, and the commencement of those works by which the representatives of the German people sought to fulfil the mission entrusted to them by the Constitution.

— Marriage of the Marquis of Lorne and the Princess Louise in St. George's Chapel, Windsor.

— Sir Henry Bulwer gazetted Baron Dalling, and Sir William Mansfield, Baron Sandhurst.

21.—The Government of Versailles issue a circular to prefects declaring the news from all parts of France to be entirely reassuring. " Disorder is nowhere triumphant. In Paris the citizens are organising the suppression of the insurrection. At Versailles the National Assembly and the Government have collected an army of 45,000 trustworthy troops around them, and are masters of the situation to-day. The National Assembly yesterday held its first sitting, showing itself calm, united, and resolute. Jointly with the Executive power, it formed a committee upon the measures demanded by the circumstances. A proclamation will be shortly published to the people. Lille, Lyons, Marseilles, and Bordeaux are tranquil. You may publish this news to the people. It is strictly true, for the Government which communicates it is a truthful Government. Let it be well understood that every Government agent who tries to make terms with disorder will be prosecuted, and will forfeit his position.—THIERS."

— The insurgent *Journal Officiel* demands that Paris shall not be separated from the provinces, nor the provinces from her. " Paris has been, is still, and must definitely remain the capital of France, the head and heart of the Democratic Republic one and indivisible. Paris has, therefore, an unquestionable right to proceed with the elections of the Communal Council, to govern herself as becomes every democratic city, and to protect herself, supported by the National Guards, composed of all citizens electing their own chiefs by universal suffrage. The Central Committee of the National Guard, in taking the necessary measures for the establishment of a Paris Communal Council and the elections of all the chiefs of the National Guards, has, therefore, taken very wise and most indispensable measures. It is now the duty of the electors and of the National Guard to support the decisions of the Government to assure the safety of France and the future of the Republic, in returning by their votes proved and devoted Republicans. To-morrow they will hold their fate in their own hands, and we are already convinced they will make a proper use of their rights. Let Paris deliver France and save the Republic. (Signed) THE DELEGATES OF THE ' OFFICIAL JOURNAL.' "

22.—The Party of Order in Paris muster in large numbers and march to the Place Vendôme, where an interview is held with insurgent leaders, ending in the latter causing the National Guards to fire on the defenceless people. Ten were said to be killed. The " Central Committee " officially explained this outrage as having its origin in an attack made upon the Guards after the Party of Order had been asked to retire.

— The Emperor William's 75th birthday celebrated at Berlin with unusual splendour, Count Bismarck, on the occasion, being created a Prince, and Count Moltke presented with the Order of the Iron Cross.

22.—M. Jules Favre reads in the Assembly a letter from Count Bismarck, complaining that the telegraph which the Germans want to use has been cut at Pantin, and requiring its restoration in twenty-four hours. Count Bismarck stated, moreover, that the condition of things in Paris offers scarcely any chance of the engagements entered into with Germany being kept, and that if the émeute be not put down forthwith Paris will be bombarded. M. Jules Favre said he had begged for time, in order that innocent people might not suffer, and had told General Fabrice that the émeute was a surprise, and that all France was faithful, but he gave it to be understood that if Paris did not submit he would concert with the Prussians in subduing it. The reading of the letter gave rise to great excitement.

23.— Found dead in his bed, Dr. Karl Schultzensteim, aged 73, German botanist and physiologist.

— Garibaldi elected General-in-Chief of France by the " Central Committee." At Versailles the Mayors of Paris appear in the Assembly, wearing their scarfs of office, to demand that permanent communication be opened up with the capital, but the tumult was so great that nothing could be settled. Two days later a communication to the same effect was laid on the table of the Assembly.

24.—Commenting, in the Lords, on the Tien-tsin Massacre, Lord Carnarvon attributed the outbreak to ill-feeling against foreigners generally, countenanced and encouraged by the local authorities. Earl Granville admitted that the massacre was wholly unjustifiable, but pointed out that the conduct of the Catholic missionaries was apt to excite misapprehensions among a jealous and irritable people like the Chinese. There could be no doubt about the prejudice of the people against foreigners, but the moral he drew from that was the necessity of avoiding hostile language as far as possible, and of showing toleration for habits and customs handed down from generation to generation, which must necessarily take much time and patience to eradicate.

25.—Vice-Chancellor Stuart retires from the Court of Chancery. He was succeeded by Mr. Wickens.

26.—Fire in a house in Pavilion Road, Chelsea, causing the death of Mrs. Winsor and four of her children.—At Blackburn, a few hours earlier, Mrs. Kilner and two assistant female confectioners were burnt to death.

— Paris elections take place, about 140,000 voting for the men on the lists of the Central Committee, and 60,000 for their opponents. Flourens, Blanqui, Félix Pyat, and Gambon, were among the elected. In abdicating its functions, to-day, the Committee advised the people to avoid those whom fortune has too greatly favoured, for it but seldom happens that he who possesses fortune is willing to look upon the working-man as a brother. " Seek men with sincere convictions; men of the people, resolute and active, who are well known for their sense of justice and honesty. Give your preference to those who do not canvass for your suffrages; the only true merit is modesty; it is for the electors to know their men, not for the candidates themselves to come forward. We are convinced that you will take note of these observations, and you will at last have inaugurated a truly popular representation; you will thus have found representatives who will never consider themselves your masters." A few of the more active members of the "Central Committee" now formed themselves into a "Sub-Committee," ultimately the real body in which the power of the Communal Assembly centred.

27.—The House of Lords reject the Marriage with a Deceased Wife's Sister Bill by 97 to 71 votes.

— Mr. Goschen introduces the Navy Estimates; the sum required for the year being 9,756,356*l.*, an increase, as compared with last year, of 385,000*l.*

— The Emperor Napoleon visits the Queen at Windsor Castle. Her Majesty returned the visit by proceeding to Chislehurst on the 3rd April.

— At a meeting in the Mansion House the Lord Mayor announces that the *Captain* Relief Fund now amounted to 54,000*l.*

28.—The Commune proclaimed in Paris in front of the Hôtel de Ville. The members of the Communal Council assembled on a platform fronting the great entrance of Henry IV., over which was placed a bust representing the Republic, wearing a Cap of Liberty, ornamented with red ribbons and flags. Numerous speeches were delivered, but amidst the hum of the crowd of National Guards who filled the square they were not much heard. Salvoes of artillery were also fired from a battery on the quay. The *Journal Officiel* had previously announced that Paris, "federated with the Communes of France already enfranchised, ought in her own name and in the names of Lyons and Marseilles, and soon, perhaps, of the other large towns, to study the clauses of the contract which ought to bind them to the nation, and to lay down an ultimatum to the treaty which they intend to sign. The ultimatum ought to contain a guarantee for their autonomy and reconquered municipal sovereignty, should secure free play for the connection existing between the Commune; and the representatives of the national unity should impose upon the Assembly, if it accepts the treaty, the promulgation of an Electoral law by which the representatives of the town shall not for the future be absorbed, and, as it were, drowned by the representatives of the country districts." Direct incitement was at the same time given to assassinate the Duke d'Aumale. "Society (writes Citizen Vaillant) has but one duty towards these Princes—Death! But one formality is required—the proof of identity.

8

The D'Orleans are in France; the Bonapartes desire to return. Let good citizens think of it." The red flag was now hoisted on all public buildings.

28.—Declining the offer made to command the National Guard of the Commune, Garibaldi writes from Caprera:—" Choose a single trustworthy citizen—and you are not without them —Victor Hugo, Louis Blanc, Félix Pyat, as well as Edgar Quinet and the other veterans of radical democracy can serve you. Generals Cremer and Billot, who, I perceive, have your confidence, may count among the number. Remember well, however, that one single trustworthy man ought to be entrusted with the supreme position with full powers. This man will choose other honourable men to aid in the rough task of saving the country. And, if you have the good fortune to find a Washington, France will rise from her shipwreck in a little time greater than ever."

29.—Died, aged 52, Louise, Queen of Sweden.

— The London School Board discuss a motion submitted by Professor Huxley for restricting Bible-reading in elementary schools to selections submitted to and approved by the Board. An amendment was proposed by the Rev. Prebendary Thorold directing the Committee on the Scheme of Education to select for approval a course of Bible readings, and giving instructions to the teachers to choose special passages as occasion might arise. The motion and also the amendment were rejected.

— Died, aged 74, Imam Schamyl, the active opponent of Russia in the Caucasus.

— The Royal Albert Hall of Arts and Sciences opened by the Queen, who was received, on entering, by the Prince of Wales as President of the Provisional Committee. A Biblical Cantata, composed for the occasion by Sir M. Costa, was afterwards given with great effect. Eight thousand people were said to be within the building on this occasion.

30.—Mr. Dilke's motion expressing regret that Government assented to a conference on the Black Sea question under the circumstances disclosed in Prince Gortschakoff's note, negatived, after debate, without a division.

— The official organ of the Commune publishes a decree abolishing the conscription, and declaring that no central force, with the exception of the National Guard, can be created or introduced into Paris. All able-bodied citizens to form part of the National Guard. Another decree grants a general remission of rent to lodgers from October 1870 until April 1871. The amounts paid during those seven months will be reckoned on for the months to come. The sale of all articles deposited at the Mont de Piété is suspended. Another decree directs all officials in the public offices to regard from henceforth as null and void all orders or communications emanating from the Government at Versailles. Every official not conforming to this decree will be immediately dismissed. Another of the many decrees now being issued almost hourly prohibited chaplains from celebrating mass in the prisons to which they were attached. The *Gaulois* afterwards mentioned that the Governor of one of the prisons, yielding to the importunities of a dying prisoner, made an exception, and gave a priest a pass thus worded :—" These presents are to authorise the Governor to allow the visit to prisoner A—— of the Citizen B——, who says he is the servant of somebody called God [*le nommé Dieu*]."

30.—Tried at Kingston Assizes, before the Lord Chief Justice, the case of Goldschmidt *v.* the printer of *Public Opinion*, in which journal had been inserted a libellous paragraph from a New York paper, imputing wasteful extravagance and domestic infelicity to the plaintiff, the husband of Jenny Lind. Verdict for the plaintiff, damages 750*l.*, the foreman of the jury adding that they felt that no amount of damages could compensate for so iniquitous a libel.

31.—The gates on the western side of Paris closed, in consequence, it was said, of the Assembly's troops mustering in great force at Neuilly and St. Cloud.

— M. Félix Pyat, in the *Vengeur*, to-day, rejoices that Paris has not returned a single moderate, temperate, or conciliatory man to the Commune, and no old men, with the exception of himself and two others. He then banters the National Assembly in language unfit for translation, adding they dare not attack Paris, but they isolate it, starve it, and cut off its work and provisions ; they annul the elections and empty the Bank and the Treasury ; they arm the peasants, and call to their aid the Bretons of Trochu, the Vendeans of Charette, and the Chouans of Cathelineau to aid the Prussians. Citizen Pyat recommended a visit to Versailles.

April 1.—University Boat-race won by Cambridge by a length.

— Engagement between the troops of Versailles and the Commune at Courbevoie, from which place the latter were ultimately shelled out by field pieces on Mont Valérien. In the evening M. Thiers issued a manifesto declaring that France—Paris excepted—was entirely pacified. In Paris the Commune, already divided, endeavours to spread everywhere false news, and pillages the public purse. It is in a doubtful position and a horror to the Parisians, who wait with impatience the moment of their deliverance. The National Assembly, rallying round the Government, is sitting peaceably at Versailles, where it is organising one of the finest armies which France has ever possessed. Good citizens, then, may reassure themselves, and hope for the approaching end of a crisis which has been sad, but short. They may be

certain that they will not be left ignorant of passing events, and that when the Government is silent, it is only because it has nothing grave or interesting to communicate.

3.—Noisy meeting in St. James's Hall, presided over by Mr. Chambers, M.P., to protest against the unconstitutional policy of the House of Lords in rejecting bills repeatedly passed by the Commons, and to demand the removal of the Bishops from Parliament.

— More fighting before Paris, again to the advantage of the Versailles troops. They were observed to treat the captured Communists with marked severity. Gustave Flourens was among the killed, and Duval taken prisoner and shot. Wild with rage at the defeat and slaughter of their leaders, the Communist party now set about schemes for making reprisals, and placed many in prison to await their pleasure in this respect.

— Died, at Postford House, Surrey, aged 74, Sir William Magnay, Bart., who filled the office of Lord Mayor in 1844, when the Queen opened the Royal Exchange.

— Mr. Secretary Bruce introduces a Licensing Bill, carrying out, as he described, two broad principles:—1. That the public have a right to a sufficient number of respectably conducted houses ; and 2. That all vested interests should be fairly considered.

— Mr. Goschen introduces two bills on the subject of local taxation, designed to provide a uniform system of local government throughout England and Wales (the metropolis excepted), and to secure uniformity of rating. The three main features of his scheme were to popularise the character and increase the efficiency of rural institutions by the establishment of parochial boards, presided over by an elective chairman, and furnishing representative members, to be associated with the magistrates in the administration of county affairs ; to give a measure of relief to tenants by a division of rates between owners and occupiers ; to give a boon, especially to urban ratepayers, by the surrender of the house-tax to local authorities in aid of local taxation. There were also provisions for subjecting to rates certain kinds of local property, such as mines, woods, and game ; for the assessment on a higher scale of country gentlemen's residences ; for the collection of all rates as one consolidated rate ; and for the simplification of the areas of local taxation. Local expenditure was said to amount to 36,000,000*l.* per annum.

— In opening the Spanish Cortes, King Amadeo said :—" We shall afford an opportunity for your patriotism to remove the difficulties which are surrounding the management of our finances, and to dissipate the apprehensions of the future. In coming to Spain, I intended to identify on the same soil the interests of the realm which has been entrusted to me with that which is dearest to me in the world—my wife and son. The mission entrusted to me is difficult, but glorious ; perhaps beyond my strength, but not above my will : and with the help of God I hope to succeed. God knows my intention, and with the co-operation of the Cortes and all good men, which will not fail me, I hope that my efforts will be crowned with the reward of achieving the happiness of the Spanish people."

3.—Eighth decennial census of the people taken throughout the kingdom.

4.—The Economic Museum, Penryn House, Twickenham, destroyed by fire.

5.—The Commune issue a proclamation to the Parisians regarding the recent engagements :—" Every day the banditti of Versailles slaughter or shoot our prisoners, and every hour we learn that another murder has been committed. Those who are guilty of such crimes—you know them ; those are the Gendarmes of the Empire, the Royalists of Charette and Cathelineau, who are marching on Paris, in shouting ' Vive le Roi !' and with a white flag at their head. The Government of Versailles is acting against the laws of warfare and humanity, and we shall be compelled to make reprisals should they continue to disregard the usual conditions of warfare between civilised peoples. If our enemies murder a single one of our soldiers we shall reply by ordering the execution of an equal number or double the number of prisoners. The people, even in its anger, detests bloodshed as it detests civil war, but it is its duty to protect itself against the savage attempts of its enemies, and whatever it may cost, it shall be an eye for an eye, a tooth for a tooth."

6.—The Princess of Wales gives birth to a son (Alexander John Charles Albert), who died the following day.

— Decree issued by the Commune setting forth that, as the Government of Versailles had trampled all the laws of humanity under foot, anyone convicted of complicity with it would be imprisoned as hostages of the people of Paris; and, upon the execution of any prisoner of war or any partisan of the Commune of Paris by the Versailles Government, three of the hostages retained by the people of Paris would be shot. On the day the decree appeared the Archbishop of Paris, the Curé of the Madéleine, and a crowd of other ecclesiastics, were lodged in the Conciergerie. The plate and other valuables found in the churches to which the Commune had been were also seized.

7.—General Cluseret, who had now come to the front as directing the military movements of the Commune, reports :—" With regard to the conduct of our troops, the soldiers are excellent, the officers of a mixed character —some good, some bad. There is much dash, but rather a want of firmness. When the war companies shall have been formed and separated from the sedentary element, we shall have an army corps *d'élite*, whose effective

strength will exceed 100,000 men. I cannot too strongly recommend the Guards to give the utmost attention to the question of the choice of officers. At present the respective positions of the two armies may be summed up thus : The Prussians of Versailles occupy the positions which were held by their allies from beyond the Rhine. We occupy the trenches of Les Moulineaux and the station of Clamart. In fine, our position is that of men who, strong in their good right, await with firmness the attack of the enemy, being satisfied with acting on the defensive In conclusion, if our troops retain their *sangfroid*, and do not waste their ammunition, the enemy will be tired out before us."

7.—Good Friday news from Paris describe the fighting continued between Neuilly and Courbevoie. At 6.30, P.M., the advantage is reported as slightly resting with the Versailles troops, "who have carried the barricade on the Paris side of Neuilly Bridge, and are also masters of the upper part of the Avenue, but the Communists are still fighting with remarkable courage and tenacity, and have just been sending down the Porte Maillot reinforcements of men and artillery strong enough possibly to turn the fortunes of the day. The excitement in Paris near the quarter in which the fighting is going on is intense. Crowds are assembled round the Arc de Triomphe, and especially at the head of the Avenue de la Grande Armée, from which much of the fighting can be distinctly seen, and which has itself received numerous shells to-day, chiefly from Mont Valérien. A few have fallen in the Avenue Uhrich, and as no house in the neighbourhood is considered safe, the consternation of the inhabitants is very great. On the other hand, in those parts of Paris which are not exposed to the bombardment the prevailing tranquillity is, under the circumstances, extraordinary. People are lounging and promenading in the Champs Elysées, and, but for the incessant marching backwards and forwards of battalions, the boulevards and principal streets would have much the same aspect that they had before the attack on Neuilly began ; yet it is believed generally that the Versailles corps are bent on taking Paris by storm, and not a few expect the assault to be made to-night, possibly with success."

— Died, Vice-Admiral Tegethoff, the Austrian officer who defeated the Italian navy off Lissa.

8.—Monument to Ernest Jones, democrat, unveiled in Ardwick cemetery, Manchester.

— The Republican League declare that Paris has no wish to destroy the work of the great French Revolution. She wishes, it was said, to continue it. "But Paris, during the last twenty years, has been more oppressed than the rest of the country. She wishes now to reconquer her privileges and to affirm her rights. The recent movement is not an insurrection, but a revolution. It is necessary that the Government should bind itself to abandon all investigations into the facts which have been accomplished since the 18th of March last. It is necessary, on the other hand, in order to assure the free expression of universal suffrage, to proceed with the general elections of the Commune of Paris. We require a great and powerful manifestation of public opinion to put an end to the struggle. Let the whole of Paris work with us to-day as she did during the siege, for the salvation of the Republic and of France is at stake. Should the Government of Versailles remain dumb to those legitimate re-vindications, let it be well aware that Paris shall rise as one man to defend them."

8.—M. Thiers, by a threat of resignation, induces the Assembly to rescind a resolution that Mayors should be elected by the Municipal Councils.

9.—General Dombrowski appointed Commandant of the Commune of Paris, in place of General Bergeret.

10.—M. Jules Favre protests in the Versailles Assembly against the calumnies brought forward "by those who pretend that an understanding exists between us and the Germans. The documents which will be laid before you will be a proof of our sincerity, and will testify on the contrary that we constantly declined the assistance which was offered to us by the Germans. It was also no less important that the position of the German authorities towards the insurrection should be clearly determined. They have always considered, as did all the other Powers, that the Government issued from universal suffrage was alone legitimate and presenting serious guarantees." M. Favre afterwards announced that the insurgents had taken away all the plate at the Foreign Office. "As to ourselves," he concluded, "we shall do our duty, and re-establish order in Paris. Our brave army can rely on our devotion as we can rely on its courage."

— Marshal MacMahon assumes command of the Versailles army.

11.—The Marquis of Normanby gazetted Governor and Commander-in-Chief of Queensland.

— Replying to a remonstrance requesting the Bishops to abstain from voting on the decision of the Privy Council in the Purchas case, the Archbishop of Canterbury writes:—"The chief pastors of our Church are of all men the very last who ought to be requested to set to this nation the example of refusing obedience to the highest tribunals. Such obedience I feel sure you consider to be the duty of all good citizens, and to be especially incumbent on all ministers of Christ, not only in our own Church, but among Nonconformists. And here I will remark that Roman Catholics, and all bodies of Dissenters, are liable to be continually called upon, like ourselves, to submit the terms of their contracts in matters most intimately affect-

ing their doctrine and discipline, to the decision of the courts of law. This is an obligation from which no section of the community can escape under a well-ordered Government. . . . The rubrics, interpreted by the Supreme Court, form the lawful rule of Divine service to which the clergy are bound to yield a loyal obedience; but certainly, as a matter of fact, not all the clergy are expected by their parishioners, or required by their bishops, rigidly to observe every point in the rubrics at all times and under all circumstances." In conclusion, his grace exhorts his brethren not to be disquieted by any strifes respecting matters affecting the vestments or posture of the clergy. "Such things," he says, "cannot touch your teaching of the Gospel of Christ, or affect the validity of His sacraments. In days when every effort is required to resist ungodliness and infidelity, all our zeal and energy ought to be directed to the promotion of real religion among our people."

11.—Another ineffectual sortie on the southern forts of Paris by Versailles troops. It had been anticipated for some time, and was made in such force as furnished ground for believing it would close the protracted strife. Fifteen thousand men, consisting of gendarmes and Pontifical Zouaves, collected during the day in the Meudon woods. The movement was detected, and 80,000 Federals drawn up within the line of the forts. General Eudes, who was in command, permitted the enemy to approach to the glacis of the Fort of Issy, when he poured a cross fire from Issy and Montrouge, repulsing the Versailles troops with slaughter. Only four men were killed within the two forts.

— Earthquake at Bathang, a village in the Chinese province of Szechuen, causing the destruction of two large temples, the offices of the collector of grain tax, the local magistrates' offices, the colonels' offices, the Ting-lin temple, with nearly 700 fathoms of wall around it, and 351 rooms in all, inside; six smaller temples, numbering 221 rooms, besides 1,849 rooms and houses of the common people. The number of people killed by the crash, including the soldiers, was 2,298, among whom were the local magistrate and his second in office. The earthquake extended from Bathang eastward to Pang-Chahe-muth, westward to Nan-Tun, on the south to Lintsah-shih, and on the north to the salt wells of Atimtoz, a circuit of over 400 miles.

— The trustees of Rugby School having had their attention directed to certain complaints of want of discipline, adopt a resolution expressive of their opinion that the irregularities referred to were not such as to call for any special interference on their part, or to cause alarm to parents. "In justice," they said, "to the head-master, they desired to impress on the under-masters generally the necessity of giving, not only a nominal, but a cordial co-operation."

12.—M. Guizot writes to the *Times* that the faults of France cause him more sorrow than her misfortunes; but he never loses faith in her good qualities, although they may seem to be obliterated by her faults, and he feels sure that the good which is in her will open up infinite resources, even when her prospects are darkest. "On the whole," he wrote, "the National Assembly and its Executive have acted with intelligence, prudence, and justice. And now, driven to the last extremity by the folly, crime, and attacks of the insurgents, it opposes them with energy, and has resolved to put an end to the revolution which oppresses Paris, and to render the guilty authors of it powerless. A new and loyal army has gathered round the representatives chosen by France, and gallantly obeys their orders and those of the generals in command. The first efforts of this army have already been crowned with success."

12.—M. Thiers informs the Prefects that "the army awaits the moment of victory, which will be gained without bloodshed. The insurrection is weary. Delegates have arrived at Versailles. If sent by the Commune they would not have been received, but they were received because they were sincere Republicans of Paris. My answer to them was invariably, ' No one menaces the Republic except assassins. The lives of the insurgents shall be spared. The unfortunate workmen shall temporarily continue to be subsidized. Paris must return into the common municipal law. All secession will be suppressed in France, as was done in America.' This was my answer."

— In Buenos Ayres 380 persons are reported to have died of yellow fever. The deaths during the week were put down at 4,000.

— Died at Grantchester, Cambridge, aged 82, Rev. Edward Pote, M.A., one of the oldest members of the University, having taken his B.A. degree in 1814 with the late Vice-Chancellor Kindersley and Mr. Justice Cresswell.

13.—Died at Dublin, aged 75, Sir Maguire Brady, Bart., three times Lord Chancellor of Ireland.

— M. Rochefort, writing in the *Mot d'Ordre*, defends the "requisition" made by the Commune in Notre Dame:—" We do not hesitate to declare them national property, for the single reason that they proceed from the generosity of those to whom the Church has promised Paradise ; and the promise of imaginary returns made to obtain any property is qualified as swindling by every code. . . . ' Your purse or hell!' Such is, in the present day, the only programme of the Catholic clergy; and as the French nation no longer believes in hell, it is natural that, in case of need, it should take back the purse."

14.—Michael Torpey apprehended in a house in Marylebone Road (where he was living with his wife) on the charge of stealing diamonds and jewellery from Messrs. London and Ryder. A portion of the stolen property w. s found in his possession.

14.—Died at Jarrow-on-the-Tyne, aged 87, Mrs. Minns, maid and confidante to Lady Byron before and after her marriage, and whose name came up recently in connection with the controversy as to the causes which led to the breaking up of that ill-assorted union.

15.—Mr. J. R. Davidson, M.P. for Durham city, and Judge-Advocate-General, found dead in his bed at the residence of Mr. St. George Burke, where he had been staying for a few days. This was Mr. Davidson's 45th birthday. At the election which subsequently took place, Government lost the seat, Mr. Wharton, Conservative, polling 814 votes to Mr. Thompson's 776.

16.—The Westmeath Committee report that, owing to the prevalence of Ribbon Societies in that district, murder and other crimes of the most serious nature have been perpetrated ; and that by reason partly of sympathy with the perpetrators of such crimes, and still more by the terror created by the existence and action of the Societies, it has been found to be almost impossible to obtain evidence on which to bring offenders to justice.

— Sunday Republican demonstration in Hyde Park to express sympathy with the Parisian Communists. Large numbers—many from curiosity—turned out on the occasion, but the gathering was generally admitted to be a failure.

— Died at Bray, aged 77, Lord Plunkett, second son of the famous Irish orator.

— Died at Bydews, near Maidstone, Rev. Beal Poste, LL.B., archæologist.

17.—Captain Chalmers, the senior officer of the Ryde and Portsmouth Steam Service, commits suicide by leaping from the deck of his vessel as she was leaving Ryde Pier.

— Billiard match in St. James's Hall between Cook, jun., and Roberts, sen., the latter receiving a start of 200 in 2,000. Cook won with an unfinished break of 268, including no less than 78 spot strokes, which his opponent had been the chief means of introducing and popularizing.

— The Versailles army capture the Château de Brem after a sharp engagement.

— M. Louis Blanc writes in the *Soir* that the solution which he judged and declared "the fittest to save us from the horrors of civil war is that which would consist in the bold proclamation of the Republic by the National Assembly, and in the adoption of a law putting Paris in full and entire possession of her municipal liberties."

18.—At the first meeting of the House, to-day, after the Easter recess, a motion submitted by Lord Henry Lennox for a Select Committee to inquire into the causes of the dismissal of Sir Spencer Robinson from the Admiralty was rejected by 153 to 104 votes.

18.—Still refusing assent to the Papal Infallibility dogma, Dr. Döllinger is formally excommunicated by the Archbishop of Munich. He asked the Archbishop to meet his disobedience, not by condemnation, but by admitting him to a conference, either at Fulda, where the German bishops were about to assemble, or before a body of theologians to be selected by the Archbishop. If in this conference he was convinced of his errors, he was ready both to accept the dogma and to withdraw everything he had written against it. If, however, this conference were allowed him, he expected to prove that the doctrine was contrary to Scripture, and based upon a misconception of the history of the Church and of her traditions. The late Council, Dr. Döllinger further maintained, enjoyed no freedom of discussion, and no pains were taken to examine authorities. "As a student of history," he said, "I cannot accept it, for as such I know that the persistent endeavour to realize this theory of universal dominion has cost Europe rivers of blood, has disordered whole countries and brought them to ruin, has shattered the beautiful structure of the earlier Church, and in the Church of modern times has generated, nurtured, and maintained the worst abuses. As a citizen I must reject it, because by its pretensions to the subjection of States and monarchs, and of the whole political system to the Papal power, it leads to endless destructive conflict between Church and State, between clergy and laity." The resolution of Dr. Döllinger was approved of in an autograph letter by the King of Bavaria, and many eminent professors in the Roman College.

— The Emperor of Germany declines the proffered resignation of General Von Steinmetz, and confers upon him the highest dignity in the army.

— Meeting of London clergy held at Sion College to secure the observance of Ascension Day by the laity as a holiday like Christmas.

— Died, aged 65, Omer Pasha, Commander-in-Chief of the Turkish army.

— Died at Montrose, aged 93, Rev. Dr. Paterson, who had acted as tutor to Lord Byron in his Aberdeen days.

19.—The *Vengeur*, conducted by Félix Pyat, publishes a decree of the Commune for destroying the Vendôme Column, its demolition to be solemnly performed by military engineers in the presence of the assembled people, the National Guard, and the members of the Commune. It was also suggested that the " History of the Empire" should on the occasion be burned at the foot of the Column by a "Mère de famille."

— Last night the Versailles troops took the church of Neuilly, and drove the Communists back some 150 yards. This morning Dombrowski attempted to rally his men and retake the position. Reinforcements, however, arrived of gendarmes and marines, who drove Dombrowski's men still farther back with considerable slaughter, causing them to occupy their most remote barricade at the junction of the Rue Peronnet with the Boulevard Inkerman. Many of the Communists were killed, being fired at in their flight through the holes in garden walls which they themselves had made in their advance. There was great loss among the officers. The Ambulance head-quarters at Neuilly was shelled, and the surgeons and waggons compelled to decamp in haste.

19.—The Communists issue another proclamation, declaring that their enemies deceive themselves or the country "when they accuse Paris of desiring to impose its will and supremacy upon the rest of the nation, and to aspire to a Dictatorship, which would be a veritable attempt to overthrow the independence and sovereignty of other Communes. They deceive themselves when they accuse Paris of seeking the destruction of French unity, established by the Revolution. The unity which has been imposed upon us up to the present by the Empire, the Monarchy, and the Parliamentary Government, is nothing but centralization, despotic, unintelligent, arbitrary, and onerous. The political unity, as desired by Paris, is a voluntary association of all local initiative, the free and spontaneous co-operation of all individual energies with the common object of the well-being, liberty, and security of all. The Communal revolution, initiated by the people on March 18, inaugurated a new era in politics, experimental, positive, and scientific. It was the end of the old official and clerical world of military supremacy and bureaucracy, of jobbing in monopolies and privileges, to which the proletariat owed its slavery, and the country its misfortunes and disasters. The strife between Paris and Versailles is one of those that cannot be ended by an illusory compromise ; the issue should not be doubtful. . . . As for ourselves, citizens of Paris, we have a mission to accomplish, a modern revolution the greatest and the most fruitful of all those which have illuminated history. It is our duty to fight and conquer."

20.—Mr. Lowe introduces the Budget, showing the estimated expenditure for 1871-72 to be 72,308,800*l.*, and the revenue 69,595,000*l.* Among the items of expenditure was 16,452,000*l.* for the army, including abolition of purchase, as against 12,965,000*l.* for 1870-71. He maintained that it was in the power of this nation, "if we were so minded, to take such measures as will enable us to have a force which is demonstrably sufficient, considering the conditions of the problem of landing a force in an enemy's country, to crush any enemy before he could possibly accumulate sufficient strength to invade us. And if that can be done, I can hardly imagine any sacrifice that it would not be worth while to make from a purely financial consideration, because if you can satisfy people that this is the one spot in the world that is safe, and that will in all probability be free from the ravages of war, think how our credit will rise, how the value of our property will increase, what a predominance it gives us over other nations." What we were now doing was virtually imposing taxes, which were in the nature of war taxes, at a time when we were not going to war, and when there was no probability of our doing so. To make up the deficiency of 2,713,000*l*., the Chancellor of the Exchequer proposed to rate all personal property liable as intestate on the principle of 2 per cent, duty, and where a man paid legacy duty he should be liable to probate duty. He also proposed to increase succession duties both on real and personal property, by raising them, for the first lineal descendant, from 1 to 2 per cent. He would raise brothers to 3½, then for others 5, and upwards to 10 per cent. He also proposed a tax on matches, bearing the box-label, "Ex luce lucellum," from which he expected 550,000*l*.; and also proposed to convert a penny in the pound on the income-tax into a rate of 100 pence, or 8*s*. 4*d*. in the 100*l*. The effect of his proposals would be, that the legacy, probate, and succession duties would yield an addition of 350,000*l*., matches 550,000*l*., and the additional income tax about 1,800,000*l*. He concluded by proposing the resolution relating to lucifer matches, which, after some adverse discussion, was agreed to.

21.—Mr. Bentinck introduces, but withdraws after debate, a resolution on the Declaration of Paris, asserting that "the maintenance of British maritime rights being essential to the power, prosperity, and independence of the Empire, this House is of opinion that her Majesty's Government should forthwith withdraw from the articles of 'The Declaration of Paris, 1856,' which are numbered respectively 1 and 2, and which are expressed in the terms following:—1. Privateering is and remains abolished. 2. The neutral flag covers enemy's goods, with the exception of contraband of war."

22.—Married according to the form of a Communal certificate, "The citizen Anet, son of Jean-Louis Anet, and the Maria Saint. She engaged to follow the said citizen everywhere, and to love him always.—Anet, Maria Saint. Witnessed by the undermentioned citizen and citizenness—Fuiherar, Laroche."

— Monument set up in York Minster to the memory of Frederick Vyner, one of the party slain a year since at Skimatari by Greek brigands.

— A Communist organ, the *Montagne*, writes:—"Our dogs that used only to growl when a bishop passed, will bite him now, and not a voice will be raised to curse the day which dawns for the sacrifice of the Archbishop of Paris. We owe it to ourselves—we owe it to the world. The Commune has promised us an eye for an eye, and has given us Monseigneur Darboy as a hostage. The justice of the tribunals shall commence, said Danton, when the wrath of the people is appeased—and he was right. Darboy! tremble in your cell, for your day is past, your end is close at hand!"

23.—Collision near the Newarp lightship between the Rotterdam steamer *Kestral* and the screw collier *Frankland*, of Newcastle. The former sank, but her crew and passengers were taken off and landed at Grimsby.

24.—Most of the newspapers this morning contain articles and letters directed against the recently-introduced Budget, the proposed match-tax in particular giving rise to hostile criticism. Bryant and May, makers of the "Safety Match," calculated that the duty which it was proposed to levy would vary from 100 to 400 per cent., and even more on the wholesale price. "On the wholesale price of 625*l*. worth of the commonest matches the duty will be 3,000*l*., or nearly 500 per cent. The effect of this imposition will be almost entirely to extinguish two important branches of the business, throwing vast numbers of workpeople out of employment, and consequently on the rates, which in the locality where the trade is principally carried on—the East-end of London—are at present almost unbearable. A great portion of the home trade will, no doubt, drift into the hands of foreigners, as the demand will be for the lowest qualities, which are principally manufactured abroad." Regarding the Terminable Annuity Sinking Fund, Mr. Hubbard supported a proposal made by the *Times* to suspend its operation for one year.

— Michael Campbell executed at Springfield gaol, Essex, for the murder of Mr. Galloway at Stratford. The prisoner had gone out with two other men on the evening of the 9th of February for the purpose of entering houses by climbing up the porticoes in front, and then plundering the upper rooms. They had made two or three unsuccessful attempts, and at length, while in the act of entering the house of the deceased gentleman, they were disturbed, and one of the prisoner's companions seized by the deceased. The prisoner then came up and stabbed the unfortunate gentleman in the eye, inflicting a wound of which he died a very few days afterwards.

— Mr. White's Budget resolution—"That the additional taxation proposed will entail burdens upon the people which are not justified by existing circumstances," rejected by 257 to 230 votes, after a discussion in which Mr. Lowe and Mr. Gladstone were found to be the only speakers who seemed inclined to support the Budget as a whole.

— The matchmakers muster in large numbers at the East-end of London, and in various sections march through the City to Westminster to present petitions against the imposition of the new tax. Some tumult naturally prevailed along the line of march, and in Palace Yard for a time members could not readily obtain entrance to the House; but it was not till returning by way of the Thames Embankment, where the police were stationed in large numbers, that any serious breach of the peace occurred. Here some stones were thrown and a few boards torn down, but even these offences were alleged to have been committed by parties who, from interested motives, had mixed themselves up with the processionists.

24.—In obtaining the sanction of the German Parliament to a proposal for a loan of 120 million thalers, Prince Bismarck remarked that their country had been forced into great financial sacrifices to maintain a force in France to meet all contingencies. "If the French Government," he said, "do not pay the amount agreed upon for the maintenance of the German troops it will be necessary again to have recourse to requisitions of food and forage. The German authorities will not interfere in the internal affairs of France, though it is hardly possible to promise complete forbearance under all circumstances. Should German rights and German interests be imperilled, it will become our duty to defend them."

25.—Mr. Lowe announces that the match-tax would be abandoned on account of the dissatisfaction it had excited. Mr. Wren Hoskyns' resolution pointing out the necessity of removing certain restrictions in the laws regulating the sale and transfer of land rejected by 79 to 39 votes.

— Came on before the Lords Justices, the case of Hawksworth *v.* Hawksworth, involving the question whether a daughter (aged eight and a half years) of a deceased Roman Catholic father named Hawksworth should be brought up as a Roman Catholic or as a member of the Church of England. The father died intestate about eight years ago, and the daughter had since been under the care of her mother, a member of the Church of England. The case was originally adjudicated upon by the Chancery Court of the Duchy of Lancaster. The Vice-Chancellor (Mr. Wickens), after having had an interview with the child in court, held that she should be brought up in the religion of her father—that is to say, as a Roman Catholic. The mother appealed from that decision. Lord Justice James now confirmed the finding of the Vice-Chancellor, declaring it to be a rule of the Court, a rule of the highest morality, that any person who had the conduct as guardian of a child on the father's death should have regard to the religion of the father in dealing with the child; and, unless under very special circumstances indeed, it was the duty of any guardian of a child, and it was the duty of this Court in controlling the conduct of that guardian, to see that the child was brought up in the religious faith of the father, whatever that religious faith might be. He (the Lord Justice) would not give the slightest encouragement to mothers or others who had access to young children to attempt to proselytize them. This appeal must therefore be dismissed with costs. Lord Justice Mellish concurred.

26.—The case of Mr. Purchas for a re-hearing of his appeal taken up by the Judicial Committee of the Privy Council. Petition dismissed with costs.

— The Paris forts of Issy and Vanves bombarded by batteries opened at Bas Meudon and Moulineaux. Skirmishing also took place on the north side between troops at Clichy and those massed on the plain of Gennevillers.

— Mr. Hughes' Sunday Trading Bill, supported by the Home Secretary, rejected by 80 votes to 47.

— Jane Maria Clousen, aged 17, found early this morning in Kidbrooke-lane, Eltham, dying from injuries inflicted by some person during the night. She was removed to Guy's Hospital, and afterwards identified by her friends as having lived in the capacity of a domestic servant with Mr. Pook, printer, Greenwich. On the evening of the 25th she was heard to say that she then intended to meet her " young man," known to be the son of her master, and afterwards apprehended on the charge of causing the death of Clousen. She was next found in the lane about four o'clock by Police-constable Gun. Seeing she was very much injured, and blood about her head and face, he asked her who had injured her, and she said faintly, "Oh, my poor head! oh, my poor head!" She afterwards lifted her left hand and said, "Take hold of my hand," at the same time turning her head to the left. On giving her his hand she fell on her face on the ground, and said, "Let me die." The officer again asked her what was the matter, but she made no further reply. On turning round he saw blood on the ground near Clousen, her gloves being also there, and her hat within two feet. There were footmarks, but not of recent occurrence. He looked round to see if he could see anyone, but nobody was near. He then obtained assistance, when she was taken to the surgery of Dr. King, and thence to Guy's Hospital. At a quarter to two the same morning this officer passed through the lane, but on the opposite side to that where he found the deceased lying, and did not notice her.

27.—Anticipating the probable result of a hostile resolution to be proposed by Mr. Disraeli, Mr. Gladstone announces that the increase of the legacy and succession duties would be abandoned, and also the proposal for computing income-tax by a percentage, the deficiency to be made up by raising the income-tax from 4*d.* to 6*d.* per 1*l.* The Prime Minister insisted that provision for the expenditure voted by the House must still be made, as originally intended, out of taxation, without disturbing the duties on articles of consumption. Mr. Disraeli protested against the admission of the principle that because they had agreed to votes in Supply they were bound to approve of the Ways and Means.

15

27.—Earl Kimberley lays on the table of the House of Lords a Bill to repress illegal combinations in Westmeath, by providing that in certain circumstances the districts named in the Bill are to be proclaimed, and this being done, the Lord Lieutenant is empowered to suspend the Habeas Corpus Act for two years, and arrests may be effected by Viceregal warrants in any portion of the United Kingdom.

— Speaking in the Assembly on the plea for clemency put forward, M. Thiers said :— " Our rigour will vanish when the insurgents lay down their arms, excepting against those persons who have been guilty of crime, and they are not numerous. When I give orders, not cruel ones, but orders such as would be dictated by a state of war, I feel under the necessity of asking myself, of asking you, whether right is on my side. (M. Thiers was here interrupted by various exclamations, but he appealed to the Assembly to listen to him, and continued): I give these orders with sorrow ; but was there ever a time when right was more evident than at the present ? Everyone knows the truth of what I say. In Paris the abstentions from voting at the recent elections show the isolation of the insurgents, while, on the other hand, the whole of France is with us, and with you, who are the free expression of her suffrages."

— The marriage of the Infante Alphonse Maria of Spain, grandson of Don Carlos, with the Princess Maria des Neves of Braganza, eldest daughter of Dom Miguel, celebrated in the castle of Prince Löwenstein, at Klein Leubach. The bridegroom was born in 1849, the bride in 1852.

— Died at Naples, aged 59, M. Sigismund Thalberg, pianist and composer.

28.—Came on in the Court of Queen's Bench, the case of Tomline *v.* Lowe, raised to test the question whether the Queen's subjects are not entitled to have gold and silver bullion converted into coin of the realm, on application at the Mint. The matter came before the Court on demurrer to the plaintiff's declaration, and the substantial question was, whether the old common law of the realm had been set aside by a Royal proclamation. On the part of the Chancellor of the Exchequer, the Solicitor-General conceded the right to have gold bullion coined. The Act of 1870 contained this clause:— " That where any person brings to the Mint any gold bullion such bullion shall be coined and delivered out to such person without any charge for the coining." That was clear and specific, and therefore the right as to gold could not be disputed. But as to silver, the Act of Charles II. was expressly repealed by the Act of George III., which required a proclamation. The contention on the part of Mr. Tomline was that a proclamation issued in 1817 was still in force, and that under it the same right exists with respect to silver as with respect to gold. This was now decided against the plaintiff, and so the

16

judgment affirmed that the public had a right to take gold to the Mint and have it coined for nothing, but that they had no such right in the case of silver.

28.—Mr. Cowper Temple submits a resolution in the Commons to secure the preservation of the unenclosed parts of Epping Forest as an open space for the enjoyment of the people of the metropolis. Mr. Lowe and Mr. Gladstone opposed the motion, on the ground that the land was the property of the Crown. The Premier stated that the Government had secured 1,000 acres of the forest as a recreation ground for the people ; but the House was not satisfied, and the resolution was carried by a large majority.

— M. Thiers telegraphs to the Prefects from Versailles :—" Our troops are proceeding with the works of approach towards Issy. The batteries on the left have been worked with powerful effect against the Parc d'Issy, which is no longer habitable by those who dwelt there. Fort Issy fires no longer. On the right our cavalry, scouring the country, came upon a band of insurgents. The *éclaireurs* of the 70th Regiment, commanded by Captain Santolini, routed this band, and brought in prisoners the captain, lieutenant, quartermaster, and ten men. Thirty or forty men were killed or wounded. The remaining insurgents were pursued almost to Hautes Bruyères. Notwithstanding the heavy fusillade, we have no losses to deplore."

— Virulent outbreak of small-pox in Hampstead district ; the report presented to the Vestry to-day showing 92 births against 210 deaths, 171 of which were attributable to the disease named.

— The Commune distinguishes itself by two decrees—one " requisitioning " 80,000*l.* from five railway companies within forty-eight hours; another directing that the church erected on the spot where General Brea was murdered in 1848 shall be destroyed, "as it is a permanent insult to the vanquished of June." (See June 23, 1848, p. 254.)

29.—The Freemasons of Paris muster in force in the Louvre, and march first to the Column of the Bastille and then along the boulevards towards Versailles, where they intended to seek an audience of M. Thiers to ask his mediation in favour of the Commune. Shells falling heavily at the moment in the Champs Elysées the procession got broken up, and only a few reached Versailles. They were there told that France could not yield to insurgents.

29.—Party riot at Whitehaven, the lecturer Murphy, announced to speak on the " Confessional," being attacked by Catholic miners, and seriously injured.

— Died at Edinburgh, Samuel Halkett, a linguist of acknowledged reputation, and librarian to the Faculty of Advocates.

30.—General Cluseret arrested by order of the Commune on the charge of mismanaging the supply of arms and ammunition along the line of the forts.

May 1.—After a debate protracted till near 2 A.M., Mr. Smith's motion, " That it is inexpedient that the income-tax should be increased to the extent contemplated in the financial proposals of the Government," was negatived by 335 votes to 250. In pleading against interference with the "ancestral system " of reducing debts by "terminable annuities," Mr. Gladstone warned the House that concessions had reached the end of their concessions. Mr. Disraeli described the income-tax as a third line of defence to the country in case of war, and said it should not be lightly meddled with, especially as it pressed severely on particular classes.

— The new International Exhibition, Royal Albert Hall, opened by the Prince of Wales as representing the Queen.

— Michael Torpey convicted of the diamond robbery in Berkeley Street, and sentenced to eight years' penal servitude.

— Versailles troops attack and carry the insurgent position embraced within the railway station at Clamart, dominating the Fort of Issy. This was amongst the sharpest encounters which had yet taken place, as many, it was said, as 300 being bayonetted in the enclosure.

2.—The Westmeath Peace Preservation Bill read a second time in the House of Lords, Lord Salisbury describing the main error of the Executive Government as the application of a system of judicature formed for a civilized nation to a Celtic nation, part of which was in the depths of barbarism. He would invest the Viceroy with adequate powers to deal with this population as if he had to deal with Indians.

— Speaking in the German Parliament on the Bill for the incorporation of Alsace and Lorraine, Prince Bismarck said that on the 6th of August, 1866, "the French Ambassador handed me an ultimatum demanding the cession of Mayence to France, and telling us, in the alternative, to expect an immediate declaration of war. It was only the illness of the Emperor Napoleon which then prevented the outbreak of war. During the late war neutral Powers made mediatory proposals. In the first instance we were asked to content ourselves with the costs of the war and the razing of a fortress. This did not satisfy us. It was necessary that the bulwark from which France could sally forth for attack should be farther pushed back. Another proposal was to neutralize Alsace and Lorraine. But that neutral State would have possessed neither the power nor the will to preserve its neutrality in case of war. We were obliged to incorporate Alsace with the territory of Germany in order to ensure the peace of Europe. It is true the aversion of

the population of Alsace and Lorraine is an obstacle to such a measure. Still, the population is thoroughly German, forming a sort of aristocracy in France by virtue of its noble and Teutonic qualities. We shall strive to win back to us this population by means of Teutonic patience and love."

3.—Mr. Jacob Bright's Women's Disabilities Bill rejected, on the proposal for a second reading, by 220 to 157 votes.

— A telegram from Bombay states that news had been received from Zanzibar describing Dr. Livingstone as alive and well at Manakozo, but destitute.

— Five youths drowned in Hartlepool Bay by the upsetting of a pleasure-boat in a sudden squall.

— Versailles troops under General Lacretelle carry the redoubt of Moulin Saquet in the evening, killing 150 Communists and making over 300 prisoners.

4.—A motion submitted in the Commons by Mr. Torrens to fix the income-tax at 5*d.* instead of 6*d.* rejected by 294 to 248 votes.

5.—Died at his residence, Devonshire-place, aged 86, George Thomas John Nugent, Marquis of Westmeath, an Irish representative peer, and the last survivor, it was thought, of the expedition to Egypt against Napoleon I.

6.—Vice-Chancellor Malins gives judgment in the case of Macbryde *v.* Eykyn, a suit heard to recover from the defendant, Mr. Roger Eykyn, M.P. for Windsor, 10,200*l.* Spanish Passive Bonds, and two sums of 400*l.* and 500*l.*, which, according to the defendant's statement, had been lost in the course of transactions with the plaintiff's husband, Mr. C. Wilson Macbryde, in speculations on the Stock Exchange. Bill dismissed with costs.

— Collision off Tynemouth between the steamer *David Burn*, out on a trial trip, and the *Earl Percy.* The former sank soon afterwards.

— Herat reported to have fallen to-day, Futteh Khan, the Governor, killed, and his son wounded.

— The High Joint Commissioners at New York, having met thirty-seven times, conclude their labours by signing a treaty providing for the establishment of two boards of arbitration— one to consider the *Alabama* and similar claims which will be recognized as national, and be settled on the principle of responsibility for depredations where Government has not exercised the utmost possible diligence and precaution to prevent the fitting out of privateers ; the other will consider miscellaneous claims of both sides, confined principally to those arising out of the civil war. No claims arising out of the Fenian invasion of Canada will be admitted. All legitimate cotton claims will be considered, except those of British subjects domiciled in the South. The

San Juan boundary question to be arbitrated upon by the Emperor of Brazil. American vessels to navigate the St. Lawrence free, and the Canadian canals on payment of the regular tolls.

6.—On the motion for going into committee on the Army Regulation Bill, Colonel Anson submits a resolution—"That in any scheme for the abolition of purchase in the army, the State, as well as the officers, must forego the advantages hitherto derived from that system; and in order to give the State that unrestricted power over the officers of the army which it is desirable it should possess, and also in justice to the officers of the army themselves, the regulation value of their commissions shall be at once returned to them."

8.—M. Thiers entreats the Parisians to aid the troops outside the walls. "The Government," he declared, "will not bombard Paris, as the Commune tells you. A bombardment threatens the entire city and renders it uninhabitable, and has for its object to intimidate citizens and to force them to surrender. The Government will only use cannon to force in one of your gates, and will endeavour to limit to one point of attack the ravages of a war of which it is not the author. As soon as the soldiers shall have passed the enceinte you will rally round the national flag to aid our valiant army in destroying this sanguinary and cruel tyranny. It depends upon you to prevent those disasters which are inseparable from an assault. You are a hundred times more numerous than the partisans of the Commune. Be united, and open the gates which they close to law and order, and to your prosperity, as well as to that of France. When once those gates are open the sound of the cannons will cease, tranquillity, order, abundance, and peace will reappear within your walls. The Germans will evacuate our territory, and the traces of our misfortune will rapidly disappear. But if you do not act, the Government will be obliged to take the most energetic and certain means to deliver you."

— In Committee on the University Tests Bill, the Marquis of Salisbury carries by a majority of five votes, a new test in the form of a resolution:—"That no person shall be appointed to the office of tutor, assistant tutor, dean, censor, or lecturer in divinity, in any college now subsisting in the said universities, until he shall have made and subscribed the following declaration in the presence of the Vice-Chancellor, or in the University of Durham of the Warden—that is to say: 'I, A. B., do solemnly declare that while holding the office of [here name the office] I will not teach anything contrary to the teaching or Divine authority of the Holy Scriptures of the Old and New Testaments.'"

— The Count de Chambord writes to a friend that he only asked to be allowed to devote every moment of his life to the security and happiness of France, and to share her distresses before sharing her honours:—"It is asserted that the independence of the Papacy is dear to me, and that I am determined to obtain efficacious guarantees for it. That is true. The liberty of the Church is the first condition of spiritual peace and of order in the State. To protect the Holy See was ever the honourable duty of our country, and the most indisputable cause of its greatness among nations. Only in the periods of its greatest misfortunes has France abandoned this glorious protectorate. Rest assured if I am called it will be, not only because I represent right, but because I am order, reform—because I am the essential basis of that authority which is required to restore that which has perished, and to govern justly and according to law with the view of remedying the evils of the past, and of paving the way for the future. I shall be told that I hold the ancient sword of France in my hand, and in my breast the heart of a king and a father which recognizes no party. I am of no party, and I do not desire to return or to reign by means of party. I have no injury to avenge, no enemy to exile, no fortune to retrieve, except that of France. It is in my power to select from every quarter the men who are anxious to associate themselves with this grand undertaking. I only bring back religion, concord, and peace. I desire to exercise no dictatorship but that of clemency, because in my hands, and in my hands alone, clemency is still justice. Thus it is, my dear friend, that I despair not of my country, and that I do not shrink from the magnitude of the task. 'La parole est à la France et l'heure à Dieu.'"

8.—Mr. Gladstone announces that Government proposed to abandon for this session Mr. Goschen's Local Rating and Local Government Bills, and also the licensing clause of the Home Secretary's Licensing Bill. It was still their intention, he said, to press forward the police clauses of that measure.

9.—Came on for trial in the Court of Queen's Bench, Westminster, before the Lord Chief Justice and a special jury, the case of the Queen *v.* Boulton, Park, and others, charged with conspiring to induce others to commit felony. The examination of witnesses and speeches of counsel protracted the case to the 15th, when a verdict of Not Guilty was entered for all the defendants. In summing up, the Lord Chief Justice expressed his disapprobation of the form in which the case had been brought before the Court. "We are trying the defendants," he said, "for conspiring to commit felonious crime, and the proof of it, if it amounts to anything, amounts to proof of the actual commission of crime; and I am clearly of opinion that where the proof intended to be submitted to a jury is proof of the actual commission of crime, it is not the proper course to charge the parties with conspiring to commit it." Coming to the actual facts of the case, the learned judge remarked that what had been proved against the defendants Boulton and Park was sufficient to stamp them with the deepest disgrace, although they might not have had any felonious intention. Their going, for example, to the ladies' rooms at theatres and other public places was an offence which the Legislature might justly visit with corporal punishment. His lordship subsequently remarked that Hurt and Fiske should have been tried in Scotland, if at all. "It is easy, however," he continued, "to see how all this happened. The police had taken up the case, and the whole course and conduct of it confirm the opinion I have always entertained as to the necessity for a public prosecutor to control and to conduct criminal prosecutions. The police seized the prisoners' letters, and found those of Hurt and Fiske; they then went to Edinburgh, and, without any authority, searched their lodgings, arrested them and put them on their trial here along with Park and Boulton, without taking them before a magistrate at all; and thus they are tried with the two other defendants for an alleged offence having no connection whatever with their conduct." A second indictment against the defendants for outraging decency by going about dressed as women was allowed to stand over, and in the meantime they were liberated on their own recognizances.

9.—Mr. Miall's motion, "That it is expedient, at the earliest practicable period, to apply the policy initiated by the disestablishment of the Irish Church, by the Act of 1869, to the other Churches established by law in the United Kingdom," rejected by 374 to 89 votes. In the course of the discussion, Mr. Disraeli admitted that the disestablishment of the Church in Ireland involved the disestablishment of the Church in Scotland and in England. But, fortunately, the country was not governed by logic. It was governed by rhetoric, and not by logic, or otherwise it would have been erased long ago from the list of leading communities. No form of religion represented more fully the national sentiment than the Established Church. For his own part, he had always believed that, organically, the English were a religious people. We had partially educated them, we were now going to educate them completely. And when they were educated they would not fly to the conventicle; they would appreciate a learned clergy, a refined ritual, and the consolation of the beautiful offices of the Church. If the Church conducted itself with wisdom and discretion, he believed that every year this motion, if it were made, would be made under worse auspices and with less prospect of success. Let the Church remain tolerant, temperate, and comprehensive, and it would then be truly national. In conclusion, he expressed a strong conviction that the time had come when, in matters of great change, the country required repose, and appealed to the Government to remove the impression created by the Home Secretary, that they opposed the motion only because they did not yet see their way to carrying it.—In closing the debate, Mr. Gladstone assured the House that the Government, in opposing the motion, did not limit that opposition to the present moment or base it on merely temporary grounds. If the movement represented by the Liberation Society had received any recent impulse, it was partly from embittered controversies in the Church, and partly also from the unfortunate error of those who insisted upon treating the case of the Church of Ireland entirely with reference to the theory of establishments, and not with reference to the broad, substantial arguments and facts upon which the Church of England was so strong. The Church of England was not a foreign Church—it was not a Church which, like the Church of Ireland, was imposed upon Ireland and maintained there by extrinsic power, but it was, whatever else it might be, the growth of the history and traditions of the country; it had existed from a period shortly after the Christian era, and for 1,300 years had never ceased to be the Church of the country; it had been in every age, as it was still, deeply rooted in the heart of the people, and intertwined with the local habits and feelings.

9.—The cases of small-pox in London during the past week rose to 288, the highest weekly number during the present epidemic, and almost three times as high as in any of the preceding epidemics during thirty-one years.

—Fort Issy captured by Versailles troops after a bombardment continued over eight days. A large quantity of ammunition and artillery were found within the fortress.

—Eliza Jane Cook, a young married woman in straitened circumstances, throws two of her children and herself into the Lea at Clapton. A little girl was rescued, but the mother and boy were drowned.

10.—Dissension among the Communist leaders, the first Committee of Public Safety being dismissed to-day, and another appointed in its place. Commander Rossel, charged with the provisional title of Delegate of War, wrote that he felt himself incapable of continuing the responsibility of a commandant where everyone wished to deliberate, and no one to obey. Delescluze succeeded to the post of Delegate of War.

—Professor Huxley carries a motion at the London School Board, "That measures be taken to ascertain whether any, and if so, what charitable or other endowments in the London school district ought to be applied, wholly or in part, to the augmentation of the school fund." The Professor took occasion to censure the management of Christ's Hospital in having so far departed from the wishes of those who founded the charity as to make it an educational institution for children belonging to the middle classes and neglecting the children of the poor.

—Found dead in his bed, Major-General Sir John Douglas, C.B., commanding **the**

Cavalry Brigade at Aldershot, and who had seen much service in the Crimea

11. — Came on in the Court of Common Pleas, before Lord Chief Justice Bovill and a jury, the gigantic case of Tichborne v. Lushington, occupying under one form or another the Courts at Westminster for the greater part of two years. Involving estates said to be worth 24,000*l.* a year, with a baronetcy attached, and depending mainly on evidence brought forward to identify the Claimant with the long-lost heir, the case excited the keenest public interest, and for a time in social circles put aside events of even national importance. The declaration stated that the plaintiff sued Franklin Lushington, as tenant of the trustees of the infant Alfred Joseph, to recover possession of the mansion known as Tichborne House, in the county of Southampton. He claimed to be the son of Sir James Doughty Tichborne, the youngest of three brothers, of whom the first died, the second took the estates and died, leaving a daughter, Miss Kate Doughty. The property was settled on the male line, and on the death of the second brother, without male issue, passed to the youngest brother James, who in August 1827, married Harriette Félicité Seymour, a French lady and a Roman Catholic, mother of Sir Roger Tichborne, born on the 5th of January, 1829. On the 4th of September, 1839, another son was born—James, who subsequently died, leaving a posthumous child, Alfred Joseph, who was the infant in possession of the estates. Sir Roger was brought up for several years in Paris, and received instruction principally from a tutor named Chatillon. In 1845 he went to Stonyhurst; was there for three years, and in October 1849, obtained a commission in the Carbineers, at that time in Ireland, and remained with his regiment three years and a half. At this time Sir Roger was light and slim in form, and extremely narrow in the chest; his pleasures, manners, and pursuits were those of a gentleman; he was fond of music; he was connected with the Seymours and the Townleys, and he visited at Sir Clifford Constable's, at Lord Camoys', and Lord Arundel of Wardour's; he was acquainted with the Radcliffes and some of the best families in the kingdom. In 1850 and 1851 he was a good deal at Tichborne, visiting his uncle Sir Edward, who had taken the name of Doughty, and whose daughter, Kate, was about Roger's age. Roger became very much attached to his cousin, and during a visit at Christmas 1851 the attachment was discovered. It was disapproved by Sir Edward, and an angry scene ensued, which led to Roger suddenly leaving Tichborne, with a resolve to go abroad. In January 1852 he made his will, and deposited a sealed packet with a gentleman named Gosford, an intimate and confidential friend, containing certain private wishes and intentions to be carried out if he lived. Roger then went to Paris to visit his parents, and at their earnest entreaty postponed the carrying

out of his design. But in December 1852 he had made up his mind to go to South America for a year and a half, and wrote to his parents to that effect. He also wrote to his cousin Kate that he hoped in three years to be united to her, and to another cousin, Mrs. Greenwood (who lived near Tichborne), that he hoped she would write to him, and that he should be always happy to answer her letters. With these intentions Roger sailed for South America, having one Moore as his valet. He arrived at Valparaiso in June 1853, and spent some months in travelling about the country. Here he heard of the death of his uncle, Sir Edward; but being desirous of further travel he communicated with his mother and friends at Tichborne, and sent home two likenesses of himself, produced in evidence. About the 20th of April, 1854, he embarked at Rio in the Bella; on the 26th a part of the wreck of the vessel was picked up, and the ship was never heard of again, nor any of the crew. The agents of Messrs. Glyns, Roger's bankers at Rio, heard of the loss of the vessel, and wrote to his family that he had embarked on board of her. For thirteen years nothing more was heard of Roger Tichborne. The will was proved by Mr. Gosford, his executor, the sealed packet was opened and destroyed, and a suit was instituted in which legal proof was given of his loss and death. The underwriters paid a heavy insurance on the vessel, and the owner never heard anything of the crew. The story of the Claimant was that he was picked up, with eight of the crew, about the 26th of April, and carried to Melbourne, where, he said, they were landed on the 24th of July, 1854; that on the day he landed he went with the captain to the Custom-house, and that the next day, leaving the wrecked sailors on board the ship, he went into the interior, where he resided for thirteen years under the name of Castro, this being, it was contended in defence, an alias for Arthur Orton, a butcher belonging to Wapping, who was known to have been at Wagga Wagga at this time. Unwilling to believe in the loss of her son, the Dowager Lady Tichborne advertised rewards for his discovery in various quarters, and one of them coming under the notice of one Cubitt, at Sydney, a friend of Gibbs, an attorney at Wagga Wagga, then acting in the bankruptcy of Castro, word was sent home to the Dowager, in December 1866, that her son was alive and well, at a place 600 miles from Sydney. Through the intervention of Gibbs and Cubitt the Claimant raised funds to proceed to England at the close of the year. He went, however, not direct, but by way of New York, and not to Paris, where the Dowager was awaiting him, but to England. He arrived on Christmas Day 1866, and the first visit he made was to Wapping, for the purpose of making inquiry regarding the Orton family. He afterwards visited Tichborne secretly, and was taken over the house and grounds. At Paris the Dowager made affidavit, that she recognized the Claimant as

20

her son Sir Roger ; but her death deprived the defendants of any opportunity for cross-examination. She had, however, arranged to allow him 1,000*l.* per annum till his claim could be established. In an interview with Gosford, the Claimant made no allusion to the sealed packet, though they conversed about the will previously seen at Doctors' Commons. During a residence of some months at Croydon the Dowager was again with him, and also many old servants and friends of the family, as well as troopers in the Carbineers,—the latter now the first witnesses produced to establish the identity of the claimant.

11.—Final Treaty of Peace signed between France and Germany.

— Died at Collingwood, near Hawkhurst, aged 79 years, Sir John F. W. Herschel, the most distinguished of modern astronomers. The funeral took place on the 18th in Westminster Abbey, in presence of a great company of mourners. The place selected for the interment was near the grave of Sir Isaac Newton.

— The property of M. Thiers seized by the Commune. A decree issued this morning set forth that "The Committee of Public Safety, considering that the proclamation of M. Thiers declares that the army will not bombard Paris, while every day women and children fall victims to the fratricidal projectiles of Versailles, and that it makes an appeal to treason in order to enter Paris, feeling it to be impossible to vanquish its heroic population by force of arms, orders that the goods and property of M. Thiers be seized by the Administration of the Domains, and his house in the Place St. Georges be razed to the ground Citizens Fontaine, Delegate of the Domains, and Andrien, Delegate of the Public Service, are charged with the immediate execution of the present decree." In the Assembly to-day M. Thiers demanded a vote of confidence from the Assembly, which was granted by 495 to 10 votes.

12.—Died at Paris, aged 89 years, M. Auber, composer of " Masaniello," and forty other operas.

13.—The Court of Session reverse a former decision in what was known as the " Paraguayan Case," and find Dr. Stewart liable in payment of the bill, chiefly on the ground that, although it had been got from him through fear and force, yet he had acknowledged his liability by eighteen months afterwards writing a letter, asking his brother to pay the amount of the bill from funds he had lodged in the Bank of Scotland. Madame Lynch was in the witness-box for nearly five hours.

14.—In consequence of a revolt in the garrison, the Communists withdraw from Fort Vanves, leaving it to be occupied by a portion of the investing force, who also retain the adjacent village after fighting through it house by house.

15.—Mr. Muntz's amendment on the Army Bill, designed to limit its operation to regulation prices, and to leave over-regulation and the bonus system untouched, rejected by 260 to 195 votes.

— The Pope issues a Brief directed against the professors in the Roman University who had presented an address to Dr. Döllinger "overflowing with errors, blasphemy, and unbelief." His Holiness urged upon parochial priests the necessity of restraining the young from attending the lectures of such professors, and of opposing, at the same time, the torrent of unbelief into which they were likely to be driven.

16.—Destruction by the Commune of the Vendôme Column, erected by Napoleon I., principally of cannon taken at Ulm, to commemorate the victory of Austerlitz in 1805. It was covered with 425 bronze plaques, moulded in bas-relief to display the chief incidents in the Austrian campaign of that year. They were each 3 feet 8 inches high, and formed a continuous band, enclosing the column twenty-two times as it circled to the top, the entire length of the spiral being 840 feet. Instead of Charlemagne, as at first intended, it was surmounted by a statue of the First Napoleon in a Roman costume and crowned with laurel. After several postponements it was brought to the ground this afternoon in the presence of many thousands who had waited for hours to witness the spectacle. Owing to some engineering difficulties in cutting through the column at the base, it could not be brought down at the time originally fixed. The members of the Commune were installed in all their state in the balconies of the Etat Major of the National Guard and of the Minister of Justice, on the Place Vendôme, to witness the affair. Sentinels were posted about half way down the Rue de la Paix to prevent the crowd from approaching too close, as up to the last moment accidents were feared. After a good deal of intermittent drumming and trumpeting, and caracoling backwards and forwards of officers on horseback, and the continual ascent and descent of workmen—now of the column, now of its pedestal simply—and sundry flourishes of red flags, at about half-past five the ropes were tightened, and it was evident the end was at hand. Suddenly the column was observed to lean forward towards the Rue de la Paix, then finally to fall, with a dull heavy thud, raising, as it did so, an immense cloud of dust. Before it touched the ground it separated into three parts by its own weight, and on reaching the bed of dung and faggots spread to receive it, broke into at least thirty pieces. The statue of Napoleon, on reaching the ground, broke off from its pedestal at the ankles, then at the knees, the waist, and the neck, while the iron railings which surrounded the summit of the monument were shivered to pieces. Shortly after the column had fallen, spectators were permitted to traverse the Place to witness the wreck, but were not permitted to take away any of the fragments.

17.—Mr. Lawson's Permissive Bill thrown out on the proposal for a second reading by 196 to 124 votes.

— Explosion of a cartridge factory in the Avenue Repp, Paris, causing the death of over fifty people employed in the works. In the present disordered condition of the city, this calamity was at once attributed to treachery, and various citizens were arrested on suspicion.

— The Commune threaten the lives of the Archbishop of Paris, and other hostages, Urbain, formerly a schoolmaster, who had installed himself, with his mistress, in the Mairie of The Seventh Arrondissement, demanding that ten of the number should be shot within twenty-four hours, in retaliation for the alleged murder of a woman attached to one of the Commune ambulances.

18.—In an unusually crowded house, Mr. Disraeli calls attention to the "general conduct" of the Chancellor of the Exchequer. Reviewing the various changes in the Budget, and the irregularities as regards the house-tax and tea duties with which it had been accompanied, he complained that the Government had vouchsafed no explanation of the reasons why they abandoned their first proposals, and threw the whole burden of the year on direct taxation, and especially on that particular tax which the highest authority had declared to be a most unpopular tax, and one which most severely pinched the poor middle classes. Mr. Lowe briefly replied, complaining that Mr. Disraeli had played off a practical joke upon him by threatening a general indictment of his financial policy, and sinking into a criticism of a few small isolated points, which he described as the "veriest pedantries of finance."

— In Committee on the Army Regulation Bill, Colonel Anson moved an amendment on Clause 2 with the object of permitting the purchase of Exchanges. Mr. Cardwell, in opposing it, explained that it was not intended to prevent exchanges, but merely to prohibit money passing in such transactions, except the payment of travelling expenses. To make an exception in favour of "exchanges" would be to strike at the abolition of purchase. After considerable debate the amendment was negatived by 183 to 146.

19.—Prince Arthur falls through a window, imperfectly fastened, in the billiard-room of Marlborough House, and is slightly injured in the head and foot.

— The Commune issues a decree suppressing additional newspapers, and declaring that all adverse criticism on its proceedings will be treated with the rigour of martial law.

— M. Rochefort arrested at Meaux and taken to Versailles.

19.—The Dutch iron steamship *William III.*, intended to open up a new trade between Holland and Java, burnt in the Channel.

20.—Fire at Woolwich Barracks, the whole of the block forming the offices of the Quartermaster-General, the Brigade-Major, the Barrack Control Department Clerk's offices and stores being destroyed.

21.—After a siege extending over nine weeks, the Versailles troops this (Sunday) afternoon succeed in entering Paris by the St. Cloud gate at Point du Jour, and by the gate of Montrouge. Captain Trèves, an officer of the navy, crept up quietly from the trenches to the rampart at the Point du Jour. To his astonishment he found the insurgents had retired. He immediately called up 300 sailors, who took possession of the gate. Other troops followed up, and before anyone really felt that the affair had commenced, it was all over. Not a rifle was fired at this point, nor was there a single man wounded. The insurgents at once run up a white flag over the Auteuil gate, but took occasion to strengthen a position of some importance they had taken up on the Arc de Triomphe. The division of General Douay entered by the gate of St. Cloud, and occupied the salient between the ramparts and the viaduct. Here there was a second bastion of considerable solidity. The soldiers entered the half-ruined barracks and casemates, and made prisoners of a number of insurgents whom they found concealed there. Immediate preparations were then made for the advance right and left, but as the enemy was still keeping up a fire from 7-pounders and mitrailleurs, along the bastions between Vaugirard and Montrouge, a regular assault of these positions by the division under General Cissey was determined upon. On the left General Ladmirault took the gates of Passy and Auteuil, and then still keeping to the left seized the Arc de Triomphe. General Vinoy, entering by the Point du Jour, passed the Seine, and opened the gate of Sèvres to General Cissey. By two o'clock General Cissey was master of the Faubourg St. Germain as far as Mont Parnasse, and General Clinchant was at the New Opera House. In the Assembly M. Thiers said:—"The slight resistance we have met with warrants us in hoping that Paris will soon be restored to its true sovereign—to France. We are honest men. We will visit with the rigour of the law those men who have been guilty of crime against France, and have not shrunk from assassination or the destruction of national monuments. The laws will be rigorously enforced. The expiation shall be complete."

23.—M. Thiers reports to the Prefects that the Assembly has now 80,000 soldiers within Paris. "General Cissey," he said, "has taken up his position from the railway station at Mont Parnasse to the École Militaire, and is proceeding along the left bank towards the Tuileries. Generals Douay and Vinoy are enclosing the Tuileries, the Louvre, and the

Place Vendôme, in order subsequently to advance upon the Hôtel de Ville. General Clinchant, having made himself master of the Opera, the St. Lazare Railway Station, and the Batignolles, has carried the barricades at Clichy. General Ladmirault is approaching the foot of Montmartre with two divisions. General Montaudan, following the movement of General Ladmirault, has taken Neuilly, Le Vallois, Perrey, and Clichy, and is attacking St. Ouen. He has taken 105 guns and crowds of prisoners. The resistance of the insurgents is gradually declining, and there is every ground for hoping that, if the struggle is not finished to-day, it will be over by to-morrow at the very latest, and for a long time. With respect to the killed and wounded it is impossible to fix the numbers, but they are considerable. The army, on the contrary, has suffered but very slight loss." About 6 P.M., a second circular gave intimation that the tricolour flag was then waving over the Buttes Montmartre and the Northern Railway Station. These decisive points were carried by the troops of Generals Ladmirault and Clinchant, who captured between 2,000 and 3,000 prisoners. General Douay took the Church of the Trinity, and marched upon the Mairie in the Rue Drouot. Generals Cissey and Vinoy advanced towards the Hôtel de Ville and the Tuileries. The losses of the insurgents up to this time were put down at 12,000 killed and wounded, and 25,000 prisoners.

24.—The morning news from Paris was that the Communists still held out at the barricades of the Place Vendôme, and the Place de la Concorde. Later in the day the startling intelligence was spread abroad that the Louvre and Tuileries had been set on fire by the insurgents. The Commune, it appeared, determined to keep its promise of perishing in a sea of blood, and under a canopy of flame, fired the greater number of the public buildings in that part of the city through which they were now being driven by the Versailles troops. The glories of Paris, the *Times* correspondent wrote, are rapidly passing away in smoke and flame, such as have never been witnessed since the burning of Moscow, and amid a roar of cannon, a screaming of mitrailleurs, a bursting of projectiles, and a horrid rattle of musketry from different quarters which are appalling. "A more lovely day it would be imp ssible to imagine, a sky of unusual brightness, blue as the clearest ever seen, a sun of surpassing brilliancy. even for Paris, scarcely a breath of wind to ruffle the Seine. Such of the great buildings as the spreading conflagration has not reached stand in the clearest relief as they are seen for probably the last time; but in a dozen spots, on both sides of the bridges, sheets of flame and awful volumes of smoke rise to the sky and positively obscure the light of the sun. As well as we can make out through the flame and smoke rushing across the gardens of the Tuileries, the fire has reached the Palais Royal.

Everyone is now crying out, 'The Palais Royal burns!' and we ascertain that it does. We cannot see Notre Dame or the Hôtel Dieu. It is probable that both are fast becoming ashes. Not an instant passes without an explosion. Stones and timber and iron are flying high into the air, and falling to the earth with horrible crashes. The very trees are on fire. They are crackling, and their leaves and branches are like tinder. The buildings in the Place de la Concorde reflect the flames, and every stone in them is like bright gold. Montmartre is still outside the circle of the flame; but the little wind that is blowing carries the smoke up to it, and in the clear heavens it rises black as Milton's Pandemonium. The new Opera House is as yet uninjured; but the smoke encircles it, and it will be next to a miracle if it escapes. We see clearly now that the Palais de Justice, the Sainte Chapelle, the Préfecture of Police, and the Hôtel de Ville are all blazing without a possibility existing of any portion of any one of them being saved from the general wreck and ruin." Exasperated at the success of the Versailles troops, the Commune in the afternoon seemed fully determined to fire, with petroleum, as much of the capital as they had in their possession. One order found on a National Guard, set forth that "The citizen delegate commanding the barracks of the Château d'Eau, is invited to give the bearer the cans of mineral oil necessary for the chief of barricades of the Faubourg du Temple. Signed, Brunel, Chef de Légion." In the evening, about nine o'clock, and when they had possession of only a small part of the city in the east, the Commune posted up the last of its long series of decrees, No. 398— "Destroy immediately every house from the windows of which there has been firing on the National Guard, and shoot all the inhabitants if they do not give up and execute the authors of the crime." As many, it was said, as 12,000 were taken prisoners before midnight, and in some quarters, where the resistance was especially stubborn, piles of corpses were built up near the barricades.

24.—Massacre of the hostages in the prison yard of La Roquette, principally at the instigation of Raoul Rigault, a ferocious profligate, whom the Commune had named Procureur-Général, and his subordinate, Ferré, who had arrived at the prison after firing the Préfecture of Police with the design of burning the prisoners alive. About half-past seven in the evening, the Director of the prison ascended at the head of fifty Federals to the gallery, where the principal prisoners were confined. An officer went round to each cell, summoning first the Archbishop, and then in succession M. Bonjean, the Abbé Allard, Fathers Ducoudray and Clair, and the Abbé Déguerry, Curé of the Madeleine. As the prisoners appeared, they were marched down to the road running round the prison, on each side of which were arranged National Guards, who received the captives with insults and injurious epithets. They were next taken into the courtyard facing the infirmary, where they found a firing party awaiting them. Monseigneur Darboy stepped forward, and, addressing his assassins, uttered a few words of pardon. "Do not," he said, "profane the word liberty; it is to us alone it belongs, for we shall die for liberty and faith." Two of these men approached the Archbishop, and, in face of their comrades, knelt before him, beseeching his forgiveness. The other Federals at once rushed upon them, drove them back with insulting reproaches, and then, turning towards the prisoners, gave vent to most violent expressions. The commander of the detachment appeared ashamed of this, and, ordering silence, uttered a frightful oath, telling his men that they were there "to shoot those people, and not to bully them." The Federals were silenced, and, upon the order of their lieutenant, loaded their weapons. Father Allard was placed against the wall and was the first shot down. Then M. Darboy, in his turn, fell. The whole six prisoners were thus shot, all evincing the utmost calmness and courage. M. Déguerry alone exhibited a momentary weakness, attributable, however, rather to his state of health than to fear. After this tragical execution, carried out without any formal witnesses and in the presence only of a number of bandits, the bodies of the unfortunate victims were placed in a cart belonging to a railway company, which had been requisitioned for the purpose, and taken to Père-la-Chaise, where they were placed in the last trench of the "fosse commune" side by side, without even an attempt to cover them with earth. The body of the Archbishop was afterwards recovered, embalmed, and laid in state. His funeral, together with that of Monseigneur Surat, Grand Vicar of the diocese, Father Déguerry, Curé of the Madeleine, and the Rev. MM. Bécourt and Sabatier, the Incumbents of Notre Dame de Bonne Nouvelle and Notre Dame de Lorette, was celebrated, on the 7th of June, in the Cathedral of Notre Dame, by the Papal Nuncio and four of the French Bishops, in the presence of the ministers of State, generals of the army, and members of the National Assembly. The two immediate predecessors of Archbishop Darboy met with violent deaths—M. Sibour, assassinated by a priest in the Church of St. Etienne du Mont, and M. Affré, shot on a barricade in June, 1848.

25.—The American Senate ratify the Treaty of Washington by 50 votes against 12.

— Inquiry at Marlborough Street Police Court, into the charge brought against Flora Davy, or Newington, of having stabbed Frederick Moon within her residence, Newton Road, Westbourne Grove. Her own account of the transaction was :—"We were sitting after dinner at table, and Fred made an observation to me about my daughter which annoyed me excessively. I begged him not to repeat it,

for I could not stand it. Mr. Moon said, 'I will say it again, and if you are not silent I will fling the bottle at your head.'" She stated that she then jumped up with a knife in her hand. They struggled and fell, and she saw the blood pouring out but she could not tell how.

25.—The summary execution of many women, in Paris, on the charge of poisoning and fire-raising by petroleum, caused much comment on the desperate measures found to be necessary for suppressing the Commune. A correspondent of the *Times* witnessed one such scene :—"I took a walk," he writes, "down the Rue Rivoli towards the Hôtel de Ville, to judge of the amount of damage done, and at the corner of the Rue Castiglione became aware of the approach of a great crowd of people yelling and shaking their fists. The cortége was headed by a company of mounted gendarmes, behind whom came two artillerymen, dragging between them a soiled bundle of rags that tottered and struggled, and fell down under the blows showered upon it by all who were within reach. It was a woman, who had been caught in the act of spreading petroleum. Her face was bleeding and her hair streaming down her back, from which her clothing had been torn. On they dragged her, followed by a hooting mob, till they reached the corner of the Louvre, and there they propped her up against a wall, already half dead from the treatment she had received. The crowd ranged itself in a circle, and I have never seen a picture more perfect and complete in its details than was presented by that scene. The gasping, shrinking figure in the centre, surrounded by a crowd who could scarce be kept from tearing her in pieces, who waved their arms crying 'A l'eau, à l'eau !' on one side a barricade, still strewn with broken guns and hats—a dead National Guard lying in the fosse—behind a group of mounted gendarmes, and then a perspective of ruined streets and blackened houses, culminating in the extreme distance in the still burning Hôtel de Ville. Presently two revolvers were discharged, and the bundle of rags fell forward in a pool of blood. The popular thirst for vengeance was satisfied, and the crowd dispersed in search of further excitement elsewhere."

26.—Miss Burdett Coutts gazetted Baroness of Highgate and Brookfield in the county of Middlesex.

— The insurgent position at Belleville stormed and taken after a sharp struggle. One extraordinary feature in the street fights at this time, was that many of them were carried on with a crowd of non-combatants, men, women, and children, as close to them on both sides as if the whole affair were a theatrical representation of a sensational melodramatic kind, where a good deal of powder and blue lights would be burnt, but no bullets or lives would be spent. "In streets in which fighting actually occurs no one of course shows except combatants, and these show as little as possible, lying down or sheltering behind extempore barricades and windows. The people indoors, as may be supposed, do not keep near them, as the bullets fired down the sides of the streets under cover of doorways or corner houses glance and ricochet about in the wildest way. Scarcely a window escapes if the fight lasts long, but adjoining streets, running at right angles to the fighting ground, are for the moment comparatively safe, and the people crowd about the doorways in these, the more venturesome getting close to street corners, and every now and then cautiously craning their necks round to see, if possible, whether shots tell."

27.—The Newcastle engineers strike in favour of the nine hours' movement, about 9,000 leaving the works of Armstrong, Stephenson and others.

. **28.**—In Paris to-day, the Commune is described as "dying hard," the fighting being unusually desperate in and around Belleville, Menilmontant, and Père-la-Chaise. Even the women fought savagely. "No quarter was given to any man, woman, or child found in arms. Numerous arrests are taking place in the streets of Paris, and military law is being applied with the utmost rigour in all cases. All prisoners are immediately sent up for judgment to the Provost-Marshal's court at the Châtelet. The executions now take place at three fixed points—the Champ de Mars, the Parc Monceaux, and near the Hôtel de Ville. Batches of as many as 50 and 100 at a time are shot. No person whatever is allowed to leave Paris on any pretext, unless bearing a special permit signed either by Marshal MacMahon or the chief of his staff. There is less difficulty in entering Paris, but all strangers are subjected to rigorous examination, and, if their papers are not satisfactory, to arrest. Great dread of incendiaries still prevails ; all cellar gratings, and area openings, through which combustible matter might be introduced, hermetically sealed."

— A proclamation, signed by Marshal MacMahon, announces the delivery of Paris. "Inhabitants of Paris !" he wrote, "The army of France has come to save you. Paris is delivered. Our soldiers at four o'clock captured the last positions occupied by the insurgents. To-day the struggle is over, and order, labour, and security revive." The fighting appears to have ceased about 3 P.M. A few shots were fired from the windows at Belleville, where frightful scenes were said to have been enacted. The more desperate characters, felons and escaped *forçats* of the worst description, turned at the last moment on their own comrades because they refused to continue the fight. Some women murdered, with knives, two young men for the same reason. In consequence of the firing from the windows an immense number of executions occurred The park of the Buttes Chaumont

was strewn with corpses. The soldiers were so furious that the officers found it necessary to warn strangers of the danger of incurring suspicion. Dombrowski died in the Hôtel de Ville, from wounds received at a barricade in the Rue d'Ornano ; and Delescluze fell fighting at the Château d'Eau. Bisson and Tavernier were captured and shot.

29.—M. Thiers orders the disarmament of Paris, and the dissolution of the National Guard of the Department of the Seine.

— Whit Monday kept, for the first time, as a Bank Holiday, under Sir J. Lubbock's Bill, recently passed.

— On a petition being brought up in the National Assembly to-day relative to the capitulation of Metz, General Changarnier made a speech in which he detailed the facts that preceded the retreat of the Army of the Rhine into that fortress, and said he must reproach the Commander-in-Chief with indecision and loss of time on that occasion, faults which led to the fortress being completely invested by the Germans. Famine alone had been the cause of the army in Metz being reduced to powerlessness. Marshal Bazaine had not been fortunate ; but the cession of Metz was neither preconcerted nor voluntary. General Changarnier concluded by urging the Assembly not to allow an odious suspicion to rest upon generals who were brave soldiers and honourable men. M. Thiers said he was happy to see General Changarnier undertake the defence of one of the most valiant soldiers of France. He assented to the proposal for an inquiry ; which, indeed, had been demanded by Marshal Bazaine himself; but he left the decision upon this question to the Sovereign Assembly. General Le Flô, the Minister for War, then ascended the tribune and said :—"The l aw upon this subject is most formal. Every Commander who surrenders a fortress to the enemy must be tried before a Council of War. I shall do my duty with regard to all the capitulations—those of Metz and Sedan as well as the others which occurred during the war."

— Victor Hugo expelled from Belgium for offering his home as an asylum to refugee Communists.

— Père Hyacinthe, writing to the *Gaulois*, declares that in the recent calamities which had overthrown France the Church had not done its duty. "Instead of the promises and teachings of the Gospel to the disinherited of this world, the Church in the noisy echoes of the press, and sometimes even by the mouth of its bishops, treated of matters of bitter controversy about the Pope-King, the dogmatisation of intolerance, and the canonisation of the Inquisition. I do not calumniate the political and religious régime that we have submitted to for more than twenty years, and which is summed up in these two words—'Scepticism at Paris ; fanaticism at Rome.'"

30.—"Paris," writes the *Times*, "the Paris of civilization, is no more. It pitted itself against France, and rather than be beaten has destroyed itself. We may look for it, but we shall find its place alone. They who have found themselves scores of times at Paris, just for a week's change, or on their way to and fro between this and mountain or classic lands, have lost the fairest vision of their lives. They can no longer interpret and unfold its glories to younger minds. All they have to make up for it, is the sorry boast that they have seen what the eye of man will never see again, for twenty Haussmanns would only make a new Paris—Paris revived, but not real or the same."

June 1.—The morning papers publish a letter from Prince Napoleon to Jules Favre, charging the Republican Minister and his colleagues with the responsibility of almost all the evils from which France is suffering, and pointing out how much better things were managed under the Empire. "The Empire," the Prince observed, "had committed great faults ; our defeats were great, but our disasters date from you. Let each bear his part. Without doubt it was a grievous error to count too much upon the forces of France, and to commit in 1870 the fault which Prussia committed in 1806 : to look too much to our victories under the great Republic and the First Empire ; to think too little of the powerful enemy we had to combat ; to contemplate the Crimea in 1854 and Italy in 1859, instead of calmly looking in the face the German forces in 1870, headed by remarkable men . . . For a new society a new symbol is required. It requires—and modern right wills it—the abdication of all before the will of the people freely and directly expressed. Besides this, once more I repeat, there is nothing but chaos. Faith in monarchy cannot be imposed. The only base upon which a Government in France can affirm its principle, the only source from which it can draw legitimacy and force, is by an appeal to the people, which we claim, and on which France ought to insist."

5.—In the Tichborne trial to-day the cross-examination of the Solicitor-General pressed hard upon the Claimant as to his intimacy with Miss Kate Doughty. He answered with great apparent reluctance, and professed forgetfulness. The Solicitor-General persisted, and directed his questions to the subject of the sealed packet left by Roger Tichborne in the hands of Vincent Gosford before he left England :—The Solicitor-General—In your affidavit made on the 14th of February, 1868, you say you gave Gosford "special instructions to hold, and not to open the same, except on two events, one of which I know has not happened, and the other I hope has not happened." What was the event you knew had not happened ?—My returning before Miss Doughty's marriage. Do you swear that ?—I can't swear. I don't know what I alluded to when I swore the affi-

davit. Do you mean to tell the jury that you did not know which of those events had not happened ? —It must have been my return before Miss Doughty's marriage. Is that what you swear ?—I may have meant my death, which has not happened. (Laughter.) What was the event which you hoped had not happened ?—If I am called upon to state by the Solicitor-General, it must be on his own head. I have written the object of the sealed packet in a paper which I have handed down. What was the event which you hoped had not happened ?—Will you look at that document ? I ask you what was the event which you hoped had not happened ? The witness said the question ought not to be put to him, and that it was not for his own sake that he objected to answer ; but upon the question being again repeated he answered, "The confinement of Miss Doughty." Do you mean to swear before the Judge and jury that you had seduced Katherine Doughty ? —I most solemnly to my God swear that I had. [This answer caused great sensation in court.] Your cousin—this lady (pointing to Mrs. Radcliffe, who sat behind the learned counsel) ?— Yes. The Solicitor-General—Let it be distinctly understood that Mrs. Radcliffe is here by her own wish. After some hours' cross-examination, the Claimant said he was exhausted, and the Court adjourned. The *Times*, in reporting the case, wrote—" Nothing but a literal report of every question and every answer given, every letter put in, including the contents of the returns (the one to Victoria, New South Wales, and Tasmania alone occupied 232 large, closely printed pages) to the Commissioners sent out, and the documents commented on, would give anything like a fair notion of this extraordinary trial. We might, if we adopted this course, fill at least one sheet of the *Times* every day, and even then it is impossible to convey to our readers a faint idea of the manner of the witness, the withering sarcasm of the Solicitor-General, the tone of his voice, the sensation in court, and the general effect of the proceedings." During the proceedings of Tuesday the 6th, the Lord Chief Justice, not being able to catch a word, asked the witness to repeat it, which he seemed unable to do, and finally said, "You have been awfully sharp upon me, my lord. You are determined I shall not have justice. The other side has not wanted a counsel at all." The Lord Chief Justice—"I must request you to be more respectful." The Claimant pleaded illness this afternoon, and the case was adjourned over a day. Next day the cross-examination was met by a general disavowal of being able to remember details.

6.—Died suddenly at his seat, Ogleworth Park, Gloucestershire, Sir John Rolt, Q.C., Attorney-General in Earl Derby's third Government.

— Died, aged 87, the Hon. Frederick Byng, a popular member of fashionable society from the days of the Regency.

6.—The slave vessel *Don Juan* takes fire sixty miles south of Hong-Kong, when the captain and crew leave the ship with 500 coolies to be suffocated and consumed in the hold, where they were battened down.

— The University of Oxford confer the degree of D.C.L. on Professor Döllinger of Munich. The proposal, advocated by Professor Liddon, was opposed by Mr. Rogers, of Magdalen Hall, and the Principal of St. Mary's Hall, who thought the present time inopportune. Professor Bernard received a similar honour on the 15th.

7.—In Committee on the Burials Bill, a proposal that the service, when not according to a published ritual, should consist of nothing but prayers and passages of Scripture, rejected by 146 to 144 votes.

— Funeral of the Archbishop of Paris, and the other murdered hostages.

8.—The National Assembly declares the proscriptive laws abolished, and that the Orleans Princes had been duly elected. On the other hand, the Princes were understood to have pledged themselves to resign their seats and refrain from taking part in politics at present. In the debate on the occasion, M. Thiers professed great friendship for the family of Orleans, but declared that his friendship for his country was superior to all others—a declaration which was loudly cheered by the Assembly ; and he added : "We have won a material victory ; we shall gain a moral triumph by our prudence."

12.—In moving an address to the Crown on the subject of the *Alabama* claims, Earl Russell defended the course he had pursued as Foreign Secretary, and censured the Commissioners for giving a retrospective effect in the recent treaty to certain rules of international law. The action of the Government was defended by Lord Granville, Lord de Grey, and the Duke of Argyll, and the motion negatived without a division.

— In the Commons Mr. Cardwell announces an intention on the part of Government to abandon part of the Army Regulation Bill, and persevere only with those clauses referring to the abolition of purchase, a course described by Mr. Disraeli as a breach of faith with the House, seeing that large sums had already been voted for purposes of the bill. After a brief debate the House went, for the ninth time, into Committee, and Clause 3 was agreed to.

— Examined by the Solicitor-General as to the details of school life at Stonyhurst, the following questions were put to the Claimant. —Did you learn the Hebrew alphabet?—I do not recollect. You learned Greek ?—Some portion of it. Did you go as far as the Greek alphabet?—I don't remember. Did you ever read a verse of the Bible in Greek?— Probably a part of it. Does any single Greek word linger in your memory?—Not a word. I

don't think I ever thought of it. Did you get as far as the article ? Could not you give me "an" in Greek?—No ; I have lost it entirely. Did you get better on in Latin?—I believe I got further in Latin. Did you learn the Latin alphabet ?—Of course I did. Could you read Latin ?—Yes. Could you read a line now?— No ; I could not. Did you do any Virgil, any Cæsar?—I don't recollect. Do you know whether Cæsar is written in prose or verse ?— I don't recollect. (A laugh.) Is Cæsar Latin or Greek ?—I should think it was Greek. (Laughter.) What is Virgil—a general or a statesman, or what ?—I have no recollection. Was he a Greek or a Latin writer?—I don't recollect. Did he write verse or prose ?—I don't recollect. Did you ever see it before (handing a Delphin edition of Virgil to the witness) ?—I don't want to look at it at all. (A laugh.) Is it Greek or Latin ?—It looks to me like Greek. (Laughter.) You learned mathematics, you say ?—Yes. Is it the same thing as chemistry ?—My memory does not serve me. Chemistry is a science by itself. Then what is mathematics ?—I have no recollection. What book have you ever read in mathematics?—My memory does not serve me. What is it— written in Greek, or Latin, or what ?—I don't recollect. Did you ever read Euclid ? Has that anything to do with mathematics ?—I don't recollect. I think not. (A laugh.) Has algebra anything to do with mathematics ?—I have no recollection. Have you read Euclid? —I believe I did, but don't recollect. Did you ever hear of the Asses' Bridge ?—I don't recollect. Did you ever try to get over it ? (Laughter.)—I don't recollect. Did you ever try to cross the Asses' Bridge?—I have no recollection of it. Did anybody try his best to help you over the Asses' Bridge? Did you make gallant efforts, as many of us have done, to get over it ?—I have no recollection. Do you remember whereabouts it is—how far from Stonyhurst ? (Laughter.)—It is only insulting me. Do you know it better by its Latin name, "*pons asinorum*"?—No. Have you forgotten that A. M. D. G. stands at the head of every exercise, and is printed at the head of every book, at Stonyhurst?—Will you vouch that as a fact? Is it so?—I don't recollect. Does A. M. D. G. mean "*Ad majorem Dei gloriam ?*" —I have no doubt it does. What does it mean in English ?—There is God and glory—the last two words. What does L. D. S. mean? —I don't know. Do they mean *Laus Deo semper ?*—(No answer.) Is that Latin or French?—(No answer.) What is the meaning of the words?—It would be "laws of God for ever." (Great laughter.) The Judge—It is difficult to restrain so large an assembly, but I hope people will not laugh or make any sign to interrupt the proceedings.

12.—Questioned by Sir Roundell Palmer regarding the second rule in the sixth article of the Treaty of Washington, defining the duty of neutrals towards belligerents, Mr. Gladstone said the new rule would prevent the fitting out or arming in British ports of vessels intended to act against belligerent powers with which this country was at peace, but it would not interfere with the exportation of arms and munitions of war in the ordinary course of commerce.

13.—The House of Lords, by a majority of 129 to 89 votes, agree not to insist on the Salisbury or new Test Clause introduced into the University Bill, and which had been rejected by the Commons.

14.—The German Catholics circulate an appeal, signed by Döllinger, Huber, Reinkens and others, declaring :—" 1. We persist in the rejection of the Vaticanian infallibility and dogmas, which concede to the Pope personal infallibility and absolute power in the Church notwithstanding the opposition of the bishops. 2. We persist in the firmly-grounded convictions that the Vaticanian decrees constitute a serious danger for the State and society, and are irreconcilable with the laws and institutions of existing States, and that their acceptance would involve us in an insoluble contradiction with our political duties and oaths. 3. The German bishops show by their differing and contradictory interpretations of the Vaticanian dogmas that they know full well their novelty and are ashamed of them. We deplore such a use of the episcopal office."

— Fourteen people drowned at Avoch, on the Moray Firth, by the upsetting of a fishing-boat.

15.—Celebration of the Tercentenary of the foundation of Harrow School, a former master, Dr. Vaughan, proposing at luncheon the toast of " Prosperity to the institution."

— The Paris Internationalists issue a manifesto to working-men, declaring that their society alone could lead them to emancipation, and drag into daylight capital and priestcraft. "At the present moment the International Society is denounced as grandly criminal; all those who capitulated, all the incapable persons of the capital, lay at its door the misfortunes of France and the fires of Paris. On the Jules Favres, on the Trochus, and on the rest, we hurl back the misfortunes of France. We accept the responsibility of the conflagration of Paris. The old social system must perish, and it shall perish. A gigantic effort has already shaken it to its foundations. A final effort must uproot it entirely."

16.—The German troops engaged in the late war enter Berlin in triumph. All business was suspended, and as many as 200,000 strangers were reported to have arrived in the city. The body of troops which entered numbered about 42,000, consisting of the Prussian Royal Guards, and picked deputations from all the regiments of the German Federal and Allied armies, infantry, cavalry, and artillery, which took three hours and a

half to march past. They were led by Marshal von Wrangel, whose great age forbade him to take part in the late French war. He was accompanied by other generals of the army superannuated from active service. Then came the Staff-officers of the commanders engaged in the late war ; General Blumenthal, Chief of the Staff to the Crown Prince, being the most distinguished. After these, and the general officers who had served, like Falkenstein, as civil governors in the conquered territories, rode the commanders of different army corps, and the illustrious men who commanded whole armies,—the Duke of Mecklenburg-Schwerin, the Crown Prince of Saxony, and Field-Marshal Steinmetz; Generals Manteuffel, Werder, Von der Tann, and Goeben, who had also commanded armies, were among the party of general officers preceding. The arrival of Bismarck, Moltke, and Roon, followed by the Emperor, was greeted with enthusiastic cheering. His Majesty appeared in his field uniform and on his war-horse, a dark bay. Behind him rode the Field Marshals of the royal house — the Crown Prince Frederick William of Prussia and of Germany, on a chestnut horse, and Prince Frederick Charles, on a bright bay charger. Following these, the central figures of the pageant, came a bevy of princes, guests of the Emperor, with their personal staff, glittering in varied uniforms and making a gallant show. Behind these came the under officers, of various German nationalities, bearing the spoils of war— the eagles and the colours. The unveiling of a statue of Frederick William III. formed a portion of the ceremonial.

17.—Giant and giantess (Captain Buren and Anna Swann) married at St. Martin's-in-the-Fields.

— H.M.S. *Megæra*, after being in a leaky condition for nine days, is run ashore on St. Paul's Island. She was an iron screw troopship, carrying six guns, of 1,395 tons, and 350 horse-power. When she sailed a series of questions respecting her were put in the House of Commons, and from the official answers it appeared that the *Megæra* was employed to take out to Sydney 33 officers and 350 men. Complaint had been made that the ship was overcrowded, and that she was unseaworthy, and it was said that her crew had twice protested against going to sea in her. On behalf of the Admiralty those allegations were denied, and occasions were cited in which the *Megæra* had taken to the Cape more than 500 souls, and to Cape Coast Castle 450, besides her crew, while she had frequently carried 400 tons of cargo. Official despatches stated that the leak was reported on the 8th ; on the 14th it became more serious, and gained on the pumps. " Steam was then used, and by the aid of the main steam pumps the water was kept in check. It was determined to steer for St. Paul's Island in order to examine the ship, where she arrived and anchored on Saturday, June 17th. A survey was then held, and a diver sent down to examine the leak. A hole was discovered worn through the centre of a plate, about 12 ft. abaft the mainmast and about 8 ft. from the keel, port side, besides other serious injuries in the immediate vicinity of the leak." The pumps were frequently choked with loose pieces of iron scaling off the bottom of the ship. Under these circumstances the chief engineer advised that it would be most unsafe to proceed on the voyage to Australia, the nearest port of which lay 1,800 miles distant. The vessel was run ashore on the 17th, but not abandoned till the 19th. The men who first landed, with their bags and hammocks, were sheltered by tents made from the ship's sails, but some sheds or huts already existing were used for store-houses, and barracks were afterwards put up. Rice was got on the island, and a little rain-water, but to avoid all risk of famine, the troops and crew were at once put on short allowance. They were first discovered by a vessel passing to Batavia, which took off an officer with mails and despatches. The whole were afterwards relieved by the steamship *Malacca*, and landed at Melbourne September 28th. Captain Thrupp returned to England, and at once reported himself at the Admiralty.

18.—Died at his residence, Savile Row, aged 77 years, George Grote, the philosophical historian of ancient Greece, Trustee of the British Museum, and Vice-Chancellor of the University of London. He was interred in Westminster Abbey on the 24th.

19.—The Commons negative after a debate the clause proposed by Mr. Torrens to be introduced into the Army Regulation Bill, providing that no soldier of the line be called upon to serve out of the United Kingdom until he shall have attained the age of twenty years.

— Died from small-pox, aged 21 years, Numa Edward Hartog, Senior Wrangler, Cambridge, 1870, and B.A., to which degree, being a Jew, he was admitted by a special grace, dispensing with part of the oath.

— Celebration of the twenty-fifth anniversary of the election of Pope Pius IX. Replying to an address presented by French Catholics, his Holiness described the Catholic Liberalism prevailing in that country as more formidable than even the Commune with its men who had fired Paris.

— Commencement of the sixth triennial Handel Festival at the Crystal Palace. The attendance at each of the great musical gatherings was : 1857.—Rehearsal, 5,844 ; first day, 8,629 ; second day, 9,149 ; third day, 14,792 —total, 38,414. 1859.—Rehearsal, 19,680 ; first day, 17,109 ; second day, 17,703 ; third day, 26,827—total, 81,319. 1862.—Rehearsal, 19,63; first day, 15,694 ; second day, 14,143 ; third day, 18,567—total, 67,567 1865.— Rehearsal, 15,420 ; first day, 13,677 ; second day, 14,915 ; third day, 15,422—total, 59,434. 1868.—Rehearsal, 18,597 ; first day, 19,217 ;

second day, 21,550 ; third day, 23,101—total, 82,465. 1871.—Rehearsal, 18,676 ; first day, 21,946; second day, 21,330; third day, 23,016 —total, 84,968.

21.—The new Hospital of St. Thomas (designed by Currey, the foundation-stone of which had been laid by the Queen in May 1868) opened by her Majesty, who arrived at Paddington from Windsor in the forenoon, and drove across the Parks to Westminster and Lambeth, accompanied by several members of the royal family. The treasurer, Mr. Hicks, received the honour of knighthood on the occasion.

23.—Garden party at Buckingham Palace, the Queen, in the language of the official accounts, giving a breakfast from half-past four to half-past seven P.M.

—Closing of the subscription lists for the French loan of 80,000,000*l*. The amount was subscribed for twice over.

24.—The decennial representation of the Passion Play commenced at Oberammergau. Two thousand spectators were present, a large number being English and American.

— Cobden Club Dinner, presided over by Earl Granville, who defined the policy of the deceased statesman as liberty in things political, in things religious, and in things material.

26.—Came on before Mr. Justice Lush and a common jury, the case of Pantaleoni *v*. Vaughan, an action for libel brought by the head of the religious hospital S. Sperito, at Rome, against the proprietor of the *Tablet*. The libel complained of was published in a letter in the *Tablet* on the 19th of November, 1870. It stated that Dr. Pantaleoni turned out all the religious in the hospital after he became director. He was banished from Rome in 1862 for complicity in the Fauste conspiracy, which had for its object the assassination of the King and Queen of Naples, the officers of the Zouaves, and the Prince Torlonia, the destruction of the Alliberta and other Pontifical theatres. On seeing the letter the plaintiff, Dr. Pantaleoni, wrote to the defendant, with whom he was personally acquainted, explaining that he was exiled from Rome at the time referred to, and that he knew nothing of the conspiracy. The paper, in again referring to the matter, stated that the correspondent in Rome justified what he had written, and the editor in a footnote said they had the evidence of their correspondent against the plaintiff's assertion, and the public could draw their own conclusions. Mr. Day this morning said that Dr. Vaughan, as soon as he became aware of the publication, expressed his sorrow, and used every means in his power to retract the statements contained in the libel, and he then took the opportunity of doing so in the fullest manner. The defendant entertained every respect for the plaintiff, and believed there was no ground whatever for the charge. A verdict was then taken for the plaintiff by consent—damages 250*l*., to cover costs.

29.—The Emperor and Empress of Brazil arrive in London, in the course of an extended tour through Europe. The Queen took an early opportunity of conferring the Order of the Garter on her illustrious visitor, who manifested unwearied activity during his sojourn in Britain. In London the royal party occupied apartments in Claridge's Hotel.

— The Ballot Bill passes into Committee by 326 votes to 232 given in support of an amendment, that the order be read that day six months.

30.—Lord Salisbury moves an address to the Crown against the scheme of the Endowed School Commissioners, for the management of Emanuel Hospital. The plan, he maintained, was part of a centralizing scheme, intended to break up the local administration, and to place the power in London in a body appointed by the Government, influenced by the particular philosophic project of the day, and out of sympathy with rural populations. The difference between old-fashioned Christian enthusiasm and the philosophic enthusiasm of the present day was that the Christian was content to give of his own money for what he desired to support, while the philosopher always tried to do it by getting hold of somebody else's. Lord Halifax maintained that the Commissioners had faithfully observed the intentions of the Legislature, and Lord Lawrence, as Chairman of the London School Board, thought the scheme of the Commissioners would give a great impulse to the primary education of the country. On a division, Lord Salisbury's motion was carried by 64 to 56 votes.

— The Household Brigade reviewed before the Queen in Bushey Park.

July 2.—King Victor Emmanuel enters Rome as the new capital of his dominions. A grand banquet was held in the afternoon, and in the evening, when the king passed to the Apollo Theatre, the greater part of the city was illuminated. He returned to Florence next day.

— Between 80 and 90 supporters of M. Thiers returned out of the 113 supplementary elections which take place in France. Bonapartists and Legitimists were beaten in most places.

3.—The Army Regulation Bill read a third time in the House of Commons, the final discussion taking place on a motion submitted by Mr. Graves:—"That the bill for the better regulation of the army having been narrowed to an object which will entail on the country an ascertained expenditure of several millions, besides a large permanent charge of which no estimate has been submitted, this House is un-

willing thus to add to the pressure of existing taxation by entering on a course of unknown expenditure, and, declining to commit itself to premature action, awaits from her Majesty's Government a mature and comprehensive scheme of army reform calculated to place the military system of the country on a sound and economical basis." The motion was rejected by 239 to 231 votes, the majority being made up of 204 English, 44 Irish, and 41 Scotch members; and the minority of 199 English, 25 Irish, and seven Scotch. The number of absent English members was 89, of Irish 33, and of Scotch 12. The only Conservatives who voted with the Government on this occasion were Colonel Napier Sturt, and Colonel Vandeleur. Seven Liberals joined with the minority.

3.—The Emperor of Brazil attends the Common Pleas to hear the continued cross-examination of the Claimant in the Tichborne case. At this time questions were being asked in Parliament in reference to the adjournment of the case till November. The Judge said he had received a letter from Lady Doughty, imploring that the trial might not be postponed. The Solicitor-General and the attorney of the defendants disclaimed any previous knowledge of the letter. The Judge spoke of it as reprehensible, but excusable. Lady Doughty said—"I take the liberty of imploring your lordship to take into consideration my advanced age—seventy-six next August—and my failing health, so increased from the intense suffering caused by the cruel charges brought against my now only child. I am also deputed, by the guardians of the infant, and every member of the Tichborne and Arundel families, to pray your lordship not to oppose the efforts we are making for no delay in the hearing of this cause. I trust that your lordship will not consider this communication in any other light than the outpouring of a mother's heart." During the day the Claimant was questioned respecting the titles of some of the books which Roger had left with Mr. Gosford. He knew nothing of either *Gustave de Beaumont, Attila,* or the *Practice of Elocution*:—The Solicitor-General—Who was Cromwell?—He was the Commonwealth man. Who did you say?—I say he was the Commonwealth. Well, not exactly. Now, here is a Life of John Bunyan. Who was he?—John Bunyan! I've read the book, I know; but I forget now who he was. What sort of a fellow was John Bunyan?—Quite the reverse of what you are But I don't recollect who he was: Was he a sportsman?—You can ask me as many foolish questions as you like. I say I don't know who he was—Was he a General, Bishop, or master of foxhounds?—I tell you I can't say.—What is a misanthrope—it is a word used by you frequently in letters?—I don't know that I made use of it. I cannot say what it is. Is it a bird, beast, or fish?—Well, I think I used it in regard to some books. Cross-examination closed to-day with information relative to the Tichborne Bonds, on which it was alleged 35,000*l*. had been raised.

5.—The Count de Chambord issues a proclamation, in which he promises not to attempt any disturbance of the existing order of things, but tells his countrymen that he holds himself in readiness to take the crown whenever they shall think fit to offer it to him, and to establish a régime combining monarchy with universal suffrage, and a parliament of two Chambers. " I will not," he concluded, " be silent because ignorant or credulous people have spoken of Privileges, of Absolutism, of Intolerance, and of I know not what besides—of tithes, of feudal rights, phantoms which the most audacious bad faith seeks to conjure up before your eyes. I will not allow the standard of Henry IV., of Francis I., and Joan of Arc to be torn from my hands. It is with that flag that our national unity was made, it was with that flag that your forefathers, led by mine, conquered that Alsace and Lorraine whose fidelity will be our consolation in our misfortunes. It conquered barbarism on that African soil, which witnessed the first deeds of valour of the princes of my family ; it is it which will conquer the new barbarism with which the world is now threatened. I shall confide it without fear to the valour of our army ; it has never, as that army knows well, been found but in the path of honour. I received it as a sacred deposit from the aged King, my grandfather, as he was dying in exile ; it has always been for me inseparable from the memory of my absent country ; it floated above my cradle, I wish it to droop over my grave. In the glorious folds of that stainless banner, I shall bring you order and liberty. Frenchmen, Henry V. cannot desert the white flag of Henry IV."

6.—Double murder in France, department of Indre-et-Loire. A man named Delalande, known for his dissipated habits, killed M. de Vonne, the Mayor of Saché, and as the curate, an old man of seventy-eight years, was bringing the holy oil to anoint the body of the deceased, the assassin fired again, and the curate fell mortally wounded. The terror caused by these murders was so great among the inhabitants that the body of the curate was suffered to remain three hours in the public road.

— Meeting of Liberal members at the residence of Mr. Gladstone, to devise measures for hastening the progress of the Ballot Bill through the House.

— In committee on the Ballot Bill, Mr. G. Bentinck, resenting what he called the curt and not very courteous remarks of the leader of the Opposition on gentlemen below the gangway, said a long career of political tergiversation and apostasy had placed the right hon. gentleman in a position which subjected him to observations. (" Order, order ! ") Many years ago the right hon. gentleman spoke of the Government of the day as an " organized hypocrisy,"

and that suggested that the proper description of the late Government would be that it was a disorganized hypocrisy. The chairman ruled that the hon. member was out of order in alluding to past events. Next, turning to the Prime Minister, Mr. Bentinck said he had complained of time being wasted, but no one had for years delayed business by speeches so much as he himself had done. In a long, didactic oration the right hon. gentleman commented upon the bad habit of imputing motives ; but he was guilty of that offence when he said that speeches were made solely for the purpose of creating delay. As soon as Mr. Newdegate rose a great many members on the Liberal side (in accordance with the tactics resolved upon at the meeting in the afternoon) immediately quitted the House, and the whole of the benches were soon empty. Only two or three Ministers on the Treasury bench, and three independent members behind them, were left to represent the party on the Speaker's right hand. In order to maintain the equilibrium of the assembly a number of the Conservatives, amid general laughter, crossed to the deserted seats and delivered strong denunciations of the Ballot from the places usually occupied by advanced Radicals. The speaking was carried on exclusively by Conservatives, and provoked no reply. About ten o'clock a division was taken, and Mr. Newdegate's motion for adjournment defeated by 154 to 63.

6. — Waverley costume ball at Willis's Rooms in aid of fund to complete the Scott Monument at Edinburgh.

7.—Adjournment of the Tichborne case after a trial of forty days—a course opposed by Mr. Serjeant Ballantine, and insisted on by Mr. Hawkins, who stated that the observations he had addressed to the court were made under a sense of responsibility to his clients, and he cared nothing for the observations of Mr. Serjeant Ballantine, knowing the quarter whence they came. The Lord Chief Justice —" I regret very much that such an observation should have fallen from any learned counsel. The observation of the learned counsel requires an apology upon the spot." (The learned counsel having made no response, his lordship proceeded, turning to the jury)— " Gentlemen, I regret that it is not made." Before the case was suspended, however, Mr. Hawkins, at the suggestion of the Judge, withdrew the expression. (See January 15, 1872.)

8.—Treaty agreed to by the Second Chamber at the Hague, transferring the Dutch settlement on the West Coast of Africa from Holland to Britain.

— Complimentary breakfast at the Crystal Palace to members of the company of the " Comédie Française," whose performances were brought to a close this evening. Lord Dufferin presided.

9.—Died, aged 76, Dr. Alexander Keith Johnstone, F.R.S., among the most eminent of modern geographers.

10.—At a meeting of Conservative Peers, it is resolved that the Duke of Richmond should give notice of an amendment expressing the unwillingness of the House to read the Army Bill a second time until a complete and comprehensive scheme of army reorganisation shall have been laid before it.

11.—The Ecclesiastical Titles Repeal Bill passes through committee in the Lords, and the Burial Bill is read a third time and passed. To meet the case of children working in brickfields, in whose behalf Lord Shaftesbury moved an address to the Crown, Lord Morley promised to introduce a clause into the Factory Act Amendment Bill, presently before the House.

— The Saxon troops engaged in the late war make a triumphal entry into Dresden. The Bavarian troops entered Munich on the 16th.

— Collision early this morning, in the Channel, off the Eddystone lighthouse, between the ship *Madagascar*, 1,311 tons, Captain Brunswick, belonging to South Shields, bound from London to Quebec, and the screw-steamer *Widgeon*, of Cork, proceeding from Liverpool, with a general cargo and passengers for Rotterdam. The bow of the *Madagascar* cut into the *Widgeon* midway between the funnel and the wheel, crushing the sailor at the wheel so severely that he was taken to the hospital. The water rushed into the stoke-hole and extinguished the fires. The steamer sank at 2.30 A.M., and the ship at 5 A.M. All hands of both vessels, sixty-one persons, were picked up by a trawling sloop, and brought into Plymouth.

— Died at Milan, the Princess Christina Belgiojoso, an enthusiastic worker for the unity of Italy.

12.—Commenced at the Central Criminal Court, before Lord Chief Justice Bovill, the trial of Edmund W. Pook, for the murder of Jane Maria Clousen, in Kidbrooke Lane, Eltham. The case was protracted to the evening of the 16th, when the jury, amid a tempest of applause, returned a verdict of Not Guilty. In his charge the Chief Justice commented in strong terms on the conduct of the police, who appeared, he said, to have from the first assumed the guilt of the prisoner, and strained every piece of evidence so as to ensure a conviction against him. The acquittal of Pook led to disorderly gatherings before his father's house at Greenwich, and to legal proceedings against parties for printing and selling accounts of his supposed connection with the murder.

— Serious Orange riots in New York, the military firing upon the disturbers of the peace, killing, it was reported, over thirty and wounding 170. Lieutenant James Fisk was among the latter.

14.—William Frank Gosney, a lad of 20, sentenced at the Central Criminal Court to fifteen years' penal servitude for attempting to murder Dr. De Meschin, of the Middle Temple, whose room had been taken possession of, and books stolen by the prisoner during the Doctor's temporary absence abroad.

16.—In the case of Harriet Newington or Davy, indicted for the manslaughter of Frederick Moon, the jury return a verdict of guilty, and Baron Channell, expressing his entire concurrence in its justice, sentenced her to eight years' penal servitude. The prisoner again declared her innocence. "We lived together," she said, "most happily. The whole of his consideration had been to promote my happiness, and I have studied his. I could not have done him any injury. It was in the struggle. He was going to throw a bottle, and I jumped up quickly. He tried to take the knife from me. I am not sure whether he got it or not. We struggled and fell. I thought at first I must be the one injured. I found blood on me—warm blood. I said, 'Oh, Fred! what have you done?' Then I found, of course, it was him, not myself. I tried all I could to do something to stop it. First of all I applied cold water; then I remembered that cold water produced blood instead of stopping it. Then I sent for ice and tried that. Then the doctors came." The prisoner fainted on hearing her sentence.

17.—The Army Bill thrown out in the House of Lords on the proposal for a second reading by 155 to 130 votes. Lord Salisbury interposed a pungent speech between those of the Duke of Argyll and the Foreign Secretary, declaring that though the Government talked of seniority tempered by selection, the more correct formula would be stagnation tempered by jobbery. By rejecting the bill, the *Times* thought, the Lords had adopted an ill-advised course, and made the abolition of purchase the question of the day.

19.—Lorraine Museum, formerly a ducal palace, destroyed by fire, the ancient *tapisserie* of Charles le Téméraire being the only portion saved.

— Signor Mario makes his farewell appearance at Covent Garden as Fernando in Donizetti's opera, "La Favorita."

20.—Marshal Serrano announces in the Cortes the resignation of the Spanish Ministry. Zorilla afterwards accepted the direction of affairs.

— In a crowded and anxious House, Mr. Gladstone announces the intentions of the Government regarding the rejection of the purchase part of the Army Bill by the Lords. Replying to Sir George Grey, he said that by statute there was no purchase but what was permitted by the Queen's Regulations. The House of Commons having condemned purchase, and a Royal Commission having declared that those regulation prices could not be put an end to except by the extinction of purchase as a system, the Government had resolved to advise her Majesty to take the decisive step of cancelling the Royal Warrant under which purchase was legal. That advice had been accepted and acted on by her Majesty. The new warrant had been framed in terms conformable with the law, and from the 1st of November next purchase in the army would no longer exist. The Government had no other object in view but simplicity, despatch, and the observance of constitutional usage. (Cries of "Oh!" from the Opposition, answered by Ministerial cheers.) Amid many disorderly interruptions, Mr. Disraeli and several other members taunted Government with having appealed to the prerogative of the Crown for the purpose of relieving them from a difficulty of their own devising. A bitter discussion broke out again in committee on the Ballot Bill, when Mr. Forster said it was necessary to pass the measure, in order to throw the responsibility of its rejection on the House of Lords, a proceeding described by the leader of the Opposition as an avowed and shameful conspiracy. On the Chairman calling attention to these words, they were at once withdrawn, and the discussion proceeded.

20.—Royal Warrant issued declaring that "On and after the 1st day of November in this present year, all regulations made by Us or any of Our Royal predecessors, or any Officers acting under Our authority, regulating or fixing the prices at which any Commissions in Our Forces may be purchased, sold, or exchanged, or in any way authorizing the purchase or sale or exchange for money of any such Commissions, shall be cancelled and determined."

21.—In the Willoughby Peerage case (involving also the dignity of Lord Great Chamberlain), the House of Lords decide that the Dowager Lady Aveland had made out her claim as the nearest co-heiress.

—The Grand Duke Constantine of Russia arrives in London.

25.—Tried at Stafford Assizes, before Mr. Baron Pigott and a special jury, the case of Hatherly *v.* Odham, an action for libel against the registered publisher of the *Guardian* newspaper. The alleged libel was in the form of letters criticizing the plaintiff's attempt, as a member of the Greek Church, to create a schism in the Church at Wolverhampton by the help, it was said, of "silver weapons." The jury gave a verdict for the plaintiff, with 40*s.* damages and costs.

26.—Commencement of court-martial on board the *Royal Adelaide* flag-ship to try Capt. Beamish, Lieut. Bell, and Staff-Commander Knight, for negligently stranding the *Agincourt* on the Pearl Rock, Gibraltar, on 1st February, Admiral Codrington presiding. The hearing of evidence and speeches in defence was continued till the 8th August, when the Court delivered judgment, finding the charge proved,

and severely admonished Capt. Beamish and Staff-Commander Knight. Lieut. Bell was simply admonished.

26.—Died at Cowes, aged 78, the Hon. J. Slidell, one of the Southern States Commissioners, seized on board the *Trent* in 1863.

27.—M. Jules Favre resigns his position as French Minister of Foreign Affairs.

29.—Professor Döllinger elected Rector of the University of Munich by 54 votes against 6.

31.—Died suddenly, from the bursting of a blood-vessel, the Very Rev. Dr. Mansel, Dean of St. Paul's, in his 51st year.

— After a sharp debate in the Lords, the Duke of Richmond carries, by 162 to 82 votes, the resolution he had submitted in connection with the second reading of the Army Bill:— "That this House, in assenting to the second reading of this bill, desires to express its opinion that the interposition of the Executive during the progress of a measure submitted to Parliament by her Majesty's Government, in order to attain, by the exercise of the prerogative, and without the aid of Parliament, the principal object included in that measure, is calculated to depreciate and neutralize the independent action of the Legislature, and is strongly to be condemned ; and this House assents to the second reading of this bill only in order to secure the officers of her Majesty's army the compensation to which they are entitled consequent on the abolition of purchase in the army."

— The Ministerial proposal for an annuity of 15,000*l.* to Prince Arthur carried by 289 votes to 51 against a proposal to reduce the amount to 10,000*l.*

— In Committee on the Ballot Bill, the Commons reject the Ministerial proposal to throw election expenses on the public rates by 253 to 162 votes.

— The Prince of Wales, accompanied by Prince Arthur, the Princess Louise, and the Marquis of Lorne, arrive in Dublin on a visit to the Lord-Lieutenant.

August 1.—Memorandum agreed to concerning a new social movement originated by Mr. Scott Russell to improve the condition of the working classes by an alliance of workmen with Conservative statesmen. "We appreciate," they said, "the confidence thus shown to be placed in us ; we fully recognize the national necessity of a hearty good feeling between the different classes of society ; we believe that this good feeling can and ought to be secured where both parties are in earnest on the subject. Awaiting communications from the Council, we readily engage to give an attentive consideration to the measures which may be hereafter submitted by them to our judgment. At the same time we do not conceal from ourselves that the task which we have been requested to undertake is not free from difficulty. We cannot become parties to any legislation which we do not believe to be consistent with the real interests of all classes. We must reserve to ourselves the most unfettered discretion in the selection of objects, and in the modification or rejection of measures proposed to us for consideration ; and we must hold ourselves free, either collectively or individually, to retire from the task to which we have been invited whenever we may be of opinion that our assistance is not likely to be for the advantage of the public or satisfactory to ourselves.—Salisbury, Carnarvon, Lichfield, Sandon, John Manners, John S. Pakington, Stafford Northcote, Gathorne Hardy."

1.—In consequence of the defeat of his Government on the Decentralization Bill, M. Thiers announces in the Salle des Conférences that the factious conduct of the Right left him no alternative but to resign. He retired from the hall with four of his Ministers, declaring that he would call for a vote of confidence on the following day.

— The M'Fadden family—husband, wife, and two children—attacked in their residence at Errandsey, Londonderry, and all but murdered by the brothers M'Callog, who had been concerned in litigation with their victims.

— The Army Bill, introduced first as a Reorganization Bill, then an Abolition of Purchase Bill, and finally a Compensation Bill, passes the House of Lords.

2.—In the course of his opening address to the British Association, the chairman for the year, Sir W. Thompson, made reference to the origin of life on the globe in terms which gave rise to considerable controversy. "I confess," he said, "to being deeply impressed by the evidence put before us by Professor Huxley, and I am ready to adopt, as an article of scientific faith, true through all space and through all time, that life proceeds from life, and from nothing but life. How, then, did life originate on the earth?" Remarking that we have no right to assume an abnormal creative act in order to answer this question, if it can be answered otherwise, the president suggested that the first germs of life were brought to this world by fragments of matter detached from other worlds in which life had previously existed, just as islands springing up in the ocean are covered with vegetation by the seeds which float in the water and the air. "Hence, and because we all confidently believe that there are at present, and have been from time immemorial, many worlds of life besides our own, we must regard it as probable in the highest degree that there are countless and seed-bearing meteoric stones moving about through space. If at the present instant no life existed upon this earth, one such stone falling upon it might, by what we blindly call natural causes, lead to its becoming covered with vegetation. I am fully conscious of the many scientific objections which may be urged against this hypothesis, but I believe them to be all answerable. The hypothesis that life originated on this earth through moss-grown fragments from the ruins of another world may seem wild and visionary ; all I maintain is that it is not unscientific."

3.—James Nimmo, Glasgow, poisons three of his children with prussic acid, and then commits suicide by swallowing a portion of the same drug.

4.—The Ballot Bill passed through Committee in the Commons.

5.—Cooper's Hill College, founded by the Secretary of State and Council of India for training civil engineers in the Indian service, opened by the Duke of Argyll.

— Colonel Hogg, as Chairman of the Metropolitan Board of Works, lays the foundation stone of the Chelsea section of the Thames Embankment, extending along the river front of the Hospital to Battersea Bridge.

6.—Riot in the Phœnix Park, Dublin, arising out of the interference of the police with a Fenian amnesty meeting, called to neutralize the loyal demonstration made in favour of the royal visitors presently residing with the Lord-Lieutenant. About sixty were injured, several of whom were policemen, struck by stones, apparently carried to the place of meeting for purposes of attack.

— Dedication services in the English Church at Zermatt, built partly as a memorial of the disastrous ascent of 'the Matterhorn by English travellers in July, 1865.

7.—Trial of the Communist prisoners commenced at Versailles. The indictment gave an account of the proceedings of the International prior to the insurrection, and of the various crimes which followed the revolt of the 18th March. Charges then followed, first against Assi, who was accused of incitement to civil war, of usurpation of civil and military powers, of having assumed Government functions, and assisted in issuing orders, the consequence of which were devastation, massacre, pillage, arson, and assassination. All the accused were further charged with conspiring for the overthrow of the Government, with incitement to civil war, and usurpation of office and power. Courbet was specially accused of complicity in the destruction of the Vendôme Column ; Lullier of attempts to carry destruction, massacre and pillage into Paris, of taking possession of city property appertaining to the State, and of inciting soldiers to join the ranks of the rebels. Grousset stood charged with active participation in the revolt, with public incitement to contempt of existing laws and of the National Assembly. Verdure, Billioray, and Ferré were arraigned for arbitrary confiscations, wanton destruction of private dwelling-houses and public monuments, sacrilegious pillage of churches, and assassination, they having voted for the execution of the hostages. Jourde was further charged with financial transactions involving the violation of the seals of the public chests and the squandering of public charities. All the members of the Commune were made responsible for the destruction of property by fire. The number of prisoners was said to be 33,000.

8.—The Ballot Bill read a third time in the House of Commons.

9.—The centenary of the birth of Sir Walter Scott celebrated in various towns in Scotland by festive gatherings. At Edinburgh, where the highest interest was naturally manifested, there was an exhibition of Scott relics—books, pictures, and manuscripts—and the day observed in the city as a holiday. The banquet there was presided over by the Earl of Dalkeith (in the absence of his father, the Duke of Buccleuch); and the toast of the evening, "The Memory of Sir Walter Scott," proposed by Sir Wm. Stirling Maxwell. Dean Stanley attended at Edinburgh, and Professor Jowett at Glasgow, where also was present Sheriff H. G. Bell, one of the few survivors of those who took part in the memorable Theatrical Fund Dinner in Edinburgh, Feb., 1827, when Sir Walter acknowledged himself to be the sole and undivided author of the Waverley Novels.

10.—Lord Shaftesbury's motion to reject the Ballot Bill, on the ground of the late period at which it was sent up to the House, carried after a brief debate by 97 to 48 votes.

— Died suddenly at Lochearnhead Hotel, Perthshire, in his 48th year, Charles Buxton, M.P. for East Surrey.

— Meeting of a council of skilled workmen to consider a report prepared by Mr. Scott Russell, detailing the result of his three months' negotiations to secure the support of Conservative leaders to his scheme for a union of workmen and noblemen. The party was reported to be thoroughly and successfully united in a representative council of peers and legislators.

11.—Explosion in Prentice's gun-cotton factory at Stowmarket, Suffolk, causing the death of twenty-four people, injury to seventy, and a great destruction of property in the neighbourhood. Two members of the firm were among the killed. During the last few weeks, experiments had been carried on by Government officials, tending to show that, under the regulations observed at Stowmarket, the cartridges made there would not explode. A dense column of smoke was observed to rise high into the air, spread itself out gradually into a fan-like shape, and then came a terrific roar, heard, it was said, at distances varying from twelve to fourteen miles. As the result of a lengthened inquiry before the coroner, a jury found—"That the explosion causing the deaths of persons on whom this inquest was held was produced by some person or persons unknown adding sulphuric acid to the gun-cotton subsequent to its passing the tests required by Government. At the same time we consider, from the evidence adduced, that there

is no danger in the manufacture of gun-cotton in the wet process, but that the drying and storing of gun-cotton should not be allowed near a town. Also, we consider that gun-cotton works should be subject to constant Government inspection." Another explosion, but less disastrous, took place at this time in the powder-works of the Schultze Company, situated in the heart of the New Forest.

12.—The Emperors of Germany and Austria have an interview at Ischl.

— Proposals submitted to the French Assembly for prolonging the power of M. Thiers. The first, brought forward by the Left Centre, gave M. Thiers the title of President of the Republic, continued his power for three years unless in the meantime the Assembly should dissolve itself, and made the Ministers (to be appointed by the President) responsible to the Assembly. The proposition of the Right simply declared the confidence of the Assembly in the wisdom and patriotism of M. Thiers, and confirmed and continued the powers conferred upon him at Bordeaux.

15.—The Commons agree to the Lords' amendments on the Army Bill, after a discussion, having reference chiefly to the Ministerial expedient of resorting to the Royal prerogative for the abolition of purchase.

16.—Fire in Burlington Arcade, resulting in the destruction of several shops.

17.—Unveiling of the statue erected on the Thames Embankment to commemorate the services of Lieut.-Gen. Sir James Outram, G.C.B. In the absence of the Secretary for India, Lord Halifax made a short speech on the occasion.

18.—Replying to some criticism made in the House on the view he privately maintained on the Army Bill, Sir Roundell Palmer writes to Mr. Cardwell:—"I have always thought and said that the issuing of such a warrant was within the undoubted power of the Crown; though to do so without having a sufficient assurance that Parliament would provide the necessary compensation for the officers, who would otherwise suffer by such an exercise of Royal power, would not be just, and therefore would not be consistent with the spirit of the Constitution, which vests all such powers in the Crown, in the confidence, and for the purpose, that right, not wrong, shall be done. I should have been glad if it had been generally and clearly understood from the beginning that, subject to the sense of Parliament being ascertained with reference to the point of compensation, the form of procedure would be that which was eventually adopted, because it is certainly an evil that the adoption of one constitutional mode of procedure, rather than another, should appear to arise from an adverse vote of the House of Lords."

—The screw-steamer *Compeer*, laden with flax, stranded on the coast, near Berwick, and breaks up early next month during a severe easterly gale.

19.—Admiralty minute in the case of the *Agincourt* issued. "Their lordships are of opinion that the primary cause of the disaster was clearly the unsafe course steered by the squadron in obedience to signals from the flag-ship. It appears that Vice-Admiral Wellesley, on l-aving Gibraltar, conducted the squadron under his command so close to the western shore of the bay that, with the weather fine and clear, and the wind light, the leading ship of the in-shore division struck on the Pearl Rock, and was in imminent danger of being wrecked. Their lordships cannot but feel that due care was not exercised by the Vice-Admiral in command to insure that a safe course should be steered by his squadron ; and they greatly regret that, with such large and valuable ships in his charge, he did not satisfy himself, by examination of the course proposed, and by seeing them laid off on the chart, that the squadron would be taken a safe distance from a well-known and dangerous shoal." As the result of their deliberations, their lordships superseded Vice-Admiral Wellesley and Rear-Admiral Wilmot, and placed Staff-Commander Kiddle on half-pay.

20.—Celebration of the Beethoven centenary, commenced at Bonn, under the direction of Franz Liszt.

21.—An insane woman at Stow Bedon, named Hamer, wife of a labourer, murders one of her own children by cutting its throat, and also a deaf and dumb idiot, 18 years of age, the daughter of her husband by a former marriage.

—Parliament prorogued by Commission the Royal Speech read on the occasion, making special reference to the Treaty of Washington, as embodying certain rules for the guidance of neutrals, "which may, I trust, ere long obtain general recognition, and form a valuable addition to the code of International Law."

— Hurricane and earthquake at St. Thomas causing the loss of much property, and the injury or death of over 100 people.

23.—Festivities at Inverary in connection with the arrival of the young Marquis, and Princess Louise, at the castle. The rejoicings extended over three days.

—Renforth, a famous Tyne oarsman, seized with a fatal attack of apoplexy while rowing in the Anglo-Canadian boat-race at St. John's, New Brunswick. It was at first thought that some drug had been maliciously administered to the champion puller, but a post-mortem examination made it clear that death resulted from causes which could be otherwise accounted for.

24.—West Surrey, vacant through the death of Mr. C. Buxton, carried by Mr. Watney, Conservative, against Mr. Leveson Gower, Liberal, the numbers being 3,912 to 2,749.

24.—Stormy debate in the French Assembly on a proposal made for the immediate dissolution of the National Guard. A compromise proposed by General Ducrot was adopted, which provided for such gradual dissolution as might be permitted by the reorganization of the army.

27.—Illness of the Queen at Balmoral. Various recent rumours as to her Majesty's health received some confirmation from the announcement in the *Court Circular* :—"The Queen has been suffering from severe sore-throat, headache, and grave general illness. Although greatly better, her Majesty was not sufficiently recovered to attend Divine service."

28.—The freedom of Glasgow presented to Lord Shaftesbury.

—Died, aged 78, Paul de Kock, French novelist.

29.—It is announced from Vienna that a "League of Peace" has been formed at Gastein, to be directed against any power seeking to disturb the peace of Europe. Not only Austria and Germany, but Italy also, and perhaps even Russia, were described as likely to join the League.

September 1.—Walter Montgomery, late manager of the Gaiety Theatre, and who had been married only two days since, committed suicide by discharging a pistol through his head in a bedroom adjoining an apartment occupied by his young wife. Deceased was interred in Brompton cemetery on the 5th, when Mrs. Montgomery dropped on the coffin the wreath of orange blossom she had worn so recently at the altar.

2.—The Court at Versailles pronounced judgment on the first group of Communist prisoners. Ferré and Lullier were condemned to death ; Urbain and Trinquet to imprisonment for life with hard labour ; Assi, Billioray, Champy, Régère, Paschal Grousset, Verdure, and Ferrat to transportation to a fortress ; Jourde and Rastoul to simple transportation ; Courbet to six months' imprisonment and a fine of 500f. ; and Clément to three months' imprisonment. Descamps and Parent were acquitted. The Court afterwards engaged in the trial of forty women, charged with being concerned in firing Paris with petroleum.

3.—Another riot in Dublin, a disorderly mob returning from an amnesty meeting attacking the police, and injuring about a score of them severely.

— Accident on the French Northern Railway at Seclin, near Lille, a Paris express running into an ordinary train from Douai. Ten passengers were killed.

—The Bishop of Winchester, presently the guest of Mr. Ellice, M.P., Invergarry, preached in the parish church, Glengarry, observing the usual Presbyterian form. The Archbishop of

York officiated in the same place the following Sunday.

6.—Explosion in the Moss Colliery, Wigan, causing the death of sixty-nine men and boys employed in what was known as the nine-feet seam. As soon as the surface damage could be repaired, a band of explorers descended one of the shafts and found that the men working in another part of the mine were safe. They were drawn up, along with some who were nearest the shaft in the part where the explosion had occurred. Another explosion took place while the explorers were below; and although they came up uninjured the sides of the pit were reported to be on fire. It then became necessary to close the shaft, so that all hope was given up of saving any other of the large body of workmen known to be in the pit.

— Meeting at Salzburg between the Emperors of Germany and Austria, to complete, it was given out, certain details of the League of Peace.

7.—Died unexpectedly, of puerperal fever, in her 22nd year, Sybil Grey, Duchess of St. Albans.

— Brighton poisoning case, the magistrates to-day committing Miss Christina Edmunds for trial on the charge of attempting to poison a lady named Boyes by sending her a cake with arsenic in it. A charge of murder in reference to the sudden death, with symptoms of strychnia poisoning, of the little boy Sidney Albert Barker was next gone into. The theory of the prosecution in this case was, that the prisoner had conceived a guilty passion for Dr. Beard, with whose family she was on visiting terms; that she had attempted to poison his wife with a chocolate cream; and that then, Dr. Beard suspecting her, she had procured a number of such sweetmeats, put strychnia upon them, and returned them to the shop of Mr. Maynard, a confectioner from whom they were procured, in order that other persons might be made ill, or even killed, and suspicion diverted from her in respect of the attempt to poison Mrs. Beard. After the inquest on the boy his father received three anonymous letters to the effect that there was a general feeling of indignation in the town at the proceedings at the inquest, blaming Mr. Maynard strongly for having sold the chocolate creams after having been warned, urging Mr. Barker to take further proceedings; and stating that if he did not prosecute Mr. Maynard other parties would, and that, having made three persons ill, he ought to be prosecuted. An expert who had examined the letters believed them to have been written by the same hand as others known to have come from the prisoner. On being committed on this capital charge she exhibited no signs of emotion or regret.

8.—The appointment of the Rev. R. W. Church to the Deanery of St. Paul's gazetted.

10.—Died, aged 77 years, Richard Bentley, publisher, founder, in conjunction with Charles Dickens, of the periodical known as "Bentley's Miscellany."

11.—Foundation-stone of a new Seaman's Orphan Institution laid at Newsham Park, Liverpool.

13.—Opening of the Mont Cenis Tunnel, the first train, with the engineer, Grattoni, and some friends, passing through to the northern outlet in 40 minutes. The maximum temperature inside the carriages was 25 deg. centigrade. Two hours later the train returned to the Italian side, the journey occupying 55 minutes. The tunnel was then found entirely clear of the steam discharged during the previous journey. The formal opening of the tunnel took place on the 18th, when a banquet was held to celebrate this great achievement of engineering skill, and a statue of Poleocapa, Minister of Public Works for Sardinia, was unveiled by the King at Turin.

— The Doncaster St. Leger won by Baron Rothschild's Hannah, which had before carried off the One Thousand Guineas and Oaks. To make the Baron's triumph unprecedented in turf annals, he had also carried off the Derby with Favonius.

— The King of Spain enters Barcelona in the course of a tour through the eastern portion of his dominions.

14.—Continued anxiety being still manifested regarding the health of the Queen, the *British Medical Journal* announces that her Majesty has passed through a trying and severe illness, from which she is now happily recovering.

16.—First mimic battle of the campaign undertaken by three divisions of regular troops, militia, and volunteers, in the district round Aldershott fixed in the "Military Manœuvres Act" of last Session. The first division, comprising the Guards, under the command of Lieutenant-General Sir Hope Grant, representing the British army in defence of the road to London, was engaged at the same time in repelling the attacks of the second division, under Major-General Carey, and of the third division, under Major-General Sir Charles Staveley.

18.—Explaining his position as mediator in the strike still pending among the engineers, the Mayor of Newcastle writes:—"I was asked by Sir William Armstrong whether I was authorized by the representatives of the men to make such a proposition. I replied that, for obvious reasons, I was not, but that, nevertheless, I believed that if I, as a neutral party, proposed it equally to both parties, they would accede to it. Some further conversation ensued, on which I retired. I believe that the unwillingness of the masters to agree to this proposition arose from the hard and fast line adopted by the men as to the nine hours, and from their great haste in commencing the struggle, as evinced by their indisposition to lengthen their notices—a great mistake, in my view, on their part. But I was then and am still of opinion that, even with both parties equally resolute in their own views, a conference of explanation, undertaken at the request, through myself, of influential inhabitants of the town, might have ended in some modification on one or both sides, and have so brought this conflict, sad in every respect, to an end, and it was with this view I proposed it." Mr. Burnett also wrote on the part of the men, blaming the employers for continuing the strike.

18.—Died, aged 69, G. A. Hamilton, for many years Permanent Secretary of the Treasury, and latterly a member of the Irish Church Temporalities Commission.

19.—Died, aged 73, Rev. Richard William Jelf, D.D., Canon of Christ Church, and formerly Principal of King's College, London.

20.—Chief Justice Norman stabbed at Calcutta by a fanatical Wahabee named Abdoola, a native of Upper Bengal. The assassination took place as Mr. Norman was entering the Calcutta High Court, when his assailant suddenly rushed upon him in the vestibule and inflicted a deep wound in the abdomen with a dagger. As there was no one at hand except a native solicitor and a court servant, Mr. Norman ran back, but was followed by the assassin brandishing his dagger, and again stabbed in the back close to the spine. After this, Mr. Norman kept off his assailant for a few seconds by picking up stones and throwing them at him, till a punkawalla connected with the court, attracted by the cries, ran up to the Mussulman and knocked him down with a piece of wood. The assassin struggled violently, but was soon disarmed and prevented from doing further injury. The stabs he had already inflicted, however, caused mortal wounds, and Mr. Norman only lingered till shortly after one o'clock next morning. The murderer, who at first pretended insanity, was quickly tried and executed, and his body burnt.

— Mr. Butt, a Home Rule candidate, returned for Limerick unopposed.

— Dr. Patteson, Bishop of Melanesia, murdered by natives of Santa Cruz, in revenge it was thought for gross outrages recently committed by Europeans engaged in the slave or "labour" trade. Mr. Brooke, with another clergyman, the Rev. J. Atkin, an *alumnus* of St. John's College, Auckland, and one or two native Christians, had been left for a few months, in pursuance of the regular plan of the Mission, at Florida, a small member of the Solomon Islands group, some distance to the north-west of Santa Cruz. At the end of August, the Bishop called for them in the *Southern Cross*, and took them aboard. After visiting several islands on the way, they made for Santa Cruz, and on the 20th of September,

reached, not the large island which gives its name to the group, but one of its small outliers, Nupaka, at which the Mission schooner had been accustomed to call first, in order to procure an interpreter for Santa Cruz itself, where the language had not yet been mastered. On this occasion no boats put off to meet them. This was an unusual circumstance, which in itself gave an indication of danger. But four canoes hovered near the reef, and the Bishop, taking with him Mr. Atkin and three natives, put off in a boat to join them. The boat could not cross the reef, and the Bishop, leaving the rest of the crew in charge, went ashore in a canoe belonging to two chiefs whom he knew, Taula and Motu. The boat remained near the reef at about ten yards distance from the canoes. Suddenly, without any warning, a volley of eight arrows was poured from them into the boat's crew. Every shot at that short distance took effect. Mr. Atkin was shot in the left shoulder, one of his companions in the right, and Stephen Taroaniara was trussed with six arrows in his shoulders and chest. The boat immediately pulled off to the ship. The wounded crew were replaced by a fresh one, with the exception of Mr. Atkin, who, in spite of his wound, was obliged to act as pilot ; and they started again, with sad presentiments, to ascertain what was become of the Bishop, who had been left ashore. The tide had risen and the boat pulled over the reef. What followed may be told in Mr. Brooke's own words:—"No canoes approached—but a tenantless one, with something like a bundle heaped up in the middle, was floating alone in the lagoon. The boat pulled up to this, and took the heap or bundle out of it and brought it away, a yell of triumph rising from the beach. As they pulled alongside, they murmured but one word — ' The body.' " That was indeed their melancholy freight ; but it had been strangely and carefully prepared for them. It was no murder or deed of blind vengeance executed in the sudden fury of the moment. It wore the aspect of a deliberate judicial act, and suggested the idea of a sacrificial victim sent forth as a ghastly herald to announce its solemn completion to the foe. There lay the body, not mutilated or insulted, but wrapped carefully in native matting, and tied at the neck and ancles. Into the breast was thrust a palm frond on which were tied five thick knots! When the covering was removed, the manner of his death became apparent. He had probably been first shot by a volley of arrows, and then despatched by the blow of a tomahawk. The right side of the skull was found to be completely shattered, the top of the head was cloven by some sharp weapon, and there were numerous arrow-wounds about the body. Yet amidst all this havoc and ruin, says the narrator of the sad spectacle, "the sweet face still smiled, the eyes closed, as if the patient martyr had had time to breathe a prayer for these his murderers. There was no sign of agony or terror. Peace reigned supreme in that sweet smile, which will live in our remembrance as the last silent blessing of our revered Bishop and our beloved friend." So fell at his post the first Bishop of Melanesia, happier in one respect by his immediate death than his two companions in martyrdom. Atkin died of his wounds on the 27th, and Stephen on the 28th. Bishop Patteson, the eldest son of the late Mr. Justice Patteson, was born on the 1st of April, 1827, went out to New Zealand with Bishop Selwyn in 1854, and was consecrated Bishop of Melanesia by Bishops Selwyn, Abraham, and Hobhouse in St. Paul's Church, Auckland, on St. Matthias's Day, 1861.

21.—M. Rochefort sentenced by the Versailles tribunal to imprisonment for life in a fortified place.

— The Chief Justice of Utah territory instructs the grand jury, that bigamy there was a crime as elsewhere in the United States, and ordered his officers of Court, if they knew of anyone practising polygamy, to bring indictments against them as criminals.

— Inquiry commenced into the charges brought against the management of Hampstead Small Pox Hospital.

— Murder and suicide in a railway carriage on the Manchester and Liverpool line, a man named Wanlen first shooting his wife, from whom he had been separated lately, and then himself.

22.—Placing the case of the Newcastle masters before the country in the *Times*, to-day, Sir William Armstrong points out the loss which would come to the employer by the shortened working of his plant. " As a mere arithmetical question, a reduction from 59 to 54 hours a week represents a money gain to the workman of about 8¼ per cent. on the price of his labour. To the employer the direct loss is of course the same ; but the indirect loss must be matter of estimate, varying in each particular instance. In my own case, I should certainly regard it as equal to the direct loss on wages, and I believe that engineers in general would concur in the substantial accuracy of this estimate. Upon this view the reduction of time claimed by our men would be attended with a gain to them of 8¼ per cent. on the amount of their wages, and of a loss to us equal to 17 per cent. on the same amount. To suppose that the average profits of the trade have of late years been such as to admit of a deduction to that extent is absurd."

— Opening of the Old Catholic Congress at Munich, presided over by Herr Wolf. A report read declared that they recognized the Roman Primate only so far as the same is recognized in accordance with the writings of the Fathers of the Church and the decisions of Councils. A hope was expressed that the re-union of the Catholic Church with the Greek and Eastern Russian Churches may be accomplished, as well as that a gradual understanding with Protestantism and the Episcopal English and American Church may be arrived at. Dr. Döllinger delivered an historical dissertation on the Church of Utrecht.

22.—The Hampshire military manœuvres brought to a close with an inspection by the Commander-in-Chief at Aldershott. The force on the ground comprised a grand total of 30,233 men, 5,701 horses, and 90 guns.

— Died, aged 52, Irwin Lewis Willis, the " Argus " of the *Post's* sporting columns.

— Transatlantic Company's ship *Lafayette* burnt at Havre.

24.—Died, aged 85, Louis I. Papineau, a leader in the Canadian revolt of 1837.

— Died, aged 66, Samuel Solly, F.R.S., surgeon.

26.—Acknowledging the compliment of the freedom of the city of Aberdeen conferred upon him to-day, Mr. Gladstone said, if the doctrine of Home Rule were to be established in Ireland, they would be just as well entitled to it in Scotland ; " and, moreover, I protest on behalf of Wales, in which I have lived a good deal, and where there are 800,000 people, who to this day, such is their sentiment of nationality, speak hardly anything but their own Celtic tongue—a larger number than speak the Celtic tongue, I apprehend, in Scotland, and a larger number than speak it, I apprehend, in Ireland —I protest on behalf of Wales that they are entitled to Home Rule there. Can any sensible man, can any rational man suppose that at this time of day, in this condition of the world, we are going to disintegrate the great capital institutions of this country for the purpose of making ourselves ridiculous in the sight of all mankind, and crippling any power we possess for bestowing benefits through legislation on the country to which we belong ? " The Prime Minister admitted one grievance—" a grievance with regard to university education, which is not so entirely free in Ireland as it has now been made in England ; but that is an exceptional subject, and it is a subject on which I am bound to say Ireland has made no united demand upon England ; still, I regard it as a subject that calls for legislation ; but there is no demand which Ireland has made and which England has refused, and I shall be very glad to see such a demand put into a practical shape in which we may make it the subject of candid and rational discussion."

— Mr. Disraeli presides at the annual dinner of the Hughenden Horticultural Society. In proposing the health of the Queen, the right hon. gentleman spoke of the state of her Majesty's health, which, he said, had for several years been the subject of anxiety to those about her ; but it was only this year that the country generally had become acquainted with the gravity of her condition. He believed there was some improvement in her Majesty's health, but he feared that a long time must elapse before her Majesty would be able to resume the performance of those public and active duties which it was once her pride and pleasure to fulfil, because they brought her in constant and immediate contact with her people. "The fact is," he added, "we cannot conceal from ourselves that her Majesty is physically and morally incapacitated from performing those duties; but it is some consolation to her Majesty's advisers to know that, with regard to those much higher duties which her Majesty is called upon to perform, she still performs them with a punctuality and a precision which have certainly never been surpassed, and rarely equalled by any monarch of these realms."

27.—Writing from Balmoral to Mr. Whalley, the Prime Minister replies to a question which the member for Peterborough had put, on the part, he said, of his constituents:—"I quite agree with those of your constituents, on whose behalf you address me, in thinking that the question 'Whether the Prime Minister of this country is a member of the Church of Rome,' and being such not only declines to avow it, but gives through a long life all the external signs of belonging to a different communion, is a 'question of great political importance,' and this not only 'in the present,' but in any possible 'condition of the Liberal,' or any other 'party.' For it involves the question whether he is the basest creature in the kingdom, which he has a share in ruling; and instant ejectment from his office would be the smallest of the punishments he would deserve. If I have said this much upon the present subject, it has been out of personal respect to you. For I am entirely convinced that, while the question you have put to me is in truth an insulting one, you have put it only from having failed to notice its true character; since I have observed, during an experience of many years, that even when you undertake the most startling duties, you perform them in the gentlest and most considerate manner."

— Emancipation Bill passed in the Brazilian Senate by 33 to 4 votes.

30.—Exhibition at South Kensington closed, having been visited during the season by 1,142,154 persons.

October 1.—The King of Spain returns to Madrid after a tour of thirty days in the provinces, where he met with an enthusiastic reception.

— Brigham Young arrested by the United States authorities, on a charge of lewdly cohabiting with sixteen young women. Troops were also despatched at this time to Salt Lake City.

— Rev. C. Voysey, deprived of the vicarage of Healaugh by the Judicial Committee of

40

the Privy Council, opens regular services in St. George's Hall, Langham Place.

2.—The Spanish Cortes abandon the proposed liquor tax, but impose a duty of 11 per cent. on travellers and merchandize conveyed by railways. Another duty was imposed on shares and bonds.

— Mechanics' Institute at Bradford, erected at a cost of 32,500l., opened by Mr. Forster, M.P., with an address, in which he reviewed the recent action of Parliament on the subject of education.

— Insurrectionary movements in the city of Mexico. The bulk of the garrison proved true to their allegiance, and shot, it was said, 150 of the insurgents.

— Died at Dublin, aged 79, Sir Thomas Deane, architect, formerly President of the Royal Hibernian Academy.

4.—Triple explosion in the premises of an oil and colourman in Manor Street, King's Road, Chelsea.

— Died, aged 77, John Scott, of Malton, the trainer of sixteen St. Leger and four Derby winners.

— Mayor Hall, of New York, attends the Nashville Police-court to offer bail for his appearance to answer the charges of appropriating and misusing the public funds of the city.

6.—Newcastle strike closed after lasting nineteen weeks. The conditions of agreement conceded fifty-four hours per week, the men to work overtime when and to what extent might be required by the employers. Wages, both as to ordinary wages and as to overtime, to remain the same in the different factories as existed prior to the strike; and to be paid weekly at 12.15 P.M. on Saturday. The agreement to be for twelve months, with permission to either party to terminate it at the end of six months, by giving one month's previous notice. The men to go to work on the arrangement now existing in the shops (fifty-seven hours), and the new terms (fifty-four) to take date from January 1, 1872.

7.—Died, aged 89, Field Marshal Sir John Burgoyne, a Peninsular veteran, and commanding engineer at the siege of New Orleans.

8.—Murder of Mrs. Watson, Stockwell Crescent, by her husband, the Rev. J. Selby Watson, for twenty-five years head-master of Stockwell Grammar School, and well known in the literary world as the biographer of Warburton and Porson. This (Sunday) evening the servant left the house, and did not return to it until nearly ten o'clock. When she returned, Mr. Watson told her that her mistress had left for the country, and would be absent five or six days. On Monday morning, Mr. Watson called at the shop of Mr. Turner, a packing-case maker, carrying on business at No. 219, Clapham Road, and requested to see the proprietor. The rev. gentleman was then very cool and collected, and upon Mr. Turner making his appearance he said to him : " I want you to make a large chest for me, and I want it done sharp ; and it must be air and water tight, for I want to send it by rail." The box was afterwards countermanded, but a measurement of the crouched body of Mrs. Watson showed that it would have gone into such a one as was ordered. On Tuesday he went to a chemist's shop, where he was well known, and asked for some prussic acid. This was refused him, but he must have obtained some kind of mixture, for on his return home he told the girl that if anything happened to him in the night she was to send at once to Dr. Rugg. On the morning of the 11th he rose as usual, and wrote some letters, which he left upon the dressing-table, one of them being addressed " To the Surgeon." He then went to bed again, and about eleven o'clock the servant heard him making a moaning noise. and she immediately went to Dr. Rugg, stating that her master was in a fit of apoplexy. Dr. Rugg went to the house, where the servant put the following letter into his hand :—" In a fit of fury I have killed my wife. Often and often have I endeavoured to restrain myself, but my rage overcame me, and I struck her down. Her body will be found in the little room off the library. I hope that she will be buried as becomes a lady of birth and position. She is an Irish lady, and her name is Anne. The key is in a letter on the table." Dr. Rugg immediately went upstairs to Mr. Watson, whom he found very weak and speechless, apparently suffering from some violent poison. As the result of medical treatment he recovered, and was removed to the police station. The body of Mrs. Watson had in the meantime been found. Both temples were beaten in, and there was a deep wound in the forehead. A document in the prisoner's handwriting explained his wishes in the event of his death, but gave no clue to a motive for the crime. " I know not," he wrote, "whose business it will be to look to property left, as my little possessions will be my books and furniture. My only brother was living when I last heard of him five or six years ago in America, at 82, Grand Street, Williamsburgh, and a niece with him. He is my heir if he is still alive. I know not if I have any other surviving relatives. One quarter's wages will soon be due to my servant, and I should wish the sum to be more than doubled for her on account of the trouble which she will have at the present time, and the patience with which she has borne other troubles. In my purse will be found 5l. 10s. I leave a number of letters, many of them very old, with which I hope that those who handle them will deal tenderly."

8.—Burning of the city of Chicago, founded in 1832, and having now a population of over 300,000. This overwhelming disaster was at first

reported to have been caused by a cow kicking over a kerosene oil lamp in a stable, and so setting fire to the straw litter gathered there ; but the official report of the Fire Commissioners appointed to investigate its origin did not favour this surmise as to the cause of the calamity. All that could be established by evidence was that a drayman named Sullivan observed the fire after it had made some progress in a two-storey frame barn, in the rear of premises No. 137, Dekoren Street, owned by Patrick Leary. This was about half-past nine P.M., when the whole of the inmates were in bed and asleep. Witnesses living near the site of the outbreak, thought that from ten to fifteen minutes elapsed between the alarm and the arrival of the first engine. On reaching the fire, three or four buildings in the block were burning fiercely, favoured by a strong breeze from the south-west, which spread the flames rapidly among the old wooden buildings in that part of the city. Early in the evening, indeed, it was seen that the entire Fire Department, though working with the utmost energy, could do little to counteract the progress of the flames. A little after ten o'clock a sudden gust carried the fire across the river, between Van Buren and Adams Streets, by means of flying brands, and set fire to Powell's roofing establishment, adjoining the gasworks. Before this time, the watchman in the Court House cupola had twice extinguished the fire caught from brands carried by the wind into the Court House balcony from the west side, a distance of a mile. At 11 o'clock the keeper of the crib of the lake tunnel, two miles from the shore and three miles from the fire, found the sky full of sparks and burning brands, and from 11.30 till morning, he testified, wrought with all his might to prevent the wooden roof of the crib from burning up and destroying himself and wife. From Powell's roofing establishment the progress of the fire was rapid and terrific, sweeping everything in its course. The engines had all been working on the west side, and they could not reel 600 feet of hose each, cross the river and get to work soon enough to prevent its spreading, literally, on the wings of the wind. Blowing up buildings in the face of the breeze was tried, and without any benefit. The Court House and waterworks, though a mile apart, were burning at the same time. Gunpowder, however, was used for blowing up buildings next day, with good effect, in cutting off the fire at the extreme south end. After the waterworks fell, the firemen could do little good with their engines, except on the banks of the river. It appeared at one time as if the flames no sooner reached a wall than they passed quite through it. A few minutes sufficed to destroy the most elaborately built structure ; the walls melted, and the very bricks were consumed. The wooden pavement took fire, making a continuous sheet of flame two miles long by a mile wide. No human being could possibly survive many minutes. Block after block fell, and the red-hot coals shot higher and higher and spread further and further, to the north side of Lake Street. It was a vast mountain of flame from the river to the lake. At one time so hemmed in were the people that it was expected thousands must perish. Sherman, Tremont, and other hotels were emptied of their guests, and a remarkable sight presented itself in the hurrying throngs with trucks, sacks, or bags on their shoulders, fleeing amid flames for their lives. Thousands of persons and horses inextricably commingled; poor people of all colours and shades and of every nationality, from Europe, China, and Africa, in the excitement, struggled with each other to get away. Hundreds were trampled under foot. Men and women loaded with bundles and household goods, and to whose skirts hung tender infants, half-dressed and barefooted, all rushed to a place of safety. Hours afterwards these might have been seen in vacant lots, or in the streets far out in the suburbs, stretched in the dust. The area over which the fire swept was put down at 2,050 acres, divided thus among the three divisions of the city :—About 160 acres in the west division, 500 acres in the south, and 1,400 acres in the north. The total loss of property, 200,000,000 dollars; number of buildings burned, between 17,000 and 18,000 ; and lives lost about 200, although not more than 117 were reported to the coroner. A calamity like this, unparalleled in magnitude, and demanding instant relief, naturally excited sympathy in every country to which the intelligence was wafted, and relief in clothing, food and money commenced to flow towards the 100,000 homeless and destitute sufferers on a most gigantic scale, the United States, Canada, and Great Britain rivalling each other in the work of benevolence. Before the flames had been subdued in several quarters, the work of rebuilding was begun.

11.—Rumours published of an alleged new "social alliance" between a body described as a "council of skilled workmen" and certain Conservative statesmen, the most of whom at once repudiated all connection with the movement. (See Aug. 1st.)

— Fenian raid into Canada under General O'Neill, who seized the Custom House at Manitoba and the Hudson's Bay Port. He was seized by American troops, and his followers scattered.

12.—Free Library at Derby opened by the Mayor and Corporation.

— Convention signed by Prince Bismarck, Count Arnim, and M. Pouyer-Quertier, concerning the annexation of the French Departments, and the position to be occupied by Alsace and Lorraine in regard to import and export duties.

13.—In the height of the consternation caused by the Chicago fire, additional calamities of the same kind continue to be reported from America. "The forest fires," it was given out, "have desolated the St. Clair, Huron, Tuscola, and Sanilac counties of Michigan. Huron City, Forestville, Whiterock, and many other villages have been destroyed. Many persons have perished in the flames, and great losses in cattle, horses, and winter stores have been sustained. News comes from Toronto that a large portion of the flourishing Canadian town of Windsor, opposite Detroit, was burned down yesterday morning." Another telegram, a few hours later, made public the startling news :— " The entire town of Mainstre, in Michigan, has been destroyed by fire. Two hundred houses and six mills have been burned, and the loss is estimated at 1,250,000 dols. In Wisconsin also four villages on the Green Bay River have been burned, with a fearful loss of life. The inhabitants were surrounded by the flames and 150 fugitives burnt alive in a barn. Hundreds of persons were driven into the river, and altogether 500 people are said to have perished." The worst of all was at Peshtego, a place of 2,000 inhabitants, which was reached by the fire soon after the people returned from the evening service at church. An ominous roaring sound was first heard ; then flakes of fire like meteors fell in different parts of the town, igniting whatever they touched. A fierce wind arose, and everything became enveloped in fire, smoke, hot sand, and cinders. Numbers who fled in affright were suffocated and burned before they could advance many steps. The storm lasted only half an hour, but the buildings and the woods burned all night. The forest surrounding the village was in a blaze ; and the flames being driven into the village, it presented one mass of fire. The people living close to the river reached it and walked in up to their necks. They remained in the water from two to four hours, and endured the heat only by wetting their heads. Many who lived one or two streets from the river were overtaken by the flames and burned to death. Whole families were thus destroyed. Next morning the streets were strewn with burned bodies ; in one case eighty or ninety being found together.

13.—M. Léon Say, Prefect of the Seine, and M. Vautrein, President of the Municipal Council of Paris, attend a meeting of the Common Council at Guildhall to present an address expressive of the thankfulness of the citizens of Paris for the sympathy and material aid sent from London on the raising of the siege.

— Died, aged 75, Sir Francis Graham Moon, Bart., fine art publisher, and Lord Mayor of London in 1855.

14.—Public funeral of the escape-conductor, Joseph Ford, who died from injuries received at a fire in Gray's Inn Road, after rescuing six of the inmates.

15.—Collision in Shields harbour, the *Providence* of Sunderland sinking with five of her crew.

16.—The brigantine *Ruth* blown up off Erith. She had on board 2,000 barrels of petroleum and 100 barrels of resin.

— In opening the German Parliament, the Emperor William explained at some length the recent friendly negotiations with Austria. "The German Empire," he said, "and the Austro-Hungarian Imperial State are, by their geographical position and their historical development, so forcibly and in so manifold a manner called upon to entertain friendly and neighbourly relations with each other, that the fact of these relations having ceased to be troubled by the reminiscence of conflicts which were the undesirable inheritance of the last thousand years, will be received by the entire German nation with sincere satisfaction. The hearty reception which I, as representative of this Empire, received in every part of the great Fatherland, and which has filled me with joyful satisfaction, but, above all, with thanks to God for the blessings which will in future not fail to our constant and honest endeavours, is a pledge that such satisfaction will, in view of the complete development of the German Empire, be felt by the great majority of the nation."

— Dr. Livingstone arrives at Ujiji.

17.—Unveiling of the statue erected to the memory of Dean Alford in a niche of the west front of Canterbury Cathedral.

— Archbishop Sumner's Memorial Schools at Lambeth opened by the Archbishop of Canterbury.

18.—Died at his residence, Manchester Square, aged 79, Charles Babbage, F.R.S., mathematician, and inventor of the "calculating machine."

— Total destruction by fire of Ashton Brothers' cotton mill at Hayfield, Derbyshire. A few hours later a similar building in Glasgow, belonging to Houston and Co., was also destroyed.

19.—Reform banquet in the Free Trade Hall, Manchester, presided over by Earl Granville. Regarding the new social movement, the Foreign Secretary said it was perfectly clear "there is a mistake and inaccuracy with regard to certain peers and distinguished commoners having signed in private certain resolutions; but we are in the dark, on the other hand, as to what was the character of those negotiations which Lord Salisbury informed the public through the press had been confidentially communicated to him. All I can say is, that whatever their character may be, I feel no alarm. I shall, on the contrary, rejoice if those who hitherto have shown too much opposition until the very last moment to the Parliamentary rights of the working classes —those who offered a consistent opposition to those great principles of freedom of trade which nowhere come so alive to one's under-

standing as sitting in this magnificent hall—I shall rejoice if, acting upon sound principles, they come forward and give hands to the working classes, and thereby greatly facilitate the work which, not only her Majesty's present Government, but, I am sure, all successive Governments will have to undertake, which is the solution of many of the most pressing social questions of the day."

19.—Various pretended biographies of Mr. Disraeli making reference to his early connection with the press, he causes his solicitors to make intimation that he had never at any time edited any newspaper, review, magazine, or other periodical publication, and rarely contributed to any, nor has he at any time received or required any remuneration for anything he has ever written, except for those works which bear his name."

21.—A jury sitting in Salt Lake City, Utah, return a verdict of guilty against a Mormon named Hawkins charged with polygamy. The announcement created much excitement. Counsel for the plaintiff moved that the defendant be taken into custody, and the motion was resisted by the defendant's attorney. The prosecution, however, were firm in their demand that the case should take the ordinary course; and the United States marshal was accordingly directed to hold Hawkins a prisoner. Time was allowed to prepare a motion for a new trial and arrest of judgment. The penalty prescribed by the Utah statute for the crime of adultery is imprisonment for not over twenty years nor less than three years, or a fine of not over 1,000 dols., or both fine and imprisonment, at the discretion of the court.

22.—Died in his 80th year, Sir Roderick Murchison, for many years the esteemed President of the Geological and Geographical Societies.

23.—Mr. Gladstone writes to Sir George Pollock that, if it was agreeable to him to accept the office of Constable of the Tower, vacant by the death of Sir John Burgoyne:— "I shall be very happy to submit your name for her Majesty's approval. And I beg that you will consider the proposal I now make as one due solely to your public services and distinction. I have not yet forgotten the description given of those services by Sir Robert Peel when head of the Government, at the climax of your military career, after the catastrophe in Affghanistan had been covered, through your exertions, with a merited and conspicuous success. But it is a great pleasure to me to have an opportunity, after the lapse of so many years, of again tendering to you a mark of honour which I feel confident will have, if accepted by you, the gracious sanction of her Majesty, and the cordial approbation of the country." The appointment was accepted, and gazetted Nov. 14.

24.—Newcastle College of Physical Science, in connection with the University of Durham, opened by the Dean of Durham.

25.—The Mansion House Fund for the relief of the Chicago sufferers reported to have reached 41,189*l*.

— Colliery explosion at Seaham, Durham, causing the death of thirty men.

28.—Mr. Gladstone addresses his constituents in an open-air meeting at Blackheath, dwelling chiefly on the important measures of the past session — abolition of purchase, education, and the ballot. In criticizing the new social movement the Prime Minister admitted that much still remained to be done, though he was of opinion that law could not do all that was promised. "Let the Government labour to its utmost ; let the Legislature labour days and nights in your service ; but, after the very best has been attained and achieved, the question whether the English father is to be the father of a happy family and the centre of a united home is a question which must depend mainly upon himself. And those who propose to you—whoever they may be—schemes like those seven points of which I have spoken ; those who promise to the dwellers in towns that every one of them shall have a house and garden in free air, with ample space ; those who tell you that there shall be markets for selling at wholesale prices retail quantities—I won't say are impostors, because I have no doubt they are sincere ; but I will say they are quacks."

30.—The Prince and Princess of Wales arrive at Scarborough, on a visit to Lord Londesborough.

— Unveiling of a memorial in Berlin erected to the memory of the Riflemen of the Guard who fell in France. The Emperor William urged the soldiers present to gain military knowledge in time of peace, so that they might be found ready to defend their country again if called on.

31.—Royal Warrant issued embodying the new regulations respecting promotion and appointments in the army, rendered necessary by the abolition of purchase.

November 1.—The P. and O. steamer *Rangoon*, with passengers and mails for Australia, wrecked in Galle harbour.

3.—Columbia Market formally transferred by Lady Burdett Coutts to the Corporation of London.

4.—Died, aged 78, Rev. Philip Wynter, D.D., President of St. John's College, Oxford.

6.—Sir James Colville and Sir Montague Smith take their seats as paid members of the Judicial Committee of Privy Council.

— Sir Charles Dilke, selected to second last year's Address, delivered a lecture at Newcastle

on the expense of Royalty, in which he severely criticized the expenditure of the Royal household, and declared that the Queen, in spite of a promise given to Parliament, had not been in the habit of paying Income-tax. This statement was afterwards disproved by Mr. Lowe. A few days later Sir Charles, in a speech at Bristol, declared himself a Republican.

6.—The Master of the Rolls delivers judgment in the suit Peek *v.* Gurney and others, in which the plaintiff sought to render the surviving directors of that company and the executors of a deceased director jointly and severally liable for the amount of the loss sustained by him through his purchase of shares to the amount of about 100,000*l*. in the company. After an elaborate summing up his Lordship dismissed the bill, but without costs, owing to the gross misconduct of the directors in issuing a false prospectus as to the state of the bank.

7.—Legal changes. Sir Robert Collier gazetted a Justice of the Court of Common Pleas, preparatory to his removal to the Judicial Committee of Privy Council. He was succeeded as Attorney-General by Sir John Coleridge, Mr. Jessel stepping into the office thus vacant of Solicitor-General.

— Monument at Vienna erected to the memory of the Emperor Maximilian of Mexico unveiled in presence of the Emperor Francis Joseph, the Archdukes, Ministers, and a large body of spectators.

— Lord Dufferin gazetted a peer of the United Kingdom, by the title of Viscount Clandeboye, of Clandeboye, in the county of Down, and Earl of Dufferin, in the county of Down.

8.—The "fall" elections in the United States announced to have resulted in large Republican gains. The Tammany candidates in New York were defeated by large majorities.

— Count Beust resigns his position as Chancellor of Austria, and accepts the London Embassy. Other changes took place in the Austrian Cabinet at this time, chiefly in connection with the refusal of the Emperor to concede the demands made by the Czechs of Bohemia, for a separate Parliament on the Hungarian model. Count Hohenwart, who favoured the Bohemian claim, resigned his position as Prime Minister in favour of Prince Udolf Auersperg, a leader of the old Liberal party. Count Beust was succeeded by Count Andrassy, and Count Lonyay became Prime Minister of Hungary.

9.—Commenced at Portsmouth, on board the *Duke of Wellington*, a court-martial on Captain Thrupp and officers of the *Megæra*. The inquiry was continued till the 17th, when the Court found the captain was "fully justified in beaching the ship, and that he would not have been justified in continuing his course to Australia, and doth therefore acquit him of all blame in respect to it. The Court is further of opinion that no blame whatever is attributable to her officers and men under trial, hereinbefore named, for the stranding and loss of her Majesty's ship *Megæra*, and doth therefore acquit them of all blame, and the said captain and other officers and men are hereby acquitted accordingly."

10.—After a trial extending over eleven days Robert Kelly is acquitted by the jury of the murder of Head-Constable Talbot in the open street, and after a threat that he intended to take the life of his victim, in retaliation for having acted the part of an informer against the Fenians. An elaborate attempt was made to show that death did not result directly from the wound, but from unskilful surgical treatment.

— Lord Chief Justice Cockburn remonstrates, in the name of the Bench and Bar, with Mr. Gladstone on the contemplated removal of the Attorney General first to the Common Pleas and then to the Judicial Committee of the Privy Council, as a subterfuge and evasion of the Act of Parliament passed last August, regulating the appointment. Disowning any desire to disparage the personal merits of Sir R. Collier, the Lord Chief Justice described the obvious meaning of the Act in question, and pointed out that no exception was made therein in favour of any law officer of the Crown. "I cannot help thinking," he wrote, "what would have been the language in which the Court of Queen's Bench would have expressed its opinion if such an evasion of a statute had been attempted for the purpose of qualifying an individual for a municipal office, and the case had been brought before it on an information in the nature of *quo warranto.* In the present instance, the Legislature having settled the qualification for the newly-created office, momentarily to invest a party, otherwise not qualified, with a qualifying office, not that he shall hold the latter, but that he may be immediately transferred to the former, appears to me, I am bound to say, to be nothing less than the manufacture of a qualification, not very dissimilar in character to the manufacture of qualifications such as we have known practised in other instances in order to evade the law. . . . From every member of the legal profession with whom I have been brought into contact in the course of the last few days, I have met with but one expression of opinion as to the proposed step— an opinion, to use the mildest term I can select, of strong and unqualified condemnation. Such I can take upon myself to say is the unanimous opinion of the profession. I have never in my time known of so strong or universal an expression, I had almost said explosion, of opinion." Mr. Gladstone replied that as the transaction was a joint one, and the completed part of it the act of the Lord Chancellor, the letter had been sent to him. The Lord Chief Justice then

wrote:—" My objection to the present appointment of Sir Robert Collier is not an objection to the appointment *in se*, but as being intended to create a factitious qualification for a seat on the Judicial Committee. It was because its ulterior object was to be your act that I took the liberty of addressing myself to you. Had I objected to the part of the transaction already completed, I should have addressed my observations to the Lord Chancellor." The Lord Chancellor in reply defended the appointment as made with a full knowledge on his part of Mr. Gladstone's intention to promote the Attorney-General to the Judicial Committee. "I have thus acted advisedly, and with the conviction that the arrangement was justified as regards both its fitness and its legality. I take upon myself the responsibility of thus concurring with Mr. Gladstone, and am prepared to vindicate the course pursued. You will not, I trust, think that I am wanting in respect if I reserve my explanation for a more suitable opportunity than could be afforded by a correspondence with yourself, either directly or through the medium of Mr. Gladstone." The Lord Chief Justice closed the correspondence with the remark that while he freely admitted he was "not entitled to any explanation of the course you have determined to adopt, I must in candour say that I think I might have expected that grave objections to a proceeding connected with the administration of justice, coming from one holding the office I have the honour to fill, would have received somewhat more consideration, and would not have been dismissed in quite so summary a manner. Under the circumstances, while you reserve your explanation till a fitting opportunity shall arise, so I, on my part, must reserve to myself the right to make public, when I may deem it proper, the fact of my protest and the grounds on which it is founded, as stated in my letter to Mr. Gladstone."

10.—Henry M. Stanley, a travelling correspondent, sent out by the proprietor of the *New York Herald,* discovers Dr. Livingstone at Ujiji. As the procession of native guides and assistants entered the town, Mr. Stanley observed a group of Arabs on the right, in the centre of which was a pale-looking, grey-bearded, white man, whose fair skin contrasted with the sun-burnt visages of those by whom he was surrounded. Passing from the rear of the procession to the front, the American traveller noticed that the white man was clad in a red woollen jacket, and wore upon his head a naval cap, with a faded gilt band. In an instant he recognised the European as none other than Dr. Livingstone himself; but a dignified Arab chieftain, standing by, confirmed Mr. Stanley in a resolution to show no symptom of rejoicing or excitement. Slowly advancing towards the great traveller, he bowed, and said, "Dr. Livingstone, I presume?" to which address the latter, who was fully equal to the occasion, simply smiled and replied, "Yes."

It was not till some hours afterwards, when alone together, seated on a goatskin, that the two white men exchanged those congratulations which both were eager to express, and recounted their respective difficulties and adventures. On the 20th they left Ujiji, and explored the northern end of Lake Tanganyika, confirming by a second inspection the observations which Dr. Livingstone had previously made; and after twenty-eight days thus pleasantly spent, they returned to Ujiji, and there passed Christmas Day together. On the 26th of December, they left for Unyanyembe, and, arriving there, stayed together till March 14, when Mr. Stanley, entrusted with letters from Dr. Livingstone, started for the coast, leaving the explorer to trace out the sources of the Lualaba. Mr. Stanley handed over to him 2,788 yards of various kinds of cloths, 992 lbs. of beads, 350 lbs. of brass wire, a waterproof tent, an air-bed, a canvas boat, a bag of carpenter's tools, arms and ammunition, cooking utensils, a medicine chest, and a sextant; forming altogether about forty loads. Dr. Livingstone also found thirty-three loads of his own stores, and Mr. Stanley calculated that the Doctor was thus supplied with sufficient to last him four years. He required a few additional articles from Zanzibar, especially a good watch and other instruments, and fifty trustworthy men as carriers. These Mr. Stanley undertook to send up from Zanzibar, and set out for the coast with Livingstone's journal and letters on the 13th of March. He performed the march of 535 miles, wading through swamps, across torrents, and wearily tramping through dense jungle, in thirty-five days, and reached Bagamozyo on the 6th of May. Thus was this great work completed, a service for the performance of which Mr. Stanley earned and received the most cordial recognition from the Queen and people of England, and especially from the President and Fellows of the Royal Geographical Society.

11.—Sir W. Stirling-Maxwell elected Lord Rector of Edinburgh University, by a majority of 92 votes over Sir Roundell Palmer.

13.—Mr. Pigott, an Irish newspaper proprietor, sentenced to four months' imprisonment for publishing comments in the *Irishman*, tending to bring the law officers of the Crown into contempt, and insinuating that Kelly, even if he was guilty, had not gone beyond his duty in shooting Head-constable Talbot.

15.—Mr. Disraeli elected Lord Rector of Glasgow University by a majority of 134 votes over Mr. Ruskin.

16.—Earl Russell, writing from Cannes, expresses his approval of the object of the Education League in so far as it contended for the unsectarian character of rate-aided schools. He was not of opinion that the Bible, when read, should be read without note or comment; "but I think this is a point of so much difficulty, and there is so much danger of slipping into sectarian comments on the part of teachers, that I

do not wonder at the opinion expressed by the League. My wish and hope is that the rising youth of England may be taught to adopt, not the Church of Rome or the Church of England, but the Church of Christ. The teaching of Christ, whether dogmatic or not, is to be found in the Bible, and those who in their infancy read the Bible may, at their own choice, when they reach the age of fifteen or sixteen years, follow the teaching of the Church of Rome or of any Protestant community they may prefer. In this manner Christianity may be purged of the corruptions which, in the course of time, and amid the conflicts of the sixteenth and seventeenth centuries, have stained its purity, and perverted its spirit of love and charity." On this the *Church Herald* remarked : "There can be no importance attached to anything that so perverse and vicious an old Whig as Lord Russell can say on religious teaching."

17.—Speaking at Lenzie, near Glasgow, on the subject of her Majesty's health, the state of which had lately caused considerable anxiety, Dr. Norman Macleod, lately returned from Balmoral, said he had never seen the remotest trace of any moral or mental weakness, but in every instance remarkable evidence of moral and mental strength and capacity. "Her Majesty has just passed through a severe attack of rheumatic gout, which so affected her hands that for a time she was utterly unable to sign her name, and from a severe neuralgia from which she has entirely recovered, and I have never seen her better in spirits or better in health or stronger in mind than she is at the present moment. At the same time, I am far from saying that she has recovered her strength so as to be able to do more than she is doing ; for I make bold to say that none of us have the slightest conception of the unceasing demand that is made upon a person in her high position of attending to innumerable details and carrying burdens upon her mind without the possibility of one moment's rest. . . . No one who knows the Queen but knows she would do all that it is possible for her to do, and no one who knows her but is amazed at her extraordinary considerateness for every one, how she occupies her thought upon every subject, and how she attends to such minute details of duty. I will take it upon me to say that the case of the poorest subject in her kingdom, if made known to her, would receive her immediate attention."

—The Spanish Minister, Zorrilla, having been defeated in the Cortes, tenders his resignation, which the King refuses to accept, and suspends the sittings of the Cortes.

— Died at Bournemouth, aged 77, Sir Joshua Walmsley, formerly M.P. for Bolton and Leicester.

20.—Mr. Chilborn, manager of the Arran Quay Branch of the Royal Bank of Ireland, commits suicide by shooting himself in a cemetery, under distress of mind produced by untoward speculations in the Wicklow Copper Mine Company.

22.—Illness of the Prince of Wales, a telegram from Sandringham intimating that he had been prevented paying a visit to the Maharajah Dhuleep Singh, by a chill resulting in a febrile attack which confined him to his room. Next day it was announced that the symptoms were not severe, but indicated an attack of typhoid fever.

— Mr. Bates, a Conservative candidate, returned for Plymouth by 1,753 votes against 1,511 given to Mr. Rooker, Liberal.

24.—7,000*l.* reported to have been collected in London in aid of the starving inhabitants of Bushire, Yezd, and other Persian towns. So terrible was this calamity that in some districts it was calculated one-third of the population had died from starvation, and two-thirds of the cattle and beasts of burden.

25.—Riotous proceedings at Dover, arising out of the election carried by the Solicitor-General, Mr. Jessel, against Mr. Barnett, a Conservative candidate.

—Disorderly meeting at Bolton, called to hear Mr. Dilke, M.P., criticize the functions and expense of Royalty. Similar disgraceful gatherings took place at Derby and Birmingham.

26.—The Count of Girgenti, brother of the ex-King of Naples, commits suicide by shooting himself in a room in the Hôtel du Cygne, Lucerne.

28.—Execution of Communist Generals. Rossel, Ferré, and Bourgeois were shot this morning at a quarter past seven, in front of the Artillery Butts at Satory, in the presence of 3,000 men belonging to the regular army. The intention having been kept perfectly secret, there were scarcely any other spectators present. All three behaved with great courage. Rossel and Bourgeois had their eyes bandaged, but Ferré refused to be blindfolded. Rossel was killed instantly, but Ferré and Bourgeois received the *coup de grâce* after the volley. After the execution the troops defiled past the three corpses. The execution of Rossel, known to be a brave soldier, enthusiastic and intelligent in his profession, gave rise to much severe criticism against the Versailles Government.

— Died, aged 67, Marshal Benedek, an Austrian General of experience in Italian campaigns, and commander of the forces at Sadowa.

— Eight Spanish medical students, varying in age from 14 to 20 years, shot at Havanna, a few hours after a hurried and informal trial, for alleged desecration of San Lazaro cemetery. About forty others, less prominently concerned in what appeared to be a juvenile freak, were sentenced to various terms of penal servitude.

28.—Came on before the Judicial Committee of the Privy Council, the appeal of the Church Association against the sentence delivered by Sir Robert Phillimore on the 23rd of July, 1870, acquitting the Rev. W. J. E. Bennett, Vicar of Frome, of the charge of erroneous doctrine on the subject of the Real Presence, the Eucharistic Sacrifice, and Adoration.

29.—The Queen proceeds to Sandringham on a visit to the Prince of Wales. An afternoon bulletin reported that his Royal Highness had passed a quiet day, the symptoms continuing without alteration. The *Times* mentions to-day that his illness dated from the recent visit to Lord Londesborough, and was likely to have arisen from poison generated by sewage. Others of the party had since been attacked by typhoid symptoms, one of them—Lord Chesterfield—with unusual severity. The Prince's case was thought likely to run for twenty-four days.

30.— Explosion of a cartridge factory within the Fort of Agra, causing the death of Conductor Ware, his son, Sergeant Upton, and twenty-three native workmen.

December 1.—Died at Bretby Hall, Burton-on-Trent, aged 40, George Philip Stanhope, Earl of Chesterfield. He was one of the visitors at Scarborough in October, and had been suffering for some days from typhoid fever.

— Mr. W. R. Grove, Q.C., gazetted to be a Judge in the Court of Common Pleas.

3.—Fire at Warwick Castle. The flames, first noticed in Lady Warwick's apartments, early in the morning, speedily extended over the whole east wing, between the grand entrance hall and the domestic offices adjoining Cæsar and Guy's Towers. This portion of the castle was completely gutted, and only the outer walls with charred and smouldering rubbish left. The fire then spread across the grand staircase, and reached the great hall, of which only the bare walls remained. At four o'clock the fire was burning so fiercely that it was feared the red drawing-room would also be destroyed. Preparations were therefore made for the worst by stripping this and the adjoining apartments of their rare treasures. The tapestry round the state bedroom, made in Brussels in 1694, was wrenched from the wall and carried to a place of security, together with the portraits of "Queen Anne," by Kneller, the "Earl of Essex," by Zucchero, and other rare paintings. The pictures by Rembrandt, Holbein, Rubens, Vandyke, Titiens, Salvator Rosa, Sir Peter Lely, and Carracci's "Dead Christ" were also taken down. The costly tables and treasures in the cabinets were carried to the remotest corner of the Castle, ready to be again moved in case of necessity. Fortunately, the efforts of the firemen practically arrested the fire at the end of the great hall, though the red drawing-room was slightly damaged about the roof and by water. The flames were not subdued until nearly ten o'clock in the morning. Most of the family were abroad.

3.—About 800 yards of the west pier of Leith destroyed by a fire originating in the up-setting of a vessel of boiling pitch, used for saturating the structure.

4.—United States Congress opened by President Grant with a Message congratu-lating the country on its increasing prosperity, the reduction of the debt by 17,000,000*l.* in one year, and the approaching settlement of all differences with Great Britain. " This year," said President Grant, "has witnessed two great nations, having one language and lineage, settling by peaceful arbitration dis-putes of long standing. which were liable at any time to bring nations to a bloody conflict. The example thus set, if successful in its final issue, will be followed by other civilized nations, and finally be the means of returning to pursuits of industry millions of men now maintained to settle disputes of nations by the sword." Regarding Cuba, the President re-gretted that the disturbed condition of the island continued to be a source of annoyance and anxiety. " The existence of a protracted struggle in such close proximity to our own territory, without any apparent prospect of an early termination, cannot be other than an object of concern to a people who, while abstaining from interference in the affairs of other Powers, naturally desire to see every country enjoying peace, liberty, and free insti-tutions. The American naval commanders in Cuban waters have been instructed, in case it should become necessary, to spare no effort to protect the lives and property of *bonâ fide* American citizens, and to maintain the dignity of the flag. It is hoped that all pending ques-tions with Spain, growing out of the state of affairs in Cuba, may be adjusted in the spirit of peace and conciliation which has hitherto guided the two Powers in their treatment of such questions."

— Judgment delivered in the Irish Court of Common Pleas in the case of " Wallace *v.* Seymour," known as the Hertford Estates case, and involving the ownership of property in the county of Antrim giving an income of about 60,000*l.* a year. The question turned on the effect of certain words in a codicil executed in June 1850 by the late Marquis of Hertford to his will, made in 1838. This codicil purported to give to the plaintiff absolutely " the residue of the real and personal estate " of the late Marquis in Ireland, while by the will under which the defendant claimed, the real estate in Ireland was given to trustees in the first instance, to make up any deficiency in the personal estate, and afterwards to the testator's brother for life, and thereafter to the defendant. The court held unanimously that the words in the codicil revoking the bequest of the real estate in the will were not sufficiently clear and explicit, and that the testator in inserting the

48

word " real " in the codicil either forgot the exact words of the residuary clause in the will or did not comprehend their meaning. Judg-ment was accordingly given for the defendant.

6.—Conference at Birmingham called to consider how the House of Lords could be best reformed and brought into greater harmony with the wishes of the country. One resolution declared—" That in a free country, the ultimate decision upon all questions of government or of the policy of the State must rest with representatives elected by the majority of the people ; and that some plan should be adopted in this nation to give constitutional effect to that decision." Another :—" That no right to legislate on the affairs of the nation ought to be conferred in consequence of the profession of any theological opinions, or of connection with any ecclesiastical establishment, and there-fore the legislative power of the Bishops of the English Church should be abolished."

— Disorderly republican meeting at Read-ing, resulting in the severe handling of Odger by a mob at the railway station.

— Died, at Bank Hall, Burnley, Lanca-shire, aged 72, General Sir James Yorke Scarlett, commander of the British cavalry in the Crimea.

7.—M. Thiers delivers his first Presidential Message to the National Assembly. The policy of France, he said, must be henceforth a policy of dignified and enduring peace. " If, contrary to all probability, events should disturb that peace, the deed will not be that of France. France must become once more what she has a right to be in the interest of all States. France will be true to her solemnly pledged word. Moreover, the States which took part in the war are fatigued ; and those that had been witnesses have become seriously alarmed." The Message then entered into details of the rela-tions between France and the other Powers of Europe :—" Our relations with Spain continue amicable. We likewise maintain a good under-standing with Italy. The independence of the Holy See must be rigorously upheld. As re-gards Rome we offer no counsels, for we give no advice to anyone, and least of all to an aged man who enjoys all our respect and sympathy. With regard to Austria, we sincerely wish her prosperity. As regards Russia, the most cordial relations exist between that country and France. They are the result of an elevated and reciprocal appreciation of the interests of both countries."

— A jury in the Court of Queen's Bench decide that Sir Joshua Reynolds's fine portrait of Francis George Hare, known as "Infancy," belonged to the defendant, who claimed under his uncle Julius Hare, and not to his sister.

— Prince Bismarck addresses Count Arnim, the German Ambassador in Paris, concerning the acquittal of criminals in the French courts charged with the murder of German soldiers. He declares that in future, should the French authorities refuse to give up assassins, the Germans will be compelled to seize French hostages, and in extreme cases even have recourse to more stringent measures, in order to enforce their demands. The Imperial Chancellor points out that recent events in Paris and Melun have proved the exasperation of the French to be so great that in the still pending negotiations with France, not only must the fulfilment of the conditions of peace be secured, but the necessary strength of the German position within the occupied Departments must also be kept in view.

8.—Contrasting somewhat with the assurance put forward by M. Thiers, the Emperor of Russia, in proposing the health of the Emperor of Germany, at a banquet given by the military order of St. George, said, "We desire and hope that the intimate friendship which unites us and the brotherhood of arms will be perpetuated in future generations. In this friendship existing between our two armies, which dates from a memorable epoch, I see the best guarantee for the maintenance of peace and loyal order in Europe."

— The hitherto favourable bulletins issued regarding the illness of the Prince of Wales were disagreeably varied to-day by the announcement made at 8 A.M., that his Royal Highness "has passed a very unquiet night. There is considerable increase in the febrile symptoms." At 1 P.M. it was announced that "there is no abatement of the graver symptoms." These, like the other bulletins with which the public were now getting familiar, were signed by the physicians in attendance, Drs. Jenner, Gull, and Lowe. The Queen left for Sandringham in the afternoon, along with other members of the Royal family.

9.—Chief Justice Bovill, as the head of the Court which "had been made use of," expresses his concurrence with Sir Alexander Cockburn as to the impropriety of the Collier appointment.

10.—The Prince of Wales prayed for in most of the churches throughout the kingdom. A special form was prepared late last night by the Archbishop of Canterbury, and circulated as widely as the limited time permitted. Early in the morning the Princess of Wales caused a touching request to be conveyed to the Vicar of Sandringham. "My husband," she wrote, "being, thank God, somewhat better, I am coming to church. I must leave, I fear, before the service is concluded, that I may watch by his bedside. Can you not say a few words in the early part of the service that I may join with you in prayer for my husband before I return to him?" The Princess attended service, reaching the church by the private path from Sandringham grounds. To meet the wishes of her Royal Highness, the Rev. Vicar, before reading the Collect, speaking in a voice trembling with emotion, which he vainly sought to suppress, said, "The prayers

of the congregation are earnestly sought for his Royal Highness the Prince of Wales, who is now most seriously ill." The bulletins, four of which were now being issued each day, still indicated great anxiety on the part of the medical attendants. At 5.30 this (Sunday) afternoon the report was that his Royal Highness "had passed an unquiet afternoon, with a return of the more urgent symptoms." Another, anxiously looked for, issued at 8.15 next morning, indicated still more the gravity of the situation. "Restless night, with a further recurrence of the graver symptoms." Two hours before this the Royal Family were reported in an unofficial telegram to have been summoned to the bedside in anticipation of the worst results.

12.—Total eclipse of the sun, carefully observed by English astronomers in southern India and Ceylon.

13.—Public anxiety regarding the condition of the Prince of Wales may be said to have reached its climax to-day, the morning bulletin announcing that his Royal Highness had "passed another very restless night. The conditions do not improve." With the exception, perhaps, of certain periods of the Crimean War and Indian Mutiny, public feeling had never been so deeply touched in the present generation; and the anxiety to obtain the latest news of the condition of the Royal sufferer was most intense among all classes of the community. Bulletins forwarded from Sandringham, and, in some cases, from the Home Office, were posted up in all places of resort; newspapers were eagerly bought up, edition after edition, as they were hourly brought out; and whenever two or three friends met, the condition of the Prince was not only the first but the single topic of discussion. In every town crowds waited anxiously for the latest news, and Government found it expedient to forward the medical bulletins to all the telegraph offices in the United Kingdom. Throughout India, in the colonies, and even in the United States, the daily progress of the disease was recorded and watched; while prayers were offered up by Hindoos, Parsees, Mussulmans, and Jews. This afternoon's bulletin, issued at five o'clock, was thought to indicate matters as in an almost hopeless state. His Royal Highness, it was reported, "has passed a very unquiet afternoon. There is no abatement in the gravity of the symptoms." A slight turn for the better came a few hours later. "10 P.M. His Royal Highness has passed a less unquiet evening." The Prince was said to have recognized the Queen this evening. Though still giving cause for much anxiety, the fever may be said to have weakened its hold of the system after this date. The bulletins, however, still continued to be expressed with the greatest caution, though the physicians were known by all about them to be honourably willing to afford competent interpreters of technical fact such material for illustrating the case as might enlighten the public mind, and thus relieve unnecessary anxiety.

13.—Intimation given of the probable retirement of Mr. Denison, Speaker of the House of Commons.

— Tried at the Central Criminal Court, before Mr. Justice Grove, William Anthony, blacksmith, charged with five cases of wilful fire-raising for the sake of the reward of 2s. 6d. paid for giving first notice. Found guilty, and sentenced to twelve years' penal servitude.

14.—Anniversary of the death of the Prince Consort celebrated at Sandringham under circumstances of mournful anxiety to the Royal family.

— Died at his residence, Churton Street, Belgrave Road, aged 70 years, George Hudson, all-powerful in commercial circles, thirty years since, as the Railway King.

— The Chancellor of the Exchequer informs the Treasury Board that her Majesty's Government had agreed to the following resolutions respecting the terms upon which the law officers of the Crown (except Sir John Duke Coleridge, in whose case no change is to be made) shall in future be remunerated for their services, that is to say :—" 1. Except as aforesaid, the Attorney-General shall receive 7,000l. a year for non-contentious business, and the Solicitor-General 6,000l. a year. 2. All fees payable for non-contentious business shall be paid into the Exchequer. 3. The law officers shall receive fees for contentious business, and for opinions connected with it, according to the ordinary professional scale. 4. All complimentary briefs and payments for services not intended to be given shall be abolished. 5. The salaries above mentioned shall be voted by the House of Commons."

16.—Dean Goulburn, Norwich, protests against the appointment of Bishop Temple as one of the Select Preachers of Oxford. "It seems to me," he wrote to the Vice-Chancellor, " a miserable apostacy from the principles which once animated the University of Oxford, that she should deliberately commit the religious instruction of her youth (a sacred trust, if any trust can be sacred) to a prelate who labours under grave suspicions of heterodoxy, whose theology is at best hazy, and who will not purge himself from complicity with the attempts of avowed Rationalists to throw doubt upon 'those things which are most surely believed amongst us.' "

18.—The Prince of Wales reported to have passed a quiet night, and making satisfactory progress. A boy named Blegg, attached to the stables at Sandringham, and who had been stricken down with typhoid fever about the same time as the Prince, dies to-day, to the grief of members of the Royal Family, who, as was natural in the circumstances, had bestowed on him a large measure of attention.

50

18.—The *Alabama* Committee hold a formal meeting at Geneva for the ratification of powers and exchange of papers.

— Forbes' oil manufactory at Port Dundas, Glasgow, destroyed by fire.

19.—The Queen leaves Sandringham for Windsor.

— The Duke d'Aumale and Prince Joinville take their seats in the National Assembly.

21.—The steamer *Delaware*, trading from Liverpool to Calcutta, wrecked in a gale off the Scilly Islands, and forty-eight of her crew drowned.

22.—Died, aged 81, the Earl of Ellenborough, President of the Board of Control in Sir Robert Peel's Ministry of 1841, and Governor-General of India 1842-44. The measures he sanctioned led to the rescue of the captives and close of the Affghan War.

23.—Field-Marshal Sir George Pollock, G.C.B., installed as Constable of the Tower. The ceremony was performed by torch-light, owing to the dense fog which prevailed.

— New market for the slaughter of foreign cattle at Deptford opened in presence of the Lord Mayor and other officials of the Corporation.

— In his rectorial address at Munich, Dr. Döllinger explained the natural influence which Germany and France had always exercised upon one another. "France," he said, "preserves even now, for the future, her importance as interpreter and carrier of scientific ideas. She owes her defeat chiefly to the absence of veracity in her literature, especially in the historical portion of it, which has prevailed for generations past. The 18th of July, 1870, brought to Germany a second war through the Roman declaration of war against German science. The decrees of the Vatican were launched only against German science, and had been prepared for twenty years by a systematic falsification of the theological text-books. Once before Rome carried on war against science. It was against the natural sciences, and she succumbed. Now she combats historical science."

— In opening the Reichsrath, the Emperor of Austria said the Crown, by permitting the different provinces to seek the remedy for their claims by such means as the Constitution offers to them, not only had in view the right of the whole empire, but also the real interests and protection of the separate kingdoms. "The first task of the Government, which is composed of men belonging to the representation of the whole country, is to strengthen the constitutional and legal basis, and to ensure everywhere absolute obedience to the laws. The Government, on its part, will accede to the wishes of Galicia so far as they are confined to that province, and are compatible with the conditions of the unity and the power of the whole empire. The complete independence of the Reichsrath must be assured by the unbiassed selection of the representatives of the empire."

26.—Concluded in the Court of Session, Edinburgh, the case of Asher, widow, *v.* Rennie, a claim for 1,000*l.* for breach of promise by a Glasgow merchant. This was the second trial of the case, a verdict having been returned, in the beginning of November last, for the defendant. That verdict was set aside by the Court as being contrary to evidence, and a new trial granted, which now ended in the jury unanimously returning a verdict for the plaintiff, with 750*l.* damages.

— In a letter dated from Windsor Castle, the Queen acknowledges the sympathy manifested by all classes of her subjects on the occasion of the alarming illness of the Prince of Wales. "The universal feeling," writes her Majesty, "shown by her people during those painful, terrible days, and the sympathy evinced by them with herself and her beloved daughter, the Princess of Wales, as well as the general joy at the improvement in the Prince of Wales's state, have made a deep and lasting impression on her heart which can never be effaced. It was, indeed, nothing new to her; for the Queen had met with the same sympathy when, just ten years ago, a similar illness removed from her side the mainstay of her life, the best, wisest, and kindest of husbands. The Queen wishes to express at the same time, on the part of the Princess of Wales, her feelings of heartfelt gratitude; for she has been as deeply touched as the Queen by the great and universal manifestation of loyalty and sympathy. The Queen cannot conclude without expressing her hope that her faithful subjects will continue their prayers to God for the complete recovery of her dear son to health and strength."

— Replying to a request for his opinion on the subject of a Church Defence Institution, the Archbishop of Canterbury writes:— "There seems little doubt that vigorous and persistent efforts are being made by those who desire to destroy that connection between the Church and the State which I regard as equally beneficial to both. I can therefore have no hesitation in saying that some systematic organization, to meet these efforts and keep the public informed on the subject, is much to be desired; and I think that the clergy and laity of our Church will do well to aid in the work which the Committee of the Church Defence Institution has undertaken."

27.—Renewed anxiety regarding the Prince of Wales, the single bulletin now issued daily at noon recording that his Royal Highness had passed the night quietly, "but convalescence is retarded by a painful affection above the left hip, attended with some feverishness."

28.—In accordance with an application made on her behalf, Christina Edmunds, charged with wholesale poisoning at Brighton, was

removed to-day from Lewes gaol to Newgate, previous to being tried, under "Palmer's Act," at the Central Criminal Court. On entering her new place of confinement, she made peremptory demands to be permitted to wear her bonnet and velvet dresses.

29.—George Cruikshank, who had illustrated Mr. Dickens' novel, "Oliver Twist," writes to the *Times*, claiming to have originated that work, and been the author of most of the characters.

— Senator Tweed arrested in the New York Metropolitan Hotel by Sheriff Brennan on a charge of felony connected with the misappropriation of City funds by the gang known as the "Tammany Ring."

30.—Boiler explosion in Glasgow, a road steam-traveller described as "Yuille's Traction Engine," bursting in Paisley Road, killing five and injuring about thirty others, chiefly children, who had gathered round the locomotive during a temporary halt.

31.—Died at Richmond, Yorkshire, Matthew Greathead, aged 102, supposed to be the oldest Freemason in the world, having entered the Lennox Lodge, No. 123, in 1797.

1872.

January 1. — Died, aged 71, William Edwardes, third Lord Kensington, one of the survivors of the battle of Navarino.

— Addressing the "Druids" at Oxford, Mr. Cardwell remarked:—"We are not a Continental Power. We are not a Transatlantic Power. We are an insular Power, with the largest foreign dominions and the most scattered dominions of any Power in the world. The natural consequence is that our first arm is afloat, and it is the navy. The next is that we desire to have at hand an army like our navy, first-rate in quality, but not large in quantity. If we were a Transatlantic nation, we should have no relations requiring an armed force with regard to Continental nations. If we were a Continental nation, we should require a larger armed force than we now possess. Being an insular country we have Continental obligations to which we may be called upon to do justice, and for that purpose we ought to be prepared." His brother member, Mr. Vernon Harcourt, spoke on the annual increase of the national expenditure.

— At the annual New-Year reception, the Emperor of Germany said that the endeavours of all ought now to be directed towards utilizing the peace, which, as he hoped, was now secured for a long time, in order to strengthen the foundations on which their present greatness had been established, and for the development and culture of all intellectual as well as material possessions.

1.—Subscription invited for a 5 per cent. Hungarian loan of 3,000,000*l.* at 81.

— The Bishop of Orleans resigns his place in the French Academy, in consequence of the election of M. Littré, whom he described as a materialist and a socialist.

2.—Died, aged 84, General Sir James Jackson, Colonel of the 6th Dragoon Guards, a veteran of the Peninsula and Waterloo, and one of the oldest officers in the British army. From his firmness with a mob at Carlow, in 1841, the General was known as " Justice-to-Ireland Jackson."

3.—A lion-tamer named M'Carthy torn to pieces at Bolton, while exhibiting his power over the animals in Manders' menagerie.

5.—Died, aged 54, Sir Francis Crossley, M.P. for the Northern Division of the West Riding.

— Died, at Westbourne Road, Edgbaston, aged 72, Joseph Gillott, the first manufacturer of steel pens by machinery.

6.—James Fisk, jun., of Erie Railway notoriety, assassinated in the corridor of the Grand Central Hotel, New York, by Edward Stokes, who fired three shots, one of which inflicted a mortal wound in the abdomen. Fisk, who retained consciousness to the last, was closely attended by Gould and Tweed. There had been a long and scandalous litigation between the assassin and his victim, originating in the arrest of Stokes for taking away a woman named Mansfield, with whom Fisk had illicit relations. Stokes gave evidence against Fisk in a libel suit in which this woman was concerned, and moreover threatened to publish letters from Fisk to her, revealing various secrets connected with the Erie Railway. Fisk had just obtained an injunction forbidding the publication of these letters, and also induced the grand jury to indict Stokes for conspiracy.

7.—M. Vautrain returned for Paris by 121,158 votes, against 93,423 given to M. Victor Hugo.

8.—Trades Union Congress at Nottingham, attended by seventy delegates, representing 255,710 constituents.

9.—Count Arnim presents his credentials as German Ambassador to M. Thiers.

— Royal Commission gazetted " to inquire into the property and income belonging to, administered, or enjoyed by, the universities of Oxford and Cambridge, and the colleges and halls therein (whether held or received for their corporate use, or in trust, or in whatsoever other manner), including the prospects of increase or decrease in such property and income ; and also to report the uses to which such property and income are applied, together with all matters of fact tending to exhibit the state and circumstances of the same, and the condition, management, and custody of the said property and income."

9.—Speaking at Liverpool to the members of a Working Man's Conservative Association, Lord Derby, who presided, explained the nature of the work before his party, and the means by which it could be best accomplished. The Conservative party ought not, he thought, to grow slack and indifferent about public affairs because they were in a minority of 100 in the House of Commons. If political life were what many people consider it—" a soaped pole," with 5,000*l.* a year and lots of patronage at the top—if the end and object of all party efforts were the holding of office for a longer or shorter time, he might agree with them ; but the holding of office was only a means. Power was the end, power over the legislative and administrative conduct of affairs ; and a party which at the lowest estimate includes two-fifths of the House of Commons, may exercise very great power when those who sit opposite to it are notoriously divided into sections which have hardly an idea in common. " Don't let us spoil our own game," his lordship said. " Don't let us lose power in running after place. If we become the majority it is our duty to accept the responsibilities of that position. But for myself I tell you frankly, though I should rejoice to see a strong Conservative Government in power, I had infinitely rather, in the public interest and that of your party, see the Conservatives forming a strong and compact Opposition, than have them, for the fourth time in twenty years, holding office without a tolerably assured majority." Lord Derby contended that recent Irish policy naturally strengthened the position of those who assailed the Church in England, advocated a reduction of the national debt in times of prosperity like the present, and expressed his strong opposition to all Ultramontane and Home Rule demands.

10.—Home Rule demonstration at Limerick, in favour of their new member, Mr. Butt, who admitted that the Church Act and Land Act had done much good, but that they had been grudgingly given. " There had been other legislation in a contrary direction—the last Coercion Bill, for instance, which, had it been enacted in England, would have driven it into rebellion. Another thing was the persistent refusal to release the political prisoners, the men who had led the forlorn hope of the Irish nation." He concluded by calling on the people to receive all classes and all creeds into their union.

— Explosion at Oakwood Colliery, Maesteg, South Wales, causing the instantaneous death of eleven men employed in the works.

— Manifesto in regard to the use of alcohol for medicinal purposes circulated among the leading members of the medical profession. Those signing it expressed an opinion that no medical practitioner should prescribe it without a sense of grave responsibility. " They believe that alcohol, in whatever form, should be prescribed with as much care as any powerful drug, and that the directions for its use should be so framed as not to be interpreted as a sanction for excess, or necessarily for the continuance of its use when the occasion is past. They are also of opinion that many people immensely exaggerate the value of alcohol as an article of diet, and since no class of men see so much of its ill-effects, and possess such power to restrain its abuse, as members of their own profession, they hold that every medical practitioner is bound to exert his utmost influence to inculcate habits of great moderation in the use of alcoholic liquids."

12.—Rev. John Selby Watson found guilty at the Central Criminal Court of the murder of his wife, and sentenced to death by Mr. Justice Byles. Regarding the plea of insanity urged on his behalf, the prisoner, before sentence was passed, said, "I only wish to say that the defence which has been maintained in my favour is a just and honest one." The Crown afterwards gave effect to the jury's recommendation to mercy, and commuted the extreme penalty to confinement for life.

— Vice-Chancellor Malins makes an order for the compulsory winding up of the European Assurance Society.

— Died at Nice, in his 64th year, the Duc de Persigny, formerly French Ambassador in London of the Emperor Napoleon III.

— Died at Cannes, aged 67, M. Jean Barthélemy Arles-Dufour, an eminent French free-trader.

13.—The Metropolitan Board of Works take formal possession of Hampstead Heath on behalf of the public.

14.—Last bulletin issued regarding the Prince of Wales, who was reported to be making satisfactory progress, and daily gaining strength.

15.—Tried at the Central Criminal Court, before Mr. Baron Martin, Christina Edmunds, charged with murder and various attempts at murder by poisoning. It was sought through medical witnesses to give effect to a plea of insanity set up on her behalf, but it was rejected by the jury, who on the 16th returned a verdict of guilty, and the prisoner was sentenced to death. She thereupon made a statement which led to the empanelling of a jury of matrons, who received the assistance of some medical gentlemen in court, and finally decided that there existed no ground for arrest of judgment. It was stated that there had been no occasion before for empanelling a jury of matrons at the Central Criminal Court for about fifteen years. The extreme sentence in this case was also commuted to imprisonment for life.

— Celebrated in the parish church of Chantilly, the marriage of the Princess Margaret of Orleans, eldest daughter of the Duc de Nemours, with Prince Ladislas Czartoryski, son of the famous Polish leader in the great insurrection against Russia.

15.—The hearing of the Tichborne case resumed, the Attorney-General commencing his speech for the defence.

16.— Mary Crawford, or Deuchars, 22 years of age, the wife of a pattern designer, drowned her three children in the Clyde, at Glasgow, the eldest being three years of age, the others two years and three months respectively. She then committed suicide by throwing herself into the river. She had been married about five years, her husband being a widower with four young children.

— The Rev. J. S. Drew, rector of Ovington, Hants, writes regarding the case of Mr. Watson, who, along with his wife, had been members of his congregation when at St. Barnabas, South Lambeth :—"She was always fretful and often violent in temper. She always sat with him in his study while he was at work, he hardly ever walked out without her, and in all their intercourse he bore himself towards her with the most admirable patience until that fatal moment when, through some outrageous provocation on her part as I cannot doubt, he gave way to literally ungovernable rage. I hoped until the last day of the trial that I should have had an opportunity to make this statement in court, and thus show the nature of an influence which was ever so dangerously near and ready to work on the morbid susceptibility of the unhappy man. Now, having also forwarded this testimony to the Home Secretary, I take the only course which remains open to help in rescuing my unfortunate friend from his melancholy doom, and to clear from infamy the name of one of the most considerate, kindly, and honourable men I have ever known."

— The first railway train connecting Turkey with Europe enters Stamboul.

17.— Roman Catholic demonstration in Dublin, in favour of denominational education. "Nothing," said Cardinal Cullen, who presided, "but the old spirit of ascendency would think of subjecting seventy or eighty Catholic children—about the average in each school—to religious restrictions in favour of a small fraction of Protestants." In such cases he claimed the fulness of religious teaching for Catholic children. On account of the Catholicity of the population, he went on to say, mixed schools do not and cannot exist. He further declared that proselytism was carried on in national schools, negatively, by keeping Catholic children from any knowledge of religious doctrine and positively by teaching anti-Catholic doctrines. Thousands, he stated, of Catholic children received religious instruction "from Presbyterian or other heterodox teachers, recite anti-Catholic prayers, and read in the schools the Protestant version of the Bible."

— Died, aged 84, Lewis Doxat, one of the oldest London journalists, having conducted the *Observer* for the long period of fifty years.

17.—Statue of Benjamin Franklin, a gift from the printers of the city, unveiled in New York on this the 166th anniversary of the philosopher's birth. Mr. Horace Greeley said on the occasion : " I love and revere him as a journeyman printer who was frugal and didn't drink ; a *parvenu* who rose from want to competence, from obscurity to fame, without losing his head ; a statesman who did not crucify mankind with long-winded documents or speeches ; a diplomatist who did not intrigue ; a philosopher who never lied ; and an office-holder who didn't steal."

— News of a rebellion in Loodiana arrives in London.

18.—The Emperor of Germany, proposing a toast at a meeting of the Chapter of the Order of the Black Eagle, said :— " We celebrate to-day a double anniversary of the most important events of Prussian history. On this day, 171 years ago, the first King of Prussia was crowned. This day last year my acceptance of the German Imperial Crown, unanimously offered me by all the princes and free towns of Germany, was proclaimed. Conscious of the obligations I have assumed, I, on the first anniversary of this great event, again express to the illustrious presenters of my new position, in presence of their representatives, my deeply-felt thanks, hoping that by our united efforts we shall succeed in fulfilling the just hopes of Germany." The Bavarian Minister then, in the name of the King of Bavaria and the illustrious federate allies in the Empire, proposed " The health of the German Emperor, William the Victorious."

— It is decided at a Cabinet Council that Great Britain would not consent to have the American indirect claims submitted for arbitration.

— Explosion in Gladstone's cartridge factory, Greenwich, injuring about thirty girls employed there.

19.—M. Rouher addresses the electors of Corsica, insisting that the country could no longer support the internal dissension prevailing. " The supreme duty of parties is to immolate to it their resistances and ambitions, to respectfully solicit the high manifestations of the national will, and then to dissolve themselves or to become reconciled under the salutary authority of the definitive Government created by the country. Order, the liberty of all, cannot henceforward have any other basis."

— The French National Assembly, by 377 to 207 votes, adopt a proposal for appointing a Commission to inquire whether it is possible to adjust the Budget without taxing raw material. M. Thiers thereupon threatened to resign.

20.—Died, aged 73, the Rev. Canon Moseley, Bristol, one of the earliest school inspectors under the old Education Act.

20.—Rumour being busy during the Kerry election with the name of Mr. Bright as an advocate for Home Rule, he now writes to The O'Donoghue : " To have two representative legislative assemblies of Parliament in the United Kingdom would be, in my opinion, an intolerable mischief, and I think no sensible man can wish for two within the limits of the present United Kingdom who does not wish the United Kingdom to become two or more nations entirely separated from each other."

— Died, aged 87, General Sir Alexander Lindsay, one of the oldest generals of the Bengal Artillery.

22.—The Versailles tribunal pronounce sentence on the murderers of the hostages in the prison of La Roquette. One, Gerson, was sentenced to death, and fourteen others to various terms of imprisonment.

23.—Sir Wm. Jenner gazetted a K.C.B., and Dr. W. W. Gull a baronet.

24.—Nonconformist Conference at Manchester, called to insist upon " united literary education by the State, and separate religious education by parents, or the voluntary agency of religious committees." In a paper on the political relation of the Nonconformists to the Liberal party, Mr. Richard, M. P., said:—"Our quarrel with those in power is one purely of principle. We have no intention to withdraw our confidence and support from Mr. Gladstone. He is the Minister of our predilection, and we are proud of his transcendent abilities. But if it comes to be a question between allegiance to a party and loyalty to principle, we cannot hesitate. We are willing to exercise patience, to make concessions ; but to adopt a course which will involve the sacrifice, or the surrender, or the serious compromise of these vital principles for the sake of any man or party is what we cannot, what we ought not, what we must not, what we dare not, and, by God's help, what we will not do." Several members of Parliament took occasion when addressing their constituents at this time to censure in strong terms this " Nonconformist revolt."

— Severe gale in London ; one of the lesser towers of the new Palace of Westminster blown down.

25.—For the first time since his illness the Prince of Wales walks for a short time in the open air. Active preparations now commence to be made for a special thanksgiving service at St. Paul's.

— Decree dissolving the Spanish Cortes read in the Chamber amid great excitement.

28.—Died, aged 81, Admiral Robert Gambier, who aided in the reduction of the Cape, Buenos Ayres, and Maldonado.

29.—The Court of Queen's Bench decide that they have power to issue a mandamus against the Treasury respecting the disallowance of the costs of criminal prosecutions.

30.—The Bishop of Bath and Wells inhibits Archdeacon Denison from continuing certain ceremonial observances in East Brent Church, and signifies his intention of revoking the licences of two assistant curates. The Archdeacon replied that the inhibition had not been complied with, nor would it be so long as he remained Vicar of East Brent.

— Meeting at the Mansion House in aid of the fund being raised for the relief of Dr. Livingstone.

— Died, aged 82, General Francis Rawdon Chesney, Royal Artillery, head of the Euphrates Exploring Expedition, 1836-8.

February 2.—Closing a series of letters on "Invasion Panics," Mr. Vernon Harcourt writes in the *Times* to-day: "I confess I am much more afraid of being run over by a hansom than I am of being slaughtered by a German. If I felt as certain that Lord Elcho would protect me against the one, as I am sure he will preserve me from the other, I should feel quite happy. But when we are asked to insure against risks, which *ex hypothesi* it is impossible to calculate, because they depend upon events which cannot be anticipated, and, therefore, cannot be measured— which defy the test of past experience or existing conditions—we are utterly helpless. It is this unintelligible system of political arithmetic which has brought us to the too intelligible sum of our public expenditure. It is a very good thing to have a large margin—but a margin presupposes some limited and known dimension which it circumscribes. I have always understood that an unknown infinity was superior to a margin."

— In the libel case of Pook *v.* Crosland, arising out of a pamphlet on the Eltham murder, the jury gave a verdict for the plaintiff —damages £50. In a similar action against the proprietor of the *Kentish Mercury*, a verdict was taken for the plaintiff by agreement.

— The National Assembly, by 366 to 310 votes, reject a motion in favour of returning to Paris. A bill authorizing the Government to "denounce" the commercial treaty with England was approved of by a large majority.

3.—Earl Granville informs Mr. Fish that the British Government do not consider it to be within the province of the Geneva tribunal to decide upon the "indirect claims." The British case now made public sought to show that the claims to be referred to the tribunal were claims "growing out of the acts" of certain vessels in respect of which the Government of the United States alleges that Great Britain has failed to fulfil some international duty. "If in the judgment of the tribunal there has been such a failure in respect of any specified vessel or vessels, the tribunal may adopt at its discretion either of two courses. It may award such a gross sum as the arbitrators may deem just, to be paid by Great Britain in full satisfaction of all well-founded claims on the part of the United States, 'growing out of the acts' of the vessel or vessels in respect of which there has been a failure of duty; or, on the other hand, it may content itself with deciding as to each or any vessel in respect of which there has been a failure of duty, the measure or extent of the liability which on general principles may justly be deemed to have been incurred by such failure. In the event of the second course being chosen, the office of examining and adjudicating on the validity of particular claims 'growing out of the acts' of the specified vessel or vessels is remitted to a board of assessors."

3.—Died at Hammersmith, Miss Julia Trelawney Leigh Hunt, daughter of the poet Leigh Hunt.

5.—It is officially announced that M. Casimir-Périer, French Minister of the Interior, and M. Léon Say, Prefect of Paris, had resigned.

— Another explosion in the "mixing-house" of Hall's powder works, Faversham. Two men were killed on the spot, and two injured.

— Sir William Stirling Maxwell installed as Lord Rector of the University of Edinburgh.

— Died at Montreux, Switzerland, Père Gratry, a popular preacher of the Gallican Church.

6.—Mr. F. S. Powell, Conservative, elected for the North-West Riding by 6,961 votes, against 6,917 given to his Liberal opponent, Isaac Holden.—Captain Nolan, a Home Rule candidate, elected for Galway by a majority of 2,165 over Mr. Trench.

— Parliament opened by Royal Commission. The Royal Speech made reference to the deliverance of the Prince of Wales from imminent danger. "I purpose," it was said, "that on Tuesday, the 27th inst., conformably to the good and becoming usage of former days, the blessings thus received shall be acknowledged on behalf of the nation by a thanksgiving in the Metropolitan Cathedral. At this celebration it is my desire and hope to be present. . . . The slave trade, and practices scarcely to be distinguished from slave-trading, still pursued in more than one quarter of the world, continue to attract the attention of my Government. In the South Sea Islands, the name of the British Empire is even now dishonoured by the connection of some of my subjects with these nefarious practices; and in one of them the murder of an exemplary prelate has cast fresh light upon some of their baleful consequences. A bill will be presented to you, for the purpose of facilitating the trial of offences of this class in Australasia." In connection with the Treaty of Washington, cases had been laid before the arbitrators on behalf of each party. "In the case so submitted on behalf of the United States, large claims have been included, which are understood on my part not to be within the province of the arbitrators. On this subject I have caused a friendly communication to be made to the Government of the United States. The Emperor of Germany has undertaken to arbitrate on the San Juan water boundary; and the cases of the two Governments have been presented to his Imperial Majesty." Bills were promised in connection with education in Scotland, regulation of mines, licensing system, secret voting, and corrupt practices at elections. The Address was agreed to in each House without a division, Mr. Disraeli criticising with some severity the misunderstanding which had been permitted to grow out of the Washington Treaty. Her Majesty's Ministers had adopted a new system of vindicating their policy during the recess, and might be said for the last six months to have lived in a blaze of apology.

6.—Died, General W. F. Beatson, chief of the Bashi-Bazouk force during the Crimean War.

7.—The Speaker, Mr. Denison, announces his intention of resigning, as the labour of the House had increased of late to an extent which greatly overtaxed his strength. Mr. Gladstone thereupon gave notice of his intention to move a vote of thanks for his fifteen years' distinguished services in the chair, and for an address to her Majesty that she would be graciously pleased to bestow some signal mark of her Royal favour upon the Speaker. On the subject of the pension usually given to retiring Speakers, Mr. Denison had previously written to the Prime Minister :—"Though without any pretensions to wealth, I have a private fortune which will suffice, and for the few years of life that remain to me I should be happier in feeling that I am not a burden to my fellow-countrymen."

— Came on before the Judicial Committee of the Privy Council, the case of the Rev. John Purchas, of Brighton, charged with not having obeyed the monitions as to the discontinuance of certain vestments in the Holy Communion service, and the performance of ceremonies he had practised in the services; as also in the use of lighted candles, incense, and mixing water with the communion wine, and likewise as to wafer bread. Mr. Purchas was further cited for not paying the taxed costs of 2,096*l.* 14*s.* 10*d.* incurred in the former proceedings. Mr. Purchas did not appear. The Lord Chancellor said their lordships were clearly of opinion that several acts of contempt had been proved against Mr. Purchas, and the order they would pronounce would be that Mr. Purchas be suspended *ab officio* for one year from the time of service of the order. As to the costs, their lordships would direct that Mr. Purchas be pronounced in contempt, and a sequestration be issued on his lay property.

7.—Convocation meets for the despatch of business, the Bishop of Winchester presenting a memorial from the Church Union to the Upper House, praying that any alterations made in the Prayer-book may be based rather upon the first Prayer-book of Edward VI. than upon any subsequent revision of that book, and that such alterations may only be made after mature deliberation by the Convocation of the two Provinces "ratified by the full authority of the whole Sacred Synod of the nation, as was done on December 20, 1661, after the last revision of the book."

— Died, at Notting Hill, aged 77, the Right Rev. S. Hinds, formerly Bishop of Norwich.

— Died at Baltimore, aged 62 years, the Most Rev. John Spalding, D.D., Roman Catholic Primate of the United States.

8.—Lord Redesdale gives notice of his intention to ask the Foreign Minister a hypothetical question on the subject of the *Alabama* claims.

— Died, aged 72, Joseph Pease, a leading member of the Society of Friends in Darlington, and connected by marriage with the Gurney and Fry families.

— Assassination of Lord Mayo, Governor-General of India. The Viceroy left Moulmein on the 6th, and reached Andaman Island this morning. After inspecting the public institutions in all the dangerous parts of the convict colony, he ascended Mount Harriet, for the view, accompanied by a superintendent, a staff of seven, and an armed police guard. They reached the top near sunset, stayed ten minutes, and walked down with Count Waldstein and Captain Lockwood in advance, the rest close together, with the Viceroy's guard on both sides and in the rear. About 300 yards from the hill darkness came on and torches were lit. No convicts were near, except on barrows, with overseers, on a line off the road. About a quarter to seven they reached the pier, a narrow erection with steep stone sides. When about twenty-five yards from the boat, the superintendent, with the Viceroy's permission, dropped a little behind to give an order. It was now quite dark. The armed escort was close to the Viceroy on both sides, the police and his body servant in the rear, and Major Burne a few paces to the left. The Viceroy advanced a few paces along the pier, when a person unseen sprang in a moment out of the darkness, and stabbed him twice, on the top of the left shoulder and under the right shoulder-blade. The assassin was immediately seized. The Viceroy ran a few paces forward and fell over the pier into shallow water on the left, but got up himself, and was helped out, his shoulder bleeding copiously. Lord Mayo walked firmly, felt his shoulder, and said, "I don't think I am much hurt." He was laid on a cart, the blood now flowing rapidly. When being carried to the boat after his wounds were bound up, the Viceroy said twice, "Lift up my head." He spoke no more, but expired shortly afterwards on his way to the ship. The assassin, who was seized on the spot, turned out to be a convict named Shere Ali, sentenced to penal servitude for a murder committed in Peshawur in 1867. Intelligence of the calamity reached London on the afternoon of the 12th, and in the evening appropriate tributes were paid to Lord Mayo's great merits in both Houses of Parliament. He was born in 1822, sat in the House of Commons as Chief Secretary for Ireland in Lord Derby's Administration, and was sent out to India by Mr. Disraeli as Viceroy in 1868. The body was taken in the first instance to Calcutta, where the utmost excitement prevailed for a time, and then conveyed by way of Suez to England.

8.—Died, aged 87, John Poole, dramatist, author of the once popular "Paul Pry."

9.—Mr. Brand elected Speaker in room of Mr. Denison, his proposer being Sir Roundell Palmer, and seconder Mr. Locke-King.

10.—Departure of the Livingstone Search Expedition, consisting of Lieut. Dawson, R.N., Lieut. Henn, R.N., and Mr. Oswald Livingstone, son of the traveller.

— The Prince and Princess of Wales leave Sandringham for Windsor and Osborne.

12.—M. Rouher elected to sit for Corsica in the National Assembly.

— Mines Regulation Bill introduced by Mr. Bruce, and the Scotch Education Bill by the Lord Advocate.

13.—The late Speaker of the House of Commons takes his seat in the Lords as Viscount Ossington.

— Lord Redesdale asked the Secretary for Foreign Affairs whether, if A and B in partnership sue C in a court of law for injury done to their firm by fraud or otherwise, and C pleads and proves that B was acting with him in all the matters complained of, such plea would not be a complete answer to the suit, and render any recovery of damages impossible? Why a plea which is good law and which common sense pronounces to be just has not been considered by her Majesty's Government applicable to a new case in international law, a d urged against the *Alabama* claims made on this country by the United States of America, in which the North and South are now partners, inasmuch as all the acts for which this country is charged with being culpably responsible were done by the South, and that partner now joins in the application to be paid for having done them? Lord Granville declined to answer hypothetical questions on English law, and stated that it would be undesirable to discuss the *Alabama* claims at the present stage of the negotiations.

— In answer to a question put by Mr. Mowbray, Mr. Gladstone explains some circumstances connected with the recent appointment to the Rectory of Ewelme. He said that the Act severing the rectory from the Regius Professorship of Divinity at Oxford did not at all limit the area over which the Crown could exercise its patronage, except that the Crown was entitled to present only a member of the University of Oxford. He admitted that it was he who had recommended Mr. Harvey, of King's College, Cambridge, to become *pro formâ* a member of the University of Oxford, and that it was no part of his duty to ascertain by inspection of original documents whether he was possessed of the various qualifications which Mr. Mowbray had enumerated. He would, however, make inquiries, and inform the House of the result.

15.—Earl Stanhope moves the sense of the House regarding the elevation of Sir Robert Collier to the Bench of Common Pleas, strongly condemning the course which the Government had taken. After explanation by Lord Granville the motion was negatived by 89 to 88 votes. In the course of the debate the Duke of Argyll declared that the letter of the Lord Chief Justice was only the letter of Sir Alexander Cockburn ; and throughout it he indulged in railing—he might almost say in ribald—accusation against the Gover, ment. When such was the case he denied that their lordships were bound to attach any more weight to the *obiter dicta* of Sir Alexander Cockburn than to those of anyone else. Sir Alexander's vocabulary was so rich and spicy, or so "sensational," as Mr. Justice Willes called it—and that meant claptrap rubbish—(a laugh)—that he hardly knew how to deal with it. "Evasion," "impropriety," "subterfuge," were some of the pretty terms that were used ; and he (the noble duke) took leave to tell him that their lordships were quite as able as he was to judge of the applicability of such phrases. The letter, then, was simply the letter of Sir Alexander Cockburn, written, too, in a state of great irritation, and even of effervescence. And why? Because this Government, which was so addicted to jobbery, had actually kept a judgeship in the Queen's Bench vacant for two years.—Lord Westbury described this attack as unjust and indecent ; and acting on the suggestion of mutual friends, his grace took an early opportunity of expressing his regret "for any words which may have justly seemed personally offensive to the Lord Chief Justice." The *Post* thereupon remarked, "With respect to the apology made by the Duke of Argyll in the House of Lords yesterday afternoon it is enough to state, as we are in a position to state, that had such an apology not been made, either by the Duke of Argyll or some other member of the Cabinet, it would have been impossible for Sir Alexander Cockburn to continue to represent the Government on the *Alabama* arbitration." In the Commons a vote of censure on the Collier case was rejected by 268 to 241 votes.

15.—In the Commons the second reading of the Ballot Bill is carried by 109 to 51 votes.

— Meeting in St. James' Hall, to promote reform in the Church of England, as opposed to disestablishment; presided over by Lord Lyttelton. Resolutions were proposed having reference to increased liberty in the use of Prayer-book services, the discontinuance of the Athanasian Creed, and lay representation for parochial work.

16.—Died, in his 90th year, the Right Rev. Dr. Daly, Protestant Bishop of Waterford and Cashel.

— Despatches from Melbourne announce that Bishop Patteson's death had been "avenged" by shelling the village where the murder was committed.

17.—Murder in Lambeth. While George Merritt, a stoker, was proceeding to his work at the Lion Brewery about three o'clock A.M., he was met by a man who at once fired a pistol at him. The first shot missed; then a second was fired, which also missed. Merritt now began to run, when a third shot was fired, which struck him in the neck. The assassin then came up, and, attacking him in a fearful manner, with a dagger, stabbed him several times, and then ran away. He was met at the top of Tennison Street by a constable, who stopped him, and took him back to the spot whence the reports of the pistol proceeded. The body of the victim was then found. On the policeman turning his lantern on the unfortunate man, the assassin said, "Why, that is not the man I wanted." The wounded man soon afterwards expired, and the assassin was taken into custody. He gave his name or names as William Chester Minor, and it was afterwards ascertained that he had at one time been a surgeon in the American army, serving with distinction during the late war. At his trial at Kingston assizes, before Chief Justice Bovill, the jury gave effect to a plea of insanity set up on the prisoner's behalf, and he was ordered to be confined during her Majesty's pleasure.

18.—Died at Jersey, aged 86 years, General Charles Richard William Lane, C.B., of the Bengal Infantry, a veteran of the Mahratta and Burmese wars.

19.—Lord Shaftesbury's Ecclesiastical Procedure Bill thrown out in the Lords by 24 votes to 14, the principal speech against the measure being made by the Bishop of Peterborough. Of all men, he said, the clergy from the very nature of their profession stand most in need of protection. A clergyman is a person brought into collision—sometimes violent collision—with the prejudices, passions, and party-spirit of the people, and yet it is proposed that he shall be liable to prosecution by these people. The squire of the parish whose wife may not have received a return visit from the clergyman's wife, may, with his gardener and bailiff, form the prosecuting trio. Or the trio may

consist of the publican, who has been offended by the vicar's last sermon against drunkenness, and two of his best customers. He admitted that some years ago there might be a necessity for Church associations, but these vigilance committees were rapidly becoming a dangerous ruling power in the Church instead of the Bishops. "The Church Association is not the only association of this kind—there is also the Church Union. I admit that the object of that society is not to undertake prosecutions—(cheers)—but after a time, when persecution has gone on incessantly upon one side, there is that in human nature, and in clerical human nature, to turn upon the other side, and what will then be the peace and harmony of the Church when it is divided between these rival persecutors, when each diocese is turned into a happy hunting ground for these rival societies—these theological Communists and Versaillists—and when each in its turn proceeds to mark out its respective hostages for ecclesiastical execution? (Cheers.) A nice state of things for the clergy—the Church Association swooping down upon them from above, the Church Union rushing on them from below, while every now and then they find themselves hooked by a neat turn of the Episcopal wrist." (Laughter.) "Make the clergy," concluded the Bishop, ": the slaves of a faction, or the victims of a party; destroy their self-respect and independence; and it will not be so much the clergy in the end as the laity who will suffer. Whatever degrades the clergy injures the laity of the Church, and therefore it is not mainly in the interests of the clergy, but quite as much in the interests of the laity, that I do most earnestly entreat your lordships not to vote for the second reading of this bill."

19.—Lady Charles Innes Kerr seriously injured in the hunting-field, her horse rolling over her when taking a fence near Langley Park. She was conveyed to Rowley Farm, and passed fully a month in a state exciting wide commiseration among all classes, from the Queen downwards.

21.—Mr. William Longman writes to the *Times* urging the propriety of following precedents observed in 1664 and 1678, by opening on the Thanksgiving day "a Book of Subscriptions for the completion of the Cathedral Church of St. Paul, made in the year 1872, as a Perpetual Memorial of Thanksgiving for the recovery of his Royal Highness the Prince of Wales from a dangerous sickness," and to keep this book, like its two predecessors, in the library of St. Paul's, as a permanent record of the year in which a crowning effort was made for the completion of the Cathedral. "In this book it is intended that the names of all those who may make contributions for this especial object shall be inscribed, and it is hoped that all who may be able to do so will, as was done by our forefathers, sign their names in it, as the interest and value of the book to future generations will thereby be greatly increased."

21.—Died, aged 80 years, Colonel W. Nicol Burns, late of the Indian Army, last surviving son of the poet.

— Lord Northbrook announced as the new Governor-General of India. The duties of Acting-Viceroy were, in the meantime, performed by Lord Napier of Merchiston.

— Mr. Chambers' Marriage with a Deceased Wife's Sister Bill read a second time in the Commons by 186 to 138 votes.

— Funeral service at Calcutta, in front of Government House, over the remains of Lord Mayo, afterwards conveyed with befitting ceremony on board her Majesty's ship *Daphne*.

— Sir John Coleridge concludes his speech for the defence in the Tichborne case, having spoken for twenty-six days.

22.—The Army Estimates moved by Mr. Cardwell—total amount, 14,824,500*l.* ; net decrease as compared with 1871, 1,027,000*l.* ; number of men 133,460, against 135,047 in 1871. One object specially kept in view under the Reconstruction Act of last year, was the localization of forces—identification with a locality for the purposes of recruiting, of training, of connecting regulars with auxiliaries, and of connecting the reserves with those who are actually under the standards. He believed that the principles of localization, wisely carried into effect, "will attract to the standards classes which do not now join them, will spread abroad a knowledge of the advantages which are offered by service in the army, and will associate the army with ties of family and kindred. It will induce men from the militia to join the army, and it will destroy competition in recruiting between the army and the militia." It was proposed to divide the country into territorial districts, in each of which there would be a battalion of the line and two militia regiments, and with them would be brigaded the volunteers of the district under the command of a lieutenant-colonel of the regulars, acting as brigadier. Each district would have a local central depôt, at which the recruiting and training would be carried on not only of the militia, but of the reserves and of the recruits for the line battalions.

— Execution at Satory of Lagrange and others, as the murderers of Generals Lecomte and Thomas.

23.—Mr. Fish answers Lord Granville's "friendly communication" regarding the indirect claims, by affirming that they are covered by the protocol and treaty. The American Government, therefore, cannot withdraw from the case which they have presented for arbitration. The abrogation of the Treaty, it was also mentioned, was left to England.

— Mr. Monckton carries for the Conservatives the seat of North Notts, vacant by the elevation of the Speaker ; the numbers being, Monckton 2,580, Laycock 1,524.

23.—Demonstration at Antwerp in favour of the Count de Chambord.

24.—Navy Estimates issued. Total sum required for the year, 9,508,149*l.*, being a decrease of 281,807*l.* as compared with last year.

27.—The Queen, with the Prince and Princess of Wales, and other members of the Royal Family, accompanied by all the high officers of the Crown, proceed in state to St. Paul's Cathedral, to join in a Thanksgiving Service for the recovery of the Prince of Wales. The feeling of loyalty excited by the long and severe illness, joined to the elaborate preparations known to have been made for this ceremonial, combined to make it one of the most enthusiastic displays seen in her Majesty's reign. If the crowds were not at all points equally large, or single decorations quite so gorgeous as on the occasion of the Princess Alexandra's arrival, there was on the other hand an equality of richness, a continued and unvarying appearance of wealth, magnificence, and taste, from Pall Mall to Fleet Street, from St. Paul's to Holborn, from Oxford Street back again to Buckingham Palace, such as had never been seen before. This was in great part owing to the provident arrangements of the citizens, by which, instead of decorations made according to the taste of each separate individual, a complete design was in most places followed out in every particular by a careful combination of means and minds beforehand, while the emulation in rich hangings, banners, lamps, and devices, which on former occasions caused a certain prodigality and waste of resource, was this year shared between whole parishes or streets, so that the loss of picturesqueness on one side was more than compensated by a sustained and long drawn out uniformity of magnificence, such as had been hitherto unknown in London. The weather had been for some days raw and gusty, and as it was known that this was the only circumstance likely to interfere with the Prince's attendance, the opening of the morning was looked forward to with some concern. The day turned out to be exceptionally dry and mild for the season, and by ten o'clock myriads had taken up their station within the barricades in the streets, at the windows overlooking the route of the procession, or on the endless platforms with which it was lined. A few minutes past twelve o'clock the procession set out from Buckingham Palace, and proceeded slowly to St. Paul's by way of the Green Park, Pall Mall, the Strand, Fleet Street, and Ludgate Hill. First came the carriages of the Speaker, the Lord Chancellor, and the Commander-in-Chief, followed by nine Royal carriages, six of them filled with ladies and gentlemen of the Court, the seventh with the younger brothers of the Prince, another by the Master of the Horse, and the last by the Queen, the Prince and Princess of Wales, Prince Albert Victor, and the Princess Beatrice. In the Park the Royal party were first saluted by a band of 30,000 children, who sung the National Anthem as the procession passed. At Temble Bar they were received by the Lord Mayor, Sheriffs, and Aldermen, and the Queen presented with the City sword, graciously returning it to its bearer. While the Court party were passing along the decorated streets, amid deafening welcomes, a vast company of 13,000 had assembled in St. Paul's, composed largely of members of both Houses of Parliament, representatives of the army and navy, the heads of the great City Companies, and civic dignitaries from all parts of the kingdom. Within the Cathedral nothing could be more complete than the arrangements, and nothing more perfect than their execution. The doors having been opened early in the morning, everybody got in without delay, and found places without confusion. At one o'clock the procession arrived at the great western entrance to the Cathedral, and streamed in through a vestibule erected on the steps, bearing the inscription, "I was glad when they said unto me, We will go into the House of the Lord." The Queen was received by the Dean and Chapter of St. Paul's, and conducted with stately reverence to the Royal pew set apart for her household. She was dressed, it was noticed, in black velvet, broadly trimmed with white ermine, and the Princess in blue covered with a black lace mantle. The Prince of Wales wore the uniform of a general officer with the collars of the Orders of the Garter and Bath. Her Majesty, leaning on the Prince, led one of her grandchildren by the hand, the Princess of Wales another. The service began with the "Te Deum," followed by a few responses from the Liturgy and Lord's Prayer ; then the ordinary prayers for the Queen and Royal Family, with a special form of thanksgiving. The Archbishop of Canterbury pronounced the benediction, and afterwards preached a short sermon from the text, Rom. xii. 5, "Members one of another." This was succeeded by a Thanksgiving Hymn specially prepared for the occasion, which brought the service to a close a few minutes before two o'clock. The procession then re-formed at the Cathedral door, and set out on the return journey by way of Ludgate Hill, Old Bailey, Holborn Viaduct, Oxford Street, to the Marble Arch, Hyde Park Corner, and Constitution Hill to Buckingham Palace, all converging thoroughfares on the way being decorated as profusely and crowded with people cheering as lustily as the route traversed before. In the evening the illuminations were on a scale commensurate with the splendour of the reception accorded to her Majesty and family during the day.

27.—Although careful inspection was made of most of the platforms lining the route of the Royal procession to-day, a general regret was felt towards evening that several spectators had been hurt at different parts of the city by the falling of scaffolding and the excited crush in the streets.

27.—Collision in the Mersey between the Cunard steamer *Parthia*, bound for Boston, and the screw steamer *Emiliano*, inward bound from Singapore and Manilla. The latter had to be beached near Tranmere, and her cargo, consisting of tobacco and sugar, was almost destroyed. The *Parthia* afterwards ran into the *Nina*, from Vigo, and did her considerable damage.

— Died, Rev. John McLeod Campbell, D.D., author of various religious treatises and sermons, some of which led to his being suspended from a charge in the Scotch Church at Row for heresy in 1831.

29.—The Queen writes from Buckingham Palace to Mr. Gladstone that she was anxious as on a previous occasion "to express publicly her own personal very deep sense of the reception she and her dear children met with on Tuesday, the 27th of February, from millions of her subjects on her way to and from St. Paul's. Words are too weak for the Queen to say how very deeply touched and gratified she has been by the immense enthusiasm and affection exhibited towards her dear son and herself, from the highest down to the lowest, in the long progress through the capital, and she would earnestly wish to convey her warmest and most heartfelt thanks to the whole nation for this great demonstration of loyalty. The Queen, as well as her son and dear daughter-in-law, felt that the whole nation joined with them in thanking God for sparing the beloved Prince of Wales's life. The remembrance of this day, and of the remarkable order maintained throughout, will for ever be affectionately cherished by the Queen and her family."

— Assault on the Queen. About half-past five o'clock, as her Majesty was entering Buckingham Palace after a drive, a lad suddenly presented himself at the side of the carriage, holding a paper in one hand and a pistol in the other. He tried at first, it was said, to attract the attention of Lady Churchill, mistaking her probably for the Queen, by whose side she sat, and then appeared to be about to address himself to her Majesty, going round the back of the carriage, when the equerries and the Queen's personal attendant, John Brown, followed him and gave him into the custody of the police sergeant on duty at the time. The Queen showed no sign whatever of fear. The lad was immediately disarmed of the pistol, which proved to be unloaded. It was an old-fashioned weapon, with a flint and steel lock, which was broken, and in the barrel a piece of greasy red rag was found. He had also a knife in his possession, and the paper to which reference has been made was found on examination to be a petition, written on parchment, for the release of the Fenian prisoners. He was taken forthwith to the King Street police-station, Westminster, where he gave the name Arthur O'Connor, and stated his age to be seventeen. Her Majesty at once caused a message to be sent to both Houses of Parliament informing members of the circumstance with a view to prevent unnecessary alarm.

29.—Intimation made to the Lord Mayor and Sheriffs of London that it was the intention of her Majesty to confer a baronetcy upon the former and knighthood upon the latter in connection with the recent Thanksgiving Service, "than which," wrote Mr. Gladstone, " the City of London has perhaps never witnessed a celebration more solemn or more satisfactory." The Deputy-Recorder, Mr. Chambers, also at this time received the honour of knighthood.

— Commenced to be heard at the Southwark Police Court the charge of libel with intent to extort money, preferred against Alexander Chaffers, solicitor, Lambeth, by Sir Travers Twiss, her Majesty's Advocate-General, and Lady Twiss. It appeared that soon after their marriage at Dresden in 1862, the defendant, who had acted for Lady Twiss in business transactions, made a demand upon her for 150*l.* Sir Travers's solicitor paid him 50*l.*, and Chaffers gave a receipt in full of all demands. He sent other letters, and brought sham actions against Lady Twiss for alleged slanders. In 1868 Lady Twiss was presented at St. James's by Lady Rutherford Alcock, and in 1869 was again at her Majesty's Drawing Room. On the 29th of April of that year the defendant wrote to the Lord Chamberlain complaining of Lady Twiss, stating that she had misconducted herself in London previous to her marriage with Sir Travers Twiss. The Lord Chamberlain made inquiries, as he was bound to do under the circumstances, the result of which was satisfactory to himself and Sir Travers and Lady Twiss. On the 4th of April, last year, the defendant, determined to carry on his malicious persecutions, made a statutory declaration at Bow Street Police Court, in which he accused Lady Twiss of the grossest immoralities; declared that her name before marriage was Marie Gelas; that she lived in London for several years at various addresses named, and was a person of notoriously immoral character; that the defendant met her in Regent Street in 1859, and accompanied her to her lodgings in Upper Berkeley Street, where he stayed some time, and eventually gave her a sovereign; that he subsequently passed whole nights in her company many times; that her conduct was notoriously bad even for the class to which she belonged, and that she was in consequence called to order at the Holborn Casino; finally, that Sir Travers Twiss had immoral relations with her before her marriage. The case was continued from time to time till the 13th March, the defendant subjecting Lady Twiss to a severe and insulting examination for several days. On that date Mr. Poland, the prosecuting counsel, announced, to the surprise of the Court, that Lady Twiss was determined not to appear again, and had left London. Mr. Benson, the presiding magistrate, thereupon dismissed Chaffers on his own recognizances to appear

to answer a second charge, with the remark, " With regard to what you have alleged touching the conduct of this unfortunate woman, who, after braving the Court for a few days, has shrunk from meeting the frightful charges you have brought against her, I assure you that your conduct in this case, which rendered it necessary for her to take steps against you, will cling to you as a reproach to the end of your days, and you will live an object of contempt to all honest men." (Loud applause.)

March 1.—Sir Roundell Palmer's resolution for the establishment of a School of Law negatived in the Commons by 116 to 103 votes.

— Fifteen persons accidentally poisoned by arsenic after attending a funeral at Saxby, Lincolnshire.

2.—Died, in his 81st year, Admiral Sir James Scott, K.C.B., an officer who had served with distinction in French, American, and Chinese wars.

3.—Sunday "demonstration " in Hyde Park against the Parks Regulation Bill.

— Died, Mr. Angus M'Pherson, Secretary to the Highland Society, and translator of the Queen's Diary in the Highlands into Gaelic.

4.—Sudden termination of the huge Tichborne case, the jury to-day submitting to the Lord Chief Justice the following brief statement :—" We have now heard the evidence regarding the tattoo marks, and, subject to your lordship's directions, and to the hearing of any further evidence that the learned counsel may desire to place before us, I am authorized to state that the jury do not require further evidence." An adjournment was therefore made to the 6th, the 103rd day of trial, when Mr. Serjeant Ballantine sought to gain further time by alleging that the plaintiff had been taken by surprise so far as the tattoo marks were concerned. Finding, however, that the decision of the jury was based upon the entire evidence as well as the tattoo marks, he ultimately advised his client to submit to a nonsuit. After some discussion a nonsuit was entered, and his lordship ordered the plaintiff to be committed to the next session at the Central Criminal Court, upon a charge of wilful and corrupt perjury, and ordered him to remain in custody until then, unless he should find bail himself in 5,000*l.* and two sureties in 2,500*l.* or four in 1,250*l.* each. He also expressed his opinion that the Government should undertake the prosecution, and be bound over Mr. Inspector Dunning as prosecutor. The Attorney-General said that the Government would undertake the prosecution, and on his application a Bench warrant was issued for the apprehension of the plaintiff, who was soon after conveyed to Newgate. His lordship thanked the jury for the unwearied attention they had bestowed on the case, and expressed a hope that in the new Jury Act a clause would be introduced exempting them from further service so long as they wished to be exempted. The Claimant's case had been supported by the oaths of eighty-five witnesses, comprising the baronet's mother, the family solicitor, one baronet, six magistrates, one general, three colonels, one major, two captains, thirty-two non-commissioned officers and privates, four clergymen, seven tenants of the estate, sixteen servants of the family, and twelve general witnesses, who all swore to his identity. His claim was denied by the oaths of seventeen witnesses.

4.—Died at his residence, Carlton House Terrace, William Lowther, Earl of Lonsdale, aged 85 years.

5.—An imperial Order in Council issued at Berlin, decreeing the foundation of a Naval Academy at Kiel.

6.—The Queen, who had contemplated instituting a medal as a reward for long or faithful service among her domestic servants, inaugurates the institution by conferring on Mr. John Brown, her Majesty's personal attendant, a medal in gold, with an annuity of 25*l.* attached to it, as a mark of her appreciation of his presence of mind and of his devotion on the occasion of the attack made upon her in Buckingham Palace Gardens on the 29th of February.

— Died at his residence, St. George's Square, Primrose Hill, Dr. Goldstücker, Professor of Sanskrit in University College, London.

7.—Report of the *Megæra* Commission laid on the table of the House of Commons. Sir Spencer Robinson was held to be "mainly responsible for the misfortune which befell the vessel," on the ground that he was answerable for the defective organisation of his department, for the imperfect scrutiny of dockyard reports, for the perfunctory inspection exercised by the dockyard officials, and specially for neglecting to have the *Megæra* examined during the five months when she lay idle at Sheerness before being re-commissioned for Australia. This conclusion the Commissioners stated they had come to with regret ; for there can be no question of the zeal and ability of Sir Spencer Robinson, and it is difficult, they think, to have taken part in this inquiry without forming "a high appreciation of his merits as a devoted public servant." Mr. Reed and Mr. Barnaby were blamed for the incomplete inspection made at Woolwich in 1866.

— The Scotch Education Bill read a second time, Mr. Auberon Herbert's amendment against applying rates to religious teaching being negatived by 238 to 6 votes.

8.—Mr. Mowbray raises the question of the Ewelme Rectory appointment, Mr. Gladstone defending the proceeding on the ground that it was not a colourable qualification which the incumbent had acquired, but one solid, substantial, and perfect. Nevertheless, he admitted that *primâ facie* the natural course would have

been to look for an Oxford man in the absence of reasons to the contrary, and these reasons Mr. Gladstone explained were the recommendations he had received as to the incumbent's eminence as a divine, and his ill-health, which made his immediate removal to a more salubrious neighbourhood desirable.

8.—Died at St. Petersburg, Prince Paul Gagarine, President of the Council of Ministers.

— Prince Bismarck carries the School Inspection Bill in the Prussian Upper House by 125 votes against 76. He cautioned the Conservatives against the machinations of the Ultramontanes, who were endeavouring to get up a popular agitation against the Government by accusing it of attempting to make Prussia "a godless state." Such manœuvres were totally at variance with the character of a Conservative opposition, and the Government could not believe that the Conservatives would give any countenance to them. The Prince then pointed out that since the defeat of Catholic Austria and France by Protestant Prussia, the German Ultramontanes had entered upon the field of foreign political intrigue, and he quoted on this subject a despatch which he had just received from "one of the most prominent German ambassadors at one of the most important posts in Europe." This despatch says that "the revenge which France desires is connected with the arousing of religious dissensions in Germany. The power and unity of Germany are to be paralysed by such dissensions, and the clergy of both countries, acting under directions from Rome, are to assist by their means in restoring the temporal power of the Pope."

9.—Meeting in the Sheldonian Theatre, Oxford, presided over by Bishop Mackarness, to direct increased attention to the claim of the Melanesian Mission as the most fitting manner of honouring the martyred Bishop Patteson. A former labourer in that field, the Bishop of Lichfield, addressed the meeting at some length, explaining the nature of mission work in that part of the world, and the self-denying labours of the late prelate. A resolution was also proposed declaring that the new slave trade in the Pacific calls for the prompt and effective interference of the Government.

— The Ewelme Rectory appointment being discussed in a manner tending to bring discredit on the Prime Minister's character for fairness, the Dean of Canterbury (Payne-Smith), who held the living before it was separated from the Divinity chair by the appointment of Dr. Mozley to the latter, writes : "Long after the arrangements between myself and Dr. Mozley were made, Mr. Gladstone offered the rectory to a distinguished member of the Convocation of Oxford ; and it was only on his declining it that Mr. Harvey was appointed. Personally, I should have liked an Oxford man for my successor. The associations connected with the place would have made it doubly valuable to an Oxford man. The memories of Van Mildert and Howley, of Lloyd and Burton and Hampden, must be dearer to us than they can be to a member of the sister University. But if a Cambridge man was to be appointed, Mr. Harvey is a ripe scholar and a good parish priest, and I rejoice that a place very dear to me should have fallen into such good hands."

9.—Banquet given by the Mayor of Winchester to Lord Northbrook, as a public expression of the respect and admiration which Hampshire men entertain for his lordship's character as a countryman, and of congratulation on his appointment as Viceroy of India. Sir John Kaye and Mr. Grant Duff attended from the India Office.

— The Prince and Princess of Wales leave London for Paris, on their way to Geneva, thence to the Mediterranean and south of France.

10.—Died at Pisa, aged about 70, Joseph Mazzini, an Italian patriot fertile in desperate stratagems, and possessed of high political and literary qualities. His funeral took place at Genoa on the 19th, when the remains were followed to the grave by a body of about 80,000 admirers.

— Died, Rev. James Wells, 40 years Baptist pastor of the Surrey Tabernacle.

11.—Mr. Holms's proposal to reduce the land forces by 20,000, negatived by 234 to 63; and Mr. Muntz's proposal to reduce them by 30,000, rejected by 216 to 67.

— Reported breaking up of the Erie Ring, General Dix being elected chairman, and General M'Clellan superintendent.

— Shere Ali, the assassin of Lord Mayo, executed. He stated before being led out that he had resolved to murder both the Viceroy and General Stewart, and when he heard the guns announcing the Viceroy's arrival he sharpened his knife in the jungle. It was now surmised that he was not hiding at the pier, but quietly joined the party, and in the dark crept close to Lord Mayo. No clue to anything like a conspiracy was discovered. Shere Ali made no other confession than that he could not resist the impulse to kill the Viceroy.

12.—Lord Romilly gives judgment in the case raised by Lord Ferrers against the receiver of the Stafford and Uttoxeter Railway. His lordship sold fifty acres of land to the company for 8,887*l.*, the price being settled by arbitration, and the company were ordered to pay 400*l.*, the taxed costs incident to the taking of the land by them. The railway is in the hands of a receiver, and no arrangement had been effected with the creditors. Earl Ferrers asked that he might be entitled to the lien and rights of an unpaid vendor; but Lord Romilly, characterising this as a new experiment on the part of a creditor of a railway company to get priority over all the other creditors declined to make

such a precedent, and dismissed the bill with costs.

13.—Mr. Salt's Public Worship Facilities Bill read a second time by 122 votes to 93, the object as explained by the proposer being to give greater elasticity and freedom to the parochial system by allowing the bishop of the diocese in certain cases to license clergymen to perform divine service in places of worship, including chapels in private houses, other than the parish church.

14.—A proposal, made in connection with the progress of the Ballot Bill through the Commons, to throw the election expenses upon the Consolidated Fund, rejected by 206 to 144 votes.

15.—Mr. Dodson submits to the House his scheme for the amendment of the system of private business and legislation, the main proposal being to transfer the preliminary investigations from Select Committees to a permanent tribunal of a judicial character, before which promoters and opponents could be heard in open court.

— Lord Northbrook gazetted Governor-General of India.

16.—Stranding of H.M.S. *Lord Clyde* on the isle of Pantelleria.

17.—Announcement made that the Secretary of State for India had resolved, "That having regard to the eminent services rendered by the late Earl of Mayo as Viceroy and Governor-General of India, to the munificence with which he maintained in that office the dignity of the Crown, and to his death by a deed of violence to which he was exposed in the discharge of his public duty, a life annuity of 1,000*l.* be conferred on the Countess of Mayo, to be paid out of the revenues of India; and, further, that there be paid out of the same revenues the sum of 20,000*l.* for the benefit of the younger children of her ladyship and of the late Earl of Mayo."

18.—Vice-Chancellor Wickens gives judgment in the case of the Attorney-General *v.* Batley Corporation—a suit brought to restrain the Town Council from providing out of the local rates a gold chain for the mayor, at a cost of 200*l.* His Honour held that the proposed expenditure was not within the scope of the Municipal Corporations' Reform Act, and that a chain was not a necessary adjunct of the magisterial position, and granted the injunction asked for.

19.—The first "free election" of a bishop for the disestablished Church of Ireland takes place at Clonmel, when the Dean of Limerick was elected to the vacant see. •

— Sir Charles Dilke's motion for an inquiry into the Civil List rejected after a disorderly scene at the division of the House, by 276 to 2 votes.

20.—Announcement made that Sir Travers Twiss had resigned his ecclesiastical appointments under the Archbishop of Canterbury and Bishop of London, as also the office of Queen's Advocate. He was succeeded in the office of Chancellor of the Diocese of London by Dr. Tristram, and as Vicar-General of Canterbury by Dr. Deane, Q.C. The office of Queen's Advocate was not filled up.

— The motion for the second reading of Mr. Fawcett's bill for the abolition of tests in Dublin University "talked out." On the 26th the proposal for a second reading was carried by 94 to 21 votes.

— Lord Granville replies to Mr. Fish's answer to a former "friendly communication," that the British Government had never recognized the indirect claims.

— Fire at Düsseldorf, destroying the Academy with its rich art treasures, and much other property.

22.—The *Gazette* contains the long-threatened "denunciation" of the French Commercial Treaty in the form of a communication from the Duc de Broglie to Earl Granville. This treaty, it was said, was the first of some others which had arrived at a term when it could be regularly annulled. "We can no longer even reckon with any certainty on the possibility of modifications which would be necessary to us. We are, therefore, obliged to prepare for its cessation by denouncing it now. Confident in our intentions, resolved to use only with great moderation the freedom which will be restored to us, either by negotiation of new conventions, or rather by our own legislation on our commercial *régime*, we have taken this step under the pressure of a public interest which cannot be misunderstood."

— Bach's "St. John" Passion music performed for the first time in England in Hanover Square Rooms.

23.—The Queen leaves Windsor Castle for Gosport on her way to Baden.

— University Boat-race, Cambridge winning by half a length, amid a heavy snow-storm.

25.—Bust of Mr. Grote, historian, unveiled in Westminster Abbey.

— The agricultural labourers of Warwickshire commence an agitation for increase of wages.

— Replying to an intimation that one of her Majesty's inspectors intended visiting East Brent school, Archdeacon Denison writes :—"I am sole manager of the East Brent parochial school, and I do not admit a government inspector inside the school. I have no 'conscience clause' of any kind, nor ever shall have. I have nothing to do with the 'Elementary Education Act,' except to denounce it as irreligious. If I am called upon to pay a 'school rate,' I shall refuse to pay it ; and the amount will have to be levied on my property under a

distress warrant. If you think it worth your while to inspect the school from outside, that is for yourself to decide upon. If you decide so to inspect the school, I shall be happy to give you luncheon, provided that no word is said to me about the school. I can make no answer to the queries contained in the paper inclosed, and return it. Nor can I answer any other letter on the subject of the school, and request that none other be written to me."

25.—Mr. Lowe introduces the annual Budget. The revenue for the current year, estimated at 72,315,000*l.* had realized 74,535,000*l.*, being an excess of 2,220,000*l.* On the estimated expenditure there had been a saving of 1,016,000*l.* For the ensuing year Mr. Lowe estimates the revenue at 74,915,000*l.* and the expenditure at 71,313,000. With the surplus at his disposal he proposed extending the present exemptions from the inhabited house-tax to shops, offices, or warehouses, which would cost 50,000*l.* a year ; to reduce the duty on coffee and chicory to about one half at a cost of 230,000*l.* ; to extend the principle of abatement in respect of incomes chargeable with income-tax from 200*l.* a year to 300*l.* a year, and to increase the amount to be deducted from the assessment from 60*l.* to 80*l.* Lastly, and most important of all, he would take off the extra twopence of income-tax imposed last year, reducing this tax from sixpence to fourpence at a cost to the revenue of 2,700,000*l.* The Budget was generally thought to be simple and felicitous, showing judicious finance, a sound fiscal system, and a just regard for the interests of the people.

27.—Fire in Glasgow, destroying the extensive range of warehouses and shops occupied by Messrs. Fraser and M'Laren in Argyll and Buchanan Streets and McGeoch's ironmongery stores in the courts adjoining.—Two days later the Lancefield Spinning Company's mill in the same city was destroyed by fire.

— William Rodway sentenced at Kingston assizes to twenty years' penal servitude for stabbing Ellen Carrington, Farnham, a woman with whom he had at one time lived and been engaged in business with.

30.—Eight young girls suffocated in a fuzee factory near Camborne, West Cornwall, by the unexpected ignition of a heap of recently-spun fuze.

April 1.—Died, at the house of his nieces, the Misses Sterling, Bolton Row, London, aged 70 years, the Rev. Frederick Denison Maurice, M.A., Professor of Moral Philosophy at Cambridge, and author of many popular volumes on theology and morals. His remains were interred in Highgate cemetery on the 5th, in the presence of a large number of his friends of all opinions.

— The 300th anniversary of the capture of Briel celebrated in Holland

1.—Easter review at Brighton ; the movements executed in the presence of many thousands of spectators, but amid showery, ungenial weather. About 20,000 volunteers took part in the display.

2.—Died at Ventnor, aged 30, Robert Morton, M.A., a promising Cambridge scholar, Senior Wrangler and first Smith's Prizeman in 1866.

— M. Villemessant and M. Vitré convicted of insulting General Trochu in the *Figaro*, and sentenced each to a fine of 3,000f. and a month's imprisonment.

3.—Mr. Disraeli, on a visit to Lancashire, addresses a large audience in the Free Trade Hall, Manchester. He spoke of the Constitution, which it was the special object of the Conservative party to maintain, of the House of Lords, Church and State, and, slightly, on contemporary politics. On foreign politics Mr. Disraeli remarked that although persons were apt to put them aside, yet the most vital consequences have been occasioned by mere inadvertence. He illustrated this point by two anecdotes. Since he had been in public life there had been for this country a great calamity and there was a great danger, and both might have been avoided. The calamity was the Crimean War. On that subject Mr. Disraeli observed : "I speak of what I know, not of what I believe, but of what I have evidence in my possession to prove—that the Crimean War would never have happened if Lord Derby had remained in office. How had the present Government treated the demand of Russia for the modification of the Treaty of Paris ? Having first threatened war, they threw over their plenipotentiary, and agreed to arrangements by which the violation of that treaty should be sanctioned by England, and, in the form of a Congress, they showed themselves guaranteeing their own humiliation." Regarding the future policy of the Conservative party, Mr. Disraeli remarked : "If I may venture to give such a hint, let us take care not to allow ourselves to be made to any extent the tools of the ambition or of the discontent of extreme politicians on the other side. I tell you what I mean. It may very likely be the game of the Radical party to try and turn out the present Ministry if they can and to put a Conservative Government in its place, that Conservative Government being in a minority, hoping that by so doing they shall be able to reconstruct their own party upon a new platform, pledged to more extreme and more violent measures, and then to have a Cabinet formed of the most thoroughgoing Radicals. These may be their tactics. But just because it is their game it ought not to be ours."

— Antioch destroyed by an earthquake, and as many as 1,600 persons reported to be killed.

4.—Replying to a deputation representing the National Association for Freedom of Worship, Mr. Disraeli said : " I look forward to the Church as I look to churchmen, as the maintainers and upholders of the institutions of the land ; but I wish as much as possible to divest that natural connection of mere party feeling, and I am prepared upon all occasions to act with churchmen heartily and cordially for the great ends which they propose, without any reference to the immediate necessities of the political connection of which I am proud to be a member." To another deputation representing a Church Defence Association, the leader of the Opposition expressed a hope of being able to defeat the Burials Bill if active exertions were at once made to petition against it. " That is the practical counsel I give you, and if we succeed in defeating that measure I think the tide will have turned, and that we shall have arrested the progress of these invasions which have been successful in too many instances, as much from the negligence of churchmen as really from the enmity of the assailants of the Church."

4.—Mr. Vernon Harcourt's motion for reducing the national expenditure rejected by 78 to 35 votes.

6.—At Bristol Assizes the Mayor of Exeter recovers ten guineas in name of damages against the *Times*, for publishing a letter insinuating that he had used official influence to obstruct inquiry regarding a disorderly Permissive Bill meeting, where Bishop Temple was rudely treated.

7.—Regarding the Constitution, Mr. Bright writes to a correspondent : "As to opinions on the question of monarchy or republicanism, I hope and believe it will be a long time before we are asked to give our opinion ; our ancestors decided the matter a good while since, and I would suggest that you and I should leave any further decision to our posterity. Now, from your letter I conclude you are willing to do this; and I can assure you I am not less willing."

8.—Mr. Dodson retires from the Chairmanship of Committees, and is succeeded by Mr. Bonham Carter. The House afterwards went into Committee on the Ballot Bill, a stormy discussion arising on clause 2, fixing the manner in which the poll should be taken. A proposition for marking the ballot paper with a view to detect personation, was rejected by 168 to 128 votes.

— Opening of the German Parliament, Prince Bismarck reading a message from the Emperor, declaring that the power acquired by Germany through becoming united in one empire " is not only a safe bulwark for the Fatherland, but likewise affords a strong guarantee for the peace of Europe."

— Madame Riel found murdered in her residence, 13, Park Lane. Her daughter, a member of the French Company performing at the St. James's Theatre, arrived from Paris early this morning, and on presenting herself at Park Lane was informed that her mother was absent. It was soon discovered that certain doors were locked, that the keys were missing, and that the cook could not be found. This led to an examination of the house, when the dead body of Madame Riel was found in the pantry, opened with duplicate keys in possession of the young lady. Her death appeared to have been caused by strangulation, as the tightened rope was still round her neck, though there were marks of extreme violence on other parts of the body. An examination of the safe showed that the murder had been accompanied by the robbery of gold, bank-notes, French bonds, and railway shares. Suspicion at once fixed upon the cook, Marguérite Dixblanc, a Belgian by birth, but some time resident in Verdun, and in Paris for a short period during the reign of the Commune. She was known to have been in the house alone with her mistress on the forenoon of Sunday the 7th, left it stealthily in the evening, and was traced as a passenger to Paris by the Continental mail train. A further clue to her movements there was soon obtained by a letter written a day before the murder, wherein Dixblanc indicated to the Sieur Dubois that she expected to be in Paris soon. It had been misdirected to Rue Saint Denis instead of Rue du Port St. Denis, and was in ordinary course opened by the post-office authorities, for the purpose of being returned to the writer. On the detectives presenting themselves at the house of Dubois, Dixblanc was found engaged in the task of measuring out charcoal, and talking at the same time, it was said, of the horrors of the Park Lane murder. She sought to evade apprehension for a brief period, but in the end confessed having committed the crime, and even gave an account of the manner in which it was accomplished. "I first tried," she said, "to conceal the body in the dustbin, but I could not. I then took it by the feet, but being unable to drag it, I got a cord and passed it round her waist. Finding the body bent double, I put it round her neck. At this moment the housemaid, who was out on an errand, knocked at the door. I sent her away for beer. Then I tried to drag the body up-stairs, but could not, and hid it in the cellar." Dixblanc described the robbery as an after-thought, suggested, she said, by the keys falling from Madame Riel's pocket. Extradition treaties having been complied with, she was brought over in custody to London, and after various examinations committed for trial.

8.—The Bishop of Lincoln having written to the Archbishop of Canterbury requesting an explanation of the remark made by his Grace in Convocation, to the effect that nobody believes in the damnatory clauses of the Athanasian Creed, the Archbishop writes : "I am confident that it is only in a modified sense, with such modifications as you allude to, that these clauses of the Creed are retained by the Church, and though I see no inconsistency in subscribing the words with such acknowledged

qualifications, I still feel that it is in itself an evil to use words which require such explanation. If these clauses remain they will always be used with such qualifications as you have alluded to, whether an explanatory rubric distinctly stating the qualification be adopted by the Church or no."

8.—The Queen arrives at Windsor from the Continent.

9.—Mr. Fowler's motion condemning the entail and strict settlement of land, rejected by 103 votes to 81.

10.—Petitions presented to the House of Commons, and ordered to lie on the table, praying that means might be provided from the public funds for defending the Claimant in the event of Government carrying out their intention of prosecuting him for perjury. To a charge upon two indictments—first, that he was the eldest son of Sir James Doughty Tichborne ; second, that he was not Arthur Orton —the Claimant, at the Central Criminal Court to-day, pleaded "I am not guilty." He was then removed in custody till bail could be arranged pending the issue of the trial, now removed by writ of *certiorari* to the Court of Queen's Bench.

11.—Came on at the Central Criminal Court, the trial of Arthur O'Connor, charged with unlawfully pointing a pistol at her Majesty, intending to alarm and cause a breach of the peace. The prisoner pleaded guilty on being first brought up on the 8th, but it was now stated his friends were anxious to establish a plea of insanity. This, however, was overruled, and O'Connor was sentenced to 12 months' imprisonment and 20 strokes from a birch-rod.

— The steamer *Oceanus* blown up on the Mississippi above Cairo, the wreck afterwards taking fire and burning to the water edge. Out of one hundred on board, sixty were reported to have lost their lives.

12.—In reply to Earl Stanhope, Earl Granville said that Government had determined to present a case excluding the indirect claims, and accompanied by a declaration to the Geneva tribunal, abiding by the position taken up by her Majesty's Government in their correspondence with the United States, and expressly reserving the right of Great Britain to withdraw from the arbitration should the present difference with the United States not be removed by the 15th of June. A similar statement was made by Mr. Gladstone in the Commons in reply to Mr. Disraeli.

13.—Died at Manchester, aged 84, Samuel Bamford, author of "Passages in the Life of a Radical."

15.—Proposed new Court of Appeal. In the House of Lords, the Lord Chancellor moves a resolution—"That it is expedient that one Imperial Supreme Court of Appeal be established which shall sit continuously for the hearing of all matters now heard by way of appeal before this House or before the Judicial Committee of the Privy Council, and that the appellate jurisdiction of this House be transferred to such Supreme Court of Appeal." It was intended that the new Court should constitute one tribunal sitting in two divisions—one representing the House of Lords, and the other the Judicial Committee of the Privy Council, the members of either division being able to sit in the other. The first division would consist of all peers who had filled the office of Lord Chancellor or any high judicial office for a specified time either in Great Britain or Ireland, and would · also include all peers who had actually practised at the bar, and Privy Councillors now capable of being appointed upon the Judicial Committee. In each division there would be no fewer than three nor more than five judges, who would be paid 6,000*l.* a year ; and peers who had filled the office of Lord Chancellor and who accepted the obligation to attend, would have their pensions augmented from 5,000*l.* to 6,000*l.* a year. The Lord Chancellor would be at the head of both divisions of the Supreme Court, and among the members of the second division would be the Lord Chief Justices of the Queen's Bench and Common Pleas, and the Lord Chief Baron of the Exchequer. The Lord Chancellor concluded by proposing that the motion be the order of the day in immediate priority to the second reading of the Bill constituting the Supreme Court of Appeal.

15.—James Nicholls, shoemaker, Maida Hill, murders four of his children and then commits suicide. In the afternoon a boy who lived in the house called the attention of one of the neighbours to a stream of blood running from under the door of one of the rooms occupied by Nicholls. A policeman was called, and on bursting open the door of the front room he found three of the children—Louisa, aged three ; Rosina, aged five, and James Henry, aged fourteen months — with their throats cut. The back room, which had been used as a workshop, was in great confusion, every article of furniture being out of its place. In it were discovered the body of the eldest daughter, Eliza Nicholls, aged nine, who had also had her throat cut, and the body of Nicholls himself, who appeared, after murdering his children, to have sat down at his bench and cut his own throat in a desperate manner. The coroner's jury found that Nicholls was of unsound mind.

— Mr. Harcourt's amendment to omit the word " wilfully " from Mr. Leatham's proposal to make the exhibition of a voting paper by a voter penal, carried against the Government by 167 to 166. Government was again in a minority the following evening, Sir Massey Lopes carrying his resolution on the subject of local taxation by 259 to 159.

— The English and American counter-cases presented to the tribunal at Geneva.

16.—Lord Kimberley introduces the Government Licensing Bill into the House of Lords. In explanation of some of the clauses it was stated that licences granted by county magistrates would not be valid until confirmed by a special committee to be appointed yearly by the court of quarter sessions. In boroughs where there were not more than nine magistrates the jurisdiction would remain with them as a body, and where there were more than nine a committee would be appointed to grant licences, which, however, would not be valid until confirmed by the whole body of justices and the Secretary of State. The bill also dealt with the adulteration of liquor, and provided for closing public-houses in the metropolis from twelve at night to seven in the morning ; in towns under 10,000 inhabitants from ten to seven ; and in towns with larger populations from eleven to seven. On Sunday licensed houses would not be opened until one o'clock ; and the hours of closing on that day would, in the three cases mentioned, be eleven, nine, and ten o'clock respectively. After a few words from the Duke of Richmond and Lord Redesdale, the bill was read a first time.

— Died at Oxford, aged 76, the Rev. Dr. Norris, President of Corpus Christi College.

— Celebrated with great pomp at the Oratory, Brompton, the marriage of the Marquis of Bute to the Hon. Gwendoline Mary Anne Howard, eldest daughter of Lord Howard of Glossop.

— Japanese Ambassadors arrive in Liverpool from New York.

— Derry Castle, situated on the shores of Lough Dergh, near Killaloe, destroyed by fire.

— The remains of Alexandre Dumas, detained at Pays since December 1870, in consequence of the Prussian occupation of the Seine Inférieure, were laid to-day, in accordance with the novelist's last wishes, in the little cemetery of Villers-Cotterets, near which he was born in 1802.

18. — Edward Mitchell, sculptor, while labouring under mental irritation, commits suicide by first stabbing himself with a sharp-pointed graving tool, and afterwards throwing himself from the upper story of his house.

— Persian famine increases in intensity, the news from Teheran to-day being that bread had risen to 6*d.* per pound.

19. — Christie and Manson commence to dispose of the famous Gillott collection of paintings. The sale continued till May 4th, when the total amount realised was found to be 180,000 guineas. Twelve drawings by Turner brought 16,430 guineas.

— Died, aged 74 years, Richard Westmacott, R.A., sculptor.

— The *Gazette* contains a notice from the Lord Chamberlain's office, announcing that the presentation at Court of Lady Twiss had been cancelled.

23.—Mr. Candlish's proposal to repeal in the interest of the Nonconformists the 25th clause of the Elementary Education Act, rejected after a debate by 316 to 115 votes.

— The Court of Probate pronounce for the will of Miss Cordelia Angelica Read, known as the "eccentric old lady" of Stamford Street, the owner of ruinous houses in that street, and in other parts of London. By her will, executed in 1858, she bequeathed the whole of her personal estate, amounting to about 100,000*l.*, to the Brompton Hospital.

— A miner named Lease, living at Charterhouse, on the slope of the Mendip Hills, beats his wife to death in a fit of passion excited by jealousy, several of the neighbours witnessing the savage attack through the windows, but too terror-stricken to interfere.

24.—Another group of Communist prisoners tried for being concerned in the murder of the hostages in May last. The woman Guyart was condemned to death ; the girl Cailleux and Léopold Viel to transportation to a fortress ; Victor Charton to penal servitude for life ; Feltesse to ten years' penal servitude ; four others to various terms of imprisonment; and twenty to imprisonment for two years.

— Discussion in the Lower House of Convocation on the Athanasian Creed. The variety of opinions expressed was fully indicated by petitions previously sent in and thus arranged : —For retention of the Creed in an unaltered form, 35,271 ; for investigating the text and a new translation, 561 ; for the removal of the use of the Creed, 10; for the omission of the Creed from the Prayer-book, 6 ; for delay in the removal of the Creed, 25 ; for omission of the damnatory clauses, 30 ; for making the use of the Creed optional, 83 ; for the retention of the three Creeds, 96. After a learned and animated debate extending over four days, divisions were taken on the various proposals. The first was on an amendment by Mr. Kempe, of St. James's, to confine its recitation to the shortened and occasional services provided by the Bill now before Parliament : this was rejected by 60 to 10. Dean Stanley then proposed to make its recitation permissive by inserting a rubric after the Apostles' Creed, allowing it as an alternative for that Creed on the appointed days : this was rejected by 60 to 12. The Dean's next proposal, placing its use at the discretion of the Ordinary, was rejected by 54 to 13 : after which Lord Alwyne Compton's motion, that the Creed should continue to be used in its integrity, was carried by 62 to 7. A proposal by Canon Blakesley, that it should be treated as a Hymn or Canticle, met with somewhat more favour—being negatived by 42 to 19. Archdeacon Denison then carried a rider by 42 to 12, that the Creed should be said on no fewer days than at present.

— The Spanish Cortes opened by King Amadeo, who expressed a hope for a prompt

termination of the insurrection, praised the discipline and services of the army and the Civic Guard, and concluded by stating that he would seek in the deliberations of the Cortes a guide for his conduct and a way to identify his feelings with those of the Spanish people. "I will never (he said) impose myself on the Spanish people ; but neither will I allow myself to be accused of deserting the post which I occupy by its will, nor of forgetting the duties which the Constitution places upon me, and which I shall fulfil with the loyalty and constancy which I owe to the honour of my name."

24.—Mr. Fawcett's proposal for throwing the expense of elections upon public funds rejected in the Commons by 263 to 171 votes.

25.—The Marquis of Lansdowne appointed Under-Secretary for War in room of Lord Northbrook, now Viceroy of India.

— Funeral obsequies over the body of Lord Mayo celebrated with great splendour in Dublin. The remains of the deceased Viceroy were afterwards interred within the ruins of the ancient church at Johnstown.

— Carlist rising in Spain, a proclamation being issued to-day by General Diaz de Ruda, who formerly held rank under Isabella II., and was lately appointed by the Pretender Commander-in-Chief of the Basque Provinces and Navarre.

— Eruption of Mount Vesuvius, attended with the loss of several lives.

26.—The little girl, Mary Winchester, rescued by the Looshai expedition, arrives in Glasgow from Liverpool on her way to Elgin, where a permanent home had been found for her among relations.

— The domestic servants of Dundee form themselves into a Protection Association for the purpose of securing shorter hours of work, higher pay, more holidays, and better feeding.

— Madame Dubourg dies in the hospital of La Pitié, Paris, from wounds inflicted by her husband in a fit of jealousy, caused by the discovery of an intrigue in which she was concerned.

27.—The Duke of Edinburgh presides at a meeting in Willis's Rooms, called to consider the propriety of raising a memorial to the late Lord Mayo. Mr. Disraeli was present, and spoke highly of the many merits centred in the Viceroy, "whose noble presence, cordial manner, the magnificence of his life, his active accomplishments, his extraordinary power of physical endurance, combined with an intuitive knowledge of mankind, inexorable love of justice, which was only tempered by the abounding generosity of his heart, produced such an effect upon those whom he ruled that all at once willingly acknowledged that he was born to command."

— Opening of the International Exhibition of 1872 at South Kensington.

29.—Proclamation of Don Carlos circulated at Madrid, thanking God for permitting him to kiss the soil of Spain, and calling upon the people to rise in arms.

30.—Died, aged 53, Horace Mayhew, author, one of the earliest contributors to *Punch*.

— The Lord Chancellor's Bill for the formation of a new Court of Appeal withdrawn after a debate, and Lord Cairns' resolution for a committee on the subject adopted.

— A band of predatory Carlists, led chiefly by priests, attack the house of the Governor of Burgos, Old Castile, but are driven back by reinforcements from the garrison, and many made prisoners.

— The Government of India resolve to dismiss Mr. Cowan and reprimand Mr. Forsyth for their summary proceedings with the rebels of Kooka, where forty-nine men were sentenced to be blown away from the guns.

— Close of the litigation between the Duke of Buccleuch and the Metropolitan Board of Works. The Duke had been awarded by an arbitrator 8,325*l.* as compensation for the construction of the Thames Embankment between Montagu House and the river. The Board of Works disputed the grounds on which the arbitrator had made his award, but on the case being taken to the Court of Exchequer, the Court decided in favour of the Duke. The Court of Exchequer Chamber reversed this decision, and the case was then referred on appeal to the House of Lords, which now reversed the judgment of the Exchequer Chamber, and affirmed that of the Court of Exchequer upholding the award of the arbitrator.

May 1.—Mr. Jacob Bright's Women's Disabilities Bill rejected by 222 to 143 votes.

— In the Lower House of Convocation, Archdeacon Denison, by a majority of 21 to 17, carries an amendment declaring that there was "no room for an explanatory note on the Athanasian Creed."

— Festival at the Crystal Palace in celebration of the recovery of the Prince of Wales, and performance of Te Deum by Sullivan.

— Telegram received describing the *Abydos* as returning from Zanzibar bringing news that Livingstone was safe with Stanley.

— Strasburg University opened with a ceremony combining courtly and academical dignity.

— Cyclone at Madras, destroying a large amount of shipping property, and also a portion of the city and suburbs.

2.—The Empress of Germany arrives at Windsor on a visit to the Queen.

— The French Government announce their intention of bringing Marshal Bazaine before a court-martial.

2.—The Licensing Bill read a second time in the Lords.

3.—Lord Northbrook, the new Viceroy of India, arrives at Calcutta, and is at once sworn into office.

— Discussion in the Upper House of Convocation on a motion submitted by the Bishop of Gloucester that it was not expedient to invite legislation on the fourth report of the Ritual Commissioners in reference to the Athanasian Creed. The Bishop of Winchester moved an amendment, expressing agreement with the resolutions transmitted by the Lower House in favour of the retention of the Creed. This was lost by the casting vote of the Archbishop of Canterbury, and in a subsequent division the original resolution was also negatived.

— The Liberal Republican Convention at Cincinnati select Mr. Horace Greeley as their candidate for the Presidency.

4.—Enthusiastic reception given by the National Assembly to the Duc d'Audriffet-Pasquier on the occasion of his presenting a report on Military Administration. He recommended the army as the best and only school in which the young generation could have a nobler and better training than that which produced such lamentable examples of want of patriotism and want of probity. The army gave an example of silent, conscientious fulfilment of duty. "Our children must all serve in it." M. Rouher took occasion some days later to answer this speech, by defending the Emperor. He called upon the Assembly to name a committee to inquire what had been done with the enormous sum voted annually for the war budget during the Empire, how the denuded state of the arsenal was to be accounted for, and what was the real sum absorbed by the Mexican Expedition.

— A court-martial at Malta dismisses from the ship and reprimands Lieuts. Wallace and Hailstone for carelessness in connection with the stranding of the *Lord Clyde.*

5.—Died, aged 64 years, G. R. Gray, ornithologist, and Assistant Keeper of the Zoological Department in the British Museum.

— The Carlist insurgents under Don Carlos defeated at Oroquieta.

6.—At the pressing request of Earl Granville, Earl Russell consents to postpone his motion regarding the Geneva arbitration till the Government were in a position to submit papers to the House or make an explanation on the 13th.

— On the proposal for going into committee on the Education (Scotland) Bill, Mr. Gordon, by a majority of 216 to 209 votes, carries a resolution—"That having regard to the principles and history of the past educational legislation and practice of Scotland, which provided for instruction in the Holy Scriptures in the public schools as an essential part of education, this House, while desirous of passing a measure during the present session for the improvement of education in Scotland, is of opinion that the law and practice of Scotland in this respect should be continued by provisions in the bill now before the House."

6.—Niblo's Theatre, New York, destroyed by fire.

7.—Sir Colman O'Loghlen submits a resolution in the Commons :—" That this House has heard with great regret that a gentleman has been appointed Lord-Lieutenant of Clare who has never resided in that county, who is a stranger to its magistrates, and who does not possess that local knowledge of the county and its residents essential to the proper discharge of the important duties of a lieutenant of a county, and that this House is of opinion that such an appointment is of evil example, and ought not to have been made." Rejected after debate by 257 to 41 votes.

8.—Literary Fund dinner presided over by the King of the Belgians, presently on a visit to England, and whose health was proposed in courtly terms by Mr. Disraeli.

9.—Rainham Church, Kent, set on fire by lightning.

— Died, aged 73 years, General Sir John Lysaght Pennefather, G.C.B., of Indian and Crimean fame, Governor of Chelsea Hospital.

12.—The surrender of Sedan being severely criticised in the National Assembly, the Emperor writes from Chislehurst :—" The honour of the army having been saved by the bravery which had been displayed, I then exercised my sovereign right, and gave orders to unfurl a flag of truce. I claim the entire responsibility of that act. The immolation of 60,000 men could not have saved France, and the sublime devotion of her chiefs and soldiers would have been uselessly sacrificed. We obeyed a cruel but inexorable necessity. My heart was broken, but my conscience was tranquil."

13.—Explanations made in both Houses regarding recent negotiations with Washington, and forbearance solicited for a few days till Government had obtained an answer to the last draught note suggesting a supplementary treaty now being considered by the Senate in Secret Executive Session.

— Earl Granville replies to Mr. Fish's argument on the indirect claims, declaring that they formed no part of the negotiations between the two countries, and were never even alluded to by the British Government. There was not a word in any letter preceding the treaty to suggest any indirect or constructive claims, and the only intimation the British Government had had of those claims was from the speech of Mr. Sumner; but they never learned that his views had been adopted by the American Government. Earl Granville then urged that the indirect claims were never admitted by the

British Commissioners, and all that were admitted were strictly defined and limited. The indirect claims were only mentioned once to the Commissioners, whereas the Fenian raids were repeatedly urged; and the withdrawal of the claims for them was only on condition that all constructive damages were abandoned by the American Government.

13.—Died at Vienna, aged 51, Moritz Hartmann, poet and journalist, but more celebrated as one of Blum's revolutionary compatriots.

14.—Marshal Bazaine constitutes himself a prisoner at Versailles.

17.—The Cunard steamer *Tripoli* wrecked near the Tuskar rocks.

20.—The Foreign Committee of the United States Senate report in favour of the Supplementary Treaty providing for the withdrawal of the indirect claims.

21.—The new Southern Hospital at Liverpool opened by Prince Arthur.

— Boat accident on the Thames, near Twickenham, and loss of four lives.

22.—Collision in the Channel off Hastings, between the North German Lloyd's steamer *Baltimore* and the Spanish steamer *Lorenzo Semprun*. Both vessels were seriously damaged, and the former run ashore.

23.—Died at Athens, aged 68, Lord Dalling and Bulwer, diplomatist.

— Explosion in Roslin powder mills, near Edinburgh, causing the loss of several lives and the destruction of much property.

26.—Died, at the family residence, Belgrave Square, William Russell, eighth Duke of Bedford, aged 63 years.

— Died suddenly, aged 65 years, Alfred Henry Forrester, known in art and literature under the *nom de plume* of " Alfred Crowquill."

27.—Mr. Justice Keogh gives a decision on the Galway election, unseating Captain Nolan, and reporting the Archbishop of Tuam, the Bishops of Galway and Clonfert, and a number of priests, as guilty of intimidation. After carefully examining the whole evidence, the judge was convinced that it presented the most astonishing attempts at ecclesiastical tyranny which the whole history of priestly intolerance afforded. Both Catholics and Protestants had been intimidated from voting. Shots had been fired into some houses. Lord Dunsandle's tenants, who had promised to vote for Trench, had been prevented, and Lord Gough's tenants likewise. Lord Delvin had been obliged to absent himself from chapel, in order that he might not hear himself defamed from the altar. The gentry were hunted through the fields by the fellows who followed that obscene monster Pat Barrett. Sir Arthur Guinness had been hounded, fighting his way at the head of twenty-seven men to vote at the booths, and several of his men were also injured. Three years ago, said

Judge Keogh when giving judgment in the Galway borough election petition, he had expressed a hope that, as Parliament was then about to strike down one ascendency, the Roman Catholics of Ireland would prevent a more galling one from being set up. The attempt had now been made, but it had been met by a spirit of independence and intelligence by the Roman Catholic gentry of this great country, and he could not say that he felt otherwise than proud of his countrymen for having had the spirit and the courage and independence to do it. This judgment, which excited the keenest feeling throughout Ireland, occupied nine hours in delivery.

27.—At the reassembling of the Commons to-day, after the Whitsuntide recess, Mr. Gladstone announces that the United States Senate had made "modifications" in the Supplementary Treaty. Earl Granville informed the American Minister next day that these "modifications" could not be accepted by the British Government.

28.—The Burmese ambassadors make a private visit to Windsor.

— Prof. Montague Bernard, one of the Commissioners for framing the Treaty of Washington, delivers a lecture on that subject to a large audience at Oxford University Museum.

29.—The long-continued and animated debate on the French Army Bill closes amid a stormy scene arising out of personal altercations between General Changarnier and Colonel Denfert, and an attack by M. du Temple on M. Gambetta. The principal speech of the day was delivered by Monsignor Dupanloup, Bishop of Orleans. He described Prussia as the first barrack in the world, but not the first nation ; and demanded guarantees for the liberty of conscience in the army and proper regulations and facilities for enabling soldiers to attend divine service. "Since you have thought it necessary," he said, "to call upon all youthful France to undertake active service, we require, at least, that the freedom of conscience should not be restricted in the army, and that soldiers should not be prevented from being Christians."

30.—A requisition, signed by about thirty subscribers to the fund for the completion of St. Paul's, having been presented to the Dean, requesting him to call a general meeting of the subscribers, with a view to expressing an opinion regarding the appointment of Mr. Burges as architect, the Dean now writes to the Lord Mayor :—"The responsibility at this stage of the business rests with the Executive Committee, and I do not think that it is right to take it out of their hands and transfer it to any meeting of subscribers, necessarily collected in a chance way. I am fully aware that we are all of us on our trial—Mr. Burges, those of us who have confidence in him, and those also who have raised an opposition against him. But Mr. Burges can do nothing in St. Paul's

till his designs—after a criticism which is not likely to be lenient—shall have been finally approved. It will be time enough to protest against him when we and the public are able to judge of what he proposes to do. Regretting extremely to find myself differing from your lordship and the subscribers who have signed the requisition, I am unable to comply with it."

30.—Third reading of the Ballot Bill carried by 274 to 216 votes.

— Died at Mossul, C. A. Rassam, British Vice-Consul.

— Explosion in the powder magazine of the Porthywain Lime Rocks, near Oswestry, causing the death of six men.

31.—Wreck of the *Halcyon* on the Tuskar rocks.

— Private Donohue stabbed in the Citadel Barracks, Devon, by another soldier, named Bradford, who was threatened with being reported for disorderly conduct.

June 1.—The Prince and Princess of Wales arrive at Marlborough House from their continental tour.

— Died at Trieste, where he discharged the duties of British Consul, Charles Lever, novelist and critic, aged 63 years.

2.—Died, aged 72, James Gordon Bennett, editor and proprietor of the *New York Herald*.

3.—Died, aged 76, Johann Rudolf Thorbecke, Prime Minister of Holland.

4.—Debate commenced in the House of Lords on the oft-deferred motion of Earl Russell for an address to the Crown praying that all proceedings on behalf of this country before the arbitrators appointed to meet at Geneva, pursuant to the Treaty of Washington, be suspended until the claims included in the case submitted on behalf of the United States, and understood on the part of her Majesty not to be within the province of the arbitrators, have been withdrawn. The discussion, conducted mainly in a spirit designed to caution the Government against dangers before them, was brought to a premature close on the evening of the 6th, when Earl Granville produced a letter from the American Minister, General Schenck, affirming the sufficiency of the Supplemental Article for closing indirect claims.

— Mr. Gordon's amendment to the Scotch Education Bill, substantially retaining the existing system of parochial schools, rejected in Committee by 222 to 167 votes.

— Flooding of the Po near Ferrara ; as many as 40,000 people said to be rendered houseless.

5.—Dublin Exhibition opened by the Duke of Edinburgh.

8.—The Judicial Committee of the Privy Council give judgment in the case of Sheppard *v.* Bennett, vicar of Frome Selwood, charged with maintaining the following heresies — " 1. The actual presence of our Lord in the Sacrament of the Lord's Supper. 2. The visible presence of our Lord upon the altar or table at the Holy Communion. 3. That there is a sacrifice at the time of the celebration of the Eucharist. 4. That adoration or worship is due to the consecrated elements in the Lord's Supper." The alleged heresies were contained in publications by Mr. Bennett, in an essay on " Some Results of the Tractarian Movement of 1833," and in " Letters to Dr. Pusey," of which there had been three editions, and in which alterations had been made. The Dean of Arches gave a judgment in July 1870, and, admitting a retractation in a corrected edition of the pamphlet as to the visible presence in the Sacrament and the adoration of the consecrated elements, he arrived at the conclusion that to describe the mode of presence as objective, real, actual, and spiritual, was not contrary to the law of the Church of England. From that judgment the promoter appealed to their lordships, and the case was argued before a committee of ten members. Their lordships had had six conferences in private to consider the question. Their lordships now dismissed the appeal, but made no order as to costs, seeing the respondent had not appeared.

9.—Died at Hoddesden, aged 77, the Rev. Wm. Ellis, widely known from his missionary labours in the South Sea Islands and Madagascar.

10.—The United States Congress adjourn without coming to any decision respecting the Supplementary Article.

— The Anglo-American four-oared race between the *London* and *Atlantic* contested on the Thames from Mortlake with ebb tide, and won easily by the former.

— The Ballot Bill read a second time in the House of Lords by 86 to 56 votes.

11.—The *Daily News* publishes a despatch from Earl Granville to Mr. Fish, proposing that on the meeting of arbitrators on the 15th a joint application should be made for an adjournment of eight months. The despatch was accompanied by a declaration that it was the intention of her Majesty's Government to cancel the appointment of the British arbitrator and withdraw from the arbitration at the close of the term fixed for the adjournment, "unless the difference which has arisen between the two Governments as to the claims for indirect losses referred to in the note which he had the honour to address to Count Sclopis on the 15th of April shall have been removed." Mr. Fish refused to unite in this arrangement, believing that the time could only be extended by a new treaty ; "but if the arbitrators consented to adjourn on the request of Great Britain, the United States Government would not object."

Explanations were made in both Houses of Parliament in the evening. Earl Granville admitted that an adjournment had been proposed, but Mr. Gladstone omitting to do so drew down strong condemnation from Mr. Disraeli, who complained of the Premier's want of frankness.

11.—The Dublin Court of Common Pleas decide that Captain Trench was entitled to the seat which Captain Nolan had been deprived of at Galway. The sitting judges were Chief Justice Monahan, and Justices Keogh, Morris, and Lawson. The three latter concurred in the judgment by which Captain Trench obtained the seat, and the Chief Justice, in stating the grounds of his dissent, took occasion to say he had no doubt as to the truth of the allegations of undue influence and intimidation by Captain Nolan and his agents. When a motion was made by Mr. Gladstone to substitute the name of Captain Trench for Nolan, in conformity with Justice Keogh's report to the Speaker, an attempt was made to raise a discussion on the point ; but it was found that by the Act of 1867 the House had parted with all jurisdiction in election matters, and had no choice but to direct the amendment of the return.

12.—The bicentenary of the birth of Peter the Great celebrated with great enthusiasm throughout Russia. At St. Petersburg the Emperor, with his brother the Grand Duke Nicholas, took part in the proceedings, while at Moscow the Imperial family were represented by the Grand Duke Constantine.

— Resignation of the Serrano Ministry in Spain, and election of Zorrilla. Carlist disturbances still continue to agitate the country.

— Opening of the first railway constructed in Japan, between Yokohama and Shinagawa.

13.—Died, aged 80, John Forrester, a well-known member of the Mansion House police force.

14.—After a trial extending over three days Marguérite Dixblanc is found guilty of the murder of Madame Riel, Park Lane, and sentenced to death by Baron Channell, who presided at the Old Bailey. Under a belief that there had been a quarrel between the mistress and her servant, the jury recommended the prisoner to the mercy of the Court. The Crown afterwards gave effect to the recommendation by commuting the extreme penalty to imprisonment for life.

15.—The Irish *Nation*, lashed into fury by the deliverance of Judge Keogh on the Galway case, declares " The man who sold them as Judas sold his God ; the man who gave them the kiss, with the thirty pieces in his pocket ; the man whose treason blasted the hopes of a confiding people, and sent thousands into exile, pauperism, or the grave, is the same who dares to come forward now in the rôle of moral censor and political headsman ! . . . Our rulers will discover ere long that a hundred ' Fenian conspirators' could not do as much in ten years as Mr. Keogh has done in one day to fill this land with hatred of the law and rule that has its representative in him ; and with resentment of the humiliation, the ignominy, the outrage of setting over us on the justice-seat, to revile our faith and destroy our liberties, a political traitor false to his country and forsworn to his oath ! "

15.—The arbitrators under the Treaty of Washington hold a private conference at Geneva.

— Owing to the death of Mr. Blenkiron, a sale of yearlings takes place at Middle Park, sixty lots bringing 17,000 guineas, or an average of nearly 300 guineas. A colt by General Peel sold for 1,750 guineas ; a bay colt by Blair Athol out of Coimbra, 1,550*l.* ; and a colt by Blair Athol out of Margery Daw, 1,150 guineas. Mr. Tattersall announced that Mr. Blenkiron's executors had received an offer from the Prussian Government for the whole of the stud, but declined it on the ground that they thought it right this country should have the opportunity of participating in its advantages.

— The old Cockhedge Factory at Warrington destroyed by a fire which broke out in the spinning department.

16.—Died, aged 82, Colonel W. H. Sykes, F.R.S., M.P. for Aberdeen since 1857, and engaged in active Indian duty as far back as 1804, when he served with Lord Lake before Bhurtpore. Colonel Sykes was twice elected a Director of the East India Company.

— Died at Glasgow, aged 60 years, Rev. Norman McLeod, D.D., a popular Scotch preacher, one of her Majesty's chaplains in Scotland, and editor of *Good Words,* to which he contributed many graphic tales and sketches of foreign travel.

17.—The Ballot Bill passes through committee in the Lords with two amendments, moved by the Duke of Richmond, designed to trace the voter, by marking on the counterfoil his number on the voting register, and to make secrecy only optional.

19.—Count Sclopis, President of the Geneva Arbitrators, states that after the most careful perusal of all that had been urged by the United States on the subject of the indirect claims, they had arrived, "individually and collectively, at the conclusion that these claims do not constitute, upon the principles of international law applicable to such cases, good foundation for an award of compensation, or computation of damages between nations, and should upon such principles be wholly excluded from the consideration of the Tribunal in making up its award, even if there were no disagreement as to the competency of the Tribunal to decide thereon, with a view to the settlement of the other claims to the consideration of which by the Tribunal no exception has been taken on the part of her Britannic Majesty's Government." On the 25th, Mr. Bancroft Davis stated that "the declaration by the Tribunal was accepted by the President of the United States as determinative of the judgment on the important question of public law involved ; and that he, as agent of the United States, was authorized to say that consequently the above-mentioned claims will not be further insisted upon before the Tribunal by the United States, and may be excluded from all consideration in any award that may be made." On the 28th the Tribunal adjourned until the 15th of July.

19.—A bill for the expulsion of the Jesuits passing the German Reichstag by 131 votes to 93 ; and another anti-clerical proposal making civil marriage and registration thereof compulsory, was approved of by 151 votes to 100.

— Strike in the London building trade for increased pay and shorter hours.

20.—The Synod of the French Reformed Church adopt M. Guizot's proposal in favour of the establishment of a definite creed to avoid the scandal of high Calvinists and Rationalists sitting together.

21.—The Burmese Embassy received by the Queen at Windsor.

— Compromise in the Thwaites will case ; the jury, under instructions from Lord Penzance, finding against the sanity of the deceased, but discharged on the plea referring to undue influence. (See page 639.)

22.—In the Treasury case of Edmunds *v.* Gladstone and others, Justice Mellor finds that the evidence had failed to prove the publication of the minute complained of, and a nonsuit was entered accordingly.

23.—Father Conway, one of the Galway priests censured by Judge Keogh, having died suddenly, Mr. Sullivan of the *Nation* declared at a meeting of Roman Catholics that he had never raised his head since the day he was made the butt of public ridicule. "He went but once since to the altar where his consecrated hands so often offered the august sacrifice to the Most High. He was consigned to a bed of fever, in his delirium repeating the sentences of contumely that had broken his noble heart, and sent him to-day a murdered priest into his grave. (Sensation.) Father Conway has gone to appeal from Judge Keogh's judgment to the judgment of One who would not deny him justice, and before whose high throne and judgment seat on the eternal day Judge Keogh would find his sentence reversed." (Sensation.)

24.—Bethnal Green Museum opened by the Prince and Princess of Wales.

25.—Addressing the Constitutional Association at the Crystal Palace, Mr. Disraeli said : "I have always been of opinion that the Tory party has three great objects. The first is to maintain the institutions of the country—not from any sentiment of political superstition, but because we believe 'hat the principles upon which a community like England can alone safely rest—the principles of liberty, of order, of law, and of religion—ought not to be entrusted to individual opinion or to the caprice and passion of multitudes, but should be embodied in a form of permanence and power. We associate with the monarchy the ideas which it represents—the majesty of the law, the administration of justice, the fountain of mercy and of honour. We know that the estates of the realm, by the privileges they enjoy, are the best security for public liberty and good government. We believe that a national profession of faith can only be attained by maintaining an Established Church, and that no society is safe unless there is a public recognition of the Providential government of the world, and of the future responsibility of man." The Reform Act of 1867-8 was founded, he said, in a confidence that the great body of the people of this country were conservative. " I use the word in its purest and loftiest sense. I mean that the people of England, and especially the working classes of England, are proud of belonging to a great country, and wish to maintain its greatness—that they are proud of belonging to an Imperial country, and are resolved to maintain, if they can, the empire of England—that they believe, on the whole, that the greatness and the empire of England are to be attributed to the ancient institutions of the land." Mr. Disraeli exhorted his hearers to do their best to secure the triumph of their principles. The time was at hand—at least it could not be long distant—when England would have to decide between national and cosmopolitan principles. This observation was received with loud and long-continued cheering, as was also the prophecy with which the speaker concluded, on the assumption that the Conservative party would put forth its united strength :—" You will maintain your country in its present position. But you will do more than that—you will deliver to your posterity a land of liberty, of prosperity, of power, and of glory."

25.—Mr. Cowper-Temple's Occasional Sermons Bill rejected by 177 to 116 votes.

— Mr. M'Arthur's motion, " That a humble address be presented to her Majesty, praying that she will be graciously pleased to take into consideration the propriety of establishing a Protectorate at Fiji, or of annexing those islands, provided that this may be effected with the consent of the inhabitants," rejected by 135 to 84 votes.

— The Burials Bill defeated on the motion to go into committee, by 100 to 78 votes.

26.—Unveiling of a stained-glass window in Berkhampstead church as a memorial to the poet Cowper, son of the rector of the parish, and born there November 15, 1731.

— The Ballot Bill read a third time in the House of Lords and passed.

74

27.—Miss Fox, adopted daughter of Lady Holland, married to Prince Liechtenstein at the Pro-Cathedral, Kensington.

— Announcement made in both Houses of Parliament that America had accepted the declaration of the Geneva arbitrators excluding the indirect claims.

28.—The Lords' amendments to the Ballot Bill considered in the Commons. The optional ballot rejected by 302 to 234 ; the scrutiny accepted by 382 to 137 ; the extension of the hours of polling rejected by 227 to 190.

30.—William Edward Taylor, dealer in old iron, Bermondsey, murders a woman with whom he lived, named Hebden, their daughter Frances, aged five years, fractures the skull of his son James, and then attempts to commit suicide. A few hours after being conveyed to the hospital the maniac jumped out of bed, evaded the constable and the nurse who were in charge of him, rushed into another ward, seized the tongs and menaced the nurse, who escaped by springing from the second-floor window to the ground, fortunately without being injured. Taylor then dashed about the ward and the corridors, and wrote in blood on the wall, " Poison me. Kill me. Let me die. Put me out of my misery." He ultimately ran to a window on the first floor and jumped out of it into the grounds beneath. The window, however, was only six feet from the ground, and he was not injured by his leap.

July 1.—The Commons reject the Lords' amendment to the Ballot Bill limiting the duration of the Act to eight years, by 246 to 165 votes. After a conference with the Upper House the Commons accepted this clause, and the Lords withdrew the power of optional secresy proposed to be given to the voter.

— Disorderly scene in the French National Assembly between M. Thiers and M. Rouher regarding the tax on raw materials.

2.—Mr. Miall's motion for a Royal Commission to inquire into the origin, nature, amount, and application of the property and revenues of the Church of England rejected by 295 to 94 votes. Mr. T. Hughes's amendment directing the inquiry to ecclesiastical purposes generally was also rejected by 270 to 41 votes.

— Inauguration of the memorial edifice at Newcastle, erected to the memory of Nicholas Wood, engineer, and coadjutor of George Stephenson in the early days of railway enterprise.

3.—The International Prison Congress assemble in the Middle Temple Hall, under the presidency of Lord Carnarvon.

— Died, aged 59, Jonathan Bagster, bible publisher.

4.—Commencement of a series of riots near Antwerp, between the military and the populace.

4.—The Acrobats Bill, framed to protect young people from engaging in entertainments dangerous to their lives or injurious to health, read a second time in the House of Lords.

— "Independence Day" celebrated by the arbitrators at Geneva, Mr. Adams responding at the banquet to the toast "The Day we celebrate."

— After a debate protracted over six days the Upper House of Convocation resolves to refer the subject of the Athanasian Creed to a committee of both Houses.

5.—Experimental firing into the *Glatton* in Portland Roads, with results favourable to turret-built ships of her strength. The gun used was the *Hotspur's* 25-ton.

— The Queen reviews the troops at Aldershot.

6.—The church of St. Mary Magdalen, Paddington, destroyed by fire.

— Mr. and Mrs. Alfred Wigan take leave of the stage at Drury Lane.

— Judge Keogh having been appointed to take the Irish north-west circuit, the Dublin *Nation* writes :—" And so, guarded by special constables, watched over by spies, and protected by detectives, with gall on his tongue and venom in his heart, he returns to the land of his birth. Deeply as we may regret this issue, it leaves us some little grounds for consolation, like the shining jewel in the forehead of the toad of adversity. The spectacle afforded by Judge Keogh and his political surroundings may not be without its uses in Ireland, and the lesson which his presence in Ireland will inculcate is not wholly devoid of advantages. Others besides temperance lecturers have found the benefit of having a 'dreadful example' to point to, and Mr. Justice Keogh will serve as a living memento to tell the aspirants to public favour in Ireland the way they should not go."

8.—Convalescent Home at Highgate opened by the Prince and Princess of Wales.

— A vote of 4,133*l.* for the legal expenses of Governor Eyre's defence against criminal prosecutions, carried by 243 to 130 votes.

— At the Central Criminal Court, Henry Benson pleaded guilty to obtaining 1,000*l.* from the late Lord Mayor on the false pretence of relieving the destitute inhabitants of Châteaudun at the close of the war, and was sentenced to twelve months' imprisonment with such hard labour as he was able to perform.

9.—Explosion in Tradeston Flour Mills, Glasgow, causing the destruction of an extensive range of buildings, the deaths of fourteen people, and serious injury to twelve others employed in the building at the time. The calamity was at first attributed to an escape of gas, but scientific and practical evidence submitted to a court of inquiry held immediately afterwards, made it more likely to have been caused by an accumulation of explosive dust generated in the process of grinding.

9.—The Democratic Convention at Baltimore nominate Mr. Horace Greeley as their candidate for the Presidency, and Mr. Gretz Brown for the Vice-Presidency.

— Justice Keogh and Justice Lawson set out from Dublin for the purpose of opening the assizes at Longford. The train by which they travelled was preceded by a pilot engine and two carriages containing a number of soldiers. At intermediate stations policemen were under arms, but there was no demonstration whatever. A large force of cavalry, infantry, and constabulary awaited the arrival of the train at Longford, where the judges were received by the high sheriff. Their lordships proceeded to their lodgings under a strong escort.

10.—The greater part of the masons on strike in London resume work.

— Mrs. Squires and her daughter Christiana, newsvendors in Hoxton, beaten to death in their shop and the premises robbed by some person unknown.

11.—Heavy floods and thunderstorm over the kingdom.

— The Royal Botanic Society of London give a fête in their gardens at the Regent's Park.

— The Prince of Wales lays the foundation-stone of the new Hospital for Sick Children in Great Ormond Street.

— A cabinet of Staffordshire ware presented to Mr. Bright by workers in the Potteries district. In acknowledging the gift he took occasion to refer to the subject of Parliamentary Reform, mentioning that within the last few days they had seen how much progress had been made. "The House of Lords—which seems to be almost the last refuge of political ignorance and passion—the House of Lords has consented to the establishment of vote by ballot, by which perfect security and independence will be given to every elector. They have, unfortunately, insisted on a reservation which shows how little they know of the signs of the times, which must infallibly create embarrassment, and contest, and party strife. This might have been avoided, for they, of all persons, have the greatest interest in dispensing with it."

15.—The Free Church Presbytery of Dundee engage in the consideration of a charge brought against the Rev. Mr. Knight, a member of their body, of having preached in the chapel of the Rev. James Martineau, London. After a long discussion, a motion was adopted, setting forth that Mr. Knight's conduct was highly censurable, but that in view of the offence being the first of the kind with which the Church had had to deal, Mr. Knight should simply be admonished, required to repudiate the Unitarian body as forming part of the Church of Christ.

and enjoined not to repeat the same act under the pain of exposing himself to the highest censure of the Church.

16.—Meeting of the English Roman Catholic, in Willis's Rooms, to protest against the suppression of religious houses in Italy and the expulsion of the Jesuits from Germany.

17.—Debate on Sir R. Blennerhassett's bill for the purchase of Irish railways by the State, Lord Hartington promising on the part of the Government that careful consideration would be given to the question.

18.—The Ballot Bill receives the Royal assent.

— Freedom of the City of London presented to the Baroness Burdett Coutts, the first lady honoured with such a distinction.

— The Marland Spinning Mill, near Rochdale, occupied by the Castleton Co-operative Spinning Company, destroyed by fire.

— Attempt made to assassinate the King and Queen of Spain in the Calle Arenal, Madrid. One of the party of five who fired was killed on the spot by attendants, and two others captured.

— National festival in Norway in celebration of the thousandth anniversary of the establishment of the kingdom. At Christiania Prince Oscar, attended by the Prime Minister, Stang, unveiled the national monument in the presence of deputations from the Storthing, the University, and the Supreme Court.

19.—Mr. Arthur Helps gazetted K.C.B.

— Came on at the Dorset Assizes, before Mr. Justice Mellor, a right of common case, in which the nominal litigants were Davis v. Thorne, but the real parties in the dispute the Earl of Shaftesbury, Lord Normanton, Lady Bingham, and other freeholders, on the one hand, and Mr. Fryer, lord of the manor of Verwood, in Dorset, on the other. The plaintiff Davis was a tenant of Lord Normanton, and before certain enclosures were made—now the subject of litigation—he could drive his cattle at once from his homestead on to the common. But by these enclosures—made by the defendant—he had been shut out, and compelled to go on to the turnpike road in order to get to a portion of his farm, thus putting him to a very great inconvenience. A great number of witnesses came forward, it being argued from the evidence that by the making of the enclosures the lord of the manor had enriched himself, while the rights of the freeholders had been destroyed. Verdict for the plaintiff, with nominal damages of 40s.

20.—The Edinburgh Court of Session give judgment in the Belhaven peerage case, finding that Mr. James Hamilton, North Leith, had established his claim, and remitted to the Sheriff of Chancery to serve him heir to the earldom.

21.—In view of the difficulty of procuring praiseworthy competitive dramas for the "T. P. Cooke National Prize," the Master of the Rolls transfers the 3,000l. bequest from that purpose to the general fund of the Royal Dramatic College.

22.—Lord Granard states in the House of Lords that, having read the papers relating to Mr. Justice Keogh's judgment on the Galway Election Petition, he was unable either to modify or retract any expressions contained in his published letter on the subject. Under these circumstances he had placed his resignation of the lord-lieutenancy of Leitrim in the hands of the Lord-Lieutenant of Ireland, and his resignation had been accepted. In the Commons Mr. Gladstone announces that Government intended to prosecute the Bishop of Clonfert and nineteen priests for illegal practices at the Galway election.

— A proposal to grant a pension of 1,000l. (in addition to an equal sum paid out of the Indian revenue) to Lady Mayo agreed to by both Houses.

— Replying to a memorial signed by 7,000 lay members of the Church of England on the subject of the Athanasian Creed, the Archbishops of Canterbury and York write to Lord Shaftesbury :—" While we think it right to pay due attention to the legitimate scruples of those who, through their zeal to maintain the truth as it has ever been taught by the Church of Christ, feel great anxiety respecting any change, we fully anticipate that, in conjunction with our brethren, we shall be able to devise some plan which will meet the wishes of that other large body of persons who object to the solemn use of words which they regard as unauthorised, in their most obvious sense, either by the letter or the spirit of Holy Scripture."

— Died, aged 60 years, General Don Benito Juarez, President of the Republic of Mexico, and the successful rival of the Emperor Maximilian, whom he put to death.

23.—Died, aged 75 years, W. Bridges Adams, mechanician.

— Henry M. Stanley, the discoverer of Dr. Livingstone, arrives at Marseilles with numerous letters and reports from the great traveller.

— Severe thunderstorm accompanied by a heavy fall of rain experienced in London and neighbourhood.

24.—Commenting on the Keogh judgment, the *Freeman's Journal* attacks the Prime Minister :—" Unhappy Ireland ! Ill-fated people ! The serpent whom the nation warmed into vitality and power, 'the people's William,' is the first among the foremost to curl his viper tail and strike his envenomed fang into the national heart, not only prosecuting the bishops and priests for being true to their people, but seeking, by a deep-laid plot, to stifle their defence." On the attention of the House being called to the words, the Irish Attorney-

General said it was not his intention to institute a prosecution in regard to that article, and ne was surprised that Colonel Knox, being an Irishman himself, should not have known that such things were customary in that country.

24.—Mr. Gilpin's bill for the abolition of capital punishment rejected by 167 votes to 54.

— Meeting of the Church Association to promote the presentation of a lay memorial to the Bishops, and a protest on the subject of the Bennett judgment.

25.—Edward E. Stokes tried for the murder of James Fisk at New York, but the jury declare themselves unable to agree upon a verdict.

26.—Mr. Vernon Harcourt's motion, "That the administration of the law under the existing system is costly, dilatory, and inefficient ; that a competent commission having reported that the judicial organisation is defective in all its branches, it is desirable that her Majesty's Government should, in the next session of Parliament, present to this House a measure for its reform and reconstruction, which, without increasing the public charge, shall provide for the more effectual, speedy, and economical administration of justice," rejected after debate by 60 votes to 45.

27.—Mdlle. Christine Nilsson married to M. Rouzaud at Westminster Abbey.

28.—Subscriptions received for the French loan of 120,000,000*l.* issued at 84f. 50c. Total amount subscribed 1,720,000,000*l.*

29.—Earl Derby calls the attention of the House of Lords to the treatment experienced by Dr. Hooker, director of Kew Gardens, at the hands of Mr. Ayrton, First Commissioner of Works. After tracing the history of Kew Gardens, and the distinguished scientific career, first of Sir W. Hooker and then of his son, he stated from the blue book the acts of which Dr. Hooker complained, and charged the First Commissioner of Works with systematic arrogance and disregard of the courtesies of official life.

31.—Died, aged 67, Augustus Smith, the lessee (under the Duchy of Cornwall) or king of the Scilly Isles, with no neighbouring proprietor nearer than the Land's End on one side and Newfoundland on the other.

— Enormous rise in the price of coals—in the metropolis to the extent of 100 per cent., and in the colliery districts to 300 per cent. on last winter's prices.

— Celebration of the 400th anniversary of the foundation of Munich University. Herr Von Lutz, the Minister of Public Instruction, was the bearer of the King's congratulations, and announced the foundation by his Majesty of a scholarship for students in history. Professor Sybel on the part of various German associations, Professor Max Müller on the part of foreign universities, and Professor Ernst Curtius on behalf of the learned societies, delivered congratulatory addresses. The Rector, Dr. Döllinger, in reply to Professor Max Müller, remarked that the many good sides of the English Universities were not unknown in Germany, and Oxford especially was venerated as a model and an elder sister.

31.—At a meeting of the Suez Canal Company the estimated revenue for the year was stated to be 22,000,000f., leaving a profit of 6,650,000f., in consequence of the new mode of applying the tariffs. Eight hundred and eighty-seven vessels passed through the canal during the first six months of 1872, producing 7,244,000f., or an increase of 45 per cent. on the preceding half-year. The calculation of the tariff on the basis of the gross tonnage instead of the net tonnage produced since the 1st of July an increase of 50 per cent. in the receipts. .

— Died, aged 19 years, François Louis Marie Philippe, Duc de Guise, only surviving child of the Duc d'Aumale, by his late consort Marie Caroline Auguste, daughter of the Prince of Salerno.

August 1.—Experiment with gun-cotton in the neighbourhood of the Treasury, Whitehall, resulting in an explosion which shattered the windows of several public offices.

— General Schenck, the American Minister, General Sherman, and the admiral and captains of the United States quadron at anchor in Southampton water, sreceived by the Queen at Osborne.

— The return from the bankers' clearing house, for the week ending to-day, shows a total of 147,553,000*l.* In the corresponding week of last year it was 116,642,000*l.* The largest return ever known previously to the present one was for the week ending the 3rd ult., when it amounted to 142,045,000*l.*

2.—The Select Committee appointed to report upon the whole subject of railway communication between the Mediterranean, the Black Sea, and the Persian Gulf, issue their report. The committee state that the evidence which they have taken has satisfied them that there is no insuperable obstacle in the way of the construction of a railway from some suitable port in the Mediterranean to some other suitable port at or near the head of the Persian Gulf ; that there is more than one port which might be selected at either end of the line ; that there are several practicable routes ; that there would be no difficulty in procuring the necessary supply of labour and of materials for constructing a railway ; and that there need be no apprehension of its being exposed to injury by natives, either during the process of its construction or after it shall have been completed. The committee think that 10,000,000*l.* would cover the expenses of the shortest route proposed. In conclusion, the report says :— "Speaking generally, your committee are of opinion that the two routes, by the Red Sea and by the Persian Gulf, might be maintained and used simultaneously ; that at certain seasons and for certain purposes the advantage would lie with the one, and at other seasons and for other purposes it would lie with the other ; that it may fairly be expected that in process of time traffic enough for the support of both would develop itself, but that this result must not be expected too soon ; that the political and commercial advantages of establishing a second route would at any time be considerable, and might, under possible circumstances, be exceedingly great ; and that it would be worth the while of the English Government to make an effort to secure them, considering the moderate pecuniary risk which they would incur."

3.—Collision at Clifton Junction, on the Lancashire and Yorkshire Railway, between an express and a goods train. Five persons killed and several seriously injured.

— Melkshott Court, Romsey, the seat of Lady Ashburton, burnt, but the greater part of the valuable works of art with which it was crowded saved.

4.—Died, aged 81 years, General Julius George Griffith, of the Royal Artillery, an old Deccan campaigner under Colonel Lionel Smith.

— Murder and suicide at Gerson near Lucerne, an American shooting a young lady walking with her mother and sister, and discharging a pistol through his own head.

5.—Publication in the *Gazette* of the official despatches from Dr. Livingstone, brought home by Mr. Stanley, who had arrived in London on the 2nd inst., after a short stay at Paris. They comprised six letters, the first addressed to Lord Stanley, being dated the 15th of November, 1870, and the last to Earl Granville, dated Unyanyembe, near the Kazeh of Sheke, February 20, 1872. In 1866 Dr. Livingstone had entered Africa from Zanzibar, but far south of the Nile system. The great valley of the Zambezi, with its tributary, Lake Nyassa, already familiar to him, was the scene of his first labours. Thence he worked northwards over the watershed in search of streams that might feed the infant Nile, and at last, deserted by his guides and worn out by toil, but rewarded by the discovery of the great river Chambezi, he reached Ujiji, the Arab trade depôt on Lake Tanganyika, in 1869. There he rested for a while, and then started again on the same quest. Again he was rewarded by the sight of a great river called Lualaba, which he succeeded in tracing back till it was identified with the Chambezi of his former discovery. But he was worn down by illness and exhaustion. His feet were sore with ulcers, his followers had mutinied, his stores were exhausted, and he had no resource but to fall back once more on Ujiji, which he reached for the second time, utterly dispirited

78

and forlorn, and, in his own expressive phrase, "a mere ruckle of bones," in the middle of October 1871. But he had not long to wait for help and comfort. On the 10th of November the discharge of many muskets announced the arrival of some distinguished party, and the old traveller's eyes and ears were soon gladdened by the sight of a white face, and the sound of the familiar English tongue. Mr. Stanley had found him out, and brought health and plenty in his company. (See Nov. 10, 1871.) Dr. Livingstone sent home his journal to his daughter Agnes. "It is," he writes, "one of Letts's large folio diaries, and is full except a few (five) pages reserved for altitudes which I cannot at present copy. It contains a few private memoranda for my family alone, and I adopt this course in order to secure it from risk in my concluding trip." Letters continued to be received from Livingstone till July of this year.

5.—Mr. Grant-Duff introduces the Indian Budget. For the regular estimate year 1871-72 the revenue was 50,013,686*l.* and the expenditure 47,282,356*l.*, and the Budget estimate for the coming year put the revenue at 48,771,000*l.* and the expenditure at 48,534,000*l.*, leaving a surplus of about a quarter of a million. The decrease in the revenue was due chiefly to opium and assessed taxes. Since the year 1861, the income drawn from India amounted to 569,000,000*l.*, and we had spent there 576,500,000*l.* But for this excess of expenditure over income of seven millions, India had obtained over thirty-seven millions of property, namely, seven millions and a half in public roads, eight millions in canals and a million and a half in harbours, six and a half millions in civil buildings, eleven millions in military buildings, and two millions and three-quarters in state railways. An amendment moved by Mr. Fawcett, condemning the income-tax, was withdrawn after discussion.

6.—Royal assent given to the Scotch Education Bill.

7.—Earl Russell, writing to the *Times*, suggests a change in the termination of the financial year. If it were to close, he said, on the 30th June, instead of the 31st March, the following advantages would be secured :—1. The months of February, March, and April might be devoted to the consideration of bills by the House of Commons, these bills being sent to the House of Lords before the end of April. The House of Commons would not then be required to give up June and July to the business of legislation. 2. The House of Commons, not having its attention occupied by the passing of bills through Committee, would be able at the beginning of May to give its attention to Estimates and to any financial measures which the Government or individual members might place before them 3. The Estimates being voted before the 30th of June, the expenditure of the year would begin with the closing of the Committee of Supply.

7.—At Guildford Assizes, before Baron Martin, the jury again return a verdict for the defendants in the action raised by Leonard Edmunds against several newspaper proprietors to recover damages for alleged libels contained in a Treasury minute published by them.

— The Countess Waldegrave presented with a portrait of her husband, Mr. Chichester Fortescue, M.P., recently retired from the office of Chief Secretary for Ireland.

8.—Mr. Fawcett calls the attention of the Commons to the dispute between Mr. Ayrton and Dr. Hooker. At the same sitting Mr. Butt's motion concerning Judge Keogh was rejected by 126 votes to 23.

— Died, aged 70, George Godolphin Osborne, Duke of Leeds.

— Died, aged 89, Colonel Thomas S. Begbie, late of the 44th Regiment, a Peninsular veteran, who had entered the army as early as 1807.

— Died at Berlin, Dr. Abeken, the Gentz of modern Germany, familiarly known as "Bismarck's pen," and described by the Emperor as "one of my most trusty counsellors, who stood by me in the most decisive moments of my life, and whose loss is to me irreparable."

9.—Mr. Childers sworn in as Chancellor of the Duchy of Lancaster.

10.—Parliament prorogued by Commission; the Royal Speech, in addition to a brief notice of the more important measures passed, making reference to the satisfactory result of the controversy raised by the Treaty of Washington and the termination of the commercial treaty with France. It was also intimated that "my Government has taken steps intended to prepare the way for dealing more effectually with the slave trade on the east coast of Africa." Previous to the formality of reading the Speech the Royal assent was given by commission to the Licensing Bill, the Mines Regulation Bill, the Public Health Bill, the Military Forces Localization (Expenses), and other bills.

— The Prince of Wales places the finishing stone of the Breakwater at Weymouth, the first stone of which was laid by the Prince Consort, July 25, 1849. The structure is a great sea-wall 100 feet high from the bottom of the sea, and 300 feet thick at the base, but narrower above, and stretches with a bend towards Weymouth, a mile and five-eighths from the east side of the island of Portland, and shelters from every wind an area of 6,745 acres of water—namely, the space for anchorage or coaling of men-of-war, 1,290 acres outside the five-fathom line, 1,590 acres between three and five fathoms, 1,758 acres between 12 feet and 19 feet, and 2,107 acres up to low-water level. The entire structure consists of an inner breakwater, 1,900 feet in length, divided from an outer or isolated breakwater, 6,200 feet in length, by an opening 400 feet wide. The whole is built in nine to ten fathoms of water,

the material used being rough blocks of Portland stone, quarried by convicts from the neighbouring shore.

10.—Marine Aquarium at Brighton opened by the Mayor of the borough. At the luncheon given afterwards in the Pavilion, Dr. Carpenter urged that the aquarium should be made a marine observatory in the interest of science. It was, he said, what naturalists had long wanted, and if properly managed would do much to advance the study of marine zoology.

11.—Died, aged 78 years, Prince Gholam Mahomed, K.C.S.I., last surviving son of Tippoo Sultan.

— Died, aged 75 years, Sir Andrew Smith, K.C.B., Director-General of the Army Medical Department, 1851-58.

12.—The Japanese Envoy presented to the Queen at Windsor.

— Died, Rev. Dr. Walsh, Roman Catholic Bishop of Ossory, defendant in the case of O'Keefe v. Walsh.

— Disorderly gathering of women at Low Green, Workington, Cumberland, to protest against the price of butcher's meat.

— James Flynn, sentenced to death at the last Manchester Assizes for the murder of Johanna Nairn at Oldham, commits suicide in the county prison by starving himself.

— Charles Holmes, a labourer at Bromsgrove, executed at Worcester for the murder of his wife, whom, during their four years of married life, he had treated with systematic brutality.

13.—Triple execution within the walls of Maidstone gaol: viz., Francis Bradford, who murdered one of his comrades at Dover; Thomas Moore, who murdered his wife at Ashford; and James Tooth, the murderer of a drummer boy at the Marine Barracks, Chatham. The three men were tried, convicted, and sentenced to death by Mr. Baron Bramwell at the recent summer assizes at Maidstone. Tooth and Moore died instantly, but Bradford, being lighter, struggled for nearly ten minutes. Christopher Edwards was also executed within Stafford prison for the murder of his wife at Willenhall.

— Mr. G. Gilbert Scott, architect, gazetted a knight.

— A woman named Venables, living in Roman Road, Islington, with a cabman named Chatterton, murders her daughter, apparently under a fit of terror at apprehended ill-usage. She was tried on the 21st, and found guilty of murder, but recommended to mercy.

14.—Inauguration of the fountain erected in the West-end Park, Glasgow, to commemorate the introduction of the Loch Katrine water supply and the services rendered in connection with that great work by the late Lord Provost Stewart.

14.—The Queen arrives in Edinburgh for a stay of three days.

— The British Association met at Brighton under the presidency of Dr. Carpenter, who delivered an address having reference chiefly to the mental processes by which are formed the fundamental conceptions of matter and force, of cause and effect, of law and order, the basis of all exact scientific reasoning. To set up those sequences, he said, which we call laws as self-acting, either excluding or rendering unnecessary the power which alone could give them effect, appeared to him as arrogant as it was unphilosophical. Modern science, fixing its attention exclusively on the order of nature, had separated itself wholly from theology, whose function it was to seek after its cause, and herein science was justified; but when science assumed to set up its own conception of the order of nature as a sufficient account of its cause, it was invading a province of thought to which it had no claim.

15.—Died, aged 73, Dr. F. C. Skey, Demonstrator, Lecturer, and latterly Professor of Anatomy, and President for a time of the Royal College of Surgeons.

— The first Parliamentary contest under the Ballot Act takes place at Pontefract, Mr. Childers, the new Chancellor of the Duchy of Lancaster, receiving 658 votes against 578 given to Lord Pollington, presently professing Conservative principles, but in 1868 said to have sought an alliance with his present opponent on Liberal views.

16.—Commencement of a week's rioting between the Orangemen and Catholics of Belfast. Public-houses were sacked, workpeople mobbed, and Protestants in considerable numbers driven forcibly out of Catholic districts. On the 21st a policeman named Moore was shot, and several Catholic schools sacked.

— Mr. Stanley details to a crowded and enthusiastic meeting at Brighton his travels in search of Dr. Livingstone, and their happy termination in the discovery, at Ujiji, of the pale, careworn, grey-headed old man "dressed in a red shirt and crimson jo-ho, with a gold band round his cap, an old tweed pair of pants, and his shoes looking the worse for wear." The ex-Emperor Napoleon was among the audience, composed for the most part of members of the British Association.

19.—In the course of a missionary speech at Carlisle the Archbishop of Canterbury referred to the many natives of heathen lands to be seen in London, at the Queen's levees, at the Temple, and at the Eastern Homes, insisting that unless steps were taken for converting them the likelihood was that these heathen would be converting us. "I am almost," said his Grace, "afraid to say it, but I cannot help thinking that this great proximity of the East to ourselves has somehow or other infected the philosophy on which the young men feed in our great seminaries of learning, and that men of learning, from rubbing shoulders with men who altogether disbelieve in Christianity, have more toleration for that denial than they had in the olden times; and that systems which have existed for centuries in the extreme lands of heathenism are finding some sort of echo even among the literature and philosophy of this Christian country."

20.—Died in Glasgow, advanced in years, William Miller, known in Scotland as the "Nursery Poet."

21.—Murder and attempted suicide in a house of ill-fame in Langton Street, Chelsea, by two young Germans named May and Nagel, natives of Berlin, the latter, by mutual arrangement it was presumed, shooting himself through the heart after seriously wounding his friend.

22.— Prince Milan Obrenovitch IV. ascends the throne of Servia in succession to Prince Michel assassinated four years since.

— The failure announced of the old firm of Gledstanes and Co., East India merchants, Austinfriars, with liabilities set down at 1,722,235*l.*

23.—Mary Ann Cotton, "the poisoner," committed for trial by the Bishop-Auckland magistrates on the charge of murdering her stepson with intent to defraud a burial society.

24.—Attempt by J. B. Johnson to swim from Dover to Calais; failed after two experiments, when the circulation was so low as to compel his friends to lift him into the steamtender.

— The Pacific Mail Company's steamer *America* destroyed by fire in the harbour of Yokohama; between sixty and seventy passengers, mostly Chinese labourers, were killed, and a valuable cargo from San Francisco destroyed.

— The Prince of Wales visits M. Thiers at his marine residence at Trouville, where the President had been staying since the breaking up of the Assembly.

— Died, aged 65 years, Nathaniel Beardmore, civil engineer.

27.—Following up the remarks of the Archbishop of Canterbury on "the heathen" in London, S. B. Thakur, a Hindoo student, writes to the *Times*:—" It is possible that the fears of the Primate were groundless; but there is every reason to believe that Eastern philosophy and literature will exercise a very great and beneficial influence on English thought, because Arabic and Sanskrit—two out of the three most important languages of Asia—are being studied at the Universities of this country—the former by the students of theology as being indispensable to a critical acquaintance with Hebrew; the latter by classical scholars, as being absolutely necessary to a sound scholarship in Greek, Latin, and philological lore. Thus a day will come when our philosophers and logicians will be eagerly studied by the English youth, just as Aristotle and Plato are."

27.—The Queen presents Mr. Stanley with a snuff-box and a letter thanking him for his services in connection with the discovery of Dr. Livingstone. The young traveller afterwards visited the Queen at Dunrobin.

— Fire at Kentish Town railway station, destroying the upper part of the premises and some adjoining properties.

— The Spanish steamer *Perseveranza* wrecked near Oporto, and thirty of those on board drowned.

28.—The residence of Mr. Panizzi, at Sydenham, attacked by burglars, and one of the servants of the family injured in a fight which ensued.

29.—Termination of the strike of London carpenters.

— The Archbishop of York preaches a sermon in connection with the 600th anniversary of the hospital at Greatham, near Stockton-on-Tees.

31.—Mr. Speaker Brand, addressing his tenants on the estate of Glynde, proposes to give labourers a share in farming profits proportionate to the amount of capital they were able to invest. " If you have got 5*l.*," he said, "in the savings bank, and you would like to lend it to my farming business, I will engage to give you, as the savings-bank does, 2½ per cent. for the money ; and I will do more than that. I will—supposing the profits of the farm exceed 2½ per cent. for the money I have invested —give you precisely the same interest upon the capital you lend me. That is to say, supposing I get 10 per cent. as profit on the capital I have invested, you shall have 10 per cent. on your 5*l.* instead of 2½. So, you see, you will be in this position—that you will never get less than the 2½ per cent. you receive now, and if the farm yields more you will have the benefit of it. I am quite sure of this, that we shall never come to a satisfactory settlement of the relation between employer and employed until the latter, according to the amount of capital and labour he has invested, has an interest in the good conduct of the concern. My sole object is to give you a personal pecuniary interest in the conduct of the farm, and to endeavour to raise you a little above the position you now occupy as labourers."

September 2.—Consulted on the disputes between the Rugby masters, the Attorney-General writes that " it seems to him equally strange and deplorable that a head master should gravely put forward such matters as had been submitted to justify the virtual dismissal and possible ruin of a gentleman of ability and education engaged with him in teaching. The evidence is of the vaguest sort. There is absolutely nothing to connect Mr. Scott with Mr. Kynnersley's expressions, except the inferences of Dr. Hayman and Mr. B. Mr. Scott, I understand, denies that his letters were hostile to Dr. Hayman ; and it is in my judgment intolerable that a gentleman should be brought to book and threatened with dismissal because he has written to his relation as to what is going on at his school, and that relation has made strong comments on the head master. If this were permitted by the governing body to affect their minds, I cannot but observe that the position of an assistant-master at Rugby School, under such conditions, is not one which they can expect a gentleman with the feelings of a gentleman to undertake."

2.—International Congress of workmen opened at the Hague.

3.—Fire in Canterbury Cathedral, originating, it was thought, in the carelessness of workmen engaged in repairing the lead roof of the fabric. Owing to the scarcity of water, about 150 feet of the roof was consumed before the flames could be got under. The shrine of Thomas à Becket, together with the interesting portion of the edifice known as Becket's Corner and the tomb of the Black Prince, were in imminent danger; telegrams, indeed, at one period giving little hope of saving any portion of the magnificent fabric.

— Father Hyacinthe married at the Marylebone Registrar's office to Mrs. Merriman.

4. — The Hungarian Diet opened by the emperor.

— A company of Mormons, numbering five hundred and ninety, leave Liverpool in the *Minnesota* for New York on their way to Utah.

— Heavy thunderstorm in the northern and western counties, with loss of several lives. At Liskeard the telegraph office was destroyed by lightning.

5.—Alice Blanche Oswald, an American governess, aged twenty years, commits suicide by throwing herself off Waterloo Bridge into the Thames. She rose more than once screaming frantically, and seemed to be swimming, but sank twice before the Thames police-boat could reach her. She was well dressed. In her pocket was found a purse containing a halfpenny, a duplicate for a shawl pledged for 2*s.*, a wedding ring, a small box key, a dress ring with white stones, a pair of gilt earrings, small brooch, and a locket containing the miniature of a gentleman ; also several papers, and addresses of the American Minister, Consul, and others. At the inquest a letter written by deceased was read explaining the motives compelling her to self-destruction :—" Alone in London, not a penny or a friend to advise or lend a helping hand, tired and weary with looking for something to do, failing in every way, footsore and heart-weary, I prefer death to the dawning of another wretched morning. I have only been in Britain nine weeks. . . . Oh, God of heaven, have mercy on a poor helpless sinner ; Thou knowest how I have striven against this, but fate is against me. I cannot tread the path of sin, for my dead mother will be watching me. Fatherless, motherless, home I have none. Oh for the rarity of Christian hearts. I am now mad ; for days I have foreseen that this would be the end. May all who hear of my death forgive me, and may God Almighty do so, before whose bar I must soon appear. Farewell to all, to this beautiful, and yet wretched world.—Alice Blanche Oswald. I am twenty years of age the 14th of this month." The jury returned a verdict of " Suicide while in a state of temporary insanity."

5.—Foundation-stone laid of new harbour works at St. Helier's, Jersey.

6.—The Queen arrives at Dunrobin on a visit to the Duke of Sutherland ; and during her stay lays the foundation-stone of a monument in honour of the late Duchess.

— Explosion in the mixing-house of Curtis and Harvey's Hounslow powder works, causing serious damage to the works and the death of five people employed therein.

7.—Conference at Berlin between the Emperors of Austria, Germany, and Russia, attended with great military display, and torchlight "tattoo" in the evening.

— Commencement of the Autumn Military Manœuvres at Wimborne and Blandford Downs, under the command of Generals Sir John Michel and Sir Robert Walpole.

8.— Died, aged 80, Rev. Dr. Bisset, minister of Bourtie, formerly Moderator of the General Assembly, and in early life teacher at Udny Grammar School, where he had for pupils lads so well known afterwards as Sir James Outram, Dr. Joseph Robertson, and Dr. Hill Burton.

9.—The State elections in Maine carried by the Republicans.

11.—Social Science Congress opened at Plymouth by the President for the year, Lord Napier and Ettrick.

12.—Replying to an address from English Protestants expressive of sympathy in his struggle with the Ultramontanes, Prince Bismarck writes :—" I am glad that I agree with you in the principle that, in a well-regulated community, every person, to whatever profession of faith he may belong, should enjoy that amount of freedom which is compatible with the liberty and security of others and the independence of the country. In the battle for this principle God will protect the German Empire from opponents who take His name as a mask for their enmity against our peace at home."

— The Autumn - manœuvres closed by a "march past" at Beacon Hill, near Amesbury.

13.—A sermon on St. Bartholomew's Day, preached by Dean Stanley in Mr. Boyd's church, St. Andrew's, having recalled attention to the controversy regarding the approval said to have been expressed by Pope Gregory XIII.,

82

Dr. Newman now writes to the *Times* :— " Craft and cruelty, and whatever is base and wicked, have a sure Nemesis, and eventually strike the heads of those who are guilty of them. Whether in matter of fact Pope Gregory XIII. had a share in the guilt of the St. Bartholomew Massacre must be proved to me before I believe it. It is commonly said in his defence that he had an untrue, one-sided account of the matter presented to him, and acted on misinformation. This involves a question of fact, which historians must decide. But, even if they decide against the Pope, his Infallibility is in no respect compromised. Infallibility is not Impeccability. Even Caiaphas prophesied, and Gregory XIII. was not quite a Caiaphas."

13.—Replying to a criticism by Mr. Capes, Dr. Newman writes :—" He assumes that I did not hold or profess the doctrine of the Pope's Infallibility till the time of the Vatican Council, whereas I have committed myself to it in print again and again, from 1845 to 1867. And, on the other hand, as it so happens—though I hold it as I ever have done—I have had no occasion to profess it, whether in print or otherwise, since that date. Anyone who knows my writings will recollect that in so saying I state the simple fact. The surprise and distress I felt at the definition was no personal matter, but was founded on serious reasons of which I feel the force still." In another letter to the *Guardian* Dr. Newman writes : " It is true I was deeply, though not personally, pained both by the fact and by the circumstances of the definition ; and, when it was in contemplation, I wrote a most confidential letter, which was surreptitiously gained and published, but of which I have not a word to retract. The feelings of surprise and concern expressed in that letter have nothing to do with a screwing one's conscience to profess what one does not believe, which is Mr. Capes's pleasant account of me. He ought to know better."

— Two sisters, Alice and Jane M'Culloch, drowned off Cumbrae in the Firth of Clyde, by the upsetting of a pleasure-boat in a squall.

— Paris papers contain the text of a judgment delivered in the Brest scandal case, concerning the Jesuit Father Dufour and the Viscomtesse de Vielmont. The judgment pointed out that the case for the prosecution rested entirely on the evidence of the guard of the train, and that his statements were inconsistent with each other, and, in some particulars specified, not conceivably true. The accused were therefore entirely acquitted of the charge of indecency. At the same time, the judgment observed that the defendants had admitted familiarities which were " very reprehensible."

14.—Frederick Clappison, late secretary of the London and County Bank, examined at the Mansion House on a charge of forging transfer shares, and committed for trial. On the 25th he was sentenced to five years' penal servitude.

14.—The Geneva Court of Arbitration issue an award unanimously finding Great Britain liable for the acts committed by the *Alabama ;* by a majority of the Italian, Swiss, Brazilian, and United States arbitrators against the arbitrator appointed by Great Britain, they find Great Britain liable for the acts committed by the *Florida ;* and by a majority of the Italian, Swiss, and United States arbitrators against the arbitrators appointed by Great Britain and Brazil, they find Great Britain liable for the acts committed by the *Shenandoah* after leaving Melbourne. They unanimously decided that, in the cases in which Great Britain was held responsible, the acts of the tenders should be considered to follow the judgment given in regard to the cruisers to which they were attached. They decided that Great Britain was not responsible for the acts committed by the *Georgia,* or by any of the other Confederate cruisers except the three above named. They rejected altogether the claim of the United States Government for expenditure incurred in pursuit and capture of the cruisers. They decided that interest should be allowed, and have awarded a gross sum of 15,500,000 dollars in gold (about 3,229,166*l.* 13*s.* 4*d.*) in satisfaction and final settlement of all claims, including interest. The amount of the claims preferred before the Tribunal, as appears from the Revised Statement of Claims presented on the part of the United States in April last, was 19,739,095 dollars in gold, to which was added a claim for expenses of pursuit and capture to the amount of 7,080,478 dollars, with interest at 7 per cent. on the whole amount for about ten years, or, in all, 45,500,000 dollars in gold (or about 9,479,166*l.* 13*s.* 4*d.*) This award was signed by all the arbitrators except Sir A. Cockburn.

— Disturbance at Oxford in connection with the carrying out of the early closing clauses of the Licensing Act.

— Died at Nuremberg, aged 69, Ludwig Feuerbach, author of "Das Wesen der Religion," and numerous other philosophical works.

— M. Edmond About arrested by Germans at his private residence, Saverne, the alleged offence being seditious speaking and writing. He was liberated in a few days.

15.—In opening the Cortes, King Victor Amadeus described the Carlist insurrection as almost at an end, and promised to despatch to Cuba all the military strength necessary to suppress the insurrection ; "and when that end is attained bills would be introduced, specially intended for that dependency, relative to finances, justice, commerce, the army, and public instruction."

— Died, aged 73, Rev. Wm. Anderson, LL.D., a well-known Glasgow preacher.

— Ghent *fêtes* attended by a number of English volunteer commanders.

17.—Died, aged 81, Joseph Johnson, fifty years since an active associate of Hunt, Cobbett, and Bamford, and who had undergone two years' imprisonment as one of the leaders at Peterloo.

18.—Died at Malmö, aged 46, Charles XV. King of Sweden and Norway. Prince Regent Oscar was proclaimed as Oscar II.

19.—Roundhay Park, Leeds, opened by Prince Arthur. Next day he laid the foundation stone of the New Exchange.

— M. Thiers sets out for Paris from Trouville, where he had been honoured by the presence of French and English war ships.

20.—Captain Burton, formerly of Damascus, gazetted to be her Majesty's Consul at Trieste.

— Old Catholic Congress at Cologne opened. One motion submitted expressed a desire that the Governments of Germany, Austria, and Switzerland will :—1, Regard the Catholics adhering to the Old Catholic Church, and who reject the Vatican decrees as innovations, as members of the Church recognized by the State, and protect them as such ; 2, Deem the bishops recognizing the Vatican innovations and their organs as having no right of jurisdiction over the Old Catholics, who, moreover, are declared in the Vatican decrees not to belong to the New Catholic sect.

22.—Liberal gathering at Antwerp known as the "Banquet des Gueux," or Beggars' League, a name assumed in honour of an ancient confederation of noblemen, who in the middle of the sixteenth century received this contemptuous designation from Margaret of Parma. They vowed that they would make the name respected, and the "Beggars" soon afterwards revolted and drove the Spaniards from the Netherlands.

— Preparations for a banquet to M. Gambetta at Chambery suddenly stopped.

23.—Died, aged 66, her Serene Highness the Princess Hohenlohe-Langenburg, daughter of the Duchess of Kent, (by her first marriage with Emich Charles, reigning Prince of Leiningen), and half-sister of Queen Victoria.

— Partial strike of London bakers.

24.—A supplement to the *Gazette* sets forth the judgment and award of the Geneva Tribunal of Arbitration, the reasons of Lord Chief Justice Cockburn for dissenting from it, and the "opinions" presented during the progress of the case by Count Sclopis, the Viscount Itajuba, M. Staempfli, and Mr. Adams. Sir Alexander Cockburn's judgment was of a most elaborate character, and filled 250 pages. Writing of the alleged unfriendly feeling said to have been shown by Great Britain to the United States, Sir Alexander explained that a strong impression could not fail to be produced on the public mind by the energy, determination, and courage displayed by the South, and the generous ardour with which its population risked life and fortune in the desperate struggle for national independence, so resolutely maintained to the last against infinitely superior force. " Whatever the cause in which they are exhibited, devotion and courage will ever command respect ; and they did so in this instance. Men could not see in the united people of these vast provinces, thus risking all in the cause of nationality and independence, the common case of rebels, disturbing peace and order on account of imaginary grievances, or actuated by the desire of overthrowing a Government in order to rise upon its ruins. They gave credit to the statesmen and warriors of the South—their cause might be right or wrong—for the higher motives which ennoble political action ; and all the opprobrious terms which might be heaped upon the cause in which he fell, could not persuade the world that the earth beneath which Stonewall Jackson rests does not cover the remains of a patriot and a hero." Again, defending Earl Russell :—" When the history of Great Britain during the nineteenth century shall be written, not only will there be none among the statesmen who have adorned it whose name will be associated with greater works in the onward path of political progress than that of Earl Russell, but there will be none to whom, personally, an admiring posterity will look back with greater veneration and respect. That this distinguished man should feel deeply aggrieved by the unworthy attack· thus made on the Government of which he was a leading member, and on himself personally, it is easy to understand ; but there are attacks which recoil upon those who make them ; and of this nature are aspersions on the honesty and sincerity of Earl Russell." Sir Alexander concurred with his colleagues as to the *Alabama*, though not for the same reasons, but protested against the allowance of interest and the amount of it. He concluded by expressing an earnest hope that the decision will be accepted by the British people "with the submission and respect which is due to the decision of a tribunal by whose award it has freely consented to abide."

26.—Acknowledging the gift of the freedom of the city of Glasgow, Mr. Lowe censures Sir Alexander Cockburn for publishing his "reasons" for differing with the other arbitrators. "I very much regret," he said, "that my learned friend the Lord Chief Justice did not take the course of simply signing the award with the other arbitrators, it being perfectly well known that he differed from them in certain respects which would appear by the transaction or the award. When the thing is decided, and when we are bound to act upon it, and when we are not really justified in any feeling, I think, of honour or good faith, in making any reclamation or quarrel at all with what has been done in such circumstances, I think it is a great pity that he should have have thought it his duty to stir up and renew the strong arguments and contes's, on which the arbitrators had decided. At any rate, I think

if it was his opinion that we ought to acquiesce quietly and without murmur in the award, he had better not have published his arguments. If he had thought it right to publish his arguments he had better have retrenched his advice."

26. — M. Gambetta delivers a speech at Grenoble, in which he demands the dissolution of the Assembly, and expresses his distrust of " Republicans of the eleventh hour." Let us, he said, have no renegades in our ranks, and nothing to do with chiefs who now come over to us.

28. — Sir Sydney Waterlow elected Lord Mayor of London.

29.—Rev. Wm. Brock, D.D., retires from the Baptist Chapel, Bloomsbury, where he had ministered for twenty-five years.

30. — Close of the "option" in Alsace-Lorraine, when 88,000 emigrants are reported to have passed through Nancy. .

October 1. — Disestablishment Conference at Birmingham, called to induce Liberal leaders to adopt a new creed demanding immediate action against the National Churches of England and Scotland. Mr. Miall argued that Nonconformists should move every stone in order that the principle may be thoroughly well represented in the next Parliament, but he did not think that in every place, and especially in county constituencies, they should lay it down as a general rule that if they could not have a man purely avowing the principle of disestablishment, they should let the next general election go in favour of the Conservative party. They must not separate themselves altogether from the Liberal party on this question until they were prepared to do far more than they could do now.

— Lord Hatherley having resolved upon retiring from the woolsack, the Attorney-General, Sir Roundell Palmer, is generally mentioned as his probable successor.

— Died, aged 63, the Right Rev. Dr. Gray, Bishop of Capetown and Metropolitan of South Africa.

2.—The Escurial, built by Philip II. of Spain in honour of St. Lawrence, struck by lightning, and partly consumed.

— Eleven persons killed and many injured by the Scotch express from London running into a mineral train while some waggons were being shunted at the Kirtlebridge station of the Caledonian Railway. The first passenger carriage was not much injured, but the next three were broken up, and most of the killed found among the fragments. The stationmaster Currie was arrested pending an inquiry as to the position and working of the signals, and afterwards committed for trial on the double charge of culpable homicide and wilful violation of duty. An official report described four causes as contributing to the accident : the forgetfulness of the stationmaster ; the want of interlocked points and signals, worked from a properly placed cabin ; the absence not only of a telegraphic block system, but even of any telegraphic warning of the approach of the delayed train ; and the unpunctuality of the passenger train. Captain Tyler said there was no blame to be attributed to the railway servants with the passenger train. The whole onus of the accident rested with the stationmaster, who was represented to be a very careful and hard-worked man ; but if the particular points, the moving of which was the cause of the accident, had been interlocked with signals, it would have been impossible for the stationmaster or anyone else to cause the accident. This, and neither the block system nor notice by telegraph, was, Captain Tyler asserted, the precaution which was really required to prevent the accident. During the year 1871, out of 159 accidents, 53 were caused by the want of locking or other defective signal arrangements, and during the year 1870, out of 122 accidents, 60 were caused by the same means.

2.—Mr. Justice Willes commits suicide by shooting himself in his bedroom, at Otterspool, near Watford, where he was spending the vacation. On the afternoon of the 1st, his clerk noticed the Judge looking miserable and depressed, and complaining of want of sleep. This morning about two o'clock he heard a fall and a scream in the direction of the Judge's room, and on entering found him lying wounded on the floor slightly conscious. He survived only a few minutes. Other evidence given at the coroner's inquest showed that the deceased had long been suffering from ailments demanding rest and relaxation. Mr. Justice Willes was born in 1814, called to the bar of the Inner Temple in 1840, when he went the Home Circuit ; in 1850 he was appointed a member of the Common Law Commission, and raised to the bench as puisne judge of the Court of Common Pleas in 1855.

— Mr. Butt addresses his constituents at Limerick on Home Rule, pressing it as the duty of the Irish people to present to England the offer of a federal union under which they should have the full right of managing all Irish affairs, while they were willing to join with England on equal terms in the management of Imperial affairs. As to how he expected to obtain Home Rule, Mr. Butt said the next general election would, if Irishmen were true, give them from seventy to eighty members pledged to Home Rule. He thought in his conscience that if they returned eighty members pledged to Home Rule, the cause was won. He believed, he said, the great majority of the Irish people would be perfectly satisfied with a form of government that would give them the perfect and free management of their own affairs ; and that if the people of Ireland demanded separation, it was because they thought that was the only way of gaining independence.

— Died at Walmer, aged 86, Sir George Pollock, G.C.B., Constable of Marshal Tower, and engaged in important services in Nepaul in 1817, and Afghanistan in 1842-3, when he forced the Khyber Pass, and relieved the garrison at Jellalabad. He routed the Afghans, released the prisoners, and carried the English flag in triumph to Cabul. (See p. 119.) For these services Sir George received the thanks of both Houses of Parliament, and was made first a member of the Supreme Council of India, and then a Crown member of the Court of Directors. Sir George was buried with honour in Westminster Abbey on the 16th.

— Died, aged 65, Lieutenant-Colonel Robert Wylie, late Military Secretary to the Government of India.

6. — Religious ceremony at Lourdes, in honour of the appearance of the Virgin, attended by 40,000 "pilgrims" from all parts of France.

7.—Explosion in the Deep Pit of Marley Colliery, near Dewsbury, causing the death of thirty-four workmen out of forty-five employed in the seam where the accident occurred. The origin of the calamity was ascribed to the incautious use of matches by several of the miners to light their pipes.

8. — The State elections in Pennsylvania, Ohio, Indiana, and Nebraska carried by Republicans.

— The twelfth Church Congress opened at Leeds, under the presidency of the Bishop of Ripon. A stormy discussion took place on the 10th, on "The just principle of the Church's comprehensiveness in matters of doctrine and ritual," when a member present, who described himself as belonging to the Protestant Reformed Church of England, mentioned other speakers as talking like Roman Catholics. Scores of clergymen bawled and gesticulated, and the President for some time could neither direct nor check the disorder.

11.—Republican rising at Ferrol, in Spain.

— Died, aged 66, his Excellency Baron de Beaulieu, Belgian Minister at the Court of St. James's.

— Bonds and coupons to the amount of 40,000l. stolen from the house of John Allan, Derby Terrace, Glasgow, during the absence of the family. The theft was afterwards traced to a man named Fraser, and the bonds recovered in a quarry on the Gareloch.

12.—On the subject of Home Rule for Ireland Earl Russell writes :—"I fear, if an Irish Parliament is set up in Ireland, all her energies will be wasted in political contention. I therefore wish to divert the forces which might give heat and comfort instead of concentrating them in a manner to produce a conflagration. This is the more necessary, as the Irish nature is so very inflammable that it

85

...onfire to the warmth of a moderate **fire.** I fear, however, that wisdom will be wanting both in England and Ireland."

12.—Died, aged 70, Vladimir Dahl, compiler of a "Dictionary of the Living Russian Tongue," and historian of Muscovite folk-lore.

— Prince Napoleon expelled from France by order of M. Thiers. He arrived at Geneva under an escort next day.

13.—Died at Kilmoran Castle, aged 79, Sir David Baxter, a generous Dundee merchant.

— Died, aged 77, Albany William Fonblanque, formerly proprietor and editor of the *Examiner*, and latterly head of the Statistical Department of the Board of Trade.

14.—Mr. J. S. Mill, writing from Avignon, explains to a Nottingham association his views on their programme described in "The Law of the Revolution." "There is no real thing called 'the revolution,' nor any 'principles of the revolution.' There are maxims which your association, in my opinion, rightly considers to be essential to just government; and there is a tendency, increasing as mankind advances in intelligence and education, towards the adoption of the doctrines of just government. These are all the facts there are in the case, and the more clearly and unambiguously these, and nothing but these, are stated, the better people will understand one another, and the more distinctly they will see what they are disputing about and what they are avowed to prove. . . . I cannot conclude without expressing the great pleasure with which I have seen the full and thoroughgoing recognition by your body of the claim of women to equal rights in every respect with men, and of minorities proportionately to their numbers with majorities, and its advocacy of the federal principle for the security of this last."

— Opening of the new Japan railway from Jeddo to Yokohama.

15.—In the course of an audience at Balmoral, Lord Hatherley formally surrenders the Great Seal, and is succeeded by Sir R. Palmer, now Lord Selborne. In taking leave of his constituents at Richmond, the latter wrote:—"In the high office to which her Majesty has been pleased to call me I trust I may be enabled, by God's blessing, so to act as not to forfeit your good opinion, nor give you any cause to regret that my name has been so long associated with the borough of Richmond."

— Died, aged 49, Rev. John Purchas, of St. James's Chapel, Brighton, a ritualist leader whose case had repeatedly occupied the attention of the Judicial Committee of Privy Council.

— Died, somewhat unexpectedly, the Countess of Shaftesbury, eldest daughter of the late Viscountess Palmerston, by her first marriage with Earl Cowper.

15.—Unveiling of a statue erected to the memory of Sir Humphrey Davy at Penzance, where the great natural philosopher was born in 1778.

— The Count de Chambord writes to La Rochette from Ebenzweyer:—"As a whole France is Catholic and Monarchical; it is for us to caution it against errors, to point out the rocks, and to direct it towards the port. I trust that I have never failed in that sacred duty, and no one will ever be able to seduce me from my path. I have not one word to retract, not an act to regret, for they have all been inspired by love of my country; and I insist upon my share of responsibility in the advice which I give to my friends. The day of triumph is still one of God's secrets, but have confidence in the mission of France. Europe has need of it, the Papacy has need of it, and therefore the old Christian nation cannot perish."

— Mr. J. A. Froude, presently lecturing to American audiences on the political relations between England and Ireland, entertained at a banquet in Delmonico's, New York, by literary men and publishers.

16.—Foreign Office circular issued to Chambers of Commerce explanatory of the negotiations with France relative to the new Commercial Treaty.

— Died at Boston, aged 61, Mrs. Parton, sister of N. P. Willis, and widely known in literary circles under the *nom de plume* of "Fanny Fern."

— The Emperor of China married at Pekin. There was no public ceremony outside the palace, beyond the procession to bring the bride, the Lady Aluto, daughter of Chungchi, a doctor of the Imperial Academy.

17.—Correspondence with Russia regarding the disputed Afghan boundaries. Earl Granville writes to-day that her Majesty's Government considers as fully belonging to the Ameer of Cabul (1) Badakshan, with its dependent district of Wakhan from the Sarikol (Woods Lake) on the east to the junction of the Kokcha River with the Oxus (or Penjah), forming the northern boundary of this Afghan province throughout its entire extent. (2) Afghan Turkestan, comprising the districts of Kunduz, Khulm, and Balkh, the northern boundary of which would be the line of the Oxus from the junction of the Kokcha River to the post of the Khoja Saleh, inclusive, on the high road from Bokhara to Balkh. Nothing to be claimed by the Afghan Ameer on the left bank of the Oxus below Khoja Saleh. (3) The internal districts of Aksha, Seripool, Maimenat, Shibberjan, and Andkoi, the latter of which would be the extreme Afghan frontier possession to the north-west, the desert beyond belonging to independent tribes of Turcomans. (4) The western Afghan frontier between the dependencies of Herat and those of the Persian province of Khorassan is well known, and need not here be defined. Prince Gortscnakoff's reply to this despatch, of date St. Petersburg, December 7, stated that General Kaufmann, owing to various difficulties, had been unable to carry out his investigation as speedily as the Russian no less than the British Government desired. The conclusions drawn by the Russian Government did not much differ substantially from those of the British Government, but Russia was unable to find any traces of sovereignty exercised by the Ameer of Cabul over Badakshan and Wakhan; "on the contrary, all our information upon the subject goes to prove that these districts should be regarded as independent."

17.—Mr. Justice Denman sworn into the vacant judgeship in the Court of Common Pleas.

— The Prince of Wales, now on a visit to the Earl of Tankerville, engages in a wild bull hunt in Chillingham Forest, and brings down with his rifle the king of the herd, about seven years old and weighing upwards of sixty stone.

— Lord Northbrook holds a public durbar at Umballa. In a brief address the Viceroy referred to the loss which the native princes had sustained by the death of Lord Mayo, and thanked them for their prompt action on the occasion of the Kooka outbreak.

— A Great Eastern express train runs off the line at a cutting near Kelvedon, killing one person, injuring twenty others, and destroying several carriages.

— Died suddenly at Campbeltown, Dr. Finlayson, Scotch clergyman.

18.—Died at Auburn, aged 70, W. H. Seward, late Foreign Secretary for the United States.

— Collision between two mineral trains at Woodhouse Junction, near Sheffield, causing the death of an engine driver and stoker, with great damage to rolling stock.

19.—A man and woman, names unknown, found dead in their lodgings in Golden Square. A phial labelled strychnine was on the table. There was also, in a man's handwriting, a note in English to the following effect :—"Our last will. We wish the trunk and the contents to be given to Mrs. Cunningham in return for the trouble given her. The rest may serve to pay the expenses of the funeral. Nobody is to blame, as we both took strychnine, and we wish to remain unknown. We have done no wrong to anybody. O Lord, forgive us all, and pardon us, for Thine infinite mercies. We leave 5*l.*, 1*l.* to be given to Mrs. Cunningham for one week's rent. The rest for the burial. 'Though I walk through the valley of the shadow of death, I will fear no evil ; for Thou art with me : Thy rod and Thy staff they comfort me.'" No papers of any description which could lead to the identity of the persons were found, but from the appearance of the grate in the room a number of papers were destroyed

before suicide was committed. A rumour was afterwards circulated that the bodies were those of Captain and Mrs. Douglas, Richmond.

19.—The *Batavier* steamer, the largest of the vessels of the Netherlands Steam Packet Company, run into in Barking Reach by the Turkish screw man-of-war *Charkec*, and sank in a few minutes.

— New chapel at Rugby School consecrated by the Bishop of Worcester.

20.—Found dead in his bed at Geneva, Dr. Merle d'Aubigné, the historian of the Reformation. The venerable divine was in his 79th year.

— Died in his lodgings near Tottenham Court Road, Dr. Frederick Welwitsch, a high authority on the flora of Africa.

21.—Telegraphic communication between London and Adelaide completed.

— Panic in Hengler's Circus, Sheffield, caused by the falling of a gallery during an acrobatic performance.

— The council of the Royal Geographical Society, with some officers of the late Abyssinian Expedition, entertain Mr. Henry M. Stanley at a banquet in Willis's Rooms. It was announced by the chairman, Sir H. Rawlinson, that the Society had that day decreed to Mr. Stanley the Victoria Medal of 1872.

— The Emperor of Germany, as arbitrator in the San Juan difficulty, gives an award that the claims of the United States fully accord with the true interpretation of the treaty of the 15th of June, 1846, and that the boundary line has, therefore, to run through the Haro Channel.

22.—Died, aged 54, George Mason, A.R.A., a prominent English landscape-painter.

— Died, aged 82, Simon Thomas Scrope, of Danby Hall, York, the representative of a house which during the last 300 years produced two earls, twenty barons, one Chancellor, four Treasurers, two Chief Justices of England, five Knights of the Garter, and numerous baronets.

23.—Died at Paris, aged 61, M. Théophile Gautier, dramatist and journalist.

24.—Addressing his constituents at Exeter, Sir John Coleridge said that no Ministry in the world ever fulfilled the expectations that were raised about it, and no man that ever lived, not Pitt, nor Peel, nor Palmerston, ever maintained the power with which he began. It therefore would not surprise him, Sir John Coleridge said, if after four years of administration the foes of the Government were found to be more active and its friends somewhat more disunited than in the winter of 1868. The Tories were always united. There are five hundred ways of going forward, but one way of standing still. To stand still and observe the Government seemed to be their best idea of a policy. To tell the persons who listen to them that the Government has alienated the colonies and humiliated the country is about the limit of their topics. Now, neither of those charges was true. The colonies are not alienated, and he could see no trace anywhere of the waning influence of England in her attitude toward foreign Powers. "I see none, for instance," he said, "in the eagerness of the French Government to conclude the new French Treaty. I can see none at all even in the Treaty of Washington, or in the Geneva award. I admit there is a good deal in the caustic language of the Chancellor of the Exchequer. I admit that there is still more in the splendid specimen of reason and eloquence which we owe to the matured vigour and extraordinary powers of the Lord Chief Justice of England. I admit that there is a good deal in this and other things to make an Englishman's face hot and his blood to tingle. I admit that when one reads some of the American arguments, though I am a man of peace, my fingers itch. I admit that it is not a matter for great pride, but it is a matter for acquiescence. I cannot help feeling that on the whole we are well out of a bad business."

26.—Lord Westbury, as arbitrator in the liquidation of the European Insurance Company, decides that shareholders who under the deed of settlement had a portion of the dividends accredited to them, as an addition to the amount paid by them on uncalled capital, are entitled to have that amount deducted from the amount of uncalled capital for which they are liable.

— John Dorrington, described as Master of Ripley College, Derbyshire, sentenced at Marlborough Street Police Court to two months' imprisonment with hard labour for fraudulently obtaining charitable subscriptions.

27.—Died, aged 61, Sir Alexander Duff Gordon, Commissioner of Inland Revenue.

28.—Died, aged 80, Miss Jeffrey, a granddaughter of Flora Macdonald, companion for a time of Prince Charles Stuart in his Highland wanderings after Culloden.

— Two Roman Catholic Bishops consecrated with great ceremony at Salford.

30.—Died, aged 57, John Chubb, inventor and maker of the well-known locks which bear his name.

— Died at Oxford suddenly, Thomas Combe, M.A., printer to the University of Oxford, and founder of St. Barnabas' Church and the Chapel of the Radcliffe Infirmary.

— Died at Hartrigge, Lord Kinloch, Senator of the College of Justice, Edinburgh.

— The Suez Canal Company erect a monument at Suez to the memory of Lieutenant Waghorn, the enterprising pioneer of the Overland and Red Sea Route to India and China.

31.—Sixty thousand persons reported to be rendered homeless in Italy by floods.

31.—The Prussian House of Peers, by 145 to 18 votes, reject a County Electoral Reform Bill, designed to establish local representative institutions in the rural districts. Count Eulenberg afterwards announced that the King was resolved to pass the measure, and would immediately close the session.

— At a luncheon given by the Lord Provost of Edinburgh, Mr. H. M. Stanley charges Dr. Kirk with speaking harshly of Dr. Livingstone.

— Died, aged 57, John Francis Maguire, M.P. for Cork, and editor of the *Cork Examiner*.

November 1.—The Oxford Music Hall destroyed by fire.

— Field-Marshal Sir William M. Gomm, G.C.B., gazetted Constable of the Tower and Custos Rotulorum of the Tower Hamlets.

— Dinner in Willis's Rooms, presided over by Earl Stanhope, to Mr. W. J. Thoms on the occasion of his retirement from the editorship of *Notes and Queries*, which he had held since its commencement in November 1849. On the same evening a dinner was given in the same place by the Royal Geographical Society to Sir Bartle Frere, previous to setting out on his special mission to Zanzibar.

— The trial of Mayor Hall at New York for participation in the Tammany frauds ends in the discharge of the jury on account of their not being able to agree upon a verdict. They were locked up from 9.30 P.M. on the 31st of October till 11 A.M. on the following day, and it was reported in court that they had spent the night in political discussion.

2.—The *Morning Post* announces that it enters this day on the 101st year of its existence, its principles having been during that time uniformly "loyal and national."

— Launch of the *Hansa*, the first German ironclad built in a German dockyard.

— Unveiling of the statue erected to the memory of Sir Walter Scott in the Mall of the Central Park, New York.

3.—Sunday meeting in Hyde Park to demand the release of Fenian prisoners.

— Rev. C. Voysey celebrates in St. George's Hall, Langham Place, for the first time, the service of "dedication and benediction of children," a substitute for the ancient ceremony of baptism.

— Correspondence between the Duke of Marlborough and the Attorney-General regarding the eviction of certain labourers from the Blenheim 'estate. "The Duke" writes Sir John, "denies that his estates have ever been granted by the State. It is hardly worth controversy; but I was under the impression that they were granted and *inalienably* settled by Act of Parliament soon after the battle of Blenheim. If I am wrong in this I shall be happy to apologize. The Duke says I am 'pleased to style him a Tory duke,' and seems annoyed that I have done so. I meant no more offence than he would mean if he called me a Liberal Attorney-General. I have heard the great leader in whose Cabinet he served speak of himself as 'the leader of the Tory party in the House of Commons;' but, as the Duke objects to the epithet, I regret that I used it, and should I have occasion to allude to him again in public I will take care to avoid it." To this the Duke made answer:—"What I denied was that the 'vast estates' to which he alluded in his speech in connection with my cottage property had ever been so granted. I beg to refer him to 3 and 4 Anne, cap. 6, an Act to enable the Queen, by letters patent, to grant to the Duke of Marlborough the honour and manor of Woodstock and Hundred of Wootton. He will there see the identical lands granted, with their names and admeasurements, and will be able to form his own opinion what proportion they bear to the total acreage of my landed property. For the information of the public I may say that they are almost exclusively park, pleasure-grounds, and woods, and comprise little over 500 acres outside and adjoining the park itself; and, with the exception of lodges and keepers' houses, there are no cottages whatever upon the lands in question. The Attorney-General, if he cares to peruse this Act, will perhaps be candid enough to admit that he has been indulging in the same strain of rhetoric to which in his letter of to-day he has already pleaded guilty."

4.—Anti-slavery meeting at the Mansion House, called to strengthen the mission about to be undertaken by Sir Bartle Frere to suppress the slave trade on the East Coast of Africa.

— Discovery of human remains at Cropton, near Pickering, Yorkshire, supposed to be those of Joseph Wood and his son James, tenants of the farm, who had been missing since May last, and whose residence was now occupied by a person named Charter, pretending to have authority to act for the Woods.

5.—Dr. Cookson, Master of St. Peter's College, elected Vice-Chancellor of Cambridge University by 40 votes against 26 tendered for Dr. Atkinson, Master of Clare College.

— The new Library and Museum erected by the Corporation of the City of London opened by the Lord Chancellor in the presence of nearly 2,000 guests. Lord Selborne, in a brief address, dwelt on the zeal for education which the City of London had uniformly manifested, even as far back as what were sometimes called "the dark ages," and said that in building this beautiful library the City was only adding the finishing touch to a work which had been going on consistently for ages. The speech of the Lord Chancellor was received throughout with much enthusiasm, and, at its close, his lordship was conducted through the building, and inspected the works of art and objects of antiquarian interest there displayed. The Crypt

and the Guildhall itself, both brilliantly lighted, were also thrown open to visitors.

5.—Electors for the Presidential contest in America chosen for the different States, the number being equal to the Senators and Representatives sent by each. Large majorities found to vote for Grant and Wilson, the former carrying thirty States with 278 votes against Mr. Greeley's seven States with 74 votes.

— A young hippopotamus, afterwards known as "Guy Fawkes," born in the Zoological Gardens, Regent's Park.

6.—Died, aged 80, Thomas Keightley, author of "Fairy Mythology" and various histories.

— M. Rochefort granted a temporary release from prison for the purpose of marrying the mother of his illegitimate children, understood to be dying at Versailles.

7.—Mr. E. J. Reed, replying to criticisms on his recent letters on the Navy, writes:— "In spite of our recent and even present strength, so many powerful ships are springing up abroad that we are falling astern in the chase, and by our total inaction, extending now over years, are losing even the chance of competing. I have not sought to excite apprehension of imminent danger. My forecasts necessarily go into the future, and I maintain that, looking to the future, our recent policy has been involving us in very serious risks and disadvantages."

8.—In his closing visitation at Tonbridge, the Archbishop of Canterbury expressed his gratification that the Church of England had worthy and prominent representatives at the recent meeting of the Old Catholics at Cologne; and while sympathizing with the endeavours that have been made and are still making to promote a better understanding among the Episcopal Churches, he looked back with pleasure to what he did ten years ago as Bishop of London towards giving a kindly welcome to pastors from Germany, from France, from Switzerland, and from the Waldensian valleys. He recognized the fact that, both historically and doctrinally, the Church of England has affinities to very different forms of Christian thought and organization, and contended that these varied affinities give the Church a particular fitness for attempting the work of reconciliation. The Archbishop also took occasion to speak of the comprehensiveness of the Church of England as combining the perfection of civil and ecclesiastical society : "There are certain names which occur to us of famous ministers of the Church of England—Archbishop Whately, Thomas Arnold, Frederick Denison Maurice, Frederick Robertson—to name only those who have gone to their rest. These are not the names of the clergy who are the most popular throughout England ; but I am bold to maintain that they. are the names of men who have done a good work in their day and generation, for their very presence among us has been a standing protest against any notion that inquiry and a fearless love of truth can be inconsistent with the Gospel which we preach. If these men had lived under another system and in another age, it might have been very difficult to say what would have become of them. They certainly could not have joined the Church of Rome without crushing their convictions, as many have done in past ages under the weight of overwhelming tyranny, or seeking relief from their doubts and scruples by a silence akin to death. But, also, I say that these men could not well have found a home in any of the ordinary sects which exist among us. It is then, I am bold to say, no blame to the Church of England, but rather it may be its pride, that it is able to inclose within its fold the most active and inquiring intellects, and that it has no fear lest a bold examination of truth should destroy those truths of God in which it teaches men to hope for their salvation."

8.—Châlons evacuated by the Germans.

— The *Gazette* sets forth the details of the new Commercial Treaty with France, Article 2 stating that the President of the French Republic having represented to her Majesty that the financial necessities of France imperatively require the imposition of new taxes in that country, and the modification for that purpose of the tariff stipulations previously in force, her Majesty, in "a spirit of friendship towards France," consents to such modification. The contracting parties guarantee to each other the treatment of the most favoured nation. The provisions with regard to tariffs are to remain in force until the 1st of January, 1877, and those with regard to navigation until the 1st of July, 1879.

— Vice-Chancellor Bacon gives judgement in the case of the assignees of the Countess d'Alteyrac against the estate of the late Lord Willoughby d'Eresby. Under the award of Mr. Vernon Harcourt, the Countess was to receive a capital sum of 5,000*l.* in respect of her action, and Lord Willoughby d'Eresby to settle upon her an annuity of 1,200*l.* within a certain time, and in the event of his failing to legally secure it to her, an additional payment of 100*l.* a month was awarded until the annuity was purchased by his lordship. The annuity not having been purchased, the payment of 100*l.* a month was made until the death of his lordship in August 1870. In 1860 the Countess was adjudicated a bankrupt, and her assignees made the present claim. It was contended that the assignees were only entitled to the value of the annuity as if it had been purchased on the day of his lordship's death, and also that the Countess was not entitled to the additional payments of 100*l.* a month, as they were in the nature of penalties, and therefore void. The Vice-Chancellor held that the assignees were entitled to have an annuity of 1,200*l.* purchased, and that until the day of payment the annuity of 100*l.* was payable in pursuance of the award.

9.—Commencement of a fire in Boston, U.S., laying waste a large portion of the business part of the city, and causing gigantic loss to those engaged in commerce. It broke out in the evening at the corner of Summer Street and Kingston Street, ran along Summer Street both ways to the north-west and to the south-east, increased greatly in intensity by a violent north-westerly gale. Block after block of substantial granite buildings crumbled before its fury. By four o'clock on Sunday morning (10th) twenty-two squares were destroyed, the burnt district at that time covering about sixty acres, bounded by Summer Street on the south-west, Big Broad Street on the south-east, Pearl Street on the north-east, Milk Street on the north, and Washington Street on the north-west. The Boston Fire Department was crippled by the epidemic among the horses, this also preventing to a great extent the removal of the goods. Aid summoned from Worcester, Providence, New York, Fall River, Lowell, Lynn, and other towns, was promptly sent. All the railways coming into Boston ran fast trains, bringing firemen from the neighbouring cities, many companies arriving before three in the morning. The police being unable to maintain order, the United States troops and marines stationed there were ordered on duty. Extensive plundering went on during the confusion ; and 200 thieves, some of them women, were arrested. The loss of life was heavy, but it was impossible to tell the number accurately. The old South Church, the most interesting monument in Boston, where Warren defied the Royal authority, delivered his oration on the Boston massacre, where resistance to the tea-tax was organized, and for a century and a half the election sermons were preached to the Governors of Massachusetts, was among the buildings destroyed. Latterly the progress of the fire could only be arrested by blowing up blocks of valuable property. At noon on Sunday it was believed the fire was under control, after lasting for twenty hours and destroying seventy acres of buildings. Shortly after midnight, however, flames broke out again, owing to explosions of gas, and destroyed six more large stores with the Exchange and Post Office. In all it was reported that 959 buildings were destroyed, 125 being private buildings ; 35 persons were reported killed, 2,043 firms and individuals suffered pecuniary loss. The insurances were estimated at 48,000,000 dols., half the policies being in Massachusetts companies.

— Mr. H. M. Stanley, the discoverer of Dr. Livingstone, leaves Liverpool for America.

— At the Lord Mayor's banquet to-night, Earl Granville, in the absence of Mr. Gladstone through indisposition, devoted the greater part of his speech to the new commercial treaty, declaring his belief that its principle and substance are strictly in accordance with free trade. On the subject of their general policy and procedure, Lord Granville claimed for the Government that they might be considered the most hard-worked set of public men he had ever known; and he had no doubt they would maintain that character till they reached what he trusted would be an honourable death.

9.—Bank rate raised from 6 per cent., at which it was fixed on the 10th October, to 7 per cent.

10.—Hadley's City Flour Mills in Upper Thames Street, near Blackfriars Bridge, destroyed by fire. The building, towering high above all its neighbours, and pierced it was said with 400 windows, was built in accordance with a plan by which it was thought that a fire if it broke out might be strictly confined to that part in which it originated. The floors sprang chiefly from massive pillars of stone resting on foundations of the utmost solidity, and each story was supported by iron girders of great strength. The fire was observed about 7 A.M., and after this the floors one by one gradually gave way from the top, falling on each other, and so bursting out the walls. One fireman was killed.

— The golden wedding of the King and Queen of Saxony celebrated at Dresden in presence of a great gathering of princes and distinguished persons, including the Emperor and Empress of Germany. Bishop Forwork pronounced the benediction, concluding by asking the King and Queen, "Do you promise, in the sight of God, to remain true till the end of your days to the indissoluble tie entered into fifty years ago, and, with conjugal unity and mutual help, to serve God until God you do part?" The King and Queen answered in a loud voice, "Yes." Thereupon the priestly blessing was bestowed. The whole party proceeded to the Court Church, where *Te Deum* was sung amid rifle firing and salvoes of artillery.

11.—Sir James Hannen, one of the justices of the Court of Queen's Bench, appointed to the Probate and Divorce Court, in room of Lord Penzance, resigned.

13.—M. Thiers delivers his Presidential Message to the National Assembly at Versailles, consisting mainly of a commercial and financial retrospect describing the condition of France in most favourable terms. Respecting finance he anticipated a deficit of about 130 millions for the current year, but thought a surplus of about 80 millions of francs might be calculated on for 1873. Regarding the Treaty of Commerce he said that England had consented to put off until the year 1876 her being placed on an equality with other countries under the most favoured nation clause. The duty on raw materials was to be enforced in March next, and other duties to come into operation on the 1st of December in the present year. M. Thiers concluded by saying: "We draw near to a decisive moment. The form of this Republic has been only an incidental form, given by events and reposing upon your wisdom and your union with the power which you have

temporarily chosen. But the public mind is awaiting your action. All are asking what day and what form you will select in order to give to the Republic that conservative strength with which she cannot dispense. It is for you to choose both the day and the form. The country, in delegating to you its powers, has evidently laid upon you the task of saving it, by procuring for it, first, peace, after peace order, and with order the restoration of its power; and, lastly, a regular Government."

14.—Twenty-two lives lost by the flooding of the Kelsall Hall Colliery, Walsall. At the time of the accident thirty men and boys were in the mine in various parts of the workings. These had gone to their work, as usual, at half-past six in the morning, and at nine had the customary interval of half an hour for breakfast. During this brief interval an immense volume of water suddenly burst into the mine and poured with great force through the workings. Two men named Stanley and Starkey were the first to perceive the inundation and gave the signal to be drawn up. On reaching the bank they announced that the pit was flooded. The cage was at once let down with an exploring party, who found that the water was already ascending the shaft, and on the surface of the flood nine men and boys were with extreme difficulty keeping themselves afloat. They clutched with great eagerness at the cage as it neared the water, and all of them were rescued. The others still remained scattered in the various workings of the mine. Notwithstanding the apparent impossibility of reaching any of these, the cage was let down a second time. But the explorers found to their dismay that the water in the shaft had risen to such a height as to render approach to the men possible by no other means than the prodigiously difficult task of pumping the whole volume of water out of the mine. This went on for several days, as much as 1,000 gallons per minute being raised at one time by the pumping apparatus; but even this did not permit the rescue of any of the workmen left in the pit. About five o'clock on the morning of the 20th, three workmen forced their way about 160 yards from the bottom, and found eighteen of the missing miners. Ten lay upon the floor of the mine, seven others were crowded together in a sitting posture on two tubs, and the eighteenth, an old man named Starkey, was just beyond. Their clothes were dry, and the appearance of the place showed that water had never reached their level, and that death must therefore have resulted from choke-damp.

15.—A recent case of "tunding" at Winchester leading to a controversy on the subject of "fagging" at public schools, the "Victim" writes in defence of the system: "The punishment I received is universally allowed (and readily by the Prefect himself) to have been excessive; at the same time I firmly believe, as everyone else here does, that there was no tyranny or brutality in the matter. On the contrary, it was done in an honest though mistaken impression that serious insubordination was intended by my refusal to obey him. That being the case, I consider that though his action may in some degree deserve condemnation, he himself and his motives deserve respect. I may add that this letter is written entirely of my own motion and under no compulsion whatever."

15.—In the case of Earl Beauchamp *v.* the Overseers of Madresfield, the Court of Common Pleas decide against the right of Peers to vote for members of the House of Commons.

— The feast of St. Eugénie celebrated at Chiselhurst by a great gathering of friends of the Empire.

16.—Mutiny among the metropolitan police owing to the dismissal of Goodchild, secretary to their movement for increase of pay. Four days later an order was issued dismissing 109 constables and reducing others in rank and pay. Inquiry into grievances had previously been promised.

— Public funeral of the fireman Guernsey, who lost his life at the burning of the City Flour Mills. The route to Abney Park Cemetery was lined with spectators.

18.—Died, aged 83, James Capel, the oldest member of the Stock Exchange, and formerly chairman of the Board of Managers.

— Questioned by General Changarnier as to his comments on M. Gambetta's Grenoble speech, M. Thiers declares that for forty years he had fought against Socialism and Demagogy; for the last two years he had shown no lack of energy. "I was not undecided under the walls of Paris." (Noise.) "I have not been undecided in repressing the 'strikes'—("Bravo," from the Left Centre) ;—but I cannot admit that I ought to be called upon to rise here to make a profession of faith which is rendered useless by my whole career. Let us be frank. It is not the Grenoble banquet which is the real question ; it is something higher. Everybody knows what it is that makes you uneasy. Well, since you complain of a Provisional Government, make a definitive one. (Shouts of applause from the Left and Left Centre.) For my own part, I declare that I will not reply. If you would have a strong Government, say that it is strong, but not that it is undecided. No, I will not reply. Since you exhibit this distrust of me, I beg of you to lose no more time. Proceed at once to a vote. I call for a vote of confidence. I demand it instantly. I am not even afraid to take the country as a judge between you and me." (Prolonged applause.) A vote of confidence in the Government was ultimately carried by 267 to 117 votes.

21.—Statue of Queen Victoria unveiled at Montreal in presence of the Governor-General, Lord Dufferin.

—Paul Julius May, the survivor of what was known as the "Chelsea Tragedy," acquitted at

the Central Criminal Court of complicity in the murder of his friend Nagel ; Mr. Justice Grove ruling that the jury in order to convict must be satisfied that the suicide was a joint act in which each assisted or encouraged the other. The prisoner, now restored to health, was afterwards committed on a charge of forgery.

21.—Died, aged 73, Richard James Lane, A.R.A., one of the two associate engravers of the "old class" in the Academy.

— Sir Bartle Frere leaves England on his mission to Zanzibar to negotiate for the suppression of the East African slave trade.

23.—Died at Claremont, Exeter, aged 80, Sir John Bowring, first editor of the *Westminster Review*, and for many years representative of British interests in China.

—Fifty-six betting-men brought before the Lord Mayor ; one was fined 50*l.*, another 5*l.*, and the rest dismissed with a caution.

25.—The *Royal Adelaide*, bound from London to Sydney, wrecked on the Chesil bank, Portland.

26.—M. Batbie presents to the Assembly the report . of the Kerdrel Commission appointed to consider M. Thiers' Message, declaring that "Freedom of deliberation, concord between the Assembly and the Executive, and the dignity of the President of the Republic—all these things are motives for organizing Ministerial responsibility, and for doing so without delay. Moreover, unity between the public powers cannot any longer be postponed. Although the observations we have made touched upon the position and person of M. Thiers, we have not feared to wound him by communicating them to him. We were sure that the great historian would not be surprised to see the representatives of his country seek means of assuring the value of their votes."

— Came on for trial at Westminster before Mr. Justice Brett and a full special jury, an action raised by Mr. Hepworth Dixon against the proprietors of the *Pall Mall Gazette* for libellous criticism contained in an article on "Free Russia," and on the plaintiff's appearance as president of a meeting called in St. George's Hall to hear Elder Evans. In the latter he was described as the "Shaker's friend," and in the former it was said—"We have received from Mr. Hepworth Dixon another of those insolent ingenious letters with which he contrives to puff his books—obscene, inaccurate, or both—as soon as they appear." The plaintiff was severely cross-examined regarding the accuracy of some of his books of travel, and on the propriety of certain views on social subjects set forth in his "Spiritual Wives ;" Sir John Karslake on the third day of trial concluding a speech of over five hours' length with the words : "As you say you are a member of a high and honourable guild or calling, I say you have prostituted that calling, that you have palmed off as being works of philosophy things which you knew were works of filth. You have injured that high calling to which you belong, and you are a writer of obscene and vamped-up books." Verdict for the plaintiff—farthing damages.

28.—Sir Donald M'Leod killed on the Metropolitan Railway when attempting to enter a train in motion at Gloucester Road station.

29.—Died, aged 61, Horace Greeley, an enterprising American journalist, recently a candidate for the Presidency.

— Died at Naples, aged 93, Mrs. Mary Somerville, authoress of "The Connection of the Physical Sciences," an honorary member of the Royal Astronomical Society, and to the closing weeks of her life a devoted enthusiast in the higher departments of mathematical science. Her last important work on Molecular and Microscopic science, was published in her ninetieth year, forty-three years after her first publication.

30.—The American Sergeant Bates enters London after his walk from the Scottish border with his national flag.

December 1.—Royal decree issued appointing twenty-five new Prussian peers to secure the passing of the new County Election Bill.

— An effort being made to reject Dean Stanley as one of the Select Preachers at Oxford, Dean Goulburn, of Norwich, writes to-day (Sunday) that his reason for joining in the protest was, that you (Stanley) "are in the habit of throwing the whole weight of your high character, your brilliant abilities, and your eminent position into the support of the Rationalistic school—a school which seeks to eliminate from Christianity both its doctrinal and its supernatural element, and to reduce it to a system of moral truth, illustrated by a bright example, and which, in regard of the written Word of God, claims the right of accepting only such parts of it as approve themselves to the natural reason and conscience of man. I hold it to be the paramount duty of every Churchman and every Christian to take every opportunity of entering his protest against the views of this school, which I honestly believe to be undermining the faith of many young men, and paving the way for the total rejection of revealed religion. . . . I am by no means insensible to your amiability and integrity, nor to sentiments of 'Auld lang syne.' Our convictions as to truth and right differ very widely; but I can sincerely say that I wish I were habitually as true to my convictions as I well know you have always been to yours."

2.—The Archbishop of Canterbury receives at Lambeth Palace a memorial from the clergy of the Northern and Southern Provinces, praying for some change either in the compulsory rubric or in the damnatory clauses of the Athanasian Creed. Of the 3,000 clergymen who signed, 2,159 did so without any reserve, thus signifying their desire to leave entirely to the discretion of the authorities to determine whether the rubric, or the clauses, or both, shall be altered ; 421 desired especially the alteration of the rubric only—218 were for optional use of the Athanasian Creed, and 203 for its entire disuse in public worship ; 292 desired only to touch the damnatory clauses—208 asked for their removal, and 84 for their alteration.

2.—Strike of 2,400 men employed in the London gas-works, the immediately inciting cause being the discharge of a " Union " stoker from the Fulham retort house.

— Discussion at Rugby School, the Governing Body desiring to express their conviction that the course taken throughout by Dr. Hayman in dealing with Mr. Scott has not been marked by that spirit of justice which the circumstances of the case required.

3.—A paper upon a cuneiform inscription setting forth the Chaldean account of the Deluge read before the Society of Biblical Archæology, by Mr. George Smith, British Museum.

— The strike of the 2,400 stokers limits the supply of gas to only a few streets in the City. As night closed in the aspect of the West end was dismal in the extreme. In many streets it was difficult to move along. From the afternoon no lights could be had at many of the underground railway stations, and at seven o'clock no little consternation was occasioned among the railway passengers at Ludgate Hill by the sudden disappearance of all the lights. The panic which would almost certainly have occurred was prevented by the fact that Messrs. Spiers and Pond's lights were just sufficient to make the darkness visible. The St. James's Theatre had to be closed, another had to use candles in " front," and a third was in a state of considerable dimness. The letter-carriers went about carrying "bull's-eye" lamps in one hand and their bundles of letters in the other. On the Surrey side of the river the gas was burning as usual.

— Judgment given by Lord Gifford in the Edinburgh Court of Session in the Murthly marriage case, wherein the plaintiff, Mrs. Margaret Robertson (formerly Wilson) sought to have it declared that she had been married to and had a son by Major Steuart, only son of the late Sir William Steuart, of Murthly and Grandtully, Perthshire. The defendants were Sir Archibald Douglas Steuart, who is heir to Sir William, and Mr. Franc Nichols Steuart, who had been butler to the deceased baronet for a long period, and who has come into possession, by will, of one o the estates. Lord Gifford, in a long and elaborate decision, held that the plaintiff's marriage with Major Steuart had been clearly established.

4.— Meeting at Willis's Rooms for the purpose of taking steps, Parliamentary or otherwise, to prevent the encroachment upon legitimate trading interests by the so-called Civil Service Co-operative Societies.

5.—The Japanese Embassy received by the Queen at Windsor.

— Died at Kensington, aged 72, Francis Charles Massingberd, D.D., Chancellor of the diocese of Lincoln, and author of a history of the Reformation.

— The French Government defeated in the election of the Dufaure Committee; nineteen members of the Right and eleven of the Left chosen.

— The Directors of the Chartered Gas Company resolve "That the men who at the various stations of the Gas Light and Coke Company without notice deserted their duties and imperilled the safety of the metropolis, are unworthy of confidence, and that none of them be hereafter employed by the company." This involved the dismissal of no fewer than 1,400 hands. The issue of summonses against the 500 stokers who turned out at the Beckton Gas-works commenced to-day, about a dozen constables being specially appointed to assist the summoning officer in the duty, and each being accompanied by a foreman, or one of the workmen acquainted with the defendants and their residences. Constables were also instructed to procure labourers where they could be got and send them in to the works to replace the men on strike — a proceeding protested against by the stokers as illegal.

8.—J. H. Gordon, formerly of the British Indian Civil Service, shoots Ada Schiani, to whom he had been paying his addresses, while walking in the garden of the Villa Nazionale, Naples, and then commits suicide by shooting himself.

—· Severe hurricane experienced generally over England. It was stated that, allowing the number 12 to represent the strongest wind ever experienced in these latitudes, the extreme force recorded at Scilly, Plymouth, and Portishead was 11 ; London, Liverpool, Holyhead, Portsmouth, and Yarmouth, 10 ; while on the Continent the gale rose to 10 at Brussels, and to 9 at Helder, Cape Gris-Nez, and L'Orient. The gale was most severe over the southern half of England and Wales. In the Midland Counties and the North there was less wind, but more rain.

9.—Four gas-stokers formerly in the service of the Commercial Gas Company at Stepney, appear at the Thames Police Court, to answer summonses which stated that "they, being under a certain contract of service not yet expired, did, on the 3rd of December, unlawfully neglect and refuse, and have ever since neglected and refused, to fulfil the said contract, without just or lawful excuse, for the non-performance of which contract by you no

compensation or damage can be assessed, and that pecuniary compensation will not meet the circumstances of the case." After hearing evidence, the magistrate, Mr. Lushington, gave it as his opinion that no pecuniary compensation, which would probably be paid out of the funds of the men's Union, would meet such a case, and he felt it his duty to sentence each of the defendants to six weeks' imprisonment, with hard labour.

9.—The Prussian Counties Reform Bill passes its final reading in the House of Lords by 116 votes to 91.

11.—The Fifth Avenue Hotel, New York, burnt, and twenty-two of the female servants suffocated at the top of the building.

— Died, aged 77, Edwin Norris, formerly secretary to the Royal Asiatic Society, and Translator to the Foreign Office, a distinguished philologist, and Assyrian scholar.

— The appointment of Dean Stanley as one of the Select Preachers at Oxford confirmed by 349 votes to 287. Dean Goulburn thereupon resigned a similar office to which he was appointed last year, "as the most forcible protest he can give against (what he must consider to be) the unfaithfulness to God's truth which the University manifested by its vote in favour of Dean Stanley." Dr. Goulburn goes on to say that he has no desire to circumscribe too closely the limits of the Church of England, and if he must err would rather err on the side of latitude than of exclusiveness. But "the line must be drawn somewhere," and his complaint against the Dean of Westminster is that he seems to draw it nowhere.

12.—President Grant officially recognizes a coloured man appointed by the Legislature of Louisiana to replace Governor Warmouth, as lawfully holding the executive power of the State of Louisiana.

— Died, at Tichborne House, the Dowager Lady Doughty Tichborne, alleged to have identified the Claimant as her son.

13.—Came on for trial in the Irish Court of Queen's Bench the case of Father O'Keefe against the Rev. Mr. Walshe, one of his curates —an action for slander in calling plaintiff a liar before his own congregation. The case had been tried before, when the plaintiff obtained 100*l.* damages. The verdict was set aside and a new trial directed. The defendant did not now appear, and the jury, after a brief deliberation, found a verdict for the plaintiff— damages, 250*l.* and costs.

14.—Animated debate in the French Assembly on the petition for a dissolution, ultimately set aside by 490 to 201 votes.

— Meeting of Liberal members at Swindon, the Chancellor of the Exchequer criticizing recent speeches made by Lord Salisbury and Mr. Disraeli ; the latter of whom, he said, "never having in his life done anything that

I am aware of, or asked anybody to do anything, in the way of public health, or taken up the subject, thinking it a harmless thing, and being hard pressed, and having a necessity to say something, says health is the great matter that the Tory party propose to deal with. They do not propose to do anything else for us, but they are going to give us all good constitutions. I can only say, coming as it did, 'Sanitas sanitatum omnia sanitas.' I propose to restore the original reading, ' Vanitas vanitatum omnia vanitas '—vanity of vanity, all is vanity." Mr. Lowe finished with a retrospect of the doings of the Tory party when in office, with a view to show, as he said, that they had two policies—one when they are in office, and the other when they are out of it. "When they are out of it their policy is to say nothing and do nothing—not to commit themselves, as far as they can help ; when they are in, it is their policy to take the policy of their predecessors, which they had opposed, and pass it."

15.—Died, aged 61, Henry G. Blagrove, violinist.

— Died at Hughenden, aged 83, after a brief illness, Mary Ann Disraeli, Countess of Beaconsfield, wife of the Right Hon. Benjamin Disraeli, M.P. Lady Beaconsfield was the daughter of Mr. John Evans, of Bampford Speke, Devon, and married first in 1815, Mr. Wyndham Lewis, Mr. Disraeli's predecessor in the representation of Maidstone. Mr. Lewis died in 1838, and in the following year his widow became the wife of Mr. Disraeli.

16.—The Japanese Embassy leave England for Paris.

17.—Four men sentenced to death at Durham for kicking a man to death outside his own house at Spennymoor. Two were afterwards respited.

19.—Came on at the Central Criminal Court, before Mr. Justice Brett, the trial of five gas stokers concerned in the late strike, and now indicted for conspiracy to intimidate the manager of the Beckton gas-works, by refusing to engage in their ordinary duties till certain dismissed servants of the company were reinstated. The trial lasted till the close of the day, when the jury found them all guilty, but strongly recommended them to mercy on account of their great ignorance, of their having been misled, and of their previous good character. In addressing the prisoners, Mr. Justice Brett said that so far from agreeing with the jury that they were misled, it seemed to him that from the course they took during the whole of these proceedings they were not the men misled, but the men misleading, and that it was they who misled the others, and most of the 500 obeyed what they had suggested. A serious punishment must be inflicted—a punishment that would teach men in their position that although without offence they might be members of a trade union, or might agree to go into an employment or to leave it without

committing any offence, yet they must take care when they agreed together that they did not agree to do anything by illegal means. If they did that they were guilty of conspiracy. The sentence he had to pass was that they be kept in prison for twelve calendar months.

20.—News from New York announce that Jay Gould has settled the claims of the Erie Railway Company against him by making restitution to the amount of 1,945,000*l.*

— Died suddenly, aged 59, George Peabody Putnam, American publisher.

21.—Addressing the students of Liverpool College, Mr. Gladstone pointed out that so far as religion was concerned, the conflict was not now between different forms of Christianity, but between Christians and men who (like Dr. Strauss, from whom Mr. Gladstone quoted at some length) reject belief in a personal God and individual immortality. He did not object to " free thought ; " on the contrary, he held with Homer that the man who does not value the freedom of his thoughts deserves to be described as but half a man. St. Paul was a preacher of free thought ; he urged men to " prove all things," but he also advised them to " hold fast that which is good." The free thought of the present day " seems too often to mean thought roving and vagrant more than free, like Delos drifting on the seas of Greece without a root, a direction, or a home." Mr. Gladstone went on to urge his hearers not to fall in too readily with the prevalent notion that this age is vastly superior to all that have gone before it. He admitted the material triumphs which it had seen accomplished, as well as the mental activity which characterized it, but it was by no means an age abounding in minds of the first order, in great immortal teachers. " It has tapped, as it were, and made disposable for man, vast natural forces ; but the mental power employed is not to be measured by the size of the results. To perfect that marvel of travel, the locomotive, has perhaps not required the expenditure of more mental strength and application than to perfect that marvel of music, the violin. In the material sphere the achievements of the age are splendid and unmixed. In the social sphere they are great and noble, but seem ever to be confronted by a succession of new problems which almost defy solution. In the sphere of pure intellect I doubt whether posterity will rate us as highly as we rate ourselves. But what I most wish to observe is this, that it is an insufferable arrogance in the men of any age to assume what I may call airs of unmeasured superiority over former ages. God, who cares for us, cared for them also. In the goods of this world we may advance by strides ; but it is by steps only and not strides, and by slow and not always steady steps, that all desirable improvement of man in the higher ranges of his being is effected."

— Prince Bismarck's resignation of the Prussian Ministry of State accepted by the

Emperor. He was succeeded by Count Von Roon.

21. — The screw-steamer *Germany*, one of the Allan company's line of vessels running between the Mersey and Canada, Baltimore and New Orleans, wrecked on a sandbank at the entrance of the Gironde, and thirty of those on board drowned.

23. — At a Consistory attended by twenty-two Cardinals, the Pope complained bitterly of the oppression exercised on the Church by the Italian Government. "Above all things," he said, "the law presented to Parliament on the subject of religious corporations deeply wounds the rights of possession of the Universal Church, and violates the right of our apostolic mission. In face of the presentation of this law, we raise our voice before you and the entire Church, and condemn any law which diminishes or suppresses religious families in Rome or the neighbouring provinces. We consequently declare void every acquisition of their property made under any title whatsoever."

24. — Died, aged 52, W. J. Macquorn Rankine, Professor of Civil Engineering and Mechanics in the University of Glasgow.

— The Rev. Dr. Wallace, of Old Greyfriars, Edinburgh, presented by the Queen to the Chair of Church History in the University of Edinburgh, vacant by the resignation of the Rev. Dr. Stevenson.

25. — Sir Sydney Waterlow, Lord Mayor, entertains 186 of his relations at the Mansion House. His lordship's father, eighty-two years old, had the gratification of dining at the same table with his 13 children, 49 grandchildren, and 14 great-grandchildren. The Lord Mayor was supported by his 4 sons and 4 daughters, 4 brothers and 6 sisters, 17 nephews, 22 nieces, 29 cousins, and 1 grandson ; and Lady Waterlow by her stepmother, 4 brothers, 3 sisters, 12 nephews, 12 nieces, and 41 cousins.

— A young woman named Harriet Buswell found murdered in her house, Great Coram Street ; the criminal not discovered, but supposed to be a German who accompanied her home, and robbed his victim of some trifling trinkets she had borrowed for use as a member of the *corps de ballet*.

— Collision between the *Northumberland* and *Hercules* ironclads at Funchal, while riding out a heavy westerly gale.

27. — Availing himself of the opportunity of handing over the prizes at the Art and Science School at Newton Abbot, Devonshire, the Duke of Somerset contrasted the real progress which had been made by Natural Science with the talk about progress in which politicians indulged. "Just look," he said, "at what the steam-engine has done and what it has added to the power and civilization of England. By sea and by land, in the depth of the mine and in the manufactory, everywhere it has added

to England's prosperity and wealth. I saw, to my great surprise, when I read the speech of the Prime Minister on education, that he said he would balance for the proof of intellect the invention of the violin against the locomotive engine. Now, I thought that was very strange. I should like to know what the violin has done for the civilization of mankind. Men have been scraping on these squeaking strings for the last 300 years, and what good has the world gained by it ? But he says the violin is a marvel of music, and therefore is equal to the locomotive engine. Now, I remember that some years ago, when Paganini, the great fiddler, died, a newspaper, published in Italy, contained an article which commenced in this style :—'Genoa has produced two great men— Paganini and Columbus.' (Laughter.) I confess that it seemed to me, when I read of Mr. Gladstone comparing the violin with the locomotive engine, that it was very much like comparing Paganini with Columbus. (Laughter.) But is that all ? Why, the locomotive engine is altering the civilization of the world. The railroad and the locomotive are going not only through Europe, but they have gone into Japan. Do you think they go there without advancing civilization ? I should like to know what fiddle has ever done the same ? (Laughter.) We hear a great deal about the science of government, but there is no such science. It is a few desultory principles people have scrambled hold of, and they are trying to apply them. The statesman who applies them in one way corrects the blunders of former statesmen, but he generally substitutes some blunders of his own. (Laughter.) Down in Plymouth there was what they call a Social Science meeting. How can they call that science ! I read the papers, and I confess I was quite surprised that they called that science. Science ought to proceed on some carefully ascertained data leading to actual conclusions. What data have they got ? I read nothing but crotchets and crudities, which poured out according to the fancy of the speaker. No doubt many of those things may eventually be of use to science, but it is not yet come to science—it is not matured sufficiently to be called science. The science of government and what they call social science are yet in their infancy, and they have not yet come to years of discretion." (Laughter.)

27. — Meetings held to memorialise the Home Secretary for a commutation of the sentence passed upon the gas stokers.

— Died at Edinburgh, aged 80, the Very Rev. Dean Ramsay, a popular preacher and author of "Reminiscences of Scottish Life and Character."

— A young woman named Britton, serving in a house at Ealing Green, severely beaten by her sweetheart, Walter Trinder, who afterwards committed suicide by cutting his throat.

28. — M. de Bourgoing, the French Minister at the Vatican, leaves Rome.

28.—In a case of libel raised by the Lord Provost of Glasgow against the *North British Daily Mail*, in which the plaintiff had been charged with "corruptly making use of his position as a trustee under the City of Glasgow Improvement Trust," the jury return a verdict in his favour, damages 575*l*.—On the same day Mr. Stannus, agent for the Hertford estates, obtained 100*l*. damages in an action for libel against the *Belfast Northern Whig*.

29. — The Duc de Gramont explains to Count Daru, as President of the Commission of Inquiry, that on the 20th July, 1870, Austria had distinctly promised to make the cause of France her own, and contribute to the success of her armies as far as she possibly could.

30.—Addressing his constituents at Oxford, Mr. Vernon Harcourt objected to the use of the word Liberty by Permissive Bill advocates. "Liberty (he said) does not consist in making others do what you think right. The difference between a free Government and a Government which is not free is principally this—that a Government which is not free interferes with everything it can, and a free Government interferes with nothing except what it must. A despotic Government tries to make everybody do what it wishes; a Liberal Government tries, as far as the safety of society will permit, to allow everybody to do as he wishes. It has been the tradition of the Liberal party consistently to maintain the doctrine of individual liberty. It is because they have done so that England is the place where people can do more what they please than in any other country in the world—more so than in Russia, far more so, I believe, than they can do in America." Regarding the Church, Mr. Harcourt asked, "But why is it safe? Because the Liberal party have dealt with the Church as they have dealt with the Throne and with the aristocracy. The Church of England is no longer the Church of Laud, nor the Church of the Non-jurors. The Church which was once a dominant hierarchy is now the servant, as it is the creature, of the State. Its doctrine and its discipline are defined by statute; its dignities are in the gift of a parliamentary Minister. From being the stronghold of intolerance it has become—we have seen it lately in Oxford—the city of refuge for freedom of opinion. Its national latitude and its tolerant creed offer a liberal shelter against the persecuting dogmatism of sects. Its communion is free to all, without money and without price. It is compulsory on none; no one now gains anything by being a Churchman or loses anything through being a Dissenter. The Church is safe. But do you think that it would have been safe if the Tory party had had their way; if the Catholics had not been emancipated; if the disabilities of Dissenters had still remained; if Parliament, the public service, the universities had not been opened to men of every creed; if the Church had not been compelled to exchange a persecuting priesthood for

a missionary clergy? The Reformed State Church of England, too, such as we know it, is the work of the Liberal party."

1873.

January 1.—The Emperor William confers upon Prince Bismarck the Order of the Black Eagle in brilliants on the Chancellor's retirement from the Prussian Premiership. An accompanying letter testified to the extreme sorrow with which the Emperor acceded to the wish of the Prince to be relieved from the Presidency of the Prussian Cabinet, but added that, after the strain of body and mind involved in its duties during the last ten years, the Emperor could no longer refrain from granting the relief asked for. The letter emphatically acknowledged how the Imperial Chancellor's counsel and assistance during the last ten years, so pregnant with important events, had enabled the Emperor to develop the power of Prussia and to lead Germany towards unity. The name of Prince Bismarck, said the Emperor, is indelibly engraved on the history of Prussia and of Germany, and the highest recognition is justly his due.

2.—The operation of lithotrity performed upon the ex-Emperor Napoleon by Sir H. Thompson. The bulletin next morning announced that his Majesty had passed a fair night, and was free from any unfavourable symptom.

4.—Suspension announced of Pawson and Company, warehousemen, St. Paul's Churchyard, with liabilities estimated at over 600,000*l*. A limited company was afterwards formed to take over the business. Another large failure announced at this time was that of Anselmo Vivanti, silk merchant, St. Mary Axe, with liabilities estimated also at 600,000*l*.

— Declining to receive a deputation on behalf of the imprisoned gas stokers, Mr. Bruce causes intimation to be made from the Home Office that the Home Secretary is not a court of appeal from the decisions of her Majesty's judges on questions of law, and has no authority to overrule them. The Court for the Consideration of Crown Cases Reserved is the proper tribunal to decide such questions; and if the correctness of the law laid down by the judge at the trial had been doubted, it was open to the counsel engaged to have asked to have a case reserved for the opinion of that court; but such a course was not adopted by them. The Secretary of State, therefore, must decline to have any such question raised before him, or to give any opinion upon it.

6.—The *Daily News* publishes a letter sent by Mr. Bright, but written some years since by Mr. Cobden, on the subject of small holdings and peasant proprietors, in which the writer contended that the result of a general study of all the best authorities is to show that there is a unanimity of opinion in favour of the French system, on moral grounds, as tending to elevate the character, promote the intelligence, and stimulate the industry of the peasantry.

— In the case of Stokes, tried for the murder of Fisk a twelvemonth since in the Great Central Hotel, New York, the jury return a verdict of wilful murder.

7. — Seventy thousand colliers and iron-workers on strike in South Wales, in resistance to a threatened reduction in wages of 10 per cent. At Dowlais works alone 10,000 men were out.

— Count Schouvaloff arrives in England on a special mission from the Czar, regarding the disputed Central Asian boundary.

8. — The Duke of Somerset, speaking at Newton Abbott, takes exception to Mr. Cobden's recently published opinion on the land laws. "In France," he said, "the land has now for fifty years or more been subdivided. There is no entail there. Well, have they improved in agriculture so much as we have? The French have a better climate than we have; they have done away with entail, and they have got subdivision of property to their hearts' content, and have they improved their agriculture as we have? Certainly not. That, at least, is the report made to the Government by the agricultural returns which they themselves called for. I want to know what are the peculiar reasons why this question of the investment of capital in land is being discussed It strikes me that it is not capital in land that these speakers want so much as to make a little capital for themselves."

— Earl Granville writes to Lord A. Loftus that Count Schouvaloff had explained the Khivan expedition as intended to punish acts of brigandage, to recover fifty Russian prisoners, and to teach the Khan that such conduct on his part could not be continued with the impunity which the moderation of Russia had led him to believe. Not only was it far from the intention of the Emperor to take possession of Khiva, but positive orders had been issued to prevent it, and directions given that the conditions imposed should be such as could not in any way lead to a prolonged occupancy of Khiva. "Count Schouvaloff repeated the surprise which the Emperor, entertaining such sentiments, felt at the uneasiness which it was said existed in England on the subject, and he gave me to understand that I might give positive assurances to Parliament on this matter."

— Bulletins issued describing the precarious condition of the ex-Emperor of France.

9. — Died in exile at Chiselhurst, this forenoon, Charles Louis Napoleon Bonaparte, ex-Emperor of France. He was the third son of Louis King of Holland, third brother of Napoleon I., and was born at the Tuileries 20th April, 1808, his mother being Hortense Eugénie Beauharnais, daughter of the Empress Joséphine, the great Napoleon's first wife, by her first husband, the Vicomte de Beauharnais.

9. — Died, at Barcelona, where he discharged the duty of British Consul, James Hannay, journalist and critic, aged 46.

10. — Despatches from Paris announce that no excitement was visible consequent on the Emperor's death. "Small notice is taken of the event, and the few evening papers whose latest news announce the Emperor's death speak of it as doubtful. The Bonapartist journals — the *Pays* and the *Ordre* — say that the Emperor's state is quite satisfactory. They continue to treat as Republican calumnies the story that he is in danger, and allege particularly that in a few days he will be able to sit on horseback without suffering as he did at Sedan. It was announced to-day as the result of a *post-mortem* examination that death had taken place by failure of the circulation, and was attributable to the general constitutional state of the patient. The disease of the kidneys, of which this state was the expression, was of such a nature and so advanced that it would in any case have shortly determined a fatal result.

— Disturbance on board H.M.S. *Aurora* off Plymouth, leading to a disrating of various petty officers and able seamen.

11. — Mr. Baron Pollock takes his seat in the Court of Exchequer.

12. — The death of the Emperor Napoleon, it is reported from Berlin, excites comparatively little attention. "The press notices are brief, and as a rule without bitterness. They chiefly turn upon the future prospects of the Imperial party. It seems to be generally thought in political circles that there will soon be two Bonapartist factions, one led by Prince Napoleon, and the other by the Empress Eugénie and the Prince Imperial. It is also thought that the death of Napoleon III. will improve the prospects of the Imperial dynasty."

— Replying to a deputation on the Temporal Power, M. Thiers said, "There is on foot at present in Europe a crusade against the Papacy. The man who has placed himself at the head of this campaign against the Holy See is indefatigable. He is one of the greatest men of this century — one of those who have made the grandeur of Germany and overwhelmed our country. I refer, of course, to M. de Bismarck. He is now bestowing his favours with profusion on Italy, which is his natural ally in the great struggle on which he has entered. It is evident that nothing is neglected by this profound politician which can induce Italy to enter into alliance with Prussia. Do you wish to promote the alliance? We respect the rights of the Holy See; we desire that it should be fully and completely independent; but we accept accomplished facts, and we shall do nothing which will separate us from a King and his Ministers with whom we can only express satisfaction "

12.—Sir Bartle Frere arrives at Zanzibar.

13.—The Chancellor of the Exchequer intimates to Sir Henry Rawlinson on the part of Mr. Goschen and himself that they saw no pressing reason why an Arctic expedition should be sent out this year. " We give no opinion as to the expediency of such an expedition at a future time, but we are clearly of opinion that it would not be right to send out a second scientific expedition precisely at the moment when the public revenue has to bear the main burden of the expenses of the operations intrusted to the *Challenger*. I believe it has been erroneously stated that the *Challenger* expedition involves very little expense. That is not so. The cost has already been considerable, and nothing has been spared to ensure success. There will further be an additional annual outlay for three years.

— Japanese Seven per Cent. Loan of 2,400,000*l*. put on the market at 92½.

— News from St. Petersburg announce that an expedition to Khiva had been resolved upon by a Council of Ministers.

— Currie, station-master, and Ramsay, pointsman, at Kirtlebridge, on 2nd October last, tried for manslaughter before the High Court of Justiciary and acquitted.

— A Papal Allocution establishes an Apostolic Vicariat for the Swiss Canton of Geneva. It was read in the Catholic Churches on the 2nd February without the sanction of the Government.

14.—Seven persons burnt to death at Lichfield, in a house occupied by Mr. Corfield, watchmaker, adjoining that in which Dr. Johnson was born.

— Apologizing for inability to address his constituents at this time, Mr. Bright writes to a friend :—" There are two questions to which you refer that are probably too large to be undertaken with any degree of completeness in the last years of a Parliament. I allude to the state of the county representation and to the land question. They seem to me the great questions of the immediate future, and the more they are discussed by the public the more will Parliament be prepared to deal with them. The question of expenditure is one which demands resolute handling. If the present Government is unable to grapple with it, it should only show us how great are the interests which oppose themselves to economy, and how much an earnest public opinion is wanted to arrest the extravagant and scandalous expenditure which every statesman in turn condemns, and which not one of them seems able to diminish."

15.—Funeral of the Emperor Napoleon at Chiselhurst. Between 2000 and 3000 of the most prominent Frenchmen in all walks of life under the Empire took part in the procession, and upwards of 50,000 English people congregated to witness the passing of the *cortège* from Camden House to the little Roman Catholic Chapel dedicated to St. Mary. The distance between these two places by the carriage road is about a quarter of a mile, and along both sides of the common there was a dense mass of people, while carriages were ranged three and four deep on one side of the way. The chief mourners were the Prince Imperial, Prince Napoleon (Jerome), Princess Joachim and Achille Murat, and M. Rouher. A deputation was also present from the army of Italy. The Prince Imperial met the friends of the Empire in the afternoon, and was saluted as Napoleon IV.

15.—Died, suddenly, J. B. Bergne, for many years head of the Treaty Department of the Foreign Office, which he entered in 1817.

— The Commission of the General Assembly of the Church of Scotland resolve, by a majority of 55 votes against 38, to forward a protest to Government regarding the appointment of the Rev. Dr. R. Wallace, of Old Greyfriars Church, to the chair of divinity and church history in the University of Edinburgh, as being likely to be prejudicial to the interests of religion in Scotland.

17.—A number of applications having been made by officers of the French army to attend the funeral of the Emperor Napoleon, the War Minister writes to Marshal McMahon :—" The Government understands and respects the feelings of gratitude and affection which a certain number of officers continue to entertain for the Imperial family. It will certainly attribute no blame to those of them who, on the occasion of the death of the Emperor, considered it their duty to address letters to the Empress individually in testimony of their respectful sympathy. Such a course only does honour to those who write them, and I am sure that it is consistent with the obligations imposed upon them by their duty towards the legal Government recognized by France, for men of feeling are always men faithful to their duty. But you will also understand that, if I may permit some individual and isolated expressions of feeling, I cannot at the same time allow the army to desert its purely military duties and mingle in an agitation full of danger to discipline and the peace of the country."

— The widow of Marshal Lauriston, a descendant of the famous Law of the South Sea Bubble Scheme, died in Paris, aged over 100 years.

— A column of United States troops defeated by Modoc Indians, intrenched in caves at Kalmath, Oregon.

18.—Died at Torquay, aged 67, Edward Bulwer-Lytton, Lord Lytton, novelist, poet, and critic, and Secretary of State for the Colonies from May 1858 to June 1859. Interred in Westminster Abbey on the 25th. " With the exception," the *Times* wrote, " of Scott, who, like Shakespeare, wrote for all men and all times, it would be hard to find a novelist who contributed more largely to popular enjoyment.

H 2

To Lord Lytton belongs the credit of first popularising what, in the modern sense of the word, may be termed the political novel. His novels, while invariably providing the reader with entertainment and diversion, invited him as invariably to turn his faculties to account by study, observation, and reflection."

18.—Died, suddenly, at Euston Hotel, Mr. S. R. Graves, M.P. for Liverpool.

— Sir Bartle Frere entertained at a banquet by the Sultan of Zanzibar.

— Dr. Gottfried Hessel, a German clergyman, arrested at Ramsgate on the charge of being the murderer of Harriet Buswell, Great Coram Street. After being repeatedly before the magistrate, he was freely acquitted of all suspicion on the 30th.

19.—Died at Ockham Park, aged 91, the Right Hon. Stephen Lushington, engaged with Brougham and Denman in the defence of Queen Caroline, and judge for thirty years of the Court of Admiralty.

20.—Died at Stanmore, aged 74, the Hon. and Rev. Baptist Noel, an Evangelical clergyman who had seceded from the Church of England to the Baptist body.

— Mr. Guildford Onslow, M.P., and Mr. Whalley, M.P., fined 100*l.* for contempt of court in speeches made at Tichborne defence meetings.

— The Pope receives a deputation from the British section of the League of St. Sebastian, recently organized to maintain the temporal powers of the Holy See.

21.—Defending Roman Catholic loyalty at Sheffield, Archbishop Manning asks: How could Catholics, who believed that the Church was one, identify themselves very closely with a State which admitted all creeds and all forms of worship on the same level? How could they be in sympathy with a State which encouraged secular education? Was there any wonder that under such circumstances as these Catholics should isolate themselves? But who was in fault? Catholics remained true to the principles which had united the Christian world, and they could not compromise those principles. But outside that circle, and in all things that did not hinge upon their duty to God, they were the staunchest and the most loyal of Englishmen. Lord Denbigh some years ago defined the position clearly when he declared that he was a Catholic first and an Englishman afterwards. Dr. Manning then went on to remark that it was said that Ultramontanism was opposed to progress, but he could not pretend to understand this assertion. The Christian world was created by Christianity. Christianity was the Church; the Popes were the head of the Church. The Papacy was Ultramontanism, and Ultramontanism, therefore, had brought about the advancement made up to the sixteenth century.

21.—The masses at Paris for the Emperor Napoleon attended by large numbers of friends of the Empire.

22.—A crime of unusual magnitude and inhumanity was committed this evening near midnight about two miles off Dungeness, by the Spanish steamer *Murillo* running down the emigrant ship *Northfleet*, and heartlessly leaving over three hundred people to perish without the slightest offer of assistance. The ship *Northfleet*, Captain Knowles, 895 tons register, bound from London to Hobart Town, with a cargo of railway iron and emigrants, was at anchor or at the tress at eleven o'clock, with mast-head light burning, when she was run into and sunk about three-quarters of an hour afterwards. The panic on board was described as terrible. The screams of the women and children were heard for miles, but the foreign steamer took no notice, nor could she be identified for several weeks. The pilot on duty said that when he was sitting in the saloon he heard the anchor watch cry out, "Pilot, pilot, come out!" He immediately rushed on deck, and was just able to see a steamer backing out from amidships. He saw that the riding light was burning properly. He instructed the captain to give orders to set the pumps to work, and then conferred with the captain as to what should be done next. The latter instructed that signals of distress should be burned. All the rockets that were on board the ship were sent up in succession. During the time there was great confusion among the passengers, and signs of distress among the women when they saw the ship was sinking. The quarter-boats were lowered, and the captain, who retained perfect self-possession, ordered that the women and children should at once be got into them. There was a great rush of male passengers towards the boats, and, as far as witness could see, a boat, full of men, was cut away from the ship's davits. Two boats put away full of people. The ship was then rapidly settling down, and witness went into the rigging. He saw a number of persons struggling in the water. On recovering himself he was just able to see the mizzentop crosstree out of the water, and swam towards it. He clung to it till he was taken off. Out of the 412 passengers and crew only 85 persons were saved, and brought in a steamer and a lugger to the Sailors' Home at Dover. The wife of the captain was among the survivors. One man was shot in the leg by the captain, while endeavouring to prevent the passengers from crowding into the boats; the unfortunate commander, who displayed great heroism, went down with his vessel. Besides Mrs. Knowles, a woman with her baby and a little girl were saved.

— What was announced as the last execution of Communist prisoners, three in number, takes place at Satory.

— The case of Baily (appellant) *v.* Williamson (respondent), raising the question of the right of public meeting in the Royal parks in the metropolis, argued in the Court of Queen's Bench, and the conviction of the police magistrate affirmed, thus establishing the validity of the new rule.

23.—Establishment of a parcel post between England and India.

— Prince Arthur of England received by the Pope at a special audience at Rome.

[**24.**— The St. Petersburg *Official Gazette* announces that the recent "exchange of ideas" between the English and Russian Governments has been friendly, and shows "no divergence of views."

— A deputation from the National Education Union wait upon Mr. Gladstone to urge "that compulsory education should be made general, but that in districts where no school boards have been elected, and where, owing to there being sufficient school accommodation, it is not desirable that any should be elected, the compulsory provisions should be carried out by the boards of guardians; and, lastly and chiefly, that the right of parents to select the school to which their children shall be sent, as embodied in the 25th section of the Education Act, shall be maintained." Mr. Gladstone thanked the deputation, and promised consideration of their requests.

[**26.**—Died, at Lisbon, the Dowager Empress Amelia of Brazil, widow of Pedro I.

— Died, at Florence, Miss Jane Blagden, authoress, the faithful companion and nurse of Mrs. Browning.

27.—Died, at Trinity College, Cambridge, aged 87, Adam Sedgwick, LL.D., an eminent geologist and Woodwardian Professor, who had graduated at Trinity as far back as 1808, when he was fifth Wrangler, the late Lord Langdale being senior, and the late Bishop of London, Dr. Blomfield, third. Professor Sedgwick was senior of his college at death.

— Sir George Honyman takes his seat in the Court of Common Pleas.

28.— The French Commission of Thirty adopt the principle of a Second Chamber, but without deciding on the way in which it is to be elected or what are to be its functions.

29.—Mr. Skipworth, barrister, sentenced to three months' imprisonment and a fine of 500*l.* for contempt of court in his speeches at various towns on the Tichborne case. The Claimant was also ordered to find bail for three months.

— Died, aged 86, the Dowager Lady Bridport, Duchess of Brontë, niece of Lord Nelson.

— A deputation complaining of the Civil Service Stores to-day waiting upon Mr. Lowe; he said the Clubs themselves were co-operating, "and I am told that persons find they save 30 per cent. by co-operation. I say you should meet this state of things in the only way you can meet it—by competing with the stores. If you have not enough capital, let several of you combine, and unless you meet these circum-

stances by competition, you must make up your mind you will be driven out of the market. If people want credit, they will go to a respectable tradesman; but when people go with ready money, they will go to the cheapest market, and no agitation you can enter upon will keep the public from doing the best with ready money."

31.—In the case of the gas stokers sentenced by Mr. Justice Brett to twelve months' imprisonment, her Majesty gives effect to a recommendation made by the Home Secretary for a remission of eight months of the punishment.

— Meeting in St. James's Hall to resist the proposals for removing the Athanasian Creed from the Prayer Book, or rendering its use optional.

February 1.—General Von Kaufmann leaves St. Petersburg for Tashkend to organize the Khivan expedition.

— The Duke of Cambridge issues a circular disapproving of officers petitioning Parliament for redress of grievances.

— Died aged 67, Commodore Maury, formerly of the United States Navy, and author of "The Physical Geography of the Sea."

2.—Heavy snow-storm in London, leading to an almost entire stoppage of street traffic.

3.—New Naval College at Greenwich opened.

— Intimation made that Government would be prepared, under the exceptional circumstances of the apprehension and examination of Dr. Hessel, to defray the reasonable costs incurred in his defence, and also to provide the necessary funds for the passage fares to Brazil of Dr. and Mrs. Hessel. "I am further," writes Mr. Cavendish, of the Treasury, "desired by Mr. Gladstone to request you to express to Dr. Hessel his sympathy for the painful position in which he has been placed." The doctor was afterwards presented with a public testimonial of over 1000*l.* as a mark of sympathy under the unmerited indignities to which he had been subjected.

4.—The London coal merchants advance the price of coals from 37*s.* to 45*s.* per ton.

— Mrs. Knowles, widow of the captain of the *Northfleet*, awarded a pension of 50*l.* per annum from the Civil List.

5.—Robert C. M. Bowles, banker, acquitted at the Central Criminal Court of the charge of unlawfully pledging and converting to his own use and that of his firm 200 Lombardo-Venetian Railway Bonds which had been deposited with the firm for a particular purpose.

— The Hawaiian Legislature proclaim Prince Lunalilo as King of the Sandwich Islands.

— Extradition Treaty concluded between Great Britain and Italy.

5.—The Burmese mission take leave of her Majesty at Osborne.

6.—Parliament opened by Commission, the Royal Speech making reference to Sir Bartle Frere's mission to Zanzibar, the decision of the German Emperor on the San Juan reference, the Geneva arbitration, and the French Commercial Treaty. On the Central Asian question it was said :—"It has been for some years felt by the Governments of Russia and the United Kingdom respectively, that it would be conducive to the tranquillity of Central Asia if the two Governments should arrive at an identity of view regarding the line which describes the northern frontier of the dominions of Affghanistan. Accordingly a correspondence has passed, of which this is the main subject. Its tenor, no less than its object, will, I trust, be approved by the public opinion of both nations." Bills were promised for settling the question of University Education in Ireland, and for the promotion of a Supreme Court of Judicature, including provision for the trial of appeals. Address agreed to without a division.

— Payment of 150,000,000fr., the second on the fourth milliard, made by the French Government to Germany.

— "Hoax" attempted upon Dr. Cumming at Brighton, a telegram intimating that the Pope had died this morning being put into his hand as he was stepping on the platform to deliver a lecture on "The Pope and his work in England."

8.—The Count de Chambord writes to Bishop Dupanloup :—"Believe me, notwithstanding all its failings, France has not so far lost the sentiment of honour. It no more understands the head of the House of Bourbon denying the standard of Algiers than it would have understood the Bishop of Orleans consenting to occupy a seat in the French Academy in company of sceptics and atheists. I have not learned with less pleasure than the true friends of the country the presence of the Princes, my cousins, at the Chapelle Expiatoire on January 20 ; for, in appearing there to pray publicly in that monument consecrated to the memory of the Martyr King, they must have felt the full influence of a place so propitious to great teaching and generous inspirations. I have, then, neither sacrifices to make nor conditions to receive. I expect little from the ability of man, and much from the justice of God. When I am too bitterly tried, a glance at the Vatican re-animates my courage and strengthens my hopes. It is at this school of the illustrious captive that one acquires the spirit of firmness, resignation, and peace—of that peace which is assured to everyone who takes his conscience as his guide, and Pius IX. as his model."

— Kew bridge opened free of toll, the Lord Mayor and Sheriffs marching across at the head of a procession.

8.—The French Committee of Thirty appoint the Duc de Broglie as their reporter.

9.—Died, at Vienna, aged 83, the Dowager Empress Caroline Augusta, widow of the Emperor Francis.

10.— Mr. Charles Reade obtains 200*l.* damages in an action against the *Morning Advertiser* for a criticism judged to be libellous on the plaintiff's dramatic piece "Shilly Shally."

— The Home Secretary submits to the Commons the new rules framed under the Parks Regulation Act, superseding those previously put in force by Mr. Ayrton. The new regulations provided that no public address of an unlawful character, or for an unlawful purpose, could be delivered in the Park, nor any assembly of persons permitted unless conducted in a decent and orderly manner.

11.—King Amadeus of Spain announces to the Cortes his intention to abdicate. It was a great honour, he said, to preside over the destinies of a country, however profoundly disturbed it might be, and he had resolved to keep his oath and respect the Constitution, believing that his loyalty would compensate for the errors due to his inexperience. "My good wishes," adds the King, "have deceived me, for Spain lives in the midst of a perpetual conflict. If my enemies had been foreigners, I would not abandon the task, but they are Spaniards. I wish neither to be the King of a party nor to act illegally ; but believing all my efforts to be sterile, I renounce the Crown for myself, my sons, and heirs." The President then proposed that the King's message should be sent to the Senate, and that both Chambers should unite and assume the sovereignty. The abdication of the King was unanimously accepted, and the Cortes appointed a commission to draw up a reply to his Majesty's message. It was therein declared that "if any human forces could restrain the inevitable course of events, your Majesty, by your constitutional education and your respect for constituted right, would have completely and absolutely averted them. Penetrated with this truth, the Cortes, if it had been in their power, would have made the utmost sacrifice to persuade your Majesty to desist from your resolution and withdraw your abdication. But the knowledge they have of the unbending character of your Majesty, the justice they do to the maturity of your ideas and to your perseverance in your resolutions, impede the Cortes from asking your Majesty to reconsider your determination, and bind them to notify you that they have assumed to themselves the supreme power and sovereignty of the nation, in order, under circumstances so critical, to provide, with the rapidity counselled by the gravity of the danger and the supreme crisis for the salvation of the democracy, the basis of our politics ; of liberty, the soul of our rights ; and of the nation, which is our mother, immortal and beloved."

11.—Convocation of the Province of Canterbury meet in the Jerusalem Chamber, Westminster, the Upper House engaging in a debate on an increase of the Episcopate, and the Lower on the Rubrics, the Burial Service, and Athanasian Creed. On the latter question, a Synodal Declaration was agreed upon after a long debate.

12.—Suspension announced of Peter Lawson and Sons, seedsmen, established in Edinburgh over a century.

— Sir T. Chambers' Marriage with a Deceased Wife's Sister Bill read a second time in the Commons by 126 to 87 votes.

— The Spanish Assembly elect a government of Republicans and Radicals under the presidency of Señor Figueras.

— King Amadeus and the Queen with their children leave Madrid for Lisbon, escorted by a guard of honour as far as the frontier.

13.—The Lord Chancellor introduces a measure for the establishment of a Supreme Court of Judicature and a Court of Appeal. The Lord Chief Justice, he explained, was to preside over the High Court, composed of four divisions, representing respectively the Court of Queen's Bench, the Court of Chancery, the Court of Common Pleas, and the Court of Exchequer. Each of these subordinate Courts was to have, in a general way, jurisdiction in all cases ; and there would, therefore, be commenced a fusion of Law and Equity. The House of Lords was to cease from its judicial functions in English appeals, which were to be transferred to the Court of Appeal, consisting exclusively of Judges under the presidency of the Lord Chancellor. But the existing procedure was still to apply to appeals from Scotland and Ireland ; and Lord Selborne abstained from touching the subject of ecclesiastical jurisdiction, this being, as he observed, *sui generis*, and interfering with it at present would only diminish the prospect of passing any measure whatever.

— Mr. Gladstone submits to the Commons his scheme for dealing with Irish University Education. He proposed to separate Trinity College, Dublin, from the Dublin University, and the Theological Faculty from Trinity College, Dublin. The precedent of England was to be followed in drawing a distinction, not merely theoretical, between the University and the College or Colleges in union with it ; and the Theological Faculty was to be handed over to the Representative Body of the disestablished Irish Church, with a fund to be administered in trust to the purposes for which the Faculty had hitherto existed. The newly constituted Dublin University was to be a teaching as well as an examining body, though, on account of the unduly sensitive state of the Irish mind, neither theology, modern history, nor moral and metaphysical philosophy were to have a recognized place in the *curriculum*. The Governing Body of the University would contain twenty-eight ordinary members, to be nominated in the first place by Parliament ; but it was hoped that in ten years' time the University itself would be in a fit state to take its share in appointing its own governors. The University funds were to come in different proportions from the revenues of Trinity College, Dublin, from the Consolidated Fund, from the fees of students, and from the surplus of Irish ecclesiastical property. Trinity College, the Colleges at Cork and Belfast, and, if the rulers of those voluntary bodies thought fit, Magee College, and the so-called Roman Catholic University, would at once become members of the new University, which might hereafter be made still more comprehensive. The scheme was favourably received at first, but latterly gave rise to much hostile criticism both in and out of the House.

14.—Señor Figueras receives General Sickles, the United States Minister at Madrid, who officially recognizes the Spanish Republic.

— Five young women burned to death at Liverpool in a fire on the premises of Rushton, Cooper, and Dunderdale, spice and rice merchants.

15.—A partial settlement of the South Wales strike effected, 4,000 men now resuming work ; the wages paid for the first fortnight to be 5 per cent. lower than in December 1872, during March to be the same as December 1872, and from March to July 5 per cent. higher than at the close of last year.

17.—Monsignor Mermillod expelled from Swiss territory by the Federal Council. He afterwards explained that the Holy See had appointed him to the office of Apostolic Vicariat because the Catholics had no longer a spiritual head, and because the form was one always used by the Holy See whenever there was a conflict of jurisdiction and it was desired to pave the way to an agreement. Monsignor Mermillod further declared that the Apostolic Vicariat was in no way identical with the erection of a diocesan see. Secondly, that the measure was temporary and provisional. Thirdly, that it attempted nothing against the rights of the State. Fourthly, that far from closing the pending negotiations between Church and State in Switzerland, it left the door open to every attempt at a treatment of the matters in dispute. The Bishop further added, that there were only three practical solutions of the problem of the relations of Church and State—viz., complete liberty, as in England and America ; an agreement in the nature of a Concordat ; or oppression. M. Mermillod was afterwards arrested and removed to Ferney.

18.—Joseph Xavier de Lizardi, of Lancaster Gate, examined at the Mansion House on a charge of obtaining 12,000*l*. by false pretences from Messrs. Glyn, Mills, Currie and Co., in so far as he had handed over as part security a bill of lading for 1,300 quarters of wheat sold some days previously to another firm. Lizardi afterwards absconded.

18.—Explosion at Talke Colliery, causing the death of twenty workmen, all engaged in the seam where the accident occurred.

19.—Dr. Duggan, Bishop of Clonfert, acquitted on the charge of inciting certain Galway electors to attack Captain Trench. This being the third acquittal in connection with the Galway election, the remaining prosecutions were abandoned.

— Army Estimates for the current year issued, showing the net charge to be 13,231,400*l.*, and the total number of men 128,968.

--- The four hundredth anniversary of the birthday of Copernicus celebrated at Thorn in Prussia.

20.—The Earl of Rosebery moves, but withdraws after debate, a motion for the appointment of a Royal Commission to inquire into the alleged scarcity and deterioration of English horses. Earl Granville suggested a Select Committee as the proper tribunal for making the necessary inquiries, a suggestion afterwards carried into effect.

— On the subject of the Athanasian Creed, the Lower House of Convocation of the Northern Province, agree " That inasmuch as Holy Scriptures, in divers places, doth promise life to them that believe, and declare the condemnation of them that believe not, so doth the Church, in sundry clauses of this confession, declare the necessity of holding fast the Christian faith, and the great peril of rejecting the same. Nevertheless, the Church doth not therein pronounce judgment upon particular persons, the Great Judge of all being alone able to discern who they are who in this matter are guilty before Him. Moreover, the warnings contained in this creed are not otherwise to be understood than as the like warnings set forth in Holy Scripture."

20. — Her Majesty visits the Empress Eugénie at Chiselhurst for the first time since the death of the Emperor.

21.—The Duc de Broglie reads to the Assembly the report of the Committee of Thirty. The document described the labours of the Commission, its relations with the Government, and the principal alternatives which have excited discussions. It dealt successively with the relations of the existing powers, Ministerial responsibility, the Second Chamber, electoral reforms, and the transmission of powers, and explained the patriotic reasons which induced the vote of the Commission. The report concluded with the *projet de loi*, and article 4, adopted at the last sitting of the Commission, in the following terms :—" 1. The National Assembly will not separate until it has made provision respecting the organization and the mode of transmission of Legislative and Executive powers. 2. Respecting the creation and

104

the functions of a Second Chamber, which is not to come into operative existence until after the separation of the present Assembly. 3. Respecting the electoral law. The Government will submit to the Assembly bills upon the subjects above-mentioned."

22.—In the case of the appeal of Mr. Edwin James to be reinstated as a member of the English bar, the judges decide that no adequate cause had been shown for reversing the decision of the benchers of the Inner Temple, and he could not therefore be re-admitted to practice at the bar.

— The report of the Emma Silver Mining Company (Limited) states that there have been paid to the shareholders thirteen monthly dividends, amounting to 193,532*l.*, while, on finally making up the accounts to the end of December, it turns out that the funds available amounted only to 185,658*l.*, leaving a deficiency of 7,874*l*. This result was attributed chiefly to the disastrous flooding of the mine in June, and the litigation consequent on the hostile action of the Illinois Tunnel Company.

23.—Died, aged 81, the Rev. Dr. Thomas Barclay, Principal of the University of Glasgow. He was succeeded by Dr. John Caird.

24.—Mr. Cardwell introduces the Army Estimates for 1873-4.

— The Japanese Government annuls the edict against the Christian religion, and liberates all Christians imprisoned under it since 1870.

— Died at St. Leonards-on-the-Sea, aged 70, the Rev. Thomas Guthrie, D.D., Free Church clergyman, and editor of the "Sunday Magazine."

— Discussing the new frontier line to the north of Affghanistan at a meeting of the Royal Geographical Society, Sir Henry Rawlinson and Lord Lawrence highly approved of fixing the line of the Oxus, and were agreed that, although invasion from the Attrak valley by way of Persia might be possible enough, on the side of Badakshan it was quite impracticable. Lord Lawrence said it would be "insanity" on the part of Russia to think of the attempt. Sir Henry explained how the doubt had arisen as to whether Badakshan, geographically and politically, had always in reality been subject to Affghanistan. Russia had always believed, or professed to believe, in maps whose falsity has been proved to demonstration. They were based partly on forgeries by a German klaproth, who described, and circumstantially mapped out, a country he had never travelled, partly on charts done in squares by a Chinese expedition ; and, as it happened, the particular squares comprising the country in dispute had been turned sideways in fitting them together. Thus a mountain range that actually runs from east to west had been represented as running from north to south.

25.—Opposition to Mr. Gladstone's Irish University Bill. At a meeting of the Senate of Dublin University, Sir Joseph Napier expressed an opinion that the governing scheme was one of the most astounding academic constitutions which it could ever have entered into the head of a man to devise. Mr. Gladstone's description of the University, as in a state of absolute servitude and bondage, from which he was anxious to deliver it, was rather a caricature to excite a laugh than a statement to form the basis of legislation. Dr. Hart proposed the adoption of a petition complaining that the proposal to substitute for the two existing Universities a single central body with a monopoly of granting degrees would lower the standard of Academic attainments, and declaring that the evil would be aggravated by the affiliation of small provincial schools or colleges. The Roman Catholic prelates also held meetings to oppose the scheme, joining in a declaration :—"That, viewing with alarm the widespread ruin caused by godless systems of education, and adhering to the declarations of the Holy See, we reiterate the condemnation of mixed education as fraught with danger to that divine faith which is to be prized above all earthly things. . . . That the distinguished proposer of this measure, proclaiming as he does in his opening speech that the condition of Roman Catholics in Ireland in regard to university education is 'miserably bad,' 'scandalously bad,' and professing to redress this admitted grievance, brings forward a measure singularly inconsistent with his professions, because, instead of redressing, it perpetuates that grievance, upholding two out of three of the Queen's Colleges, and planting in the metropolis two other great teaching institutions the same in principle with the Queen's Colleges. . . . That, as the legal owners of the Catholic University, and at the same time acting on behalf of the Catholic people of Ireland, for whose advantage and by whose generosity it has been established, in the exercise of that right of ownership, we will not consent to the affiliation of the Catholic University to the new University, unless the proposed scheme be largely modified ; and we have the same objection to the affiliation of other Catholic Colleges in Ireland."

— Died, aged 81, Henry Lester Horn, the oldest midshipman in the Navy, having been present with the fleet at Corunna in 1809, and again on a perilous service in Quiberon Bay. His father, Lieutenant James Horn, when stationed at Gravesend, in charge of the pressgang, during the Mutiny at the Nore, performed the hazardous service of carrying a despatch from the Lords of the Admiralty to the admiral, which resulted in the termination of the mutiny, and the re-opening of the navigation of the Thames. For this he received a silver salver from the merchants of the City of London.

26.—Died, aged 69, Sir William Fry Channell, formerly a Baron of the Court of Exchequer.

27.—The House of Lords reject the Chelsea Waterworks Bill by 70 votes against 29, thus seeking to preserve the beauty of the Thames between Hampton Court and Ditton.

28.—The first contested School Board election in Scotland takes place in the parish of Eastwood.

— Died, aged 74, Robert Graves, the last member of the Associate Engravers of the old class of the Royal Academy. Mr. Graves was elected a member of the Royal Academy in 1836, at which election (the only time in one hundred years) a ballot was not necessary, the candidate having obtained the whole of the votes of the academicians present.

March 1.—Collision in the Irish Channel soon after midnight between the sailing vessel *Chacabuco* from San Francisco to Liverpool, and the steamer *Torch* from Liverpool to Dublin. The captain, pilot, and twenty-two of the crew went down with the sailing ship.

— Discovery of extensive forgeries of bills on City houses, discounted by the Bank of England ; and a reward issued for the apprehension of Frederick Albert Warren, one of the Bidwell gang.

3.—Mr. Gladstone's motion for the second reading of the Irish University Bill met with an amendment by Mr. Bourke, expressing regret that the Government had not stated the names of the twenty-eight members of the governing body. In anticipation of this objection, the Prime Minister remarked that it would be the wish of the Government to select men of the greatest weight to serve on the governing body without reference to their political opinions or to the course they might have taken with regard to the bill, but it would be impossible to ask such men to undertake the duty until the bill had made some way in Committee. If, indeed, they were willing to serve before they knew what shape the bill would take, they would not be fit for the position. That the refusal of the Government to take this course should be made the subject of a vote of censure was a fact worthy of commemoration in parliamentary history. Debate adjourned.

— Died, Dr. Robert Buchanan, M.A., late Professor of Logic in Glasgow University.

4.—Mr. Plimsoll moves for a Royal Commission to inquire into the condition of, and certain practices connected with, the commercial marine of the United Kingdom, mentioning in connection with his proposal that there had perished at sea in 1868, 2,488 men ; 1869, 2,821 ; 1870, 3,411 ; 1871, 2,205 ; making a total of 11,016, or an average of 2,754 lives per annum. Mr. Fortescue, on the part of the Government, assented to the appointment of a

Royal Commission, but suggested such a change in the language of the motion as would point the attention of the Commission to the various causes of shipwreck, with the view of suggesting remedies.

4.—After a two hours' speech from M. Thiers, the Assembly votes the preamble of the Duc de Broglie's bill by 475 to 199 votes. "I am," said M. Thiers, "the President of the Republic, and I promised you to restore intact the powers entrusted to me. (Bravos from the Left). I shall not allow it to be interfered with by any interest ; but it is an incontestable and undeniable fact that what has been entrusted to me was the Conservative Republic. There are very respectable men who prefer the monarchy to the Republic, but if we speak as honest men, it must be confessed that it would be very difficult at present to establish a monarchy. (A cry from the Right of 'difficult, thanks to you !') Gentlemen, let us have political as we have religious toleration. Political toleration does not mean the abandonment of Faith, just as religious toleration is not apostasy. It is a respect for the opinion of others ; it is admitting that a man may serve another form of government to ours without being a bad citizen. Monarchy is impossible, and the definitive and immediate Republic is wanted."

— President Grant enters on his second term of office with a message to Congress, declaring that his efforts "will be directed to the re-establishment of good feeling between the different sections of our common country, the restoration of the currency to a fixed value compared with the standard value of gold, possibly to a par with it ; the construction of cheap routes, the maintenance of friendly relations with all our neighbours, as well as with distant nations, the re-establishment of our commerce, and the recovery of our share of the carrying trade on the ocean, the encouragement of manufacturing industries, the elevation of labour, and the civilization of the aborigines under the benign influence of education— either this, or war to extermination. Our superiority in strength and the advantages we derive from civilization should make us lenient towards the Indian ; the wrong already inflicted leaves a balance to his credit, and the question to be considered is, 'Cannot the Indian be made a useful member of society by proper teaching and treatment !' For the future, while I hold office, the subject of the acquisition of territory must have the support of the American people before I recommend it. I do not share the apprehension that there is a danger of governments becoming weakened or destroyed by extension. As commerce, education, and the rapid transit of thought and matter by telegraph and steam have changed everything ; I rather think that the Great Maker is preparing the world to become one nation, speaking one language—a consummation which will render armies and navies no
106

longer necessary. 'I will encourage and support any recommendations of Congress tending towards such ends."

4.—Sir James Fergusson, Bart., gazetted to be Governor and Commander-in-Chief of New Zealand and its dependencies.

— In his evidence before the Select Committee on Endowed Schools, Lord Lyttelton said he held that no man ought after his death to be able to direct the application of his property ; "It should be left to the commonwealth to deal with it after a certain time, and so all restrictions in section 19 should be removed. Nothing is more sacred than a trust, but it ought not to be perpetual. The time will come when it will be held to be a superstition that a dying man may direct what is to be done with his property."

— Replying to remonstrances forwarded to him from the Mess of the Northern Circuit, regarding a supposed slight on the Attorney-General of the County Palatine, who had been passed over in the case of the Queen v. Cotton, Sir John Coleridge writes :—"There either is a right in Mr. Aspinall or there is not ; and although it is for the Treasury and not for me to decide, I certainly think that the Treasury have decided rightly in the negative. If then, as I think, there is no right, I am unable to perceive upon what ground the Mess of the Northern Circuit should apply to the Attorney-General that any particular gentleman should represent him in any particular case. It would be highly inconvenient if in any instance where the choice of the Attorney-General was disapproved of by the Mess he should be applied to by resolution to alter his choice, and direct a gentleman indicated to him by such resolution to be instructed to represent him. With a very earnest wish to avoid offence, I must decline to be a party to any such proceeding."

5.—Speaking at Croydon on the occasion of presenting a portrait to Mr. Locke King, M.P. for East Surrey, Mr. Gladstone praised the guest of the evening as combining political independence with that regard to party ties without which political progress was impossible. "We are in the middle," he said, "of an adjourned debate, and that adjourned debate is upon a vote of censure. What is it about? It may seem strange to some that all this row should exist about an Irish University Bill ; but somehow or other an Irish question is very commonly found to be a suitable and convenient subject for a row, and as to this Irish question in particular, it seems to have acquired a peculiar aptitude for this purpose, arising out of the joint operation of two circumstances— firstly, that it is rooted in a real necessity for legislation ; and, secondly, that this legislation has been pressed upon the Government for, I think, three, if not four, of the successive years of its existence with such eagerness and urgency, and our plea that we were otherwise occupied has been so scornfully rejected by some, that it has only been by an appeal to the confidence of the House of Commons—by what is called staking our existence on the issue—that we have been able to secure for ourselves the opportunity of dealing with it at all, and presenting to that House the views which we might conscientiously entertain. Well, we have done that, and in the midst of the din of the battle I am not going to anticipate the issue. To-day a measure may be upon the crest of the wave, and to-morrow it may be in the trough ; but the same measure which was one day on the crest of the wave and the next day in the trough, may on the third day be on the crest of the wave again." In subsequent observations the right hon. gentleman said that " when the hour of dissolution—not of Parliament, but of the Cabinet—should come, it would find him and his colleagues not unwilling victims. But we will not," he added, " abandon our positions unnecessarily."

5.—Died, at Glasgow, aged 103 years, Miss Ann Wallace, a lineal descendant of the Scottish patriot, registered in the Barony parish as born in July, 1770.

6.—Debate resumed on Irish University Bill, Mr. Horsman, Mr. Hardy, and Dr. Playfair objecting to the measure, the latter also protesting against the exclusion of mental science and modern history as a sacrifice of free inquiry to ecclesiastical dictation, which could only end in making the students bigots or infidels. Mr. Fortescue and Mr. Lowe replied, the latter creating some amusement by declaring that the "gagging clauses" were " not of the essence of the bill," and might be amended or removed in Committee.

— A deputation of Irish members wait upon Mr. Gladstone to inform him that they felt bound by every sense of honour to support denominational and religious education as against secularisation. They added that the Roman Catholic body, though vastly in the majority, did not demand endowments, but that if any class were to be endowed they claimed a proportionate endowment. If, therefore, the Government did not see their way to making such alterations in the University Education Bill as would meet the objections of their constituents, the Irish members belonging to the Liberal party would be bound to vote against the bill. This would pain them much, but they were inflexible in their determination. Mr. Gladstone replied that the Government must be considered as much masters of their own position as the Irish members were of their own actions, but that if they would put their views into writing he would submit them to his colleagues in the Cabinet.

— The National Assembly pass the second clause of the Duc de Broglie's bill relating to the promulgation of "urgent" bills by the President, and to the President's right of veto.

— Died, aged 70, the Right Hon. F. L. Corry, M.P. for Tyrone, formerly First Lord of the Admiralty.

6.—The Lord Chamberlain prohibits the performance of the "Happy Land" at the Court Theatre on the alleged ground of the piece making free with various members of the Cabinet.

7.—Died, at Ossington Hall, Notts, aged 73, John Evelyn Denison, Viscount Ossington, late Speaker of the House of Commons.

— Mid-Cheshire election, the first English county contest under the ballot, results in the return of a Conservative, Mr. Egerton Leigh, who polled 3,508 against 2,118 tendered for Mr. Latham, Liberal.

— Mary Ann Cotton charged with wholesale poisoning at Bishop Auckland, tried at Durham, found guilty, and sentenced to death. It was thought this wretched criminal had caused the death of no fewer than eighteen people—husbands, children, step-children, and lodgers.

8.—Died, aged 72, Sir Frederick Madden, F.R.S., K.H., for many years keeper of the MSS. at the British Museum, and a high authority in historical and antiquarian literature.

— Died, aged 50, Robert W. Thomson, C.E., inventor of locomotive traction steam-engines.

9.—Pastoral by Cardinal Cullen read in Irish Roman Catholic churches, in which Mr. Gladstone's bill was described as richly endowing "non-Catholic and godless colleges to those who for centuries have enjoyed the great public endowments for higher education in Ireland, and then, without giving one farthing to Catholics, it invites them to compete in their poverty, produced by penal laws and confiscations, with others who, as the Prime Minister states, are left in possession of enormous wealth. The New University scheme only increases the number of Queen's Colleges, so often and so solemnly condemned by the Catholic Church and by all Ireland, and gives a new impulse to that sort of teaching which separates education from religion and its holy influences, and banishes God, the author of all good, from our schools."

— Died, at Addlestone, Surrey, aged 81, Charles Knight, an early labourer in the field of cheap literature, and a writer of various historical works of standard excellence.

10.—An application having been made to the Exchequer by Earl Stanhope on behalf of the Society of Antiquaries, that examination should be made at the public cost of the tumuli on the plains of Troy, Mr. Lowe replies:— "The question is, are excavations undertaken for the purpose of illustrating the 'Iliad' a proper object for the expenditure of public money? I am sorry to say that in my judgment they are not. It is a new head of expense. It has no practical object, but aims at satisfying the curiosity of those who believe that the narrative of Homer was a true history, and not the creation of a poet's imagination. But while I regret to be unable to accede to your lordship's suggestion, I submit that there is a way open by which the money may be provided. It is said that the schoolboy enthusiasm of Europe liberated Greece from Turkey. Is not the literary enthusiasm of wealthy England equal to the enterprise of exploring scenes which are ever recurring to the imagination of everyone who has received a classical education? The *Daily Telegraph*, with my hearty approbation, is exploring without any assistance from the public purse the secrets that lie buried under the mounds of Mesopotamia. Shall it be said that a large number of wealthy English noblemen and gentlemen can find no better expedient for the gratification of a liberal curiosity than to ask the Chancellor of the Exchequer to employ for its satisfaction money wrung from the earnings of the poorest of the community? I sincerely regret that the spirit of Herodes Atticus has not descended to modern times, and feel convinced that if one-half the energy which is devoted in attempts to obtain aid from Government were given to create a spirit of private munificence, this and many similar objects might be attained with the utmost facility and completeness."

10.—Adjourned debate on the Irish University bill resumed by Mr. Vernon Harcourt, who declared his intention of supporting the bill, although he admitted that it was not a successful specimen of legislating according to Irish ideas, and that it had been received in Ireland with a unanimity of disapprobation. Mr. Bernal Osborne also spoke against the bill to-night, and Mr Cardwell in its support.

11.—Defeat of Mr. Gladstone's Government on the Irish University Bill, a division taking place about 2 A.M. on the morning of the 12th, on the motion that the bill be read a second time, when 287 voted against and 284 in favour. The announcement of a majority of 3 against the Ministers was the signal for a tumultuous burst of cheering. Besides the Prime Minister and Mr. Disraeli the principal speakers to-night were Col. Wilson Patten, Mr. Dodson, and Mr. Bouverie, the latter denouncing the bill as scandalously inadequate, pleasing nobody in Ireland, and yet likely within twenty years to hand over the University to priests. Mr. Disraeli rose at half-past ten to comment on the bewildering character of the debate. "Here is the hon. member for Surrey," he said, "Mr. Locke King, who, after recent proceedings, could scarcely refuse to propose a vote of confidence. (Laughter.) But this I can say for myself, and many gentlemen on this side, we have no wish to oppose it. If her Majesty's Government have not the confidence of the House of Commons, I want to know what have they the confidence of? It is a House returned under their auspices. (Loud cries of 'No, no,' from the Ministerial benches.) Well, elected under the exciting eloquence

of the right hon. gentleman. (Cheers and laughter.) When I remember that campaign of rhetoric, I must say I think this House was formally as well as spiritually its creation. (Laughter.) . . . This is essentially a material age; the opinions which are now afloat, which have often been afloat before, and which have died away as I have no doubt these will die in due time, are opposed in my opinion to all those sound convictions which the proper study of moral and mental philosophy has long established. But that such a proposition should be made in the land of the University which has produced Berkeley and Hutchinson makes it still more surprising. We live in an age when young men prattle about Protoplasm, and when young ladies in gilded saloons unconsciously talk Atheism. (Laughter.) And this is the moment when a Minister, called upon to fulfil one of the noblest duties which can fall upon the most ambitious statesman—namely, the formation of a great University, formally comes forward and proposes the omission from public study of moral and mental philosophy." (Cheers.) Mr. Disraeli next amused the House by his reference to the proposed Council of twenty-eight persons. "They are all to be distinguished men. They are all to be—and I thought the expression was a happy one—they are all to be 'eminent men of moderate opinions.' (Laughter.) The House is pretty well aware how twenty-eight gentlemen would be obtained under the circumstances. I suppose that Cardinal Cullen would be one of them, and his Eminence would be paired off with the Primate of the Protestant Church. (Laughter.) Then, under the circumstances in which we are placed, the Provost of Trinity College would be a most admirable councillor, and Monsignor Woodlock would be another. Then would come Lord Chancellor O'Hagan, who would probably pair off with the right hon. gentleman who filled the same office for us. (Laughter.) And you would have in your council very much what you have in this House—two parties organized and arrayed against each other, with two or three trimmers thrown in on each side." (Cheers and laughter.) Describing the commencement of Mr. Gladstone's policy of confiscation when he mistook the clamour of the Nonconformists for the voice of the nation— "You have now," continued Mr. Disraeli, "had four years of it. You have despoiled churches. You have threatened every corporation and endowment in the country. (Cheers.) You have examined into everybody's affairs. You have criticised every profession and vexed every trade. (A laugh.) No one is certain of his property, and nobody knows what duties he may have to perform to-morrow. I believe that the people of this country have had enough of the policy of confiscation. From what I can see, the House of Commons elected to carry out that policy are beginning to experience some of the inconvenience of satiety, and if I am not mistaken, they will give some intimation to the Government to-night that that is their opinion also." (Cheers.) Mr. Disraeli concluded :—" Although I have not wished to make this a party question, although I have no wish to disturb the right hon. gentleman in his seat, although I have no communication with any section or with any party in this House, I may say with any individual of my own immediate colleagues, I must do my duty when I am asked, ' Do you or do you not approve this measure ?' (Cheers.) I must vote against a measure which I believe to be monstrous in its general principles, pernicious in many of its details, and utterly futile as a measure of practical legislation." (Continued cheers.) Mr. Gladstone wound up the debate by defending all the essential details of the measure, declaring that " where we have earnestly sought and toiled for peace we find only contention ; if our tenders of relief are thrust aside with scorn, let us still remember that there is a voice which is not heard in the crackling of the fire or in the roaring of the whirlwind or the storm, the still, small voice of justice, which is heard after they have passed away. To mete out justice to Ireland, according to the best view that with human infirmity we could form, has been the work, I will almost say the sacred work, of this Parliament. (' No, no,' and cheers.) Having put our hand to the plough, let us not turn back. Let not what we think the fault or perverseness of those whom we are attempting to assist have the slightest effect in turning us from the path on which we have entered. As we have begun, so let us go through, and with firm and resolute hand let us efface from the law and the practice of the country the last—I believe it is the last —of the religious and social grievances of Ireland." (Loud and prolonged cheering.) On the result of the division being made known, Mr. Gladstone said : —" I think, Sir, after the division that has just taken place, the House will expect to hear a word from me. I apprehend that the effect of the vote is to lay the bill aside for the moment. It is capable of revival, but it requires a motion for the purpose of reviving the order. The vote of the House has been a vote of a grave character, I need hardly say ; and as the House never wishes to enter into deliberations upon secondary matters while the question of the existence of the Government is in doubt, probably the best thing I can do is to move that we now adjourn, and that we adjourn until Thursday." (Cheers.) The house accordingly adjourned at twenty-five minutes past two o'clock till Thursday the 13th. Thirty-six Irish Liberals voted against the bill, and fifteen Irish members in its favour.

11.—The Supreme Court of Judicature Bill read a second time in the Lords.

— Died, aged 85, Reginald George Macdonald, captain and chief of Clanranald.

13.—In the Commons this afternoon Mr. Gladstone, amid much cheering, announces, that in consequence of the vote on the Irish University Bill, her Majesty's Ministers had tendered their resignation ; and to permit of the necessary new arrangements being made, he begged to move that the House at its rising should adjourn till Monday the 17th.

13.—On entering the House this afternoon a Royal Messenger waits on Mr. Disraeli commanding his presence at Buckingham Palace. " Her Majesty (the right hon. gentleman explained) did me the honour of consulting me upon the subject of the ministerial difficulty. She inquired of me whether I was prepared to form a Government and carry on her affairs. I then informed her Majesty distinctly that I was quite prepared to form an administration which I believed would conduct her Majesty's affairs efficiently and in a manner entitled to her confidence, but that I could not undertake to conduct the government of the country in the present House of Commons. That was the information I gave distinctly and clearly to her Majesty, and from that position I have never for a moment faltered."

— Marriage with a Deceased Wife's Sister Bill rejected in the House of Lords by 74 to 49 votes.

— Died, at the Cloisters, aged 72, the Rev. Evan Nepean, canon of Westminster and chaplain in ordinary to the Queen.

14. — Letters from Zanzibar describe Sir Bartle Frere's mission as a failure ; the Sultan maintaining that he and his Arab chiefs must reject the treaty, not only for the financial reasons which he had previously put forward as his main objection, but also on the ground that slavery was a time-honoured institution, sanctioned alike by the Mohammedan religion and ancient custom, and its abolition would lead to insurrection and disaster ; and that, moreover, no confidence could be placed in any new treaties.

15.—Died, aged 68, Rev. Henry Wall, M.A., professor of logic in the University of Oxford.

— Treaty signed at Berlin for the speedy evacuation of French territory by the Germans.

— Dispute between the Greek and Latin Christians at Bethlehem concerning the curtains in the Grotto of the Nativity, burned in 1871, and which the Ottoman Government were to have replaced in order to end the traditional jealousy of the two bodies. To-day the Greek Patriarch formally protested "against the violations committed by the Latin clergy, who rely upon the right of the stronger, and tread under foot the secular rights of the Greek nation to the Grotto of the Nativity of Jesus Christ, at Bethlehem. We ask the Supreme Government not to allow this outrage against the nation."

17.—Mr. Gladstone announces in the Commons that, while passing Sunday (yesterday) in the country, he received a communication from her Majesty to an effect which led him finally to abandon any expectation that upon the present occasion the party in opposition would construct a Government to carry on the affairs of the country. At the same time, in reply to an inquiry from her Majesty, he at once stated that he placed any services he could render at her Majesty's disposal, and that he would take steps forthwith to proceed to consider, together with those who had been his colleagues in the Cabinet, how far they were disposed to resume their offices, and at the same time to consider the state of public affairs and the business of this House after the events of last week. In conformity with Mr. Gladstone's desire the House, at its rising, adjourned to Thursday the 20th.

18.—Mr Mill presides at a meeting of the Land Tenure Reform Association held in Exeter Hall, and explains its two main principles—first, no more land, under any pretext, to become the private property of individuals ; secondly, taxation on the land, in order to give the benefit of its natural increase of value to the whole community, instead of to the proprietors, these being allowed the option of relinquishing the land at its present money value.

— Close of the strike in South Wales, the remaining workmen agreeing to-day to resume work on what were known as the "Dowlais terms."

19.—Testimonial of the value of 5,800*l.* presented to the Rev. Dr. Moffatt in recognition of his services as a missionary in Africa.

— The Committee appointed to report on the column of the Place Vendôme decide to re-erect the monument as it stood, and to record by two inscriptions the date of its demolition and of its reconstruction.

20.—Intimation made in both Houses of Parliament that Mr. Gladstone and his colleagues were now in a position to carry on the Government as formerly. Quoting from a "Memorandum" submitted to the Queen, Mr. Gladstone said he "will not and does not suppose that the efforts of the Opposition to defeat the Government on Wednesday morning were made with a previously formed intention on their part to refuse any aid to your Majesty, if the need should arise, in providing for the government of the country ; and the summary refusal, which is the only fact before him, he takes to be not in full correspondence, either with the exigencies of the case, or, as he has shown, with Parliamentary usage." To this charge Mr. Disraeli replied in another "Memorandum :"—"The charge against the leader of the Opposition personally that by 'his summary refusal' to undertake your Majesty's Government he was failing in his duty to your Majesty and the country is founded altogether on a gratuitous assumption by Mr. Gladstone, which pervades his letter, that the means of Mr. Disraeli to carry on the Government were

110

not 'exhausted.' A brief statement of facts will at once dispose of this charge. Before Mr. Disraeli, with due deference, offered his decision to your Majesty, he had the opportunity of consulting those gentlemen with whom he acts in public life, and they were unanimously of opinion that it would be prejudicial to the interests of the country for a Conservative Administration to attempt to conduct your Majesty's affairs in the present House of Commons. What other means were at Mr. Disraeli's disposal ? Was he to open negotiations with a section of the late Ministry, and waste days in barren interviews, vain applications and the device of impossible combinations ? Was he to make overtures to the considerable section of the Liberal party who had voted against the Government—namely, the Irish Roman Catholic gentlemen ? Surely Mr. Gladstone could not seriously contemplate this ? Impressed from experience, obtained in the very instances to which Mr. Gladstone refers, of the detrimental influence upon Government of a crisis unnecessarily prolonged by hollow negotiations, Mr. Disraeli humbly conceived that he was taking a course at once advantageous to the public interests, and tending to spare your Majesty unnecessary anxiety by at once laying before your Majesty the real position of affairs." Mr. Disraeli now assured the House that "the Tory party at the present time occupies the most satisfactory position which it has held since the days of its greatest statesmen, Mr. Pitt and Lord Grenville. It has divested itself of those excrescences which are not indigenous to its native growth, but which in a time of long prosperity were the consequence sometimes of negligence, and sometimes, perhaps, in a certain degree, of ignorance. (Laughter from the Ministerial side.) We are now emerging from a fiscal period in which almost all the public men of this generation have been brought up. All the questions of trade and navigation, of the incidence of taxation and of public economy, are settled. But there were other questions not less important, and of deeper and higher reach and range, which must engage the attention of a Constitutional Minister. There is the question whether the aristocratic principle should be recognised in our Constitution, and if so in what form ; whether the Commons of England shall remain an estate of the realm, numerous but privileged and qualified, or whether they should degenerate into an indiscriminate multitude — (a laugh, and 'Hear, hear')—whether a National Church shall be maintained, and if so, what shall be its rights and duties ; the functions of corporations, the sacredness of endowments— (cheers)—the tenure of landed property, the free disposal and even the existence of any kind of property. (Cheers and laughter.) All these institutions and all these principles, which have made this country free and famous, and conspicuous for its union of order with liberty, are now impugned, and in due time will become great and 'burning' questions. (Cheers.)

I think it of the utmost importance that when that time – which may be nearer at hand than we imagine – arrives, there shall be in this country a great constitutional party, distinguished for its intelligence as well as for its organization, which shall lead and direct the public mind of the people. And, sir, when that time arrives, and when they enter upon a career which must be noble, and which I hope and believe will be triumphant, I think they may perhaps remember, and not, I trust, with unkindness, that I at least prevented one obstacle from being placed in their way, and that I, as the trustee of their honour and interests, declined to form a weak and discredited Administration."

20.—Died at Westfield, Ross-shire, William Brydon, C.B., late surgeon-major Bengal army and Highland Rifle Militia; a name remarkable in Indian history as that of the one solitary individual of the 13,000 soldiers and camp-followers of the British army at Cabul who was neither killed nor taken prisoner in the memorable retreat from Cabul in January 1842. Dr. Brydon, after some hair-breadth escapes from the Affghans, reached Jelalabad alive, though wounded and exhausted, all the other persons composing the British force having being either killed or taken prisoners Dr. Brydon went through the rest of the siege of Jelalabad with the garrison under the command of Sir Robert Sale. It was his singular fate to be again shut up with Sir Henry Lawrence at Lucknow, and to pass uninjured through that long and trying siege.

— Died at Athens, aged 88, Sir Richard Church, G.C.H., one of the heroes of the Greek War of Independence.

— France declares a protectorate over the empire of Anam.

21.—Mr. Gathorne Hardy moves for an address to the Crown praying that the Queen in communicating the "Three New Rules" of the Treaty of Washington to Foreign Powers will declare to them her dissent from the principles set forth by the Geneva Tribunal as the basis of their award. The motion was withdrawn after debate, on Mr. Gladstone undertaking that when these rules were presented to foreign powers they should be accompanied by an expression of the dissent of the British Government from the recital of the award.

— Died at Croydon, aged 68, Henry Dorling, who had for many years been engaged in promoting the success of the Epsom race meetings.

22.—Came on at York Assizes, before Chief Justice Bovill, the trial of the Rev. Vyvyan Moyle, late Vicar of Eston, near Middlesbrough, charged with forging and uttering certain scrip certificates and an impression of a seal, purporting to be of the firm of Jackson, Gill, and Co., Limited ; also forging a certain deed, purporting to be a transfer of 220 shares of and in the firm of Jackson, Gill, and Co. ; also forging the signature of Edward

Stickley White ; and also forging a certain letter, dated 16th December, 1872, purporting to be written by the said E. S. White, with intent to defraud, at the township of Normanby, in the North Riding. On the indictment being read over, the prisoner, who appeared to feel his position very keenly, pleaded guilty to each of the counts. The Court at the time was densely crowded, many clergymen being present. Mr. Digby Seymour pleaded in mitigation of punishment the many charitable labours in which the prisoner had been engaged and the extreme temptation to which he had been subjected. In an evil hour, he said, his client had his eye attracted to the announcement of a society in London known as the Mutual Society, the dealings of the prisoner with which the learned counsel proceeded to state. He said that Mr. Moyle flattered himself that he might be able to increase his own means and the means of doing good to others. He took a large number of shares with this object in view, and borrowed the large sum of about 11,000*l.*, expecting to be able to pay this sum back again. He showed how in this he had been disappointed, and becoming involved, he had vainly sought to extricate himself by the commission of the offence with which he was charged. Mr. Seymour referred to the prisoner's connection with the firm of Jackson, Gill, and Co., and his belief that in about a year they would have issued their scrip to the general public, and that then he would have tangible scrip to offer to the secretary. In a fatal moment it occurred to him that if he anticipated that future which must shortly arise, and if he himself issued the scrip of Jackson, Gill, and Co. to the Mutual Society, he might, when the real scrip was issued, replace it, and substitute it for the other, which proceeding would have enabled him to realize large profits. Thus he fondly reasoned with himself ; and this led to the commission of the offence to which he had pleaded guilty. Next day the prisoner was sentenced to seven years' penal servitude.

22.—Meeting in Exeter Hall, presided over by the Earl of Shaftesbury, to support the "appeal" made by Mr. Plimsoll on behalf of British merchant seamen.

— The seventy-sixth birthday of the Emperor William celebrated with great rejoicings throughout the chief cities of Germany.

24.—The prisoner Mary Ann Cotton executed within the precincts of Durham jail. She slept well during the night, walked to the drop with a firm step, and spent several minutes there in earnest prayer. The prisoner had previously made a statement admitting having used poison, but with no evil intention. The Under-sheriff fainted when the drop fell, and had to be supported by two warders.

— Under the title of "Notes on Khiva," Sir H. Rawlinson read a paper on Central Asia to the Royal Geographical Society. Sir Henry contended that great political difficulties would begin with Russia when she began to occupy the country. "She would be committed to an enormous expenditure without any commensurate results. Considering the peculiar position of Khiva, the impoverished state of the country, and the difficulty of sustaining positions against the Turkomans, and constructing forts and wells to keep a good connection with the Caspian, he could not expect that Russia could occupy Khiva at a less cost than that involved by her occupation of Turkestan. Those who wished Russia ill would desire that she should pursue her present course. In the interests of peace, perhaps it would have been better had Russia not entered into the line of the Jaxartes; but as yet he saw nothing to cause us to apprehend danger. Our position was quiescent, while hers was progressive; we must go on our way conscious that, if real dangers approached us from any quarter, we were strong enough to resist them."

— The Navy Estimates introduced by Mr. Goschen, the gross amount being 9,633,000*l.*, an excess of 134,000*l.* over the vote of 1872.

25.—Lord Romilly retires from the office of Master of the Rolls, Sir Richard Baggallay, Q.C., a senior member of the bar of that court, expressing the respect and esteem entertained for his lordship's unvarying courtesy during the twenty-two years he had held that post.

— Died, aged 69, Professor Partridge, F.R.S., surgeon.

— Died, aged 76, Amédée Thierry, French historian.

26.—The Burial Bill read a second time in the Commons by 283 to 217 votes. "The bill," said Mr. Disraeli, in opposing the measure, "assumed that the sacred fabric and its consecrated precincts were national property. But this was the exact reverse of what the Nonconformists contended for when they succeeded in getting rid of church-rates on the ground that they had no concern in the maintenance of the church and the churchyard. That controversy was settled on the footing that the church and the churchyard were the property of Churchmen, and if Dissenters used them, it must be on the same conditions as Churchmen." The Nonconformists, Mr. Disraeli thought, had committed an error of late years in making war against the Church. The Reform Act of 1832 gave them an electoral power out of proportion to their numbers and wealth, which they must be conscious that at the next general election they could not retain. He earnestly desired a cessation of the war between Church and Dissent, and that they should join together in combating the common enemy to all Churches and all religious bodies which was abroad, and which, if it succeeded, would degrade the country and destroy all religion.

— Mr. Gladstone and other ministers attend a banquet given at the Mansion House to 200 provincial mayors.

26.—Died, aged 64, Arthur, Count von Bernstorff, formerly Prussian minister to this country, and latterly ambassador of the German Empire.

— The Dutch East India Company declare war against the Atchinese of Sumatra, a native race in the north of the island, with whom differences had arisen regarding the right of possession and the power to erect lighthouses at different points.

28.—Mr. Fortescue announces the appointment of a Royal Commission to inquire into and suggest remedies with regard to the alleged unseaworthiness of British shipping, whether arising from overloading or deck-loading, from defective construction or equipment, &c.; also to inquire into the system of marine insurance, the liability of shipowners to those whom they employ, and the practice of undermanning. The commissioners to be—the Duke of Somerset, chairman; the Duke of Edinburgh, Mr. Milner Gibson, Admiral Hope, Mr. Liddell, M.P., Mr. T. Brassey, M.P., Mr. Rothery, Mr. Cohen, Mr. Denny, Mr. Duncan, Captain Edgell of Lloyd's, and Mr. Merrifield of the Royal Naval School of Architecture. Commission to inquire and suggest.

29.—Oxford and Cambridge boat-race, the latter again coming in first by three lengths.

— The French National Assembly depart from the consideration of Prince Napoleon's petition against his expulsion by 334 to 278 votes.

31.—Extradition treaty concluded between the British and Danish Governments.

April 1.—Died, aged 84, General Sir William Bell, K.C.B., a Peninsular and Waterloo officer, whose commission of second lieutenant dated as far back as Nov. 1804.

— The steamer *Atlantic* of the White Star line wrecked off Halifax, into which port she was running, short of coal, and about 560 of her passengers drowned or frozen to death. The night was dark and the sea rough, and it was thought the watch on duty had mistaken Peggy's Point light for Sambro. So sudden was the catastrophe that most of the persons on board—and there were nearly 1,000 —went down in their berths; and many probably did not awake until they found themselves drowning through the ship having struck. The surviving passengers were crowded on the bows, and clinging to the rigging. Some of the more adventurous made their way to the rock by a line, but the situation there was one of great peril, as the tide was rising. The fishermen, however, came to the rescue, and by noon all the survivors were got ashore at Cape Prospect. The official inquiry at Halifax into the cause of the disaster resulted in a verdict commending the conduct of the officers after the ship struck, but condemning her management from the time her course was changed, and especially the captain's conduct in leaving the deck at midnight. His certificate might have been cancelled, but, considering the efforts he made to save life, it was only revoked for two years. The fourth officer was suspended for three months. The court was also of opinion that the *Atlantic* had been permitted to start on her voyage with a dangerously small supply of coal.

2.—The Queen visits Victoria Park, and receives an enthusiastic reception from the inhabitants of the eastern part of London.

— M. Grévy resigns the presidency of the French Assembly, and is succeeded by M. Buffet.

3.—Mr. Munster withdraws, after debate, a complaint of breach of privilege submitted to the House in so far as an article in the *Pall Mall Gazette* declared that "it was not surprising that the Irish Ultramontane members should resort to every quibble discoverable in the technicalities of the law of parliament to delay or defeat a measure like Mr. Fawcett's, which cuts the ground from under their venal agitations and their traffic in noisy disloyalty."

— The Duc d'Aumale received into the Frence Academy, and pronounces an eloquent eulogium upon his predecessor, the Count de Montalembert.

4.—Edwin Noyes and a man supposed to be George Bidwell, but who refused to give his name, examined before the Lord Mayor on the charge of forging and uttering bills of exchange for upwards of 100,000*l.* Bidwell had been captured in Edinburgh by detective M'Kelvie. The others known to be concerned in this gigantic·fraud were Warren *alias* Horton, and Macdonnell *alias* Swift. From the evidence now submitted it appeared that on the 4th of May last, an account was opened at the West End Branch of the Bank of England by Austin Bidwell in the name of "F. A. Warren," and it was evident that through this account the forged bills were to be discounted. From the 4th of May up to January last the account was kept alive, and on the 17th of January a genuine bill of Messrs. Rothschild was paid in. The account at the Continental Bank was opened in December for the purpose, it was alleged, of having Warren's cheques paid in there, and then drawn out again by drafts signed by Horton—the money being eventually expended in the systematic purchase of American bonds. It had been proved beyond all question that Austin Bidwell was both Warren and Horton. It was necessary, in order to carry out the gigantic fraud which was to follow, that there should be a division of labour, and persons were accordingly engaged to concoct the fictitious bills, to present the cheques, and to change bank-notes into gold. After the first genuine bill had been presented, the forged bills came up regularly to the West End Branch in letters dated from Birmingham and signed by Warren. The scheme

evidently was that all the persons who could be identified in the matter should be absent in the latter part of the proceedings; and so they found that in February Warren (or Horton) left London, and was not seen again by any of the Bank authorities. Macdonnell and George Bidwell, who had not been seen by them, remained in London and transacted the requisite business for Warren, he leaving with them a number of cheques on the Bank of England and the Continental Bank signed in blank. After he left, Noyes paid in and drew out the money at Horton's account.

4.—Japanese Embassy received by the Czar at St. Petersburg. The Grand Duke Alexis left Shanghai a few days later on a visit to Japan.

— Sir George Jenkinson's motion calling upon Government to adopt the recommendation of the Select Committee regarding the construction of a railway to connect the head of the Persian Gulf with the Mediterranean negatived by 103 to 29 votes.

6.—Anniversary of the day of the birth and death of Raphael Sanzio celebrated at Urbino.

7.—Mr. Lowe introduces the Budget, estimating the revenue for the ensuing year at 76,617,000*l.*; the expenditure at 71,871,000*l.* With the surplus of 4,746,000*l.* he proposed to meet the Geneva award claim of 3,200,000*l.* due at Washington 1st Oct., to reduce the sugar duty one-half, and take one penny off the income-tax. Mr. Lowe's statement was favourably received.

— The Prince of Wales installed as Grand Master of the Knights Templars at a conclave of the order held in Willis's Rooms.

9.—Salt Lake news mentions Brigham Young as on the eve of surrendering his trusteeship over the Mormon community preparatory to forming a new settlement in Arizona among the Apaches.

— Henry Pearson, described as a physician, sentenced at the Central Criminal Court to two years' imprisonment and a fine of 50*l.* for a libel upon his niece, Miss Roper, in that he had industriously circulated reports that she led an immoral life.

— Died, aged 46, Charles Allston Collins, artist and novelist.

11.—Mary and Charlotte Rea tried at Downpatrick on the charge of murdering Isabella Kerr at Holywood, in December last. Chiefly on the ground that the deceased was known to be a person of violent temper, the jury brought in a verdict of manslaughter, and Mr. Justice Keogh sentenced each of the prisoners to penal servitude for life.

— Came on before the High Court of Justiciary, Edinburgh, the trial of Henry Reid, a strolling piper, charged with murdering a young man named M'Callum, an engineer belonging to Glasgow, on an Ayr race-night in

September last. After inflicting the wound Reid made his escape through woods and by-ways to Perthshire, and remained concealed there several weeks. The principal witness against the prisoner was a woman named Townsby, who had lived with him as his wife, and his counsel objected to her evidence on the ground that a marriage, although irregular, had taken place. To decide this point the woman was put into the witness-box and questioned. She stated that she had agreed before a number of their friends to take the prisoner for her husband only so long as he would treat her well, but as he had not done so she did not now consider herself to be his wife. The objection not being admitted, the woman's evidence against the prisoner was taken, when the jury unanimously found the prisoner guilty of murder, and he was sentenced to death.

11.—Died, Major-General Dwight and Major-General Goodwyn, formerly of the Bengal Army, each having served with distinction in the Affghan campaign of 1843.

— General Canby, the American Peace Commissioner to the Modoc Indians, killed by "Captain Jack" and his followers.

14.—Died, aged 77, General Charles Richard Fox, son of the third Lord Holland, and grand-nephew to Charles James Fox.

— Official advices from Atchin, announce the repulse of the Dutch troops, and the death of their commander, General Koller.

15.—The Spencer Docks at Dublin formally opened by the Lord-Lieutenant.

— Workmen's demonstration at Maidstone to welcome the gas-stokers now liberated from prison there.

— Mr. Arch, Mr. Cox, and others, representing agricultural labourers at present on strike, tried before the Faringdon magistrates on a charge of obstructing the highway by holding a meeting in the market-place at Faringdon. Mr. Fitzjames Stephen argued that the defendants had a legal right to do what they had done. The Act never contemplated such an obstruction as that under which the defendants were charged, and it was monstrous to call it one. Before the charge could be proved against them it must be shown that they had committed some wrong and improper act in the nature of a trespass. The market-place was the only place where such men could hold their meetings. If they were convicted they would be prevented meeting at all, as they could not obtain rooms and were not allowed to go into fields. The summons was ultimately dismissed, amid the applause of many present to hear the case.

16.—Fight at Grant Parish, Louisiana, between the whites and negroes, the latter defending the Court-house, which had been set on fire. It was reported that as many as 100 were shot down when escaping from the burning building.

17.—The *Times* gives currency to a rumour that a serious calamity had befallen Sir Samuel Baker's expedition, the leader himself, with Lady Baker and a few survivors having, it was said, been murdered by a savage tribe to whom they had previously been forced to surrender.

— Her Majesty presents new colours to the 79th Cameron Highlanders at Parkhurst, Isle of Wight. "It gives me great pleasure," said her Majesty, "to present these new colours to you. In thus intrusting you with this honourable charge, I have the fullest confidence that you will, with the true loyalty and the well-known devotion of Highlanders, preserve the honour and reputation of your regiment, which have been so brilliantly earned and so nobly maintained." A gift of the old colours having been made to her Majesty, she said :—"I accept these colours with much pleasure, and shall ever value them in remembrance of the gallant services of the 79th Cameron Highlanders. I will take them to Scotland, and place them in my dear Highland home at Balmoral."

18.—Died at Munich, aged 70, Baron Justus von Liebig, a high authority in chemical science.

19.—The marriage of Prince Albrecht of Prussia with the Princess Mary of Saxe Altenburg, solemnized at Berlin.

— Died, aged 47, Augustus Harris, stage director of the Royal Italian Opera.

— The Shah leaves Teheran on a visit to the Courts of Europe. His Majesty arrived at Moscow on the 19th, St. Petersburg on the 22nd, Berlin on the 31st, and London on the 18th June.

20.—Marriage of Prince Leopold of Bavaria to the Princess Gisela, daughter of the Emperor of Austria.

— Died at Torquay, aged 72, Sir Wm. Tite, M.P. for Bath, and architect of the Royal Exchange.

— Died, aged 60, Dr. H. Bence Jones, F.R.S., consulting physican at St. George's Hospital, and secretary to the Royal Institution.

— The Duke of Edinburgh has an audience of the Pope, and congratulates his Holiness on recovery from recent illness.

21.—In his annual report as deputy-keeper of the Public Records, Sir T. Duffus Hardy writes that he had been asked by the Master of the Rolls to prepare a report on a photograph of the MS. known as the "Utrecht Psalter," containing a copy of the Athanasian Creed, and had come to the following conclusions :— That the date of the manuscript may be assigned to the close of the sixth century ; that there are no sufficiently valid objections against this date ; and that as the Utrecht Psalter is a Gallican, and not a Roman, Psalter, objections to it based upon the Roman usage are of no force.

21.—Mr. Fawcett's Dublin University Tests Bill read a second time in the Commons.

— Rule *nisi* granted in the Court of Queen's Bench to file a criminal information against Mr. Plimsoll, M.P., for imputing cruel and criminal practices to Mr. Norwood, M.P., in so far as the latter was alleged to have sent vessels to sea in an unseaworthy condition.

22.—Debate in the Commons on the Central Asian question raised by Mr. Eastwick on a motion, afterwards withdrawn, for the production of papers.

— Rev. E. C. Wickham, fellow and tutor of New College, Oxford, elected head-master of Wellington College, in succession to Dr. Benson, appointed chancellor of Lincoln cathedral.

— Earl Delawarr commits suicide by drowning himself at Cambridge while suffering from mental affliction, apparently induced by the death of a young woman living under his protection.

23.—Came on in the Court of Queen's Bench, before Lord Chief-Justice Cockburn, Justice Mellor, and Justice Lush, the trial at bar of the Tichborne Claimant, charged with perjury, for having sworn that he was Roger Charles Tichborne, supposed to have been drowned ; that he had seduced his uncle's daughter, his own cousin ; and that he was not Arthur Orton, son of a Wapping butcher. Mr. Hawkins opened the case for the Crown; the Claimant being defended by Dr. Kenealy.

— Despatches from Khartoum announce that Sir Samuel Baker and his party were well at Fatookra.

— Fancy dress ball at the Mansion House, the Lord Mayor and Lady Waterlow appearing in dresses of the Louis Quatorze period.

— Disturbances at Madrid caused by an attempt of the " Permanent Committee " to overthrow the Government. The Committee was dissolved next day.

— Died, aged 65, H. W. Wilberforce, formerly vicar of East Farleigh, but a member for about twenty years of the Romish communion.

24.—Riotous proceedings at Frankfort, arising out of advances recently made by brewers in the price of beer.

26.—Two hundred United States soldiers fall into an ambuscade prepared by Modoc Indians, and suffer a loss of nineteen killed and twenty-two wounded.

27.—The Emperor of Germany arrives at St. Petersburg on a visit to the Czar.

— Carriage works of the Lancashire and Yorkshire Railway Company at Miles Platting, Manchester, destroyed by fire.

— The Hon. Beatrice Mary Catherine, third daughter of Lord Clifford of Ugbrooke, Chudleigh, dies from injuries received by fire.

— M. Barodet elected member for Paris by a majority of 40,000 over M. de Rémusat. Four Republicans returned at provincial elections.

— Died, at Cheltenham, aged 80, William C. Macready, an English tragedian of rare merit, and a theatrical lessee who elevated a national amusement into a means of public education and permanent good.

28.—Accident, presumed to be from an overcharge of powder, in the Wynnstay Colliery, Ruabon, causing the death of seven workmen, all who were employed in the pit at the time.

— Discussion in the Commons on Mr. Smith's motion that, before deciding further on the reduction of indirect taxation, the Government ought to put the House in possession of its views on the maintenance and adjustment of direct taxation, local and imperial.

— The Prince of Wales and Prince Arthur arrive at Vienna to take part in the ceremonies attending the opening of the Exhibition.

29.—The Lord Chancellor introduces a bill for the amendment of the law relating to the title and transfer of land.

— Lord Claud Hamilton's motion for the purchase of Irish railways negatived in the Commons by 197 to 65 votes.

— The Grosvenor Club for workmen opened by the Marquis of Westminster.

— Died, aged 60, J. R. Hope Scott, Q.C., possessor of Abbotsford in virtue of his first wife, daughter of J. Gibson Lockhart, and granddaughter of Sir Walter Scott.

30.—The Women's Disabilities Bill rejected in the Commons by 222 to 155 votes.

May 1.—The Vienna Exhibition opened by the Emperor. Though the weather was unfavourable and the building known to be far from finished, great crowds assembled to cheer the imperial family and the royal visitors present from most of the European Courts.

— The Italian Ministry resign, in consequence of a defeat on a vote involving military expenditure.

4.—Closing days of Dr. Livingstone. On arriving at Ulala, the capital of the district, where Kitambo the Sultan lived, the party were refused permission to stay, and Livingstone had to be carried three hours' march back towards Ukabende, where they erected for him a rude hut and fence. He would not allow any one to approach him for the remaining days of his life except Majwara and Susi, although they all called daily at his door to say "Good morning." During these days the traveller was in great pain, and could keep nothing, even for a moment, on his stomach. He so far lost his sight as hardly to be able to distinguish when a light was kindled, and he found this entry to be dated of the 4th of May. Only Majwara was present when the Doctor died, and he was unable to say when breathing ceased. Susi, hearing that he was dead, told Jacob Wainwright to make a note in the Doctor's diary of the things found by him. Wainwright was not quite certain as to the day of the month, and as Susi told him the Doctor had last written the day before, and he found this entry to be dated 27th April, he wrote 28th; but on comparing his own diary on arrival at Unyanyembe, he found it to be the 4th of May: and this was confirmed by Majwara, who said Livingstone was unable to write for the last four or five days of his life. The closing entry in the traveller's diary was a touching reference to the loss of his servants:—" Very weak to-day. The good boys have carried me to the vil" (village). The spot where Livingstone breathed his last was put down at 11° 25" S. and 27° E.

5.—International Commission appointed at Constantinople to determine on matters relating to Suez Canal shipping dues.

— The Greek Government abolishes all its foreign legations except one at Constantinople.

— Fall of a bridge at Dixon, Illinois, crowded with people witnessing a baptism; fifty persons, mostly women, reported to be drowned.

— Anti-Ritualist memorial presented to the Archbishop at Lambeth Palace, praying the Bishops—" 1. To exercise all the authority vested in your lordships for the entire suppression of ceremonies and practices adjudged to be illegal, and in the event of that authority proving insufficient, to afford all other needful facilities for the due enforcement of the law. 2. To take especial care that in the consecration of new and in the restoration of old churches, no form of architectural arrangements and no ornaments be allowed that may facilitate the introduction of the superstitious practices and erroneous doctrines which the Church at the Reformation did disown and reject. 3. And, lastly, in the admission of candidates to Holy Orders, in the licensing of curates, and also in the distribution of patronage, to protect us and our families from teaching which—though it may not subject the individual offender to judicial condemnation—is, when taken in its plain and obvious meaning, subversive of those truths to which our Protestant Church, as Keeper and Witness of Holy Writ, has ever borne its faithful testimony."

116

5.—On the proposal to read the new Judicature Bill a third time, the Marquis of Salisbury moved an amendment intended to transfer ecclesiastical appeals to the new Court of Appeal constituted by the bill, and thus put an end to the ecclesiastical jurisdiction of the Judicial Committee of Privy Council. The Marquis objected to the present constitution of the committee when dealing with ecclesiastical appeals, on the ground that among its members were bishops, who, though unlearned in the law, were called on to decide legal questions, and who were also, for the most part, pledged beforehand to a particular view on the subjects which came before them as Judges. The arguments of the Archbishop of Canterbury, in reply, tended to show that in a Court of Ecclesiastical Appeal bishops should be present as Assessors rather than as Judges; while the Bishop of Winchester expressed a wish for the removal of the Episcopal element from the Judicial Committee, as likely to cause the decisions of the committee to be received more impartially by the great body of the clergy —an opinion shared by Lord Cairns and Earl Carnarvon. Ultimately, the Marquis of Salisbury assenting to the objection of the Lord Chancellor that the subject was too large for discussion at that late stage, withdrew his motion, and the bill passed.

— Mr. Fawcett's University Bill passed by the Commons.

6.—Sir Charles Dilke's motion calling for redress in the inequalities of the distribution of electoral power over the kingdom rejected by 268 to 77 votes; and Mr. Trevelyan's resolution against honorary colonelcies ,rejected by 80 to 40 votes.

— A train on the Austrian States Railway thrown off the line not far from Pesth, smashing six of the carriages. Twenty-one persons were killed and forty wounded, the victims in most instances belonging to the working classes.

7.—Died, aged 65, Simon Portland Chase, Chief-Justice of the United States.

— The Irish Court of Queen's Bench pronounces judgment in the O'Keeffe demurrer case. The Roman Catholic Judges Barry, Fitzgerald, and O'Brien, held that the rescript of the Pope under which Cardinal Cullen acted in suspending Father O'Keeffe was illegal, but that Father O'Keeffe under his contract with the Church had submitted beforehand to the Cardinal's authority, and that, therefore, he could not allege that in publishing in Callan the suspension pronounced upon him, although under an illegal rescript, the Cardinal had libelled him. Judge Fitzgerald contended that an agreement to refrain from having recourse to the public tribunals is not against the public interest or any contravention of the law, and is a very wholesome rule of practice and discipline.— Chief-Justice Whiteside, on the contrary, insisted that the communication was not privileged, and that the object—one which the Courts could not sanction—was to exempt a numerous clergy from "intercourse with the civil magistrate." He also said it was "apparently thought that the present was a favourable time and Ireland a favourable country" for reasserting the foreign authority, which many ancient and modern statutes had repudiated and forbidden. His lordship also held that a priest could not be suspended even for criminal conduct without regular proceedings, except in time of visitation, and never after induction could the priest be removed at the mere discretion of the bishop.— As the other three Judges were of the opposite opinion, the case was unaffected by the Chief-Justice's view.

7.—Sir W. Lawson's Permissive Bill thrown out in the Commons by 321 to 81 votes.

— The Marquis of Lorne proposes to the Archbishop of Canterbury to raise amongst the laity a central fund large enough to make it certain that no incumbent of any living belonging to the Church of England should have less than 200*l.* a year. "Should your grace approve the establishment of such a fund, the Princess and I would be anxious to assist in raising a subscription." His grace promised to co-operate in the scheme, and secure also the countenance of the episcopal bench generally.

— The Upper House of Convocation adopt a "declaration" for the removal of doubts and to prevent disquietude in the use of the Athanasian Creed, solemnly declaring "that the Confession of our Christian faith, commonly called the Creed of St. Athanasius, is not to be understood as making any addition to the faith as contained in Holy Scripture, but as a warning against errors which from time to time have arisen in the Church of Christ ; secondly, inasmuch as Holy Scripture in divers places doth promise life to them that believe, and declares condemnation of them that believe not, so doth the Church in this Confession declare the necessity for all who would be in a state of salvation of holding fast the Christian faith, and the great peril of rejecting the same. So that the warnings in this Confession of faith are to be understood in no otherwise than like warnings in Holy Scripture. Moreover, as all judgments belong to God alone, we are not required or allowed to pronounce judgment upon any particular person or persons. Furthermore, we are to receive God's threatenings, even as his promises, as they are set forth in Holy Scripture." The Bishops of Norwich and Exeter opposed the Declaration, being desirous to abolish the use of the Creed in public worship.

8.—Died, at Avignon, from erysipelas, aged 67, John Stuart Mill, author of many valuable works on logic and political economy.

— William Alexander Roberts, stockbroker, sentenced at the Old Bailey to twelve years' penal servitude for attempting to pass a forged cheque for 11,500*l.*

9.—The Upper House of Convocation discusses a petition signed by 480 members of the Church of England, praying for the appointment of "duly qualified confessors."

— Panic on the Vienna Bourse, leading to the fall of over 200 firms, and the suspension of the Bank Act.

12.—Apologizing to Mr. Cubitt, M.P., for his inability to attend a Lambeth Conservative banquet, Mr. Disraeli writes :—"You will have an opportunity of impressing on the metropolitan constituencies that at the impending general election the country will have to decide whether they will maintain the integrity of the kingdom, as well as of the empire, and whether they will uphold and cherish that great body of laws and customs and traditions which have converted a small island into one of the mighty Powers of the world. There is no part of the Queen's dominions in which Conservative elements are more rife than in her capital city. But as happens frequently, when the area and population are alike vast, there is a want of leaders and organization. But without leaders and organization nothing can be done ; and the metropolitan constituencies must show themselves equal to the occasion, and rise to the emergency."

— Mr. Stansfeld carries a motion in the Commons for the appointment of a Select Committee to inquire and report whether the existing areas and boundaries of parishes, unions, and counties may be so altered as to prevent the inconveniences which now arise from their subdivision.

— At the meeting of the Royal Geographical Society, Mr. N. Elias, the gold medalist of the year, and the first European who had travelled through Western Mongolia, reads an interesting paper on that remote region.

13.—The Dublin University Bill read a second time in the Lords.

— Mr. Crawford's motion for an address to the Queen condemning the scheme of the Endowed Schools Commissioners for dealing with Emanuel Hospital, Westminster, rejected by 286 to 238 votes. Anne, Lady Dacre, widow of Gregory, the last Lord Dacre of the South, and sister of Thomas Sackville, Lord Buckhurst and Earl of Dorset, the poet, in pursuance of whose will the Hospital in Tothill Street was erected, died on the 14th of May 1595, having survived her husband only a few months.

— Died, in the hospital of the Prussian Deaconesses, Alexandria, aged 42, Emanuel Oscar Deutsch, an accomplished authority in Rabbinical and general oriental literature.

14.—One quarter of a King's share in the New River Company sold in four lots for 12,240*l.*, the income for the last year having been on this quarter-share 448*l.* In 1858 a share sold in the open market at the rate of 19,000*l.* Twelve years after the share was sold in lots at 38,000*l*., and the result of this last sale shows the price of a share to be now nearly 49,000*l*.

14.—New Guildhall at Winchester opened by the Lord Chancellor.

— Mr. Cowper's Occasional Sermons Bill rejected by 199 to 53 votes.

— The *Times* announces the approaching marriage of the Duke of Edinburgh with the Grand Duchess Marie of Russia.

— Intimation given of a concession granted by the Shah to Baron Reuter, and to any company which he may establish, of the exclusive right to construct railways, tramways, and other public works throughout his dominions, together with the exclusive right of working the mines and utilizing the forests of the country. By the second article of the concession, Baron Reuter's company obtained the exclusive right of making, and of working for seventy years, railways throughout the country. The lands necessary for the purpose to be given by the State, so far as possible ; and in case lands which are private property should be required, the Persian Government undertook to use its influence to prevent exorbitant prices being charged, and would, if necessary, compel the owners to consent to a forced sale. All materials to be free from import duties, and all persons engaged in the works to be exempt from taxation. The company to pay to the Government 20 per cent. on the net profits of the working of the line.

15.—The Australian Colonies (Customs Duties) Bill, designed to repeal the Act forbidding the colonial legislatures to enforce differential duties as between the colonies and the rest of the world, read a second time.

— Lord Hartington's motion for a Select Committee to inquire into the case of the Irish National Board of Education, Mr. O'Keeffe, and the Callan School, carried by 159 to 131 votes ; Mr. Bouverie protesting against the proposal, as contrary to all precedent, seeing the House was or would soon be in possession of all papers bearing on the case.

— The German State Council unanimously determines to expel the monastic orders of Redemptorists and Lazarists, and the Congregations of the Holy Ghost and the Most Holy Heart, as coming under the law against the Jesuits.

— Died, at Heidelberg, aged 53, Prince Couza, formerly Hospodar of Roumania.

16.—Mr. Miall's Disestablishment motion rejected by 356 to 61 votes.

18.—The *Daily Telegraph* prints a despatch dated Tiflis, yesterday, announcing that Khiva was taken, and the Khan a prisoner in the hands of the Russians.

18.—Reconstruction of the French Ministry announced. M. Casimir-Périer, Minister of the Interior, and M. Waddington, Minister of Public Instruction.

19.—Lord Salisbury's motion for an address condemning the scheme of the Endowed Schools Commissioners respecting King Edward's Grammar School, Birmingham, carried by 106 to 60 votes.

— Mr. George Smith, of the British Museum, at present engaged in Assyrian researches on behalf of the *Daily Telegraph*, writes from Mosul :—"I am excavating the site of the King's Library, at Nineveh, which I found without much difficulty. Many fresh objects of high importance have rewarded my search. Since my last message I have come upon numerous valuable inscriptions and fragments of all classes, including very curious syllabaries and bilingual records. Among them is a remarkable table of the penalties for neglect or infraction of the laws. But my most fortunate discovery is that of a broken tablet containing the very portion of the text which was missing from the Deluge tablet. Immense masses of earth and débris overlie whatever remains to be brought to light in this part of the great Mound,"

21.—Mr. W. Fowler's bill for the repeal of the Contagious Diseases Act rejected by 251 to 128 votes.

— The Chipping Norton bench of magistrates commit sixteen women to prison for several days on a charge of intimidating labourers employed in the room of others on strike.

22.—Died, aged 58, the Right Rev. Alexander Ewing, D.C.L., Bishop of Argyll and the Isles.

23.—Died, aged 90, Alessandro Manzoni, Italian novelist and poet.

— The Land Titles and Transfer Bill and Real Property Limitation Bill read a second time in the Lords.

24.—The new Alexandra Palace on Muswell Hill opened.

— By a majority of 360 to 344 the French Assembly adopt a vote of want of confidence in the new Ministry. M. Theirs thereupon resigned, and Marshal MacMahon was elected President. In accepting office, the latter wrote :—"I obey the will of the Assembly, the depositary of the national Sovereignty, and accept the functions of President of the Republic. A heavy responsibility is thrust upon my patriotism ; but with the aid of God and the devotion of the army, which will always be an army of the law and the supporter of all honest men, we will continue together the work of liberating the territory, and restoring moral order throughout the country ; we will maintain internal peace, and the principles upon which society rests. That this shall be the case I pledge my word as an honest man and a soldier."

24.—The Dutch Chamber vote supplies for the expedition against Atchin.

26.—President MacMahon submits his first message to the Assembly, expressing a desire for the maintenance of peace, and the reorganization of the army, which "we shall actively persevere in effecting, animated only by a legitimate desire to repair the strength and retain the rank which belong to France. The home policy of the Government will be imbued with a character of social Conservatism. All the laws you have voted possess that characteristic. The Government is resolutely Conservative. We have numerous laws to enact. The bills on the reorganization of the army and municipalities and educational reform are drawn up, and I believe I have selected Ministers who are competent to discuss them. You will discuss the bills which you instructed our predecessor to submit to you and those already before you, and the Government will examine them and give you the result of thier careful consideration. But previously to that the Government must act, and introduce into and impress upon the Administration the spirit of Conservatism, and cause the laws to be respected by appointing agents who will make them respected and themselves respect them. The Government will not fail in this duty, and will defend society against all factions. The post in which you have placed me is that of a sentinel who has to watch over the integrity of your sovereign power."

— M. Thiers resumes his place as a member of the French National Assembly.

27.—The Italian Chamber of Deputies passes the Religious Corporations Bill by 196 to 46 votes.

— The trial of the libel case of O'Keeffe *v.* Cullen terminates in a verdict for the plaintiff —damages one farthing.

— Fire in Grosvenor Mews, Berkeley Square, causing the death of six persons, and serious injury to several others in attempting to escape from the building.

— New railway project submitted by M. de Lesseps, the main feature being to connect the lines of Russia with those of India, the first section extending from the north-east of the Caspian Sea to Samarkand, and the second from Samarkand to Peshawur.

28.—Austin Byron Bidwell, captured at Havana, examined at the Mansion House on the charge of being concerned with others now in custody in the recent forgeries on the Bank of England.

— Died, aged 81, Alderman Sir James Duke, Lord Mayor of London in 1848.

29.—The General Assembly of the Church of Scotland carry a resolution disapproving of the "course taken by the Commission on 15th of January last in regard to the appointment of the chair of Church History in the University of Edinburgh, as being in itself an illegal exercise of authority, and as calculated to weaken the position of the Church of Scotland, and injuriously to affect the rights of the clergy."

29.—Prince Frederick William, second son of the Prince Louis of Hesse and the Princess Alice, fatally injured by falling out of a window in the royal castle at Darmstadt.

30.—Another serious fire at Boston, U.S., about forty different buildings being consumed in the block between Washington and Tyler Streets. The Clickering piano manufactory and the International Hotel were among the more extensive properties destroyed.

31.—Explosion of fire-damp in the Bryn Hall colliery, near Wigan, causing the death of six shot-lighters, being the whole of the workmen employed at the time.

June 1.—The Modoc war ended by the capture of "Captain" Jack and his companions.

2.—Prince Amadeus presented with the civic crown of Turin.

4.—Opening of the new Infirmary at Wigan by the Prince and Princess of Wales. Next day their Royal Highnesses opened the new Town Hall, Bolton, built at a cost of 150,000*l.*

— An obituary notice in the *Times* of the late J. S. Mill by Mr. Hayward, severely commented upon by the Rev. Stopford Brooke, leads to a split among the philosopher's friends regarding the committee of a Mill Memorial Institute.

5.—The Juries Bill considered in the Commons, and various exemptions from service agreed to.

— The Sultan of Zanzibar ratifies a treaty with England abolishing the slave trade, and clears the bazaar the same day.

— Died, at Frosinone, aged 65, Signor Ratazzi, a distinguished Italian statesman, at one time Prime Minister of the kingdom, but more frequently in opposition.

— Marshal MacMahon holds his first reception as French President. An immense number of friends were present, including all the members of the Diplomatic Body (with the exception of Count Arnim), the Ministers, all the deputies of the majority, some members of the Left Centre (such as M. Target), all the generals of the armies of Paris and Versailles with their staffs, the admirals at present in Versailles, numerous officers of all arms, the Princes of Orleans, the directors of all the State Departments, numerous eminent merchants and bankers, the leading members of the clergy, the editors of the Conservative newspapers, the members of the Court of Cassation, the Court of Accounts, the Court of Appeal, and the Tribunals of First Instance and Commerce, as well as several ladies.

6.—Died at Carlsbad, Adalbert, Prince of Prussia.

— Military banquet at Vienna in honour of the Czar's visit. The Emperor Francis Joseph, in his own name and in that of the army, proposed the health of the Czar and the valorous army of Russia. The assembled guests received the toast with loud cheers, and the Czar, in reply, proposed the health of the Emperor of Austria and his brave and faithful soldiers.

— Close of the four days' sale of the Perkins Library at Hanworth Park, the total proceeds amounting to upwards of 26,000*l.*

7.—Disorderly proceedings in Dublin, occasioned by a mob availing itself for a brief period of the confusion caused by a fire in Thomas Street.

8.—The Spanish Cortes adopt the Democratic Federal Republic by 210 to 2. After a prolonged crisis a new Ministry was formed under Señor Pi-y-Margall.

— Firman granted by the Sultan of Turkey to the Khedive of Egypt, sanctioning the full autonomy of that country, and enacting the law of primogeniture in favour of Ismail Pacha's family.

— The *Great Eastern* leaves Portland Roads to lay a fourth telegraph cable between Europe and America.

9.—The recently opened Alexandra Palace on Muswell-hill destroyed by fire. It broke out a little before one o'clock, and owed its origin in all probability to the carelessness of a workman leaving a brazier of lighted coal on the roof when he went to his dinner. The fire found its way into some crevice of the roof amid inflammable materials, and half a dozen other men who were at work on the roof had barely time to escape before the whole dome was enveloped in flames. When the news of the fire was telegraphed to London, Captain Shaw speedily set out for the palace with a full complement of men and engines, but they had some six or eight miles of ground to cover, much of it being up-hill, and by the time they reached their destination, the ruin which had been effected was complete and irreparable. The supply of water was very inadequate, and although there were numerous hydrants in the building, with a large reservoir and the New River at the foot of the hill, there did not seem to be any arrangement for pumping the water up in quantities. By three o'clock nothing was left of the building but the outside walls. Most of the pictures, water-colour drawings, tapestry, and music were saved, but the loan collection of china was destroyed, with the exception of two vases contributed by the Queen. During the fire several accidents occurred.

10.—Circumstantial accounts received of the capture of Khiva by General Kauffmann.

— Died at Liverpool, aged 79, Michael James Whitty, newspaper proprietor.

11.—General Kauffmann enters Khiva without any opposition being offered. In their march the Russian troops traversed altogether 707 versts in eighty-nine days. The halts and the works executed *en route* occupied forty-five days, thus reducing the actual marching time to forty-four days. The average daily march was 16 versts, the longest march being 40 and the shortest 6½ versts. It was ascertained that the Amoo Daria deviates in its course, and flows in a more easterly direction than is laid down in the maps.

— In explanation of his retirement, M. Thiers writes to a friend of his at Nancy :—
" A government acting energetically against all disorder, and moderately, amicably, and peaceably towards all parties which are not factious, is the only government capable of appeasing political passions, and of restoring to France a certain amount of unity and well-being. Consequently, I have preferred to retire rather than to pursue a policy which was not my own, and which, in siding with the Right, was far from siding with the majority of the country. I turn to the repose of my books and to my friends, desiring nothing but the restoration of France."

12.—Replying to an address presented by the generals of monastic orders, the Pope said he fully shared in their sorrow at the sad position in which the religious bodies had been placed. At the same time, he derived comfort from two reflections—namely, that souls beloved by God must be tried by tribulations, and that there were signs that the spirit of prayer was everywhere reawakening. The censures of the Church renewed against the authors of these acts would become a powerful weapon which God would employ for the defeat of his enemies. His Holiness concluded by exhorting the " generals " to trust in God and pray.

13. — A company of British seamen and marines repulse an attack by Ashantees on the castle of Elmina. The town had previously been burnt, in consequence of the inhabitants giving arms and shelter to the Ashantees, some 3,000 of whom advanced upon the castle. They were met by the marines sent out from England in her Majesty's ship *Barracouta*, by small-arm men and marines landed from her Majesty's ships, and also a body of Houssas. The action lasted some hours, and the Ashantees were driven back with the loss of about 300 killed and a large number wounded. News from other than Admiralty sources made mention of an impending attack on Cape Coast Castle by Ashantees, mustering 30,000 strong, about fifteen miles from the town.

— Died, at Crossmyloof, near Glasgow, aged 84, Mrs. Thomson, daughter of the poet Burns by Helen Ann Park—" Annie wi' the gowden locks "—a servant at the Globe tavern, Dumfries, whose child was rocked in the same cradle with Mrs. Burns's own infant as " a neibour's bairn."

13.—Died, aged 93, Frederick von Raumer, German historian.

— Lord Derby, speaking at the Society of Arts, disputes the wisdom of the proposal that the State should take over the railways. The public, he said, "had no security that railways would not be superseded as coaches and canals had been. The inventive powers of the human mind could not be limited. What would have happened if the Government of the day had bought up stage coaches and canals?" Lord Derby thought also there was much in the argument that the State administration of the railways would put the Government in possession of a powerful engine of corruption. Still, he did not deny that the question might have to be entertained hereafter.

14.—The Court of Queen's Bench declines to grant a criminal information against Mr. Plimsoll for a libel on Mr. Norwood, M.P., but refuses Mr. Plimsoll his costs.

15.—The first "Hospital Sunday" held in London ; above 27,400*l.* collected in connection with the different services.

— Engagement between Republican and Carlist troops near Prista, Catalonia, the latter having slightly the advantage.

16.—Replying to a memorial with 60,200 signatures against Romish teaching in the Church of England, the Archbishops of Canterbury and York write :—"We wish to state that we do not consider it to be the duty of the bishops to undertake judicial proceedings upon every complaint of a violation of the rubrics, or upon every charge of unsound doctrine that may be laid before them ; obviously it cannot be desirable that the Church should be harassed by the bishops being dragged into an unlimited number of judicial investigations founded upon charges and counter-charges made by contending theological parties against their opponents, on the ground of alleged excess or defect in conforming to the ritual and preaching the doctrine of the Church. . . . With regard to the particular matters of ceremonial and doctrine to which you direct our attention, we wish we saw a readiness everywhere manifested on the part of the laity to use all the legitimate authority which is vested in them, through the election of churchwardens, and all their personal influence to check the growth of Romanizing tendencies. The laity in many parishes possess a power, more effectual than any dread of prosecution, of preventing improper changes in ritual and extravagance in doctrine ; and we must add that they occasionally show a great reluctance to use their power. . . . We live in an age when all opinions and beliefs are keenly criticised, and when there is less inclination than there ever was before to respect authority in matters of opinion. In every state, in every religious community, almost in every family, the effects of this unsettled condition may be traced. The evils of this kind which meet us on every side are by no means restricted to such as your petition has brought prominently before us. It is an open question whether the tendencies to superstition or to infidelity, or those old tendencies of unregenerate human nature to a dull and heartless indifference, which, more than either superstition or unbelief, leave the heart open to the assaults of immorality, are most to be deprecated. But we rejoice to trace many hopeful signs in the Church of which we are ministers, and to note an increase of religious life in the whole nation."

16.—The Grand Duke Czarewitch and the Grand Duchess Czarevna, with two sons, arrive at Woolwich on a visit to her Majesty and the Prince and Princess of Wales.

— Members of the Middlesex Bicycle Club who left London on Whit-Monday (the 2nd inst.) complete their journey to John O'Groat's, a distance of 800 miles, showing an average daily speed of about 60 miles.

— The London Nonconformist Committee form resolutions expressing "the utmost dissatisfaction" at the Government proposals for the amendment of the Education Act, which the committee regard as "conceived in the interests of Denominationalism, calculated to disappoint the just expectations of Nonconformists, and interposing new difficulties in the establishment of a really national system of education."

17.—Sir Robert Anstruther introduces, but withdraws after debate, a motion favouring the abolition of patronage in the Church of Scotland, Mr. Gladstone suggesting a Parliamentary inquiry into the subject next year.

18.—His Majesty the Shah arrives at Dover, and is received by the Duke of Edinburgh and Prince Arthur on behalf of her Majesty. Charing Cross was reached late in the afternoon, and a triumphal progress made along the route to Buckingham Palace.

— Mr. Fawcett's bill for transferring the expense of Parliamentary elections from candidates to the local rates thrown out in the Commons on the proposal for a second reading by 205 to 91 votes.

— Dr. Heurtley, Margaret Professor of Divinity, Oxford, publishes a protest against conferring an honorary degree on Professor Tyndall, on the ground that he had signalized himself by denying the credibility of miracles and the efficacy of prayer.

19.—The Cape and Zanzibar mail contracts referred to a Select Committee.

— Died, Mr. David Robertson, of Ladykirk, recently elevated to the peerage with the title of Lord Marjoribanks.

— The Shah receives the members of the Diplomatic Body and her Majesty's Ministers at Buckingham Palace. In the evening the Prince of Wales gave a dinner in honour of his Majesty at Marlborough House.

20.—The crew of the *Polaris*, American Arctic Expedition, picked up by the *Ravenscraig* (Dundee whaler) twenty miles south of Cape York, proceeding southward in boats.

— The Shah is received by the Queen at Winds r, and afterwards attends a grand ball given in his honour at the Guildhall.

21.—The Czarewitch and Czarevna received by the Queen at Windsor.

— Came on for trial, before Mr. Justice Denman and a special jury, the case of Littleton *v.* Gounod, in which the plaintiff, representing the firm of Novello and Company, sued the musical composer for damages in so far as he had written that he had been "mulcted" of certain sums of money, and otherwise made imputations upon plaintiff's taste as a music publisher. Verdict for plaintiff—damages 40*s.* with costs.

23.—Naval review at Spithead in honour of the Shah; and "reception" at the Albert Hall in the evening. Next day the troops were reviewed in Windsor Park before the Queen and her illustrious guest.

24.—Died, aged 63, Thornton Leigh Hunt, journalist, eldest son of Leigh Hunt, poet and essayist.

— Sir Arthur Guinness magnanimously withdraws from further prosecuting the libel charge preferred before a Dublin bench against Sir John Gray, for a paragraph in the *Freeman's Journal* making erroneous reflections on Sir Arthur's domestic life.

— The Khan of Khiva issues a proclamation abolishing slavery :—"Penetrated by veneration for the Emperor of Russia, I declare all slaves in the empire of Khiva to be free, and the slave trade abolished for ever. I command the immediate execution of this order, and severe punishment will be inflicted in case of refusal. All liberated slaves enjoy equal rights with my other subjects, and are permitted to remain in the Khanate. Should they wish to return to their native country, special measures will be taken. The liberated slaves are to assemble at the nearest market towns, and to present themselves to the authorities, who will inscribe their names on lists and inform the Khan of the number of liberated slaves."

25.—The German Parliament prorogued by Prince Bismarck in name of the Emperor.

— Decree published in the Italian official *Gazette* putting in force the bill for the suppression of religious bodies in Rome.

26.—The Public Worship Facilities Bill framed to enable the diocesan, with the consent in writing of the incumbent of a parish, and, in certain circumstances, on the application in writing of twenty-five or more of the parishioners, to license a clergyman of the Church of England to officiate in any schoolroom or other suitable building, consecrated or unconsecrated, rejected in the House of Lords on the proposal for a second reading by 62 to 26 votes.

26.—Mr. Forster moves the annual Education vote—1,299,603*l.*

27.—Died, at Florence, Hiram Powers, an American sculptor, whose "Greek Slave" excited much interest in the Exhibition of 1851.

— Lord Stanhope's motion for an address to the Queen, praying her Majesty to take into consideration the institution of an Order of Merit to be bestowed by her Majesty as a sign of her royal approbation upon men who have deserved well of their country in science, literature, and art, negatived after a brief discussion.

29.—The *Deerhound*, detained some days at Plymouth, on suspicion of being laden with arms for the Carlists, permitted to sail.

— Reception of the foreign ambassadors in audience for the first time by the Emperor of China at Pekin.

30.—Mr. Gladstone announces amendments to the Judicature Bill, with the view of establishing one final Court of Appeal for the United Kingdom.

— Intelligence received of the safe arrival of Sir Samuel Baker at Khartoum. The country, he reported, as far as the equator, had been annexed to the Egyptian dominion, and the slave trade completely put down. Sir Samuel, Lady Baker, and party had sailed from Gondokoro in one of the steamers which had been taken up country for the navigation of the lakes, occupying about thirty-two days on the journey.

— The Chief Secretary for Ireland suggests to the Commissioners of National Education an addition to their rules to meet such cases as Mr. O'Keeffe's :—"The Commissioners also reserve to themselves the power of withdrawing the recognition of a patron or local manager, if he shall fail to observe the rules of the Board, or if it shall appear to them that the educational interest of the district require it; but such recognition will not be withdrawn without an investigation into the above matters, held after due notice to the patron or local manager, and to all parties concerned." The Commissioners unanimously agree to accept the new rule.

— Anti-Confessional meeting in Exeter Hall presided over by the Earl of Shaftesbury, who spoke of the decision of the bishops as "mealymouthed" and "contemptible," and after speaking of the confessional in strong language, concluded by saying :—"There was one test he would apply to those who were labouring to introduce the confessional into the Church. Would they appoint female confessors? (Prolonged cheering followed this question.) That was a test by which it would fall to the winds, because, if female confessors were appointed every confessional-box in England would be broken up for firewood in six weeks. Who was to blame for all the scandal in the Church? (Here there were cries which lasted some time, 'The bishops, the bishops.') If the Church of England wavered in allegiance to her principles, then let her go. (This was received with loud cheers, and cries of 'All the bishops with her,' renewed vociferous cheering, which lasted for some time.)"

30.—Public reception of his Majesty the Shah at the Crystal Palace.

— Died, aged 82, Matthew Marshall, for nearly thirty years chief cashier of the Bank of England.

— Sir Charles Wheatstone elected an Associate of the French Academy of Sciences in room of the late Baron Liebig.

July 1.—Came on before the House of Lords the appeal case of Mordaunt *v.* Moncrieffe, guardian, the pleadings ending in a reference to the Judges, suggested by Lord Chelmsford, "Whether, under the Act 20 and 21 Vict., proceedings for the dissolution of a marriage can be instituted or proceeded with, either on behalf of or against a husband or wife who, before the proceedings were instituted, has become incurably lunatic?" The learned Judges having requested time to consider their answer, the further consideration was adjourned.

— Meeting of the Education League and Nonconformists at the Westminster Palace Hotel, for the purpose of considering proposed amendments in the Education Act. Mr. Bright remarked, that while he thought the Act of 1870 was the very worst Act which had ever been passed by any Liberal Government since the Reform Act of 1832, still it was now a question of what amendment was practicable, and there was no doubt that it was not possible to pass such a measure as the meeting wanted. He warned them against an impulsive breaking away from the Liberal party. It was easier to smash up than to restore, and they might possibly find, when they had shattered the party, as some of the speakers had threatened to do, they would be in a worse and weaker position than they were before.— Resolutions were passed condemning the bill, and respectfully urging upon Liberal members of the House of Commons the desirability of offering it the most strenuous opposition.

— Isle of Man Railway opened by the Duke of Sutherland.

— Died at Paris, aged 75, the Marquis de St. Simon, descendant of the author of the celebrated " Mémoires."

2.—The Shah proceeds again to Windsor to pay a second visit to her Majesty.

3. — In Committee on the Judicature Bill, Mr. Disraeli referred to the anomalies to which the measure must give rise, and advised the Government to withdraw it this year for the purpose of re-introducing it next session in a more perfect form. Mr. Gladstone described

these objections as going to the root of the bill, and were inseparable from the constitution of a Court of Appeal. He anticipated great advantage from the mixture of judges, and derided the notion that the ablest men could not be obtained from the Scotch and Irish bars. As to the intermediate appeal, he did not admit the necessity·for its abolition, but it was a point about which no decision had yet been arrived at. There would be ample opportunity for discussing the whole question when the bill was recommitted, and there was no necessity, therefore, for postponement.

3.—Discovery of a comet by M. Temple, from the Observatory, Milan.

— New Atlantic Telegraph cable successfully laid.

— Died. suddenly, aged 57, Prince Poniatowski, a distinguished musical amateur.

— New Spanish Constitution promulgated. The president to be elected for four years, and not to be eligible for re-election. Deputies not to hold office as Ministers. The army, navy, railways, telegraphs, customs, and finances to be under the control of the Central Government. A national militia, with compulsory service, to be established. Two sessions of the Cortes every year, and the members to be paid.

4.—Lord Redesdale introduces, but withdraws after discussion, a motion for an address to the Crown, praying her Majesty to attach official peerages to the offices of Lord Chancellor, of the two Chief Justices, and of the Chief Baron of Exchequer.

5.—The Shah leaves London, and embarks at Dover for Cherbourg, arriving at Paris next day.

— The French National Assembly decide that a bill for instituting a parliamentary inquiry into the condition of the French collieries, and the best means of augmenting their productive capacity in accordance with the requirements of commerce, should be treated as "urgent."

— The Inman steamer *City of Washington* wrecked in a fog on the Gull Rock Bar, Nova Scotia ; crew and passengers saved.

7.—Mr. Gladstone announces the abandonment of various Government measures for the present session.

— Duel at Essanges, on the border of the Luxembourg territory, between M. Ranc and M. Paul Cassagnac, each receiving a slight sword-cut in the arm.

— Replying to an appeal on behalf of the National (Education) Society, Earl Russell writes that he was "aware it was founded in 1811 with the view of superseding the British and Foreign Society in the work of education, and excluding the children of all parents who embrace the Christian faith without belonging to the Church from the benefits of education. I am aware, also, that many of the parochial clergy of the present day are friendly to the restoration of those practices which led to gross abuses, and to the reformation of the Church. I fear that if encouragement to the practice of confession be fostered, the desire to subvert the principles of the Reformation will gain ground. I therefore remain steadfast in the conviction that the daily reading of a portion of the Bible is a necessary condition of any sound education for the general mass of the people."

8.—Lord Cairns states in the House of Lords that the changes proposed by the Government in the Judicature Bill were violations of the privileges of the Upper House, in so far as the extension of the new court to Scotland and Ireland was a palpable infringement of the rule that any enactment affecting the jurisdiction of their lordships must commence in their own House, and could not be altered elsewhere. It was afterwards intimated by Mr. Gladstone that, to avoid a conflict between the two Houses, Government would propose that it be left to the Lords voluntarily to surrender their appellate jurisdiction in England and Scotland. This proposal was afterwards abandoned.

— Mr. Richards carries a resolution in the Commons in favour of international arbitration as a means of preventing wars, by 98 to 88 votes.

— In the case of Farrell and Harting *v.* Gordon, in which it was sought to set aside the will of the late Baroness Weld on the ground of undue influence, the Court of Probate pronounces in favour of the will and codicils, with costs against the defendants.

— The brothers Goldsmith and their sister Rebecca sentenced at the Central Criminal Court to various terms of penal servitude for obtaining jewellery under false pretences, and uttering various forged bills of exchange.

— Lord Gifford delivers judgment at Edinburgh in the action for separation and aliment by Lady Pollok of Pollok against her husband, Sir Hew Crawfurd Pollok, which had been before the Scotch courts for some time. His lordship found that the defender acted cruelly to his wife, and granted the separation asked for, with 500*l.* per annum aliment. The aliment claimed was 1,000*l.* a year.

— The Spanish Government issues a manifesto declaring that the most pressing and important task before it is "to put an end to the civil war now devastating Catalonia, Navarre, and the Basque Provinces. We are preparing to make a supreme effort for that purpose by the application of the extraordinary powers granted by the Cortes." The manifesto stated, that in order to achieve liberty the Government had resolved to exact the inexorable execution of the law, and to compel soldiers to remain with their colours until the complete pacification of the country shall be accomplished. The Government asked the support of all volunteer corps already organized, and urged them "to display against the partisans of Absolutism the warlike spirit of which they have already given so many proofs."

8.—Died at Frankfort, aged 68, Herr Winterhalter, German painter.

— Died at Oxford, aged 83, Rev. John Wilson, D.D., formerly President of Trinity. Dr. Wilson took a first-class in classics in 1809 (the late Dean Gaisford being one of his examiners), the year after Sir Robert Peel had obtained a double-first, while Mr. Keble took his degree in the subsequent year. He was appointed president of his college in 1850, but resigned the office in 1866.

9.—Diplomatic reception in uniform, in honour of the Shah, held in Paris for the first time since the fall of the Empire.

10.—Prince Bismarck ceases to be a member of the Prussian cabinet, and is succeeded by Herr von Balan as Foreign Secretary.

— A Communist rising at Alcoy, in Spain, where the mayor, with other officers, were murdered, and several public buildings set on fire. A new Ministry was soon afterwards formed.

11.—Mr. Mitchell Henry calls attention in the Commons to the presence of "strangers," which leads to the reporters being turned out of their gallery, and a complaint by himself and Mr. Whalley as to the imperfect manner in which their speeches were reported—a result which the hon. member for Peterborough attributed to the circumstance that many of the reporters were Roman Catholics.

— The Duke of Edinburgh betrothed to the Grand Duchess Marie of Russia, at Ingenheim.

12.—Loss of the steamer *Singapore* off Cape Guardafui, East Africa.

14.—In Committee on the Judicature Bill, the Attorney-General, by 174 to 129 votes, carries a clause providing that no Lord Chancellor hereafter shall receive a pension who has not sat ten years on the woolsack, or served fifteen years as an ordinary judge, unless he give his consent in writing to serve as an additional judge of the Court of Appeal.—Mr. Ward Hunt objected to this limitation, contending that it would prevent the Government from obtaining the best men.—The Attorney-General replied that the ex-Chancellors would be relieved from the legal duties which they had hitherto performed, and pointed to the engagement of Lord Westbury and Lord Cairns in arbitration cases as grounds for depriving Lord Chancellors of their pensions. —Mr. Gathorne Hardy reminded the Attorney-General that these duties had been imposed on Lord Westbury and Lord Cairns by Acts of Parliament. — Mr. Bouverie was of opinion that this circumstance had nothing to do with the question. The proposed arrangement would degrade the office of Lord Chancellor by reducing the holder of it to the position of an ordinary judge.—Mr. Gladstone and Mr. Lowe denied that this limitation would deter the very foremost men at the bar from accepting the Great Seal, and defended the justice of it now that the law lords were relieved from their legal duties.

14.—The Uhland monument at Tübingen unveiled.

— The Marquis of Bute lectures in a Roman Catholic schoolroom, Tower Hill, on "The Shrines of the Holy Land."

16.—Baronetcy conferred on Lord Mayor Waterlow, in connection with the visit of the Shah to the city, and for having (wrote Mr. Gladstone) "deserved so well of the people of this great metropolis for his intelligent and indefatigable philanthropy." Each of the sheriffs received the honour of knighthood.

— Don Carlos re-enters Spain, and issues a proclamation to the volunteers fighting in his name deploring the blindness of the army, "forgetful of fifteen centuries of glory under the monarchical flag." Leaving the French village of Ustaritz early in the morning, Don Carlos and his party travelled for three hours through the hills and forests of St. Pé and Sare. At a small inn just on the other side of the frontier, and close to the foot of Peña de la Plata, the Marquis Valdespina and General Lizarraga were waiting by appointment with their staff and an escort. These officers having saluted Don Carlos as their king and kissed his hand, he proceeded to change his travelling costume for a brilliant uniform that had been brought over beforehand, and then, attended by those already named, continued his journey till he reached the village of Zugarramurdy, where a hearty reception awaited him.

17.—In moving the second reading of the Education Act Amendment Bill, Mr. Forster explained the course which Ministers contemplated in the face of the objections raised in various quarters against some of its provisions, and particularly to the third clause. The object of the clause was twofold—first, to secure education for all the children of outdoor paupers; and, secondly, to transfer to poor-law guardians, upon certain conditions, the onus of paying, wholly or in part, school fees for the children of indigent parents. It was to the latter proposal that objection had been raised by boards of guardians, school boards, and certain religious denominations, and the Government was not prepared to persist in opposition to these bodies. He proposed, therefore, to take out of the clause all that portion relating to the transfer of the powers under the 25th section of the Education Act to the boards of guardians. It was also proposed to extend the provisions of Denison's Act, and make education compulsory in the case of pauper children. The proposal for a second reading was carried by 343 to 72 votes.

17.—Promulgation of the new Spanish constitution, declaring Cuba, Porto Rico, the Philippines, and Fernando Po as two territories.

— Her Majesty in Council signifies her assent to the marriage between the Duke of Edinburgh and the Grand Duchess Marie of Russia.

18.—Died, aged 76, Alderman Sir David Salomons, Bart., M.P., the first Jew permitted to take his seat in the House of Commons.

— Coronation of King Oscar and Queen Sophia at the cathedral of Drontheim, Norway.

— Resignation of Pi-y-Margall's Ministry at Madrid; a new Ministry formed by Salmeron.

19.—Died, through the effects of a fall from his horse, the Right Rev. Samuel Wilberforce, D.D., Bishop of Winchester. Accompanied by Lord Granville the Bishop left London to-day (Saturday) by the South-Western Railway, with the intention of paying a short visit to the Hon. Edward Frederick Leveson-Gower, of Holmbury, near Dorking, where Mr. Gladstone had arrived to meet them. At Leatherhead they were met by a groom with horses. The Bishop mounted one which, on account of its quietness, was a special favourite with Lord Granville. After passing Burford Bridge Hotel they went off the high road, and, leaving Dorking in the valley, made their way over Ranmove Common. From this point they pursued the bridle-road towards Leith-hill. Beyond Ackhurst Downs, Lord Granville, being very familiar with this part of the country, led the way down the hill towards Abinger, and arrived on a piece of moorland locally known as "Eversheds rough." The waggon road here being full of ruts, they left it for the turf, which was light and springy, but not good galloping ground. The Bishop and Lord Granville were in conversation when the Bishop's horse stumbled, it was believed over a stone, and threw its rider forward. Death appeared to have been instantaneous, as the Bishop fell on his head, and, turning completely over, dislocated his neck. The body was conveyed to Abinger Hall, the seat of Mr. Farrer, Secretary of the Board of Trade. The Bishop, who was born on the 7th September, 1805, was third son of William Wilberforce, celebrated for the part he took in the abolition of the slave trade. Dr. Wilberforce was consecrated Bishop of Oxford in 1854 and translated to Winchester in 1869. His last public utterance was in the House of Lords on the 15th inst., when, in reply to Lord Oranmore's accusation of complicity with the Ritualists, he closed with the words, "I hate and abhor the attempt to Romanize the Church of England; and I will never hear any one make such a charge without telling him to his face that he is guilty of gross misrepresentation."

— Died at Venice, aged 75, M. Philaréte Chasles, French essayist and critic.

19.—The Shah leaves Paris for Vienna by way of Geneva.

20.—Died at his residence, Lancaster Gate, aged 73, Richard Bethell, Lord Westbury, Lord Chancellor 1861–65, one of the most distinguished of modern lawyers, and a zealous advocate of reform in his profession. His lordship was busily engaged during the past twelve months as arbitrator under the European Assurance Society Arbitration Act of 1872, and had in that short time heard and decided many of the principal points brought before him. His decisions gave great satisfaction to the policyholders, especially his interpretation of the novation question, and the decisive way in which he dealt with attempted fraudulent transfers of shares. At the last sitting his lordship was so unwell as to require to be supported on his couch by pillows, and since that time he suffered acutely from inflammation of the upper vertebræ, and latterly from a cerebral disease.

21.—Most of the newspapers comment this (Monday) morning on the death of Dr. Wilberforce and Lord Westbury, the *Times* remarking that it was seldom that within one day England suffered such an intellectual loss. In the House of Lords the Duke of Richmond described the latter as attaining to the highest rank which it was possible for a layman in this country to occupy by his overwhelming talents and his great eloquence, while the former he had for many years the privilege and gratification of claiming as a most intimate personal friend, whose genial social qualities would leave a great gap among a wide circle of sorrowing acquaintances. Next evening Lord Granville said that, sometimes in the House and sometimes out of it, their lordships were apt to depreciate themselves ; but he thought it remarkable that two such losses should have occurred to that assembly within twenty four hours, and yet should have left the House not entirely bare.

— Writing to the *Times* on the subject of the Zanzibar Mail Contract, not with reference to its philanthropic or political aspect, but as regards the utility of the East African line as a postal service, Sir Bartle Frere says that he found on the East African coast during his late mission an amount of commerce far exceeding what he had been led to expect. All this commerce was increasing, and was capable of great and rapid development. The greatest obstacle to its increase was the want of regular postal communication.

— The Duke of Richmond's motion for a Royal Commission to inquire into the grievances which the officers of the army allege they suffer from the abolition of purchase, carried against Government by 129 to 46 votes. His Grace afterwards commented on a speech attributed to the Duke of St. Albans at Nottingham, where he was said to have affirmed that the Queen's earliest views of government were guided by the Liberal leader of the day, Lord

Melbourne, and that "she is supposed never to have forgotten the principles and party of her teacher;" his Grace declaring that he had "never heard anything more irregular, more unconstitutional, or more uncommon" than the remarks attributed to the Duke of St. Albans, and "without desiring to make too much of them," he protested that they were an insult to the Queen. The Duke of St. Albans defended his speech at Nottingham, but disclaimed any wish to make his observations personal.

22.—Mr. Candlish's proposal to repeal the 25th clause of the Educational Act rejected in the Commons by 200 to 98 votes.

23.—Mr. Trevelyan's Household Suffrage in Counties Bill "talked out," but not before Mr. Forster, and through him Mr. Gladstone, confined to his room by illness, had expressed their approval of the measure.

— Died, aged 77, George Carr Glyn, Lord Wolverton, leading to the elevation to the Upper House of the Liberal "whipper-in," the Hon. G. G. Glyn, M.P. for Shaftesbury. (See Aug. 30.)

— A Committee of the Upper House of Convocation submit a report describing the position of the Church with reference to confession and the exceptional cases in which she permitted its use. Such special provisions, however, it was said, "do not authorize the ministers of the Church to require from any who may repair to them to open their grief in a particular or detailed examination of all their sins, or to require private confession as a condition previous to receiving the Holy Communion, or to enjoin or even encourage any practice of habitual confession to a priest, or to teach that such practice or habitual confession, or the being subject to what has been termed the direction of a priest, is a condition of attaining to the highest spiritual life."

— Treaty of Commerce between England and France, signed at Versailles.

24.—The Zanzibar Mail Contracts Committee report that they are of opinion that the contracts of the 8th of May should not be confirmed ; "but, seeing that the Union Steamship Company has incurred expenses, and has for six months carried out a service, the terms of which they only accepted in consideration of other advantages, consider that before offering the service to a rival company or putting it up to public tender, the Government should afford the Union Steamship Company the opportunity of electing to retain the service on fair and reasonable terms."

— The Shah arrives at Turin, and is received by the King, Princes, Ministers, and municipal authorities.

25.—The Rating (Liability and Value) Bill rejected in the Lords by 59 to 43 votes.

— The Education Act Amendment Bill read a third time in the Commons.

25.—Fighting at Malaga, in Spain, between General Solier, military governor of the city, and Carbajal, chief of the insurgents, in which the former is victorious. Cadiz bombarded next day.

— Fire at Baltimore, destroying property in the centre of the city estimated to be worth one million dollars.

— The late Bishop of Winchester buried at Woolavington, near Petworth, Sussex, of which manor he was lord, in virtue of his wife, Miss Sargent. The Queen and Royal Family were represented on the occasion, and most of the Winchester and Oxford clergy were present.

28.—The forthcoming marriage of the Duke of Edinburgh announced in both Houses of Parliament, and a day fixed to make additional provision for his Royal Highness.

— Message brought down from the Crown in answer to the recent address of the House of Lords relative to discontent in the army. The message concluded with a statement that certain cases which have appeared to fall within the principle of the Army Regulation Act, though they were not formally included within its words, would be submitted in annual votes to the favourable consideration of Parliament, and that her Majesty has also directed that the allegations contained in the memorials of the officers of the army should be carefully examined by a Royal Commission, in order to ascertain whether any of them fall within the principle of, and may be properly dealt with by, the same form of proceedings.

— After three trials Sub-Inspector Montgomery is found guilty of the murder of Mr. Glass, bank cashier, Newtonstewart, and sentenced to be executed on the 26th of August. On the verdict being announced the prisoner made a long statement, confessing the murder, and saying that he had been a drunken man for twelve months previously. The weapon, he afterwards explained, was lying on the bank table, unconcealed. Mr. Glass saw it and asked him what he was going to do with it. The prisoner replied that he was dangerous, and commenced brandishing it about his head, but the deceased only laughed. Mr. Glass then turned round to look at a map on the wall, and the prisoner struck him a heavy blow on the head. He turned round and looked, but he was powerless to do anything. Afterwards he fell on the floor. Montgomery sat down and began to read the *Belfast Newsletter* till Mr. Glass was dead. He hid the weapon and money in his sleeve in the exact way shown by Sergeant Armstrong. He was splashed all over with blood with the exception of his boots, and the notes were also stained. He washed the marks out the next morning with a sponge and water. One of the bundles of notes had not been recovered, and he did not know what had become of it. He hid the notes in Grange Wood immediately after the murder, but he did not place either the sovereigns or the weapon in the place where they were found.

29.—The French Assembly prorogued, President MacMahon causing a Message to be read, intimating that before they met again foreign occupation would have ceased.

— Mr. Cross's motion of censure on the Post-Office administration rejected by 161 to 111, and Sir John Lubbock's amendment expressing regret at the appropriation of money without the consent of Parliament agreed to.

30.—Discussion raised by Mr. Bouverie in the Commons on Ministerial responsibility, arising out of differences in the departments presided over by Mr. Ayrton and Mr. Lowe.

— Archbishop Manning expresses approval of a desire manifested among the Catholic laity to enter upon a pilgrimage to Paray-le-Monial, a small village some distance from Paris, which acquired its reputation as a centre for pilgrimages from the fact that, according to the Roman Catholic belief, just 200 years ago the Saviour appeared there to the "blessed" Mary Margaret Alacoque, and intrusted to her a message to propagate the worship of the Sacred Heart. "It is," wrote the Archbishop, "an act of faith in the sight of the world, which seems every day becoming more and more unconscious of the presence and power of God. The defiance and derision with which the world has treated the pilgrimages in Italy, Germany, Belgium, and France is an explicit reason for the Catholics of England to claim their share also in their inheritance of our common cause. Moreover, it will be a witness to the power of prayer, which has, of late, like all other supernatural facts, been tossed to and fro in the hands of our men of culture. Lastly, it will not fail to hasten the day when the reign of wrong shall cease. The present state of Europe cannot last long; and men will find that they will have to pay dear for the dishonour they have heaped upon the Vicar of Jesus Christ." The pilgrimage was advertised to start from London on Tuesday, September 2 : the pilgrims to reach Paray-le-Monial next day, and having performed their devotions at the shrine on the 4th, might, if so disposed, find themselves back in London by the Friday night or Saturday morning.

— The Shah arrives at Vienna.

31.—The second reading of the bill for adding 10,000*l.* to the Duke of Edinburgh's annuity of 15,000*l.* carried by 162 to 18 votes.

— The House of Lords affirm the decision of the Master of the Rolls in the case of Peek *v.* Gurney.

— The Indian Budget introduced by Mr. Grant-Duff. Taking the actual year ending March 1872, the regular estimate for the year just ended, and the budget estimate for the year ending next March, he showed, with regard to the first period, that there had been a surplus of over three millions—the largest known since the China trade was thrown open. The second period showed a surplus of nearly a million and a half, and for the coming year it was estimated that there would be a virtual equilibrium, the revenue being 48,286,000*l.*, against an expenditure of 48,066,000*l.* The disappearance of the surplus Mr. Grant-Duff attributed to the cessation of the income tax.

August 1.—Died at Kensington Palace, aged 84, Cecilia Letitia, Duchess of Inverness, formerly Lady Buggin, and afterwards privately married to the late Duke of Sussex.

2.—Early this morning a serious accident happened to the express known as the tourist train from London to Scotland, consisting of twenty-five carriages, one of the heaviest of the season. As it was approaching Wigan at the rate of thirty-five miles an hour, seven carriages at the end of the train were, through some cause never ascertained, wrenched from the others at a pair of facing points, and rushed up a siding at the London and North Western station at Wigan. Four carriages were destroyed, one bounded on to the platform and turned bottom uppermost, two others followed and heeled over, and a portion of one was thrown over a high wall into a foundry yard, a female passenger dropping with it. Ten persons were killed and thirty injured.

— Constantinople news makes mention of the proposed canalization of the Isthmus of Corinth The Greek Government granted to the concessionaires, Lubini and Xenos, 30,000,000 square yards of building land for the construction of the new town and docks, the mines, woods, forests near the canal, the mineral waters of Lutraki, the railways and tramways, the Lake of Stymphalia, for the irrigation, monopoly of shipping, and numerous other privileges.

— Mr. Boord, Conservative, elected M.P. for Greenwich by a majority of 745 over all the other five candidates put together.

— Died, Lady Trevelyan, sister of Lord Macaulay, and his literary executor.

— The Germans withdraw from Belfort.

3. — Pastoral issued by Cardinal Cullen, directing the performance of a "Novena," preparatory to the Feast of the Assumption.

4. — Collision between the State liner *Alabama* and the steamer *Abeona*, off Instrahull, Ireland, the latter sinking with all on board excepting three picked up by the boats of the *Alabama*. A Board of Trade inquiry resulted in a verdict that Flint, master of the *Alabama*, merited the severest censure for the lack of judgment he displayed in this calamity after the collision, and he was accordingly severely reprimanded. Further, that George Hutchings, second officer of the *Alabama*, was guilty of a grave default in the performance of his duty as officer of the watch on the night of the collision, and therefore his certificate as master was suspended for eighteen months. The court intimated that it would

call the attention of the Board of Trade to the practice of passenger ships carrying the whole of their boats turned in on the chocks and covered. The court recommended that such boats be turned outwards.

5.—Parliament prorogued by Commission, the Royal Speech making reference to the Zanzibar, French, and Brazilian treaties, and to the Supreme Court of Judicature and Education Amendment Act, among the useful measures passed during the session. The *Standard* described the speech as fitly closing the record of a barren session, and reflecting the exhaustion of an expiring Ministry. "In this empty catalogue of feeble achievements, these long-drawn-out platitudes, these sounding commonplaces, these disjointed conclusions and inarticulate congratulations, we may trace the spirit of an Administration which, after living as long as it can on the faith of a few energetic acts at the beginning of its career, is consciously approaching its dissolution." "The army," wrote the *Pall Mall Gazette*, "the police, the civil service, the diplomatic service, the public spirit, the public conscience, the independence of the Legislature, even the judicial bench have every one of them been wounded and dispirited by Mr. Gladstone's Government ; and that is something far more serious than passing a bad bill, or neglecting to pass a good one, or failing to advance some 'fundamental principle.'"

— Mr. Baxter resigns his office of Secretary to the Treasury, on the ground that Mr. Lowe had not consulted him with reference to recent contracts, and declined to follow his advice.

— The Comte de Paris visits the Comte de Chambord at Frohsdorf, and acknowledges him as the head of the royal house.

— Mr. James Baird, of Auchmeddan, a member of the Scotch firm of ironmasters, passes over to a body described as the "Baird Trust" the sum of 500,000*l.* "to assist in providing the means of meeting, or at least as far as possible promoting, the mitigation of spiritual destitution among the population of Scotland through efforts for securing the godly upbringing of the young, the establishing of parochial pastoral work, and the stimulating of ministers and all agencies of the Church of Scotland to sustained devotedness in the work of carrying the Gospel to the homes and hearts of all."

5.—The Pope writes to the Emperor of Germany that the measures recently adopted by his Majesty's Government aimed at nothing short of the destruction of Catholicism, and could have no other effect than that of undermining his Majesty's throne. "I speak," said his Holiness, "with frankness, for my banner is truth ; I speak in order to fulfil one of my duties, which consists in telling the truth to all, even to those who are not Catholics ; for every one who has been baptized belongs in some way or other, which to define more precisely would be here out of place—belongs, I say, to the Pope. I cherish the conviction that your

Majesty will receive my observations with your usual goodness, and will adopt the measures necessary in the present case. While offering to your most gracious Majesty the expression of my devotion and esteem, I pray to God that He may enfold your Majesty and myself in one and the same bond of mercy." On the 3rd of September the Emperor replied that Catholic priests in Italy sought by intrigue to disturb the peace which had existed for centuries. "I willingly entertain the hope that your Holiness, upon being informed of the true position of affairs, will use your authority to put an end to the agitation carried on amid deplorable distortion of the truth and abuse of priestly authority. The religion of Jesus Christ has, as I attest to your Holiness before God, nothing to do with these intrigues, any more than has truth, to whose banner invoked by your Holiness I unreservedly subscribe. There is one more expression in the letter of your Holiness which I cannot pass over without contradiction, although it is not based upon the previous information, but upon the belief of your Holiness— namely, the expression that every one that has received baptism belongs to the Pope. The Evangelical creed, which, as must be known to your Holiness, I, like my ancestors and the majority of my subjects, profess, does not permit us to accept in our relations to God any other mediator than our Lord Jesus Christ. The difference of belief does not prevent me living in peace with those who do not share mine, and offering your Holiness the expression of my personal devotion and esteem."

6.—Duel at Creteil between M. About and M. Hervé, arising out of comments, said to be disrespectful, made by the former regarding the Comte de Paris. M. About was wounded in the hand, and declared unable to continue the contest.

— Mr. Allsopp, Conservative, elected M.P. for East Staffordshire by 3,630 votes to 2,693 given in favour of Mr. Jaffray, Liberal.

— Died, aged 82, M. Odillon Barrot, French statesman.

7.—Application having been made by the minister and churchwardens of St. Barnabas, Pimlico, to be allowed to erect a baldacchino in the church, the Bishop of London writes :— "The question of the legality of a baldacchino as an ornament of a church has never, I understand, been raised ; and it is the more important that it should be decided once for all, because a structure of this kind was proposed by Dean Milman to be erected over the communion table in St. Paul's Cathedral, in accordance, as it is stated, with the design of Sir Christopher Wren, and has not, I believe, been abandoned by the present Restoration Committee."

8.—Increasing dissensions in the Ministry lead to a re-arrangement of offices, the *Times* making the announcement to-day that Lord Ripon and Mr. Childers would retire. "Mr.

Bruce," it was said, "will receive a peerage, and succeed Lord Ripon as Lord President of the Council. Mr. Bright will succeed Mr. Childers in the Duchy of Lancaster. Mr. Lowe, who will leave the Exchequer, will succeed Mr. Bruce in the office of Home Secretary. The Chancellorship of the Exchequer will be held by Mr. Gladstone together with the office of First Lord of the Treasury." In a few days Mr. Ayrton was made Judge-Advocate, and Mr. Adam First Commissioner of Public Works.

8.—The Shah leaves Vienna for Brindisi, on his way to Constantinople.

9.—The Potomac river steamer *Wawasset* destroyed by fire, and over forty of the passengers suffocated, burnt, or drowned.

10.—The clipper-ship *Dunmail*, belonging to the White Star Line, wrecked at the mouth of the Mersey, having become unmanageable in a heavy sea.

11.— Professor Reinkens consecrated Old Catholic Bishop at Rotterdam by Bishop Heykamp of Deventer, and two assistants.

12.— Sir George Jessel appointed to the Mastership of the Rolls.

— Died, aged 58, Mr. Chisholm Anstey, who represented Youghal for several years in the House of Commons, where he made himself conspicuous by persistent attacks on the policy of Lord Palmerston.

13.—The English yacht *Deerhound* seized by a Spanish gunboat off Fuentarrabia, laden with arms and ammunition for the Carlists.

14.—An African West Coast naval expedition, while exploring the river Prah, fall into an ambuscade and suffer great loss at the hands of the Ashantee tribe. Commodore Commerell was severely wounded.

— The Lord-Lieutenant of Ireland turns the first sod of a new graving dock at Waterford.

— Sudden prorogation of the Parliament of Canada, the Governor-General announcing the appointment of a Royal Commission to inquire into the Pacific Railway scandal.

15.—The Right Rev. Dr. Edward Harold Browne, Bishop of Ely, recommended to be elected to the see of Winchester, in room of the late Dr. Wilberforce.

— Imperialist *fête* at Chiselhurst, about 1,000 Bonapartists being received at Camden House by the Empress and Prince Imperial, the latter of whom affirmed the principle of national sovereignty.

16.—The London Carlist Committee issue a despatch that "the Royal forces of Tristany and Saballs, under the command of his Royal Highness the Infante Don Alfonso, and numbering 2,400 men, after evacuating Berga, engaged and completely routed three columns of the enemy, numbering 7,000 men, between Caserras, Gironella, and Berga. We have taken one cannon and a large quantity of rifles and munitions. The loss of the enemy is estimated at more than 200 killed and a large number wounded."

16.—Five lives lost on Windermere by the upsetting of a sailing skiff hired out for a day's pleasure by Mr. Cooper and party.

— The equestrian statue of Mehemet Ali Pasha, erected in the Grand Square at Alexandria, is unveiled, and the new Imperial Firman is publicly read.

17.—Walter Howard, formerly page to an elderly lady named Miss Warren, charged with obtaining sums of money from his mistress under the false pretence of consulting Dr. Gull and others, is dismissed at the Middlesex Sessions, the jury not being able to agree upon a verdict.

18.—The British Iron and Steel Institute commence sitting at Liege.

— The Shah arrives at Constantinople. His Majesty left for Teheran on the 25th.

— Died at Geneva, aged 69, Charles, ex-Duke of Brunswick. He left the greater part of his large fortune to the city in which he died, subject only to the charge of a princely funeral and the erection of a magnificent mausoleum in which his remains were to be entombed amidst statues of bronze and marble. Among the gems discovered in his treasure-chest was the famous onyx vase of Mantua.

— Commenced at the Central Criminal Court, before Mr. Justice Archibald, the trial of Austin Biron Bidwell, aged 27, no occupation ; George Macdonnell, 28, clerk ; George Bidwell, 34, merchant ; and Edward Noyes, 29, clerk, who were placed at the bar to take their trial upon several indictments charging them with forging foreign bills of exchange, and thereby defrauding the Bank of England of over 100,000*l.* The trial lasted till the 26th, when the whole of the prisoners were found guilty, and sentenced to transportation for life. The chief evidence was given by bank officials who had transacted business for the prisoners, engravers who had prepared plates under their inspection, hotel-keepers where they had resided, and a young woman named Ellen Vernon, who had lived some time with George Bidwell.

19.—Mr. Gladstone presides at the Welsh National Eisteddfod opened at Mold, complimenting his hearers on the fact that 800,000 people still clung to their native tongue in spite of all the pressure which had been put upon them. Such was the loyalty of Welsh people, however, that their heart never had been alienated from the throne and the laws of the country. The Welsh were a people of deep and strong religious sympathies, but on those sympathies they had been deeply, most unjustly, and even madly thwarted. To their own great honour they had made provision themselves for their own religious wants.

What a lesson that was upon the false policy that had been pursued ! We had endeavoured to hector them into the abandonment of their language ; they had clung to it with unexampled fidelity. In conclusion, Mr. Gladstone said there was no greater folly circulating upon the earth at the present moment than the disposition to undervalue the relics of the past, and to break those links which unite human beings of the present day with the generations that had passed away.

19.—Sir Garnet Wolseley appointed to the chief command of stations on the Gold Coast, and Commander Glover, R.N., gazetted "Special Commissioner to the Friendly Native Chiefs in the Eastern District of the Protected Territories near or adjacent to her Majesty's Settlement on the Gold Coast."

— Formal opening of the harbour of refuge at Holyhead by the Prince of Wales and the Duke of Edinburgh.

20.—Narrow escape of Prince Arthur from drowning at Trouville, in Normandy.

21.—Died, aged 95, Charles Bridgman, for eighty-one years organist of All Saints' Church, Hertford.

— Dr. Kenealy concludes his opening speech for the defence in the Tichborne case, having spoken for twenty-one days.

22.—Mr. Bruce gazetted to the peerage as Lord Aberdare.

23.—Opening of Albert Bridge, crossing the Thames from Chelsea to Battersea.

— Collision near Retford, on the Great Northern line, between an excursion train running from Sheffield to Cleethorpe and a fish train leaving Doncaster at 7.20 A.M. Three persons were killed and over twenty injured.

— Inquest at Wood Green respecting the deaths of Mrs. Maria Constable, aged 55, and her sister, Mrs. Sarah Everett, aged 47, who disappeared from their homes on the 25th of June, and were found on the 21st instant buried in the ruins of the Alexandra Palace. The jury returned a verdict that death had resulted by suffocation caused from a brick wall falling upon them. How they got into the ruins there was no evidence to show.

25.—Archdeacon Denison calls attention to the fact that certain bishops propose to exterminate the Catholic element in the Church. "Well," he writes, "if the Bishop of Gloucester and Bristol, or any other bishop or bishops, will have open war, let it come. If they like to 'snub' every Catholic and 'pat on the back' every ultra-Protestant, let them follow their inclination. If they elect to stimulate popular ignorance and passion by calling us 'dishonest,' 'disloyal,' 'plotters,' 'traitors,' so let it be. If they prefer to administer their dioceses inequitably, let them so administer, as some are doing now. If they propose to repeat the policy which drove out Wesley a century ago, let them try its effect upon us. If they think it will promote God's truth and the good of souls to see what can be done towards procuring persecuting Acts of Parliament, let them try their hand. We are quite ready, and we should fear nothing if they should succeed. But they will not succeed."

25. — Señor Castelar elected President of the Spanish Cortes.

— Details published of an attempt to rescue the American bank forgers presently on their trial by bribing three of the warders in Newgate.

26. — Inspector Montgomery executed in Omagh Gaol for the murder of Andrew Glass, bank cashier, at Newtonstewart.

— At Posen, Monsignor Ledochowski is condemned to a fine of 200 thalers, or four months' imprisonment, for making illegal clerical appointments. The public prosecutor had asked that the bishop should be fined 500 thalers, in consequence of his obstinate and hostile attitude towards the State. At Fulda, Bishop Koel was fined 400 thalers for appointing clergymen without the sanction of the State.

— Died, Carl Wilhelm, composer of the famous German war-song "Wacht am Rhein."

27.—The citadel of Estella taken by Don Carlos, who commanded in person.

— Opening of the new pier at Herne Bay by Lord Mayor Waterlow.

29.—Blockade proclamation issued by Col. Harley at the Gold Coast :—"Whereas, hostile forces of Ashantees and other tribes are encamped and are waging war against her Majesty the Queen in and about the western portion of the protected territories on the Gold Coast ; and whereas warlike munitions, provisions, and articles useful to the enemy in the carrying on of their hostile purposes have been supplied to them from vessels trading on the coast : Now know ye that we hereby proclaim and declare that from and after the date hereof until our pleasure herein shall be further known, the entire blockade of the coast between Cape Coast Castle and the River Assinee, and of all the ports thereon with the exception of the port of Cape Coast, is and shall be in force."

30.—The Conservatives carry Shaftesbury, Mr. Benet-Stanford polling 603 votes against 534 tendered for Mr. Danby Seymour, Liberal.

September 1. — The captured insurgent frigates towed away from Carthagena by Admiral Yelverton, in defiance of the threats of the insurgents. The vessels were afterwards given up to the Madrid Government.

2.—Six hundred pilgrims leave London for Paray-le-Monial, to visit the shrine of the Sacred Heart. Before starting many of them attended mass celebrated for their convenience in various churches as early as four and five

o'clock. The general appearance of the pilgrims presented no difference whatever from that of an ordinary excursion party, and would have been in no way distinguishable but for the great number of priests who thronged the railway platform, and from the badge of the Sacred Heart worn by almost all present. The demeanour of the pilgrims, notwithstanding their errand, was quite in keeping with nineteenth-century customs, and though they were all armed with the special manual of devotion for use by the way, many of them were careful to provide themselves with the morning papers. The pilgrims crossed the channel to Dieppe in two boats, over which floated the English Union Jack, the Papal flag, and the flag of the Sacred Heart. Mass was celebrated during the passage by Monsignor Capel. At Paray-le-Monial the pilgrims were met by the whole population of the town, bearing torches. The procession—a mile in length—was headed by the flag of the Sacred Heart, and closed by the Union Jack borne by Admiral Jerningham. The banner of England was borne by the Duke of Norfolk, that of Scotland by Lord Walter Kerr. The Bishops of Salford and Oran conducted the pilgrims to the parish church from the railway station, where benediction was said, followed by confessions. Masses and communions were afterwards celebrated every half-hour from midnight.

2.—The anniversary of the battle of Sedan celebrated at Berlin by unveiling the monument of "Victory" in presence of the Emperor, the Imperial Prince, and military deputations from various German States.

3.—Sir George Jessel takes his seat for the first time as Master of the Rolls. Though not disqualified to sit in the House of Commons, Sir George, as he explained, having regard to the spirit of the Judicature Act, thought it best not to solicit the suffrages of the Dover electors again.

— News received of the wreck of the *Ethiopia* off Negrais, on her voyage from Calcutta to Rangoon. Mails lost ; passengers saved.

— The proposal made in the Spanish Cortes by Señor Olave that death sentences of military tribunals should be referred to the Cortes before execution, rejected by 88 votes to 82.

4.—Defending Government at a Sheffield Cutlers' Feast, Mr. Lowe said that during the Liberal tenure of office the finances of the country had been so prosperous as to permit of 3,600,000*l.* of special claims being paid off without borrowing a sixpence or imposing a tax at all. "That is the answer which I have to give to those who have been so liberal in criticizing. Can it be said in exercising this strict economy in your public service that anything has been shirked, or that anything which ought to have been done has been neglected? Look at the army. In 1859 the army numbered 84,000 men. Now it numbers 98,000, being an increase of 14,000, and this amendment with this great reduction in the expenditure. If you look at the fine arts, I have spent 8,000*l.* in buying Sir Robert Peel's pictures, and 50,000*l.* in splendid collections of antiquity for the British Museum ; so far from my having been stingy, I consider that these payments have been liberal in the extreme. . . . We are not tenacious of office. We are wearied with the labour of anxious and eventful years. It is a small matter for us whether we retain power or not. It is for you to consider whether it is a small matter for you. On that I offer no opinion. But this I will venture to say, that, if the decision of the country should be against us, we shall then carry into private life the applause of our own consciences, as having done in our judgment the best we could for our country, and the consciousness that we have left on the statute-book and in the history of this country records which calumny cannot permanently distort, and which envy, with all her efforts, can never obliterate."

5.—The mutilated remains of a female found in different parts of the Thames between Battersea and Limehouse. A reward of 200*l.* was afterwards offered by Government for the discovery of the murderer, and a free pardon to any accomplice not the actual perpetrator of the presumed crime.

— Apologising for his inability to be present at the opening of the Roman Catholic cathedral, Armagh, Archbishop Manning expresses an opinion that Ireland is in a happier condition in regard to religion than any other country, and also maintains that the country was never in so good a condition materially, and was never so influential in the British Empire and in the world as at present. But "when I look upon foreign nations, and I may say also upon England, I see cause for grave foreboding." Regarding Home Rule, the Archbishop thought the Parliament of the future will be broader, and more in sympathy with the constituencies of the three kingdoms. "England and Scotland will not claim to legislate for Ireland according to English and Scotch interests and prejudices ; and Ireland, when it is justly treated, will have no more will then than it has now to make or meddle in the local affairs of England or Scotland. The three peoples are distinct in blood, in religion, in character, and in local interests. They will soon learn to 'live and let live,' when the vanquishing reliquiæ of the Tudor tyranny shall have died out, unless the insane example of Germany shall for a time inflame the heads of certain violent politicians to try their hand at what they call an Imperial policy."

— Died, at Coolavin, aged 75, Charles J. Macdermot, "Prince of Coolavin," a fellow-labourer with O'Connell in the cause of Catholic emancipation.

8.—New docks at Flushing opened by the King of Holland.

9.—The *Alabama* indemnity paid at Washington.

9.—Señor Salmeron, now elected President of the Executive Power, submits the names of a new Ministry to the Cortes.

— Colossal statue of Nelson unveiled at Plas Llanfair, the marine seat of Lord Clarence Paget.

— Three persons killed and twelve injured through an accident to a South-Western train near Guildford, caused by a bullock straying on the line.

10.—The Conservatives win Renfrewshire, vacant by the elevation of the late Home Secretary to the peerage, the numbers being, Campbell, 1,885 ; Mure, 1,677.

12.—Sir Garnet Wolseley and his staff sail from Liverpool for the Gold Coast.

— Free library, museum, and picture gallery opened at Brighton.

— Old Catholic Congress opened at Constance.

13.—Died, aged 63, the Duke de Rianzares, husband of the ex-Queen of Spain, formerly a soldier in her guard.

15. — Brief official despatch received announcing disaster to the exploring expedition on the Prah in August.

16.—The last of the German troops cross the French frontier between nine and ten o'clock this morning.

17.—The King of Italy arrives at Vienna on a visit to the Emperor, and afterwards proceeds to Berlin.

— Another fire at Chicago, laying waste a line of property nearly a mile in extent.

— The British Association commences its sittings at Bradford, Professor Williamson (in room of Dr. Joule, absent through illness) delivering the opening address as President.

18.—Commercial panic in America leading to the suspension of Jay, Cooke, and Company, of New York, and of the First National Bank at Washington. The English Funds in consequence opened at a decline of $\frac{1}{4}$, and United States Government Bonds were generally depressed to the extent of $\frac{1}{2}$ per cent., the Funded Loan falling to 90$\frac{3}{4}$ and 90$\frac{5}{8}$, but subsequently recovering to 90$\frac{3}{4}$ to 91$\frac{1}{4}$, while Erie Shares fell 2 per cent., to 44 to 44$\frac{1}{2}$ ex div., and Illinois Railway Shares 1 dol.

— Died, aged 70, Sidi Muley Mohammed, Emperor of Morocco.

19.—Died, at Florence, from an attack of cholera, Professor Donati, astronomer.

— The Comte de Chambord writes from Frohsdorf to a friend advising him to appeal to all honest people on the footing of the social reconstruction. "You know that I am not a party, and that I will not come back to reign by means of a party. I need the co-operation of all, and all have need of me. As for the reconciliation which has been so loyally accomplished in the House of France, tell those who are trying to distort that great event that everything done on the 5th of August was really done for the sole purpose of giving France its proper rank in the dearest interests alike of her prosperity, her glory, and her greatness."

21.—Burning of the Black Lion Inn, Exeter, leading to the death of three out of five people sleeping in the premises at the time.

— Died, at Paris, aged 66, M. J. J. Coste, French naturalist.

— Died, aged 66, Dr. Auguste Nélaton, surgeon to the Emperor Napoleon III.

22.—The Spanish Government release the *Deerhound* and her crew.

— The Shah of Persia arrives at his palace at Teheran on his return from Europe.

— The steamer *Murillo* seized at Dover at the instance of the owner and shippers of the *Northfleet*.

— Henry James Cochrane, proprietor of the *Cheltenham Chronicle*, fined 150*l.* for contempt of court in publishing an article designed to influence the jury in favour of the Tichborne claimant.

24. — Manchester Athenæum Library destroyed by fire.

25.—Banquet given at York by provincial Mayors to the Lord Mayor of London.

— The *Challenger* exploring expedition arrives at Bahia. Having thoroughly explored the rocky desolate islands of St. Vincent and San Jago, belonging to Portugal, a long stretch across the Atlantic ensued, through depths averaging 2,000 fathoms, to the vicinity of the African shores. With a view to investigate the currents the course was shaped for St. Paul's Rocks, a lonely cluster in mid-ocean, one square mile in area, and sixty feet above the sea level. Thence the vessel sailed (Aug. 30) for another cluster, 300 miles distant, known as Fernando de Noronha. On arrival, great disappointment was experienced by refusal of permission to land, the islands being used as a penal settlement by Brazil. America was then made for, and Pernambuco reached on September 14.

26.—Mr. Henry James announced as the new Solicitor-General.

— Opening of Wandsworth Bridge, connecting Wandsworth with Chelsea.

— Died, aged 70, Salustiano de Olozaga, Spanish statesman and diplomatist.

— Died, aged 59, Mrs. Clara Mundt (Louisa Muhlbach), German authoress.

28.—Alicante bombarded for five hours by the Carthagena insurgent frigates.

— Mr. Bright receives the seals as Chancellor of the Duchy of Lancaster.

29. — M. Thiers writes to the Municipal Council of Nancy:—"Very soon we shall be called upon to defend, not alone the Republic which, in my opinion, is the only Government capable of rallying in the name of the common interest parties now so profoundly divided, which alone can speak to democracy with sufficient authority, and which now, far from troubling France, has appeared only to restore order, the army, finance, credit; to redeem the territory, and, in a word, to heal with one exception all the wounds of the war—we shall have, I say, to defend not only the Republic, but all the rights of France, her civil, political, and religious liberties, her social state, and her principles, which, after being proclaimed in 1789, have become those of the whole world; and, lastly, her flag, under which she is known to the whole universe, under which her soldiers, conquerors or conquered, have covered themselves with glory, and which, however, dear as it is to our hearts, will not suffice if all the things of which it is the emblem are to be taken away from us; for of these sacred things it is not the image alone, but the reality itself that we must have; and the tricolored flag, if remaining only to mask the counter-revolution, would be the most odious and revolting of lies."

30.—Died at Fox How, near Ambleside, aged 82, Mary Penrose, widow of Dr. Arnold.

— The Royal Commission appointed at the instance of Mr. Plimsoll to inquire into the alleged unseaworthiness of British registered ships, issue a preliminary report, recapitulating the schemes suggested for a compulsory survey and classification of merchant shipping under Lloyd's or Government, with counter evidence throwing doubt upon all such proposals, and tending to show that Government interference would only make matters worse, and "Amid these conflicting opinions, it is impossible, in the present state of our knowledge, to offer with any confidence any recommendation on this subject. We have referred to it here in the hope of directing public attention to a question which has often been treated as if it were of easy solution; it involves, however, a great principle of public policy, which should not be adopted or rejected without comprehensive and searching examination." The commissioners drew attention to the material change in the law which had occurred since their appointment, giving the Board of Trade full power to detain unseaworthy ships. Before recommending further legislation, they thought it would be well to observe the effect of the new enactment. The commissioners stated that, in their opinion, "there is no ground for the imputation made by Mr. Plimsoll that the Board of Trade desired to screen the ship-owners."

October 1.—The Social Science Congress opens at Norwich with Lord Houghton as President.

1.—Died, aged 71, Sir Edwin Landseer, painter. He was admitted as a student to the Royal Academy in 1816, when fourteen years of age, and in the following year exhibited "Brutus—a Portrait of a Mastiff," at the Academy. He was elected an A.R.A. in 1826, an R.A. in 1831, and received the honour of knighthood in 1850. When Sir Charles Eastlake died in 1866 Landseer was chosen to succeed him as President of the Royal Academy, but he refused to accept the honour. Sir Edwin was buried in St. Paul's cathedral on the 11th.

2.—Died, aged 92, Cornelius Varley, one of the original members of the Water Colour Society.

3.—Mr. Disraeli writes to Lord Grey de Wilton regarding the Bath election contested by Mr. Forsyth, Q.C., in the Conservative interest : "My dear Grey,—I am much obliged to you for your Bath news. It is most interesting. It is rare a constituency has the opportunity of not only leading, but sustaining, public opinion at a critical period. That has been the high fortune of the people of Bath, and they have proved themselves worthy of it by the spirit and constancy they have shown. I cannot doubt they will continue their patriotic course by supporting Mr. Forsyth, an able and accomplished man, who will do honour to those who send him to Parliament. For nearly five years the present Ministers have harassed every trade, worried every profession, and assailed or menaced every class, institution, and species of property in the country. Occasionally they have varied this state of civil warfare by perpetrating some job which outraged public opinion, or by stumbling into mistakes which have been always discreditable, and sometimes ruinous. All this they call a policy, and seem quite proud of it ; but the country has, I think, made up its mind to close this career of plundering and blundering."

— Execution of "Captain" Jack and three other Modoc Indians at Fort Kalomath, Oregon, for the murder of General Canby.

4.—Sir Garnet Wolseley addresses the native chiefs of the Gold Coast, stating that her Majesty having been informed of the injuries inflicted on her allies in that part of the world by the Ashantees, "who, without any just cause, have invaded your country, and, having learnt that you were unable to repulse your enemies without assistance, has sent me to unite in one person the chief military and civil administrations, so that, as a general officer, I may be able to help you. It was not an English war, but a Fantee war. The English forts were so strong that we ourselves had nothing to fear from the Ashantees; but, as it had become evident that a merely defensive policy would result in the destruction of the Fantees, the Queen was willing to assist them. The only interest she had in the Gold Coast was the promotion of their welfare by spreading

among them the arts and blessings of civilization."

4.—Died, aged 64, Mrs. Alfred Gatty, authoress of various stories suited for young people.

6.—Died, aged 77, the Count de Strzelecki, an early Australian explorer.

— The Danish Rigsdag opened at Copenhagen, and the colossal statue of King Frederick VII. unveiled in connection with the ceremony.

— Commencement of the trial of Marshal Bazaine at the Trianon Palace, Versailles, under the Presidency of the Duc d'Aumale. The charges against the Marshal were, that after urging Marshal MacMahon to march to his relief, he did not create a serious diversion, and was therefore answerable in a measure for the disaster of Sedan ; that he did not do everything prescribed by duty and honour to save Metz and the army of 150,000 men he commanded ; that he accepted conditions without any example in history ; that he did not destroy his matériel ; that he accepted a clause permitting officers to return home on giving their parole not to serve against Germany during the war ; that he did not obtain proper conditions for the sick and wounded, and that he neglected to destroy his flags.

— Mr. Bright issues an address to his constituents, a re-election being necessary through his acceptance of the Chancellorship of the Duchy of Lancaster. "The office," he wrote, "I have accepted is not one of heavy departmental duty, or I could not have ventured upon it, but it will enable me to take part in the deliberations of the Cabinet and to render services to principles which I have often expounded in your hearing, and which you have generally approved, more important, I believe, than any I could render in the House of Commons unconnected with the Government. I do not write to you a long address, for I am not a stranger to you. I hold the principles when in office that I have constantly professed since you gave me your confidence sixteen years ago. When I find myself unable to advance those principles, and to serve you honestly as a Minister, I shall abandon a position which demands of me sacrifices which I cannot make." Mr. Bright was re-elected without opposition.

7.—Bishop Reinkens, the Old Catholic Bishop, of Germany, takes the oaths required by the Constitution at Berlin. "I promise," he said, "to observe all this all the more inviolate as I am certain that my episcopal office requires me to do nothing which can be in contradiction to the oath of fidelity and allegiance to his Majesty the King, or to the obedience due to the laws of the country."

8.—Speaking at the Bath Congress on the present position of the Church, Archdeacon Denison said he had come to the conclusion that it is almost hopeless to continue the struggle against disestablishment. "I have no doubt as to the duty of a nation to have a national church, but looking at the peculiar circumstances of these times, and the present constitution of the House of Commons, I am convinced that unless church-people make a different fight for their church, I do not see how it is possible for anything to happen but disestablishment."

8.—Bath election carried by Captain Hayter, Liberal, the numbers being—Hayter, 2,210; Forsyth, 2,071.

— Captain James Brown examined in the Tichborne trial, this witness swearing to having accompanied the Claimant on board the *Bella*, at Rio.

9.—Sir Samuel and Lady Baker arrive in London from Egypt.

— Discussion in the Edinburgh Presbytery on the case of Dr. Wallace, charged with expressing opinions in his sermons and writings calculated "to unsettle the minds of ordinary hearers on the truth and importance of essential doctrines of Christianity, as the Trinity, the union of the Divine and human natures in the person of Jesus Christ—His incarnation, miracles, and resurrection, the Ascension, and the Second Advent." Dr. Wallace, in his answers, gave such explanations that the Presbytery agreed to a resolution in which they stated that they considered it unnecessary to take further steps in the matter.

— Died, aged 74, Lieutenant-General Lord Howden, formerly Ambassador at Madrid.

— Died, aged 64, John Evan Thomas, F.S.A., sculptor, Brecon.

10.—The Education Department issue new regulations for the election of borough and parish school-boards; providing that all board elections, as well as the poll taken on the resolution to apply for a board made by the ratepayers of a parish, shall in future be by ballot.

11.—The Intransigente war-ships defeated off Carthagena, in an action with Admiral Lobo's fleet. Two days later the admiral withdrew his force in the direction of Gibraltar.

— First stage of the Bazaine trial concluded by the reading of General de Rivière's report, closing with a brief account of the chief accusations against the incriminated officer.

12. — Died, aged 87, George Ormerod, author of the "History of Cheshire."

13. — The Solicitor-General, Mr. James, elected for Taunton by 899 votes against 812 tendered for Sir Alfred Slade.

14.—This, the 115th day of the Tichborne trial, is signalized by the production of what was looked upon as the missing link in the case, Jean Luie, a Dane, one of the crew of the *Osprey*, said to have picked up the defendant at sea. He was examined by Dr. Kenealy, and gave his evidence in good Eng-

lish, but with a foreign accent. "We crossed the line," he said, "some part of April, and got into the trade winds. When we were off the coast of the Brazils something attracted my attention. Early in the morning our attention was directed to a boat. We had had a very rough night, with squalls and rain. We noticed a boat on our port bow, and hauled to the wind as near as we could; but we could not get to her on that tack. We were too much to the wind. We made another tack, and then had the boat on our quarter. At that time the boat put up a spar with a red signal. A red shirt it turned out to be. The boat, when we first saw her, was about two miles to windward. We had left her astern about the same distance when we saw the signal. Our ship must have been about 400 or 500 miles from the Brazilian coast, and eighteen or twenty south latitude. We went about again and got up to the boat, and found six men in her. They were all in a delirious condition except two, who were paddling towards us. . . . My attention was attracted to one of the men in particular. He was not a sailor. He was one of the four. When we got the men on board, we washed them all and supplied them with food. Captain Bennett—that was the name of our captain— directed me to take the young man who was not a sailor into the cabin and place him on a sofa, but instead of doing that I put him in my own berth, and there I kept him all the time until our arrival in Melbourne. It took us three months to get to Melbourne, where we arrived in the early part of July. I noticed a good deal about him. I had to wash him nearly every day during the whole voyage. He was a small-made man, and not very bony. He had small hands, and dark-brown hair and big eyebrows. He had a habit of raising his forehead and eyes. His conversation with me was generally in Spanish. I speak that language. Sometimes he talked with me in broken French. . . . We picked them up in April. I asked the young man several times for his name, and he gave me the same answer. Once he told me that his name was Roger. He told me he had been in the Brazils, and went on board a vessel of the name of *Bella*, in Rio, and that they were bound for some part of America with a cargo of coffee. I asked him if he had been staying in the Brazils for any length of time, and he said only a short time. . . . In London, in consequence of what I heard on the 5th of July, I put myself in communication with the man whom it was said had been saved from the *Bella*. On the 7th I went to a house and asked if a gentleman was living there who went by the name of the Claimant. The servant, after going inside, said I could not see him, and I was told to go to Poet's Corner. I met Mr. Hendriks and Mr. O'Brien, and they took down my statement about the *Osprey*. Mr. Whalley came in, and he took me and O'Brien in a cab to No. 34 in a street. We were shown into a room, and I saw the defendant sitting at the window. He said,

'How do you do, Luie?' in Spanish. I had not given my name except to Hendriks; but he knew me at once. I recognized his voice immediately."

14.—Father Hyacinthe and M. Chavard, the newly-elected Old Catholic curés at Geneva, take the oaths before the Council of State. The ceremony was performed at the St. Germain Church, which had been placed at their disposal. There was some excitement in the neighbourhood, but no disturbance.

— Publication at Berlin of the correspondence between the Pope and the Emperor of Germany.

15.—The Congregational Union at Ipswich discuss a letter from Lord Shaftesbury's Vigilance Committee, in which the aid of Congregationalists was requested in an endeavour to rouse the country to some common action in regard to the advance of Ritualism and the practice of the Confessional in the Church of England. A series of resolutions was proposed, expressing the grave concern with which the Union regarded the Romanizing efforts of some of the clergy and other members of the Church of England, but stating that it could not, consistently with its views of the rightful relation of the Legislature to the Church of Christ, unite with the Vigilance Committee in any political action which contemplated the strengthening of the discipline of the Church of England by means of new laws, or which assumed that the Church should continue as a national establishment; further, that the Union regarded the defection of so large a portion of the clergy as a natural result of the retention in the formularies of the Church of some of the cardinal errors of the Church of Rome.

— The first Budget ever published in Egypt issued by authority of the Khedive. It gave details of the estimated revenue and expenditure for the twelve months from the 10th of September, 1873, to the 10th of September, 1874, and showed revenue equal to 10,166,000*l.*, and expenditure equal to 9,046,000*l.*, leaving a surplus of 1,120,000*l.*

— The castle of Ardverikie, formerly the residence of the Duke of Abercorn, and in which her Majesty and the Prince Consort passed the autumn of 1847, almost totally destroyed by fire. Sir Edwin Landseer, when a guest at the castle, decorated three sides of the walls of the drawing-room with sketches, all the subjects being connected with the chase.

— The right bank of the Amou-Daria, in Khiva, with the delta from the Sea of Aral to the extreme western arm of the river, incorporated with Russia by order of the Czar.

— Inundation at St. Petersburg, the waters of the Neva rising ten feet above their usual level.

— Dismissal of Admiral Lobo by the Madrid Government.

16.—Speaking at a banquet in Liverpool,

Earl Derby described the Ashantee war as a doctor's war and an engineer's war quite as much as a soldier's war. He doubted whether it was wise to take over the Dutch forts, "and I greatly doubt whether any man in or out of the Colonial Office exactly knows, or could define, the limits of our authority and of our responsibility in regard to tribes included within the protected territory. No doubt pledges must be kept, but the narrower the limits within which we contract our relations with those tribes the better, I believe, it will be. I have no great faith in that kind of moral influence which you acquire by burning a man's house over his head, and telling him he is to be your subject, whether he likes it or not. I believe, as a matter of fact, that trade is found to grow quite as fast, if not rather faster, in places where we do not exercise political power as in those where we do; and while I firmly believe in the value to the empire of colonies to which our own people can go out, and where they can work, I think, to put the thing plainly, that we have got quite black men enough, and that we had better not go in for more."

17.—Celebration of the 1200th anniversary of the foundation of Ely Cathedral, the city of Queen Etheldreda.

— Commission gazetted for inquiring into grievances alleged to be suffered by officers in the army.

— The Emperor of Germany again visits the Emperor of Austria at Vienna.

— Speaking at a Conservative banquet at Hertford, the Marquis of Salisbury criticized at some length the action of Mr. Gladstone's Ministry, which he said had this peculiarity, that it had been, in contrast to all English Ministries of many generations past—a Ministry of heroic measures. "Far be it from me" (the noble lord said) "to accuse them of heroism. They keep their heroism to the Home Office. They don't let it transgress the threshold of the Foreign Office. They offer to us a remarkable instance of Christian meekness and humility; but I am afraid it is that kind of Christian meekness which turns the left cheek to Russia and America, and demands the uttermost farthing of Ashantee. This, however, is to be said for their heroism, that outside these islands there is no doubt it has been heroism approaching to sternness towards every interest that happened to belong to the minority defeated at the poll. . . . There may be some doubt as to what the result of the next election upon the composition of Ministries may be. I confess I do not regard that question as one of the first importance. If it may be that we are to have a strong Government, I wish that it may be a Conservative Government; but if we are to have a weak Government, I wish that it may be a Liberal one. It may not be in your power to drive this Ministry from place—you may not be able to terminate its official life; but you will be able to draw its teeth and clip its claws ; and after all, though there are better things that we can imagine—after all, government by a toothless Liberal Ministry is not so bad a thing as many others, because it does this : it ensures that Parliament shall be too divided to give its attention to projects of revolutionary innovation, and it binds over the Liberal leaders in heavy security not to agitate."

17.—Died, aged 66, Vice-Admiral Sir Robert J. Le M'Clure, the dauntless explorer of the North-West passage.

18.—The insurgent ship *Fernando el Catolica* accidentally run into and sunk by the *Numancia,* off Alicante, and the greater part of the crew drowned.

— The Comte de Chambord reported to have made concessions of a nature to give satisfaction to all the exigencies of the Liberal party.

— Died, Dr. Thomas Smethurst, tried in 1859 for the murder of Isabella Banks, and sentenced to death but afterwards reprieved (see p. 555.)

19.—Died, aged 68, the Rev. R. S. Candlish, D.D., a Free Church theologian of great prominence in the Disruption controversy, and since that time the trusted guide of its general policy. His mother was the Miss Smith immortalized by Burns as one of the "six proper young belles" of Mauchline.

20.—The first Scientific Congress held in modern Rome assembles in the Great Hall of the Horatii and the Curatii on the Capitol. Count Mamiani presided on the occasion, and delivered the opening address.

— At Warrington, Mr. Butt declares that what the Home Rulers wanted was an Irish Parliament, which should have the right of legislating and regulating all matters relating to the internal affairs of Ireland, and have control over Irish resources and revenues, subject to the obligation of contributing their just proportion of Imperial taxes. By internal affairs they did not mean the management of railways or gasworks, but the higher life of the nation —their own system of education, passing their own university laws and grand jury laws.

— The Italian Government takes possession of six convents at Rome.

21.—Marshal MacMahon declares that he will not separate himself from the Conservative party which placed him in power in France.

22.—News from Calcutta indicates a famine as threatening Bengal.

— The Conservatives carry Hull, 6,873 votes being given to Colonel Pease, against 6,594 to E. J. Reed.

— Celebration of the 50th anniversary of the Oxford University Union.

— Mr. Bright addresses his constituents on re-election, reviewing the chief measures passed by the present Government, and condemning the Education Act on the ground that it extended and confirmed the system which it ought to have superseded. It really encouraged denominational education, and it established Boards only where that system did not exist, whereas it should have attempted to establish Boards everywhere, and to bring the denominational schools under their control. The denominational system, Mr. Bright said, in consequence of the parochial organization of the Church, must be said to be a Church system ; hence the Nonconformists were aggrieved, and justly aggrieved. Speaking of policy, "What, asked Mr. Bright, is the policy of the Opposition ? Why, we were told the other day that the leader of the Opposition was 'in a state of strict seclusion.' And but for that strange and unfortunate epistolary outburst we should have had no idea of the desperate state of mind in which he has been. But still, if we ask for the policy of the Opposition, all is dark, dark, impenetrably dark, and all that we know is, that nothing can be known. I beg pardon, though ; I am wrong in that. We know that, according to the Opposition, all the work of the past five years, and if you like, of the past forty years, is evil ; but as to the future, you will see it when it comes. Now, let me tell you this, that that great statesmanship which consists in silence and secrecy is not original, it is a mere copy of thirty or forty years ago." The history, Mr. Bright concluded, "of the last forty years of this country —judge it fairly — speaks of its legislation, which is mainly a history of the conquests of freedom. It will be a grand volume that tells the story, and your name and mine, if I mistake not, will be found on some of its pages. For me the final chapter is now writing. It may be already written. But for you, this great constituency, there is a perpetual youth and a perpetual future. I pray Heaven that in the years to come, and when my voice is hushed, you may be granted strength and moderation and wisdom to influence the councils of your country by righteous means to none other than to noble and to righteous ends." Mr. Bright was said to have spoken with much of his old animation for one hour and ten minutes to an audience thought to have numbered over 15,000.

23.—Died, aged 58, Vice-Chancellor Wickens, who had taken his Bachelor's degree at Oxford in 1836 as a Double First Class.

— The Carthagena Intransigentes bring four steamers as prizes into harbour, and leave two sailing vessels outside after ransacking them.

— At the opening of the Canadian Parliament the Governor-General announces that the Pacific Railway Company had surrendered their charter.

— Attempted murder and suicide by a man named Peacock, a cooper, in Walworth, thought to be amongst the oldest of those continuing to believe in the pretensions of Joanna Southcote.

137

25.—Seven men drowned in the Thames, by the upsetting of a boat in a fog while crossing from Woolwich.

26.—Died, on the Pacific Railway, J. C. Heenan, the antagonist of Sayers in the memorable international fight at Farnborough, in April, 1860.

— Five hundred British troops sent from Aden to Lahadj, in consequence of a threatened occupation by the Turks.

27.—The evidence for the defence in the Tichborne case closes on this the 124th day of trial.

— A force of Ashantees defeated by Sir Garnet Wolseley, and several villages destroyed.

— The monarchial scheming in France suddenly checked by a letter from the Comte de Chambord to M. Chesnelong, declining to make any concession on the subject of the flag. "For forty-three years," he wrote, "I have preserved intact the sacred deposit of our traditions and our liberties. I have, therefore, a right to reckon upon equal confidence, and I ought to inspire the same sense of security. My personality is nothing; my principle is everything. France will see the end of her trials when she is willing to understand this. I am a necessary pilot, the only one capable of guiding the ship to port, because I have for that a mission of authority. You, sir, are able to do much to remove misunderstandings and prevent weaknesses in the hour of struggle. Your consoling words on leaving Salzburg are ever present to my mind. France cannot perish, for Christ still loves His Franks; and when God has resolved to save a people, He takes care that the sceptre of justice is only put into hands strong enough to hold it."

28. — Died, through the effects of a cold caught in returning from Paris, in the 85th year of his age, Sir Henry Holland, appointed Physician in Ordinary to the Queen in 1852, a traveller of wide reputation and unwearied activity.

— The old Opera House in the Rue Lepelletier, Paris, destroyed by fire.

29.—Died, aged 72, John, King of Saxony. He was succeeded by King Albert.

30.—Stokes, who shot Colonel Fisk of the Erie Railway, found guilty of manslaughter in the third degree, and sentenced to four years' imprisonment.

— The French Minister of War issues an order announcing that General Bellemare has been placed on the retired list for having written a letter the spirit of which was opposed to national sovereignty. An order of the day to the army was also issued by Marshal MacMahon, in which he stated :—"A single act of insubordination has been committed in the army, but the President of the Republic is firmly convinced it will not be repeated. He

is aware of the spirit of devotion which animates you : you know how to maintain in the army that union and discipline of which you have always set an example, and which, while constituting its strength, alone can assure the tranquillity and independence of the country. As soldiers, our duty is clearly laid down for us, and is indisputable. Under all circumstances we are to maintain order and cause legal decisions to be respected."

30.—Choral festival in St. Paul's Cathedral.

— Died, aged 52, M. Ernest Aimé Feydeau, French novelist.

31. — The filibustering steamer *Virginius*, with a crew of 135 men, captured near Jamaica by the Spanish gunboat *Tornado*, and taken to St. Jago de Cuba.

November 1.—Died, aged 60, the Right Hon. Sir William Bovill, Lord Chief-Justice of the Court of Common Pleas.

2.—The Vienna Exhibition closes, having been visited since its opening in May by 7,254,687 people.

— Died, at Coatbridge, Lanarkshire, aged 78, Mrs. Janet Hamilton, the daughter of a shoemaker, without education, mother of a large family, and for many years totally blind, yet who, by patient effort in the way of self-culture, produced poems and stories of high merit.

— Completion of the International Bridge of the Grand Trunk Railway between Canada and the United States.

— Replying to a correspondent as to the use of the term "free land," Mr. Bright writes that it means "the abolition of the law of primogeniture and the limitation of the system of entails and settlements, so that 'life interests' may be for the most part got rid of, and a real ownership substituted for them. It means also that it shall be as easy to buy or sell land as to buy or sell a ship, or, at least, as easy as it is in Australia and in many or in all the states of the American Union. It means that no legal encouragement shall be given to great estates and great farms, and that the natural forces of accumulation and dispersion shall have free play, as they have with regard to ships and shares, and machinery, and stock-in-trade, and money. It means, too, that while the lawyer shall be well paid for his work, unnecessary work shall not be made for him, involving an enormous tax on all transactions in connection with the purchase and sale of lands and houses. A thorough reform in this matter would complete, with regard to land, the great work accomplished by the Anti-Corn Law League in 1846. It would give an endless renown to the Minister who made it, and would bless to an incalculable extent all classes connected with and dependent on honest industry."

3.—The Pope writes to Ledochowski that he sees with sorrow the professors of the Church designated as rebels; "its bishops are condemned by lay courts as agitators, persecuted with fines, deprived of their offices and expelled the country, the spiritual orders are prohibited, the clergy is gagged, and, by arbitrary measures, prevented from exercising its office; education of the youth in the spirit of the Church is forbidden, in order that, on the one hand, the population may not be confirmed in the principles of religion, and that, on the other, the hope may vanish of able and faithful servants of the altar being trained up. In order to undermine the glory of God, the property dedicated to God is robbed; even the chief helmsman of the Church is kept in bondage in order that, though utterly despoiled, he may not govern the Church with freedom, according to his powers."

3.—Died, Rios Rosas, ex-Minister and President of the Spanish Cortes.

— Died, at Mecca, Abd-el-Kader, formerly Chief of Oran, Northern Africa, and a formidable foe to French rule in that country.

— Seven British seamen drowned at Santander by the upsetting of a life-boat which they had manned to save the shipwrecked crew of the Spanish schooner *Union*.

4.—Came on for hearing in the Court of Admiralty the case of the *Murillo*, two actions for 24,000*l*. by the owners of the *Northfleet* and the owners of the cargo, for the loss of both by the collision in January last. No one represented the owners of the *Murillo*. In giving judgment, Sir R. Phillimore said:—"I grant the prayer of the motion, but I don't think I ought to content myself with that single part of my judicial duty. I find it difficult to express in adequate terms the indignation which the brutality and meanness of conduct of those who had the charge of the *Murillo* must excite in the bosom of every man not void of the ordinary feelings of humanity. This case, indeed, represents all the cruelty without any of the courage of the pirate."

— Explosion in the premises of a firework maker, Broad Street, Lambeth, causing the death of eight people, being the whole of the occupants at the time the calamity occurred.

5.—The Democrats carry the New York and Virginia State elections with heavy gains over previous majorities, while in Massachusetts the Republicans were successful, but with a reduced majority. The Republican candidates were successful in New Jersey, Arkansas, and Minnesota. Democratic candidates carried Maryland. In Wisconsin the Fusionist party were successful. Generally the returns up to this date showed heavy losses to the Republican party.

— At the opening of the French Assembly, a message is read from Marshal MacMahon, stating for a sure guarantee of peace "the present Government lacks two essential conditions which could not be longer overlooked without

danger. It has neither sufficient vitality nor authority. Whoever the holder of power may be, that power can do nothing durable if its right to govern is daily called into question, if it has not before it the guarantee of a sufficiently long existence to spare the country the perspective of incessantly recurring agitation. With a power that might be changed at any moment, it is possible to secure peace to-day, but not safety for the morrow. Every great undertaking is thus rendered impossible, and industry languishes." A proposal for prolonging the President's power for ten years was thereupon carried by 360 to 348 votes.

— Opening of the Austrian Reichsrath, the Emperor speaking of the Exhibition as having drawn together sovereigns of distant states, and so increased the pledges of peace and strengthened the influence of Austria. His Majesty further exhorted the Reichsrath to work with united energy at the solution of the great task of uniting the people of Austria, so that she might become a powerful state, strong in ideas of justice and liberty.

— The Ashantees attack the British position at Abrakrampa, but are repulsed and finally retreated.

— The strong feeling in the Dominion regarding the Pacific Railway contract, and the expenditure of the funds obtained under the Allan concession, leads to the resignation of the Prime Minister, Sir John Macdonald. Mr. Mackenzie undertook the task of forming a new Ministry.

6.—The Irish National Board of Education, by 9 votes to 7, finally refuse to recognize Mr. O'Keeffe as manager of the Callan schools.

7.—The Bank rate of discount raised from 8 to 9 per cent.

— Fifty-three of the crew of the *Virginius*, including sixteen British subjects, shot at Santiago.

— The Diet at Munich resolves to extend the jurisdiction of the German Empire over the whole civil legislation of Bavaria.

— Earl Grey details in the *Times* a policy which he thinks ought to have been pursued by the British Government in Western Africa, and might, in his opinion, have avoided the Ashantee war.

8.—Monument to Count Cavour unveiled at Turin, in presence of King Victor Emmanuel, the Princes of the Royal Family, members of the Cabinet, deputations from the Senate and the Chamber of Deputies, the members of the Diplomatic Body, the civil and military authorities at Turin, and deputations from the Municipal Councils. The weather was extremely unfavourable, and the illuminations had to be postponed. At the banquet given in the evening by the municipality to 500 guests, the British Minister, Sir Augustus Paget, assured the Italians of the sympathy of England with the Italian cause, and its high admiration of the great statesman who insured its success.

8.—Died, at Paris, aged 77, Auguste de Metz, founder of the Reformatory at Mettray.

9.—Burning of the ship *Nagpore* in Kingstown harbour, attended with serious damage to other vessels in port.

— Royal order issued, relieving Count von Roon from the presidency of the Prussian Ministry, and appointing Prince Bismarck his successor.

10.—At the Lord Mayor's banquet this evening, Mr. Gladstone and Mr. Lowe defended the policy of Ministers, the latter, in addition, expressing himself as confident that the dissolution of Parliament would not necessarily be the dissolution of Government.

— Died, aged 73, Robert Vernon Smith, Lord Lyveden, M. P. for Northampton from 1831 till his elevation to the peerage in 1859.

12.—Mr. Knight, of Dundee, having withdrawn with his congregation from all connection with the Free Church, the Presbytery now formally declare that he has ceased to belong to their body.

— Prussian Diet opened.

13.—Mr. Charles Hall takes his seat in court as successor to Vice-Chancellor Wickens.

— Died, aged 76, John Gough Nichols, F.S.A., one of the founders of the Camden Society, the editor of many of its volumes, and a prolific contributor to genealogical and topographical literature.

14.—In consequence of the excitement manifested throughout the States at the *Virginius* executions, Mr. Fish urges the American Minister at Madrid to protest against them as an outrage to humanity, and an insult to the American Government. The Spanish Government in reply admitted its responsibility, and reiterated assurances of its friendly feeling towards the United States. It disapproved the executions, and promised to shape its course accordingly. Sections of the New York press urged that a declaration of war should be issued at once, and possession taken of Cuba.

15.—More changes announced in the Ministry, Sir John Coleridge accepting the Court of Common Pleas, Mr. James the post of Attorney-General, and Mr. Vernon Harcourt that of Solicitor-General. Dr. Lyon Playfair became Postmaster-General.

— M. Laboulaye presents to the Assembly the report of the Committee of Fifteen proposing to prolong Marshal MacMahon's power for five years. The President rejected this proposal, and on the 19th the Assembly by 383 to 317 votes confirmed his power for seven years.

— Opening of the Italian Parliament, the King declaring in his Speech from the Throne that Italy and Germany have both constituted

themselves in the name of the principle of nationality; "they have both been able to establish Liberal Constitutions based upon a monarchy associated for centuries with the national sorrows as well as the national glories. The relations between the two Governments are in conformity with the sympathies existing between the two peoples, and are a guarantee for the maintenance of peace. It is our desire to live in harmony with all nations. Nevertheless, I shall firmly guard the rights and dignity of the nation."

18.—Home-Rule Conference in London, called to discuss and adopt a series of resolutions. The first declared the prosperity of Ireland to be only possible under self-government; the second asserted a right to self-government; the third claimed a Parliament in Ireland composed of the Sovereign, Lords, and Commons of Ireland; the fourth affirmed the principle of a federal arrangement for internal affairs, leaving to the Imperial Crown and Parliament legislation respecting the colonies and other dependencies of the Crown, the relations of the Empire with foreign Powers, and all matters appertaining to the defence and stability of the Empire at large, as well as the power of granting and providing the supplies necessary for Imperial purposes; the fifth declared that such a change effects no change in the Constitution or disturbance of the prerogatives of the Crown; the sixth stated that it would be necessary to have in Ireland an administration for Irish purposes, conducted by Ministers constitutionally responsible to the Irish Parliament.

— The President of the Board of Trade addresses a circular to railway companies, calling attention to the opinion expressed in Colonel Tyler's report that the great proportion of accidents during the past year arose from causes entirely within their own control.

19.—Sir John Coleridge sworn in as Lord Chief-Justice of the Common Pleas. To his constituents he wrote :—"I will not affect to deny that I quit political life reluctantly, and resign the seat for Exeter with great regret. It has been the pride and honour of my life to represent the capital of my county, and my political principles are as strong and my political sympathies as keen as ever, though henceforward I can allow them, as a judge, neither influence nor expression."

— Mr. Disraeli installed as Lord Rector of Glasgow University, delivering thereafter to an immense audience assembled in the conservatory of the Botanic Gardens an address explanatory chiefly of principles to be observed by the students for attaining success in life. Self-knowledge, he said, was the first condition. Bitter disappointment and perhaps failure followed the revelation of the harsh reality which belied the golden promise of youth as to our own powers. Acquaintance with the spirit of the age was the second condition of success—not obedience to it, for it might be an evil spirit, but acquaintance with it—an acquaintance necessary to all. What was the spirit of the age? The spirit of equality. He believed in political equality. He held that equality before the law was the only true foundation of a commonwealth. It had long prevailed in Britain, and to it more than to geographical distinctions, of which we have heard so much lately, the patriotism of the people was due. He did not believe in social equality. France had tried social equality for eighty years, with what result they knew. The experiment made there showed that social equality was not a safe principle upon which to rely in the hour of trial or of danger. But social equality did not satisfy the latest philosophers. They wanted material equality. They believed only in material happiness; they would destroy private property, and acknowledge only the rights of labour. "The insurmountable obstacle," he concluded, "to the establishment of the new opinions will be furnished by the essential elements of the human mind. Our idiosyncrasy is not bounded by the planet which we inhabit. We can investigate space, and we can comprehend eternity. No considerations limited to this sphere have hitherto furnished the excitement which man requires, or the sanction for his conduct which his nature imperatively demands. The spiritual nature of man is stronger than codes or constitutions. No government can endure which does not recognize that for its foundation, and no legislation last which does not flow from that fountain. The principle may develop itself in manifest forms, shape of many creeds and many churches, but the principle is Divine. As time is divided into day and night, so religion rests upon the providence of God and the responsibility of man. (Loud cheers.) One is manifest, the others mysterious, but both are facts. Nor is there, as some would teach you, anything in these convictions that tends to contract our intelligence or our sympathies. On the contrary, religion invigorates the intellect and expands the heart. He who has a due sense of his relations to God is best qualified to fulfil his duties to man." Speaking at a banquet given in his honour by the city in the evening, Mr. Disraeli said: "It has been my fortune to be the leader in the House of Commons of one of the great political parties in the State for five-and-twenty years, and there is no record, I believe, in the parliamentary history of this country of a duration of a leadership equal to it. There have been in my time two illustrious instances of the great parties being led by most eminent men. One was the instance of Sir Robert Peel, who led the Tory party for eighteen years, though unfortunately it twice broke asunder. There was also the instance of one who is still spared to us, and who, I hope, may be long spared to us, for he is the pride of this country, as he was the honour of the House of Commons,—Lord John Russell. He led one of the great parties of

the State in the House of Commons for seventeen years, though at last it slipped out of his hands. Do not suppose for a moment that I am making these observations as any boast. The reason that I have been able to lead a party for so long a period, and under circumstances of some difficulty and discouragement, is, that the party I lead is really the most generous and most indulgent party that ever existed. I cannot help smiling sometimes when I hear the constant intimations that are given by those who are in the secrets of the political world of the extreme anxiety of the Conservative party to get rid of my services. The fact is, the Conservative party can get rid of my services whenever they give me the intimation that they wish it. Whenever I have desired to leave the leadership of the party they have too kindly requested me to remain where I was, and if I make a mistake, the only difference in their conduct to me is that they are more indulgent and more kind." Mr. Disraeli went on to speak at length on the subject of the present commercial perturbation and the high value of money, which he attributed almost wholly to the great changes which various countries in Europe and various Governments in Europe are making with reference to their standard of value. Mr. Disraeli was presented next day with the freedom of the city.

21. — The Washington Cabinet grant the extension of time asked for by Spain to inquire into the details of the *Virginius* executions, and at the same time admit that consideration should be shown for the impossibility in which Spain has been placed of ascertaining the facts of the outrage in time to make satisfactory reparation.

22.—Addressing the Glasgow Conservative Association, Mr. Disraeli defended the Bath letter as a correct description of the conduct of the Government, well weighed, and in support of which ample testimony could be adduced. "There was only one characteristic," he said —"it was not original, for six months before in the House of Commons I had used the same expressions and made the same statement—not in a hole or corner, but on the most memorable night of the session, when there were 600 members of the House of Commons present, when on the debate that took place avowedly the fate of the Ministry depended. It was at midnight that I rose to speak, and made the statement almost similar in expression, though perhaps stronger and more lengthened than the one which has become the cause of recent controversy. The Prime Minister followed me in that debate. The House of Commons knew what was depending upon the verdict about to be taken, and with all that knowledge they came to a division, and by a majority terminated the existence of the Government. . . . . There was an illustrious writer, one of the greatest masters of our language, who wrote the history of the last four years of the reign of Queen Anne, which was the duration of an illustrious Ministry. I have written the history of a Ministry that has lasted five years, and I have immortalized the spirit of their policy in five lines." Mr. Disraeli spoke of Mr. Lowe as having attacked the Government of the day for imprudence in interfering in the affairs of Abyssinia. "He laughed at the honour of the country; he laughed at the interests of a few enslaved subjects of the Queen of England, compared, as he said, with the certain destruction and disaster which must attend any interference on our part. He described the horrors of the country and the terrors of the clime. He said that there was no possibility, by any means, by which success could be obtained, and that the people of England must prepare themselves for the most horrible catastrophe. He described not merely the fatal influence of the climate, but I remember that he described one pink fly alone—(laughter)—which, he said, would eat up the whole British Army. (Great laughter.) He was as vituperative of the insects of Abyssinia as if they had been British workmen." In closing his address, Mr. Disraeli drew attention to the contest commencing in Europe between the spiritual and temporal power. "And here," he said, "I must say that if we have before us the prospect of struggles—perhaps of wars and anarchy, ultimately —caused by the great question that is now rising in Europe, it will not easily be in the power of England entirely to withhold itself from such circumstances. Our connection with Ireland will then be brought painfully to our consciousness, and I should not be at all surprised if the visor of Home-Rule should fall off some day, and you beheld a very different countenance. Now I think we ought to be prepared for those circumstances. The position of England is one which is indicated, if dangers arise, of holding a middle course upon those matters. It may be open to England again to take a stand upon the Reformation which 300 years ago was the source of her greatness and her glory, and it may be her proud destiny to guard civilization alike from the withering blast of atheism and from the simoom of sacerdotal usurpation. These things may be far off, but we live in a rapid age, and my apprehension is that they are nearer than some suppose. If that struggle comes, we must look to Scotland to aid us. It was once, and I hope is still, a land of liberty, of patriotism, and of religion. I think the time has come when it really should leave off mumbling the dry bones of political economy and munching the remainder biscuit of an effete Liberalism. . . . We all know that a general election is at hand. I do not ask you to consider, on such an occasion, the fate of parties or of Ministries; but I ask you to consider this—that it is very probable the future of Europe depends greatly on the character of the next Parliament of England. (Hear, hear, and cheers.) And I ask you, when the occasion comes, to act as becomes an ancient and famous nation, and give all your energies to the cause of faith and freedom."

22.—Boiler explosion at Cameron's engineering works, Glasgow, causing the death of four men.

— W. M. Tweed sentenced to twelve months' imprisonment and a fine of 127,500 dollars for the New York municipal frauds.

— Disastrous collision between the Transatlantic steamer *Ville du Havre*, from New York for Brest, and the English ship *Lochearn*. The steamer was struck amidships, and as she showed signs of sinking almost immediately, two of her boats were hurriedly let down, but, even with the aid of the *Lochearn's* crew, only 87 out of a total of 313 on board could be saved. The *Ville du Havre* sunk within twelve minutes after being struck. Fifty-three of the crew were rescued, including the captain. Among the passengers saved were ten ladies. All the survivors were on the same day transhipped on board the American ship *Tremountain*, bound to Bristol, where they were landed on the 1st December.

23.—Died, at sea, from fever contracted in his services against the Ashantees, Lieutenant the Hon. A. W. Charteris, eldest surviving son of Lord Elcho.

25.—Availing himself of the opportunity afforded in laying the first stone of the first school erected by the Liverpool School Board, Mr. Forster defends the principles of the Elementary Education Act, and the way in which it was carried out.

— Mr. Justice Blackburn gives judgment in the case of Bolton *v.* Maddox, involving the question whether a promise to give votes for a charitable institution was a good consideration, so as to make a corresponding promise enforceable at law. Two subscribers to a charitable institution mutually agreed to support each other's candidates for admission. At the first ensuing election the plaintiff gave his votes to the defendant's candidates; but as at the next election the defendant declined to support the plaintiff's candidate, the latter subscribed seven guineas to the institution, and was thus under its rules entitled to the requisite number of votes. For the seven guineas he brought an action against the defendant. For the latter it was contended that such a promise could not be enforced, as there was a duty on the subscriber to give his votes to the best qualified candidates for admission. If, then, the best qualified were the ones for whom he was required to vote, there was no consideration; but if they were not, the promise was against public policy, and, therefore, not enforceable at law. While some members of the Court desired to express their disapprobation of this traffic in votes, there was no principle of law which made such a promise other than a good consideration for a corresponding promise. Judgment for the plaintiff.

— Archbishop Ledochowski again fined for the unlawful institution of priests.

26. — Bombardment of Carthagena commences.

— The French Cabinet reconstituted.

27. — Came on in the Court of Common Pleas, before Mr. Justice Brett and a special jury, the case of Gilbert *v.* Enoch, an action raised by Mr. Gilbert, dramatist, against the publisher of the *Pall Mall Gazette*, in so far as a correspondent had therein described "The Wicked World" as a play too indecent to be represented in any theatre. Verdict for the defendant.

— The hearing of the Tichborne case resumed.

— Died, aged 70, the Rev. John Dymoke, hereditary "Queen's Champion."

-— The second London School Board elected.

29. — Duel in the Grunewald, near Berlin, between Generals Manteuffel and Von Gröben, arising out of misunderstandings between the two officers during the late war. Count Groben was seriously wounded by a shot in the stomach.

— General Ducrot resigns his seat in the French Assembly, with the view of devoting himself entirely to the duties of his military position.

December 1. — The Duke of Northumberland elected President of the Royal Institution in succession to the late Sir Henry Holland.

— Witnesses examined in the Tichborne case to prove the identity of Jean Luie with a person convicted of fraud under the name of Sorensen and Lundgren, and in prison at the date of the alleged rescue from the *Bella*.

— The Emperor of Austria celebrates the twenty-fifth anniversary of his accession. An amnesty was granted to all persons under sentence for offences against his Majesty's person, and a speedy report was at the same time ordered to be made respecting other condemned persons whose conduct warranted leniency being shown them.

— The *Gazette* contains Sir Garnet Wolseley's despatches from the Gold Coast. The principal points dwelt upon were the gallantry of the officers engaged, the miserable behaviour of the native auxiliaries, and the urgent necessity for reinforcements of English troops. Both Sir Garnet Wolseley and Colonel Festing spoke in high terms of Lieutenant Eardley-Wilmot. In his despatch to Mr. Cardwell, Sir Garnet said : "I regret that one young officer has lost his life, Lieutenant Eardley-Wilmot, a fine promising soldier. He was badly hit early in the skirmish, but, like an English gentleman, continued in the field at his post, until subsequently shot through the heart, when he died almost immediately."

2. — Dr. Kenealy commences his speech in defence of the Claimant.

— Fall of a clothing and outfitting establishment in Fargate, Sheffield.

— Meeting in Willis's Rooms to take steps for carrying out the proposal that Bishop Wilberforce's memory should be perpetuated by the raising of a fund for the maintenance of a body of missionary clergymen in South London. The Bishop of Chichester was in the chair, and Mr. Gladstone and Mr. Gathorne Hardy among the speakers.

— In his Message to Congress, President Grant said that the present involvement with Spain through the capture of the *Virginius* was now in the way of being adjusted on conditions equally honourable to both nations. The Spanish Government, it was said, had recognized the justice of the demand made by the United States, and arranged for the immediate delivery of the vessel and the surrender of the survivors. In addition to this, the American flag was to be saluted, the guilty persons punished, and those entitled to be indemnified.

— Ancrum House, near Jedburgh, the seat of Sir William Scott, Bart., destroyed by fire.

3. — Day of Intercession for foreign missions, Professor Max Müller delivering a lecture on the subject in Westminster Abbey in the evening.

— Died, at Brighton, aged 92, Sir George Rose, among the last survivors of the "Old Westminsters" of the last century.

4. — Earl Russell writes to Sir George Bowyer :—"I am very sorry to differ from you in the step which I have taken of consenting to preside at a meeting at which it will be proposed to express our sympathy with the Emperor of Germany in the declaration he has made in his letter to the Pope. I conceive that the time has come, foreseen by Sir Robert Peel, when the Roman Catholic Church disclaims equality and will be satisfied with nothing but ascendency. To this ascendency, openly asserted to extend to all baptized persons, and therefore including our Queen, the Prince of Wales, our bishops and clergy, I refuse to submit. The autonomy of Ireland is asserted at Rome. I decline the Pope's temporal rule over Ireland."

— The Yarkund Embassy reach Kashgar, and are cordially received by the Atalikh Ghazee. The Queen's letter with presents from the Governor-General of India was presented on the 11th.

5. — The new Solicitor-General, Mr. Vernon Harcourt, re-elected for Oxford without opposition.

6. — The Governor-General of India informs the Secretary for India that supplies of rice were now being pushed forward to the districts affected by the scarcity.

8.—Sir Samuel Baker gives an account of his expedition into Central Africa to the members of the Royal Geographical Society.

— Fire at Yeddo, destroying buildings extending over two miles and a half of the city.

9.—Mr. Mills, Conservative, elected M.P. for Exeter by 2,346 votes, against 2,055 given to Sir Edward Watkin, Liberal.

— Dense fog in London, seriously interfering with traffic, and affecting to an appreciable extent the health of the prize cattle on show at Islington. As many as fourteen people were reported to have been drowned in the docks during its continuance. The death-rate for the week was sixty above the usual average.

— Mr. Bright denies that he had ever applied the word "residuum" to the working classes. "I do not," he writes to a correspondent, "remember the time when, or the speech in which, I used the word 'residuum,' or I would refer you to the passage. You would at once see how utterly unjust and false is the construction which Mr. Read has put upon it. I do not know what Mr. Read is in his pulpit, but I would advise him to stay there, where he cannot be contradicted. On the platform, he is, what is not uncommon in the hot partisan priest, ignorant and scurrilous, and a guide whom no sensible man would wish to follow. His congregation should pray for him." The speech in which the objectionable phrase occurred was understood to be one delivered in the House during the discussion on the Reform Bill of 1867. "At this moment," said Mr. Bright, "in all or nearly all boroughs, as many of us know, sometimes to our sorrow, there is a small class which it would be much better for themselves if they were not enfranchised, because they have no independence whatever, and it would be much better for the constituency also that they should be excluded, and there is no class so much interested in having that small class excluded as the intelligent and honest working man. I call this class the residuum, which there is in almost every constituency, of almost hopeless poverty and dependence."

10.— Marshal Bazaine found guilty, and sentenced to death. At half-past four o'clock Maître Lachaud concluded his speech in defence. The Duc d'Aumale then rose and asked the Marshal if he had anything more to add. In the midst of profound silence, the Marshal rose. He said : "I bear on my breast two words, 'Honour' and 'Country.' They have been my motto for the forty years during which I have served France, alike at Metz and elsewhere. I swear it before Christ." The Marshal was pale, and he appeared deeply moved. The Court having spent some hours in deliberation, the President, on returning, said :—"In the name of the French people, the Council of War, &c., delivers the following judgment :—François Achille Bazaine, Marshal of France, is he guilty, firstly, of having capitulated before the enemy in the open field?—Unanimously, Yes. Secondly, had this capitulation the effect of making those under his command lay down their arms?—Unanimously, Yes. Thirdly, is he guilty of having negotiated with the enemy before having done everything prescribed by duty and honour?—Unanimously, Yes. Fourthly, is he guilty of having surrendered a fortified place, the protection of which had been intrusted to him?—Unanimously, Yes. In consequence of this, Marshal Bazaine is condemned to the penalty of death, with military degradation, and ceases to belong to the Legion of Honour, and, besides, is condemned to pay the expense of the trial as regards the State. The Council orders that the sentence shall be read to the Marshal in the prison, in presence of the assembled guard under arms." This sentence was in two days commuted by President MacMahon on the recommendation of the Court into twenty years of seclusion on the Isle St. Marguerite. Marshal Bazaine thereupon wrote to the President :—" You have remembered the days in which we served our country together, and I fear that the impulse of your heart overmastered State considerations. I should have died without regret, since the recommendation to mercy made to you by my judges vindicates my honour."

11. — The Claimant's witness, Jean Luie, committed for trial on the charge of perjury. Pending further proceedings against him, the prisoner was sent back to undergo the remainder of his sentence as a convict.

— Died, aged 57, William de Courcy O'Grady, known in Ireland as "The O'Grady," head of an ancient Milesian family.

— Charles Dawson sentenced to death at Durham Assizes for the murder of his wife by beating her with a champagne bottle, and then dancing upon the body of his unhappy victim.

— Meeting in London to establish a National Federation of Employers of Labour.

13.—Died, at Rome, aged 36, H. S. P. Winterbotham, M.P., Under-Secretary of State for the Home Department.

14.—Died, aged 73, the Queen Dowager Elizabeth of Prussia, widow of the late King Frederick William IV.

— The Pope's last Encyclical on the present persecution of the Catholic Church read in the Roman Catholic Churches in London by order of Archbishop Manning. By desire of the Archbishop, the "faithful" were at the same time formally warned, in their several congregations, that those who dispute or deny the definition of the Infallibility of the Roman Pontiff, or impugn the decrees and dogmatical constitutions of the late Vatican Council, incur the penalties attaching to the sin of heresy, and are in danger of being excommunicated from the unity of the Church and from the fold of Christ.

15.—Dr. Tristram, Chancellor of the Diocese of London, gives judgment against the erection of a baldacchino over the communion-table of St. Barnabas Church, Pimlico. After much consideration, he said he had come to the conclusion that the proposed ornament did not come within the rubrics, and that it was not necessary or subsidiary to the services of the Church. It was not in the province of this court to sanction the erection of an ornament that was not sanctioned, and as the law did not provide for such an ornament to the communion-table, it was not for this court to issue a faculty to give greater dignity and honour to the holy table than the simple dignity prescribed by the law. He should, therefore, refuse the application for a faculty, and grant Mr. Bowron his costs. As he had decided the question on the legal ground, it was not necessary to go into the question of discretion.

16.—The surrender of the *Virginius* and the surviving prisoners to American officers at Bahia Honda.

— Disastrous storm at Sheffield, a lofty tower in Trippet-lane falling through a portion of the works with which it was connected, and burying about a score of workmen in its ruins. A high chimney in Milton Street was also blown down, and in other parts of the town various workshops were unroofed.

— A Committee of Ministers of the Church of Scotland, concerned at the insufficient number of qualified probationers presently available, issue a circular announcing an intent on to adopt energetic means for maintaining her efficiency. "They contemplate aiding and encouraging, by pecuniary grants, young men of ability and character, who desire to study for the ministry. They consider it of vital importance that every such student should, throughout his university curriculum, be a regular worshipper in some particular congregation, from the minister, elders, and members of which he should experience friendship and attention. With a view to all this (writes the Secretary), I have to beg that you will kindly inform me, on or before the 8th proximo, whether you know of any youth in your parish or congregation who is inclined to become a minister, and whom you believe to be fitted for the office by his talents and dispositions."

18.—The Tichborne case adjourned on this the 145th day of trial until after Christmas.

— The first stone of the National Training School for Music laid by the Duke of Edinburgh at South Kensington.

— Sir James Colquhoun, Bart., of Luss, with two of his gamekeepers and a boy, drowned in Lochlomond when returning to his mansion at Rossdhu, after a day's shooting with his brother on Inchloanig.

— A paper in *London Society* forming one of a series known as "The Chesterfield Letters of 1873," being considered injurious to the

character of Colonel Charles White, Lord Desart acknowledges responsibility by signing a document denying that Colonel White or his family were referred to in the article. "Had it been so, I freely admit that that article would have been defamatory, unwarranted, unwarrantable, blackguard, infamous, and utterly unworthy of a gentleman's pen. I hope that Colonel White will give the utmost publicity to this statement."

19.—The Governing Body of Rugby School resolve to remove Dr. Hayman from the Head Mastership.

20.—The Civil Marriages Bill read a second time in the Prussian Lower House.

— Eight men drowned in the Thames at West Moulsey, by the sinking of a boat engaged to convey them across the river from the works of the Lambeth Water Company.

21.—Died, at Lambeth, aged 89, Major George Rawlinson, who had obtained an ensign's commission in 1805, and been on the half-pay list since 1816.

22.—Announcement made of the creation of four new peers—Mr. Monsell, Lord Emly, of Tervoe, in the county of Limerick; Sir James Welwood Moncreiff, Lord Moncreiff, of Tulliebole, Kinross-shire; Admiral the Hon. Edward George Granville Howard, heir presumptive to the Earl of Carlisle, Lord Lamerton, of Lamerton, in the county of Cumberland; and Sir John Duke Coleridge, Baron Coleridge, of Ottery St. Mary.

— Died, at Dublin, aged 77, Lord Chief Baron Pigott.

— The Pope holds a Consistory, at which he creates twelve new Cardinals.

— The Attorney-General for the United States pronounces an opinion that the *Virginius* was not entitled to carry the American flag, her papers having been obtained by perjury. The American Government accepted the consequences in accordance with the stipulations of the protocol upon the subject signed by Spain and the United States.

— A jury in the Court of Exchequer gives a verdict carrying 350*l.* damages against the proprietor of the *Gloucester Mercury*, for publishing a libel against Mr. Edmunds, solicitor, Newent, charged last year with the murder of his wife, and, as appeared to the Lord Chief Baron, the victim of a species of persecution under circumstances which, but that they appeared in evidence, he should have thought impossible to have existed in this country.

23.—Archbishop Manning reads a paper before a Society known as the "Academia of the Catholic Religion," on Cæsarism and Ultramontanism, to prove that the antagonist of the Church has always been Cæsarism, or the supremacy of the civil over the spiritual. "If the Church," said the Archbishop, "be Antichrist, every Cæsar from Nero to this day is justified. If it be Christ, it is the Supreme Power among men; that is to say: (1) it holds its commission and authority from God; (2) it holds in custody the faith and the law of Jesus Christ; (3) it is the sole interpreter of that faith and the sole expositor of that law. It has within the sphere of that commission a power to legislate with authority; to bind the consciences of all men born again in the baptism of Jesus Christ; it alone can fix the limits of the faith and law entrusted to it, and therefore the sphere of its own jurisdiction; it alone can decide in questions where its power is in contact with the civil power—that is, in mixed questions; for it alone can determine how far its own Divine office, or its own Divine trust, enter into and are implicated in such questions; and it is precisely that element in any mixed question of disputed jurisdiction which belongs to a higher order and to a higher tribunal."

24.—The Supreme Court of the Brazilian Empire finds the Bishop of Pernambuco guilty of attempting to set aside an Article of the Constitution, an offence punishable by imprisonment, and orders him to surrender to the court to receive judgment.

— Charles Edward Butt, a young farmer living at Arlington, sentenced to death at Gloucester Assizes for shooting a young woman named Phipps, whom he had courted for some time, and who appeared to have aroused his jealousy by attentions shown to other young men at Longney Feast.

— Died suddenly, aged 47, Dr. F. C. Webb, editor of the *Medical Times and Gazette.*

26.—Twenty men drowned in the Tyne, through the sinking of the steam-tug *Gipsy Queen*, after striking upon the wreck of a sunken lighter near Northumberland Dock.

— The liberated vessel *Virginius* founders in a gale off Cape Fear.

27.—Naval Brigade, 200 strong, land on the Gold Coast and proceed to Prahsu. Sir Garnet Wolseley and his staff proceed to the front.

— Mr. Caleb Cushing appointed American Minister to Spain in succession to General Sickles.

28.—Popular demonstration in Paris, at the funeral of M. François Victor Hugo, son of Victor Hugo.

— New Bourse at Brussels opened with a ball attended by the royal household and members of the diplomatic circle.

30.—A Berlin telegram to the *Times* reports that the Chapter of the Civil Class of the Prussian Royal Order "For Merit" has been presented to Mr. Thomas Carlyle, the vacancy having been created by the death of Alesandro Manzoni.

— The Duke of Edinburgh leaves London or St. Petersburg.

31.—Treaty between Russia and Bokhara published at St. Petersburg. One Article provided for Russian merchants having the right to construct harbours on the banks of the Amou Daria, in the territory of Bokhara, the Government of Bokhara to be responsible for the security of such harbours, and the sites chosen for them to be approved by the Russian authorities; another that Russian merchants shall be permitted to establish factories and commercial agencies in any part of Bokhara, and the merchants of the latter shall be entitled to possess such establishments in Turkestan territory. Both Governments engaged to consider all commercial treaties as sacred, and faithfully to fulfil them.

— The French National Assembly, after voting 80,000,000f. new taxes, adjourns for the recess.

— Telegram received from Hong Kong, announcing that the Portuguese Government had abolished the Macao coolie trade.

1874.

January 1.—Died, aged 53, David Morier Evans, journalist, for over thirty years connected with the City department of the *Times* and *Standard* newspapers.

2.—Parliament of Portugal opened by the King, who thanked the British and German Governments for the supply of arms furnished to his country in the course of last year to complete her military armament.

— The Spanish Cortes opened with a message from Señor Castelar, describing the insurgents at Carthagena as engaged in a criminal insurrection tending to break up the unity of the Fatherland, the marvellous work of so many centuries, "seizing upon one of our strongest places, the best provided of our arsenals, and our most formidable war vessels, maintaining its accursed flag under the protection of impregnable fortresses, and thereby encouraging the revival of demagogic passions. The want of troops and resources delays the capture of the place, but, considering the energy and activity of the besiegers and the prostration and penury of the besieged, it must soon fall at the feet of the Assembly." Papers were promised relating to the *Virginius* difficulty, settled, it was said, according to the first principles of international law.

3.—Died, aged 61, William Telbin, scene painter.

— A new Revolution in Spain, Señor Castelar, twice defeated in the Cortes, being succeeded by a military Dictatorship. Castelar thereupon wrote:—"I protest with all the energy of my soul against the brutal act of violence committed against the Constitutional Cortes by the Captain-General of Madrid. My conscience will not permit me to associate myself with demagogues ; but, on the other hand, my conscience and my honour keep me aloof from the state of things which has just been created by the force of bayonets."

5.—Dawson, Gough, and Thompson executed at Durham.

6.—The Conservatives gain a seat at Stroud, the poll showing 2,817 for Dorrington, against 2,426 for Havelock, Liberal.

— The Duke of Cambridge assaulted in Pall Mall by a retired captain named Maunsell, whose mind had become affected through what he considered a denial of justice by officials at the Horse Guards.

7.—Addressing his constituents at Elgin, Mr. Grant Duff expresses an opinion that for a Conservative Cabinet to be possible not as a mere stop-gap, but to live with its own life, he held "that not one or two men like Lord Derby are necessary, but half a dozen, and I do not see the men, nor any of them, an assertion which I make without forgetting the merits of politicians like Mr. Cave or Sir Charles Adderley." After some remarks on Mr. Disraeli's speech at Glasgow, Mr. Grant Duff discussed the possibility of a middle party in English politics, and contended that there were not men enough to form such a party. Just at present he did not think the country wanted a coalition, much less a Conservative Government.

— Died, aged 69, Henry Glassford Bell, Sheriff of Lanarkshire, and author of a volume of graceful verses. Sheriff Bell's illness gave rise to a disagreeable controversy regarding a somewhat brusque request made to him by the Home Secretary to resign, which was thought to have even damaged the closing days of the Liberal Ministry.

— The Glasgow Presbytery appoint a committee to inquire into the relations in which that body stood to Principal Caird, preparatory to dealing with him on a charge of heresy on the subject of responsibility for belief.

— The Prussian Judicial Tribunal for the trial of ecclesiastical causes sit for the first time, the case for decision being the complaint of a chaplain who had been removed from his office by the Bishop of Paderborn. The court decided that the act of the bishop was null and void.

— Explosion in Carthagena of a powder magazine, fired by the besieging batteries.

8.—President MacMahon delivers the Cardinals' hats to the new Cardinals in the chapel of the Palace of Versailles. The recipients were Monsignor Chigi, Papal Nuncio, and the Archbishops of Paris and Cambrai. "The Pope," said the Marshal, "knows our filial attachment and our admiration at the manner in which he supports his trials. His sympathy did not fail us in our misfortunes, and his good wishes are with us now in the work of pacific regeneration which my Government pursues."

9.—The Prince of Wales unveils the statue of his father the Prince Consort, set up at Holborn Circus by a private person and presented to the Corporation of the City.

— Died, aged 51, George Colwall Oke, chief clerk at the Mansion House police court, and author of various legal works.

10.—The Prince and Princess of Wales, with Prince Arthur and a numerous suite, leave London for St. Petersburg to attend the marriage of the Duke of Edinburgh.

— The Bishop of Troyes having forbidden the clergy of his diocese to celebrate masses for the soul of the Emperor Napoleon, the Empress writes that she can hardly believe it, "because the Church has never refused a prayer for the dead. The spirit of charity and brotherly love form one long chain which binds us the one to the other—the rich or the poor, those in prosperity or those in adversity, the living and the dead ! No, it is impossible that you can have refused a prayer for him who founded the institution of almoners for saying the prayers after death. No, it is impossible, when you protest against those civil burials which deprive a Christian of the prayers of the Church, that you can have refused those same prayers when asked for. Moreover, it is impossible that you can have forgotten the oath which you took in the presence of him who is no more."

11.—Carthagena surrenders to the troops of the Madrid Government. The town had suffered severely, though not so much as was supposed, except near the Madrid Gate, where the damage was very great. There scarcely one house escaped untouched, and some were riddled with shell ; two houses had been thrown down, and the street pavement ploughed up. Immense damage was found to have been done by the recent explosion of the powder magazine, where over 200 persons were said to have been killed. The walls near the Madrid Gate suffered much, but there was nothing approaching to a breach. The *Numencia*, with the insurgent Junta on board, escaped to Oran, and surrendered to French authorities.

12. — Three convicts, Butt, Bailey, and Barry, executed within the precincts of Gloucester gaol.

— A vote of confidence in Ministers carried in the French Assembly by a majority of 58 in a house of 700 members.

13.—Mr. Justice Grove, the judge appointed to inquire into the petition against the return of Sir Henry James, Attorney-General, opens proceedings in the Nisi Prius Court of Taunton Shire-hall.

14.—Iwokura, the second President of the Japanese Council of State, attacked in Yeddo, and slightly wounded.

— Dr. Kenealy concludes his speech in defence of the Tichborne Claimant, having spoken twenty-four days. Mr. Hawkins commenced his reply next day, and in the afternoon, when proceeding homeward, narrowly escaped from the attentions of an excited mob pretending sympathy with the Claimant.

14.—The French Assembly express approval of the Government bill relative to the nomination of mayors.

— The Rev. George Richardson Mackarness elected Bishop of Argyll by an absolute majority in both Chambers. The candidature of Provost Cazenove was withdrawn.

15.—The Baroness Burdett-Coutts presented with the freedom of the city of Edinburgh, "in recognition of her ladyship's devoted zeal and patriotism in the promotion and munificent support of useful and charitable institutions, and also in consideration of her ladyship's association with Edinburgh as the honoured descendant of one of its chief magistrates."

16.—The allegations against Prince Bismarck in a book recently issued by General Della Marmora, lead to a scene in the Prussian Lower House. In the course of a debate on education, Herr von Malinckrodt declared that the Ultramontanes were as faithful patriots as Prince Bismarck, and he asked, amid considerable uproar, "Were they present at the conference between Prince Bismarck and M. Govone when a cession of territory on the left bank of the Rhine was discussed?" adding, "I myself was not present, but I met with this statement of the interview in a reliable quarter." After a reply from Herr Kleoppel, the motion was allowed to drop, and the debate on the Civil Marriage Bill resumed. Prince Bismarck shortly afterwards entered the House, and obtained leave to speak on a matter of privilege. He characterized the statement of Herr von Malinckrodt as an audacious and lying invention, made in a malignant and calumniatory manner. The Imperial Chancellor added:—"I never uttered a syllable of the sort. I have never spoken of ceding a village or a meadow of German territory. The whole accusation is throughout an audaciously invented falsehood concocted to blacken my character. (Loud cheers.) I ask for no special consideration from my opponents, but I am entitled to ask that they shall behave more decently in the sight of foreign countries and our own Sovereign." Later in the discussion Prince Bismarck said:—"It is remarkable that Herr Malinckrodt attaches greater value to the testimony of a foreigner than to mine. It would require a man's lifetime to contradict all that my enemies write against me. I may safely say, and I am proud to be able to say it, that I am the most strongly and the best hated man of any country in Europe. Has not Herr Malinckrodt sought to keep you and the country in the belief that Della Marmora's book tells the truth? I do not wish to convince him, but I ask you, could I not have obtained the most immense results if I had been willing to cede a portion of German territory to France?

Did I do so? You have no right to ask the leader of the Government to justify himself against calumny in the open tribune. That is a proceeding to characterize which no parliamentary expression can be found. The public press will, no doubt, find one to supply the deficiency."

16.—Died, at Bonn, Dr. Max Schultze, anatomist.

17. — Narrow escape of the De Broglie Government on the Nomination of Mayors Bill. An amendment by M. Ducarre, of the Left, enacting that the mayors should not be selected except from the members of the municipal councils, was lost by only fourteen votes, the numbers being 343 and 329. A subsequent amendment, proposed by M. Feray, of the Left Centre, that the mayors should be selected from the municipal councils in communes having a population of less than 3,000, was rejected by 341 against 336, showing a majority for the Government of five only.

— The German Emperor writes to the Old Catholic Bishop, Dr. Reinkens:—"I thank you for the hearty congratulations which you have offered to me on the occasion of the renewing of the year. May God's blessing advance the work begun by you in His name, also in the new year. May continually widening circles be penetrated by the unquestionably right conviction, shared by you, that in my States respect for the law is reconcilable with the exercise of the religion of every community which pursues no worldly purposes, but only the one purpose—to seek man's peace with God."

18.—Died, aged 78, James Matthew Cope, for over fifty years connected with the London press.

— Died, in North Carolina, aged 63, the Siamese twins, Chang and Eng.

19.—The Swedish Parliament opened by the King in person.

— Died, Dr. George E. Biber, for many years incumbent of Roehampton, and a prolific controversialist.

— The Corporation of Brighton entertain Sir Samuel Baker at a banquet in the hall of the Royal Pavilion. Addressing the assembly after dinner, Sir Samuel said there was now a fair prospect for the development of the country of the White Nile, but the future would of course depend upon the energy and intelligence of the Governor, who should be perfectly unfettered by Egypt, and should be furnished with supreme power. He much feared that the Viceroy was rather too impatient for quick returns from his new territories; but as he had now intrusted his (Sir Samuel's) late command to an English officer of high reputation—Colonel Gordon—he felt sure all would be done that was possible with the means furnished by the Viceroy. The good work had been begun and must be continued by Englishmen. Should that element be withdrawn, the slave trade would reappear like a cancer that has been vainly extirpated.

19.—Apologising for his inability through ill health to attend the meeting in St. James's Hall, called to express sympathy with the Emperor of Germany, in his conflict with the Pope, Earl Russell writes:—"The very same principles which bound me to ask for equal freedom for the Roman Catholic, the Protestant Dissenter, and the Jew, bind me to protest against a conspiracy which aims at confining the German Empire in chains never, it is hoped, to be shaken off. I hasten to declare, with all friends of freedom, and, I trust, with the great majority of the English nation, that I could no longer call myself a lover of civil and religious liberty were I not to proclaim my sympathy with the Emperor of Germany in the noble struggle in which he is engaged. We have nothing to do with the details of the German laws; they may be just, they may be harsh; we can only leave it to the German people to decide for themselves, as we have decided for ourselves. At all events, we are able to see that the cause of the German Emperor is the cause of liberty, and the cause of the Pope is the cause of slavery."

— Circular, signed by Mr. Disraeli, sent to the Conservative members of the House, intimating that "Her Majesty having been pleased to direct that Parliament should reassemble on the 5th of February, I trust that you may find it convenient to be in your place on that day."

— The French Government suspend the *Univers* two months for publishing in its last number a pastoral letter from the Bishop of Périgueux, and for the publication of certain leading articles commenting upon the recent circular of the Minister of Public Worship to the French bishops.

— Died of fever in the camp at Prahsu, Captain Huyshe of the Rifle Brigade, a volunteer for service in the field against the Ashantees.

21.—Replying to a deputation in favour of conceding household suffrage to counties, Mr. Gladstone said the question should not be lightly taken up by any Government, and should be undertaken only when a Government is determined and reasonably believes it can carry it to a successful and satisfactory result. Mr. Gladstone concluded by saying he should be glad when the period was reached to give effect to those views which he had from time to time expressed, impressed as he was with the conscientious opinion that the object sought for by the deputation would form an additional strength to the throne and to the laws, and add to the general happiness of the country.

— Manifesto issued by the Nonconformist Liberation Society, insisting that testing-questions be applied to candidates for Parliament regarding Religious Equality, the Education Act, and Disestablishment.

21.—A body of Chinese labourers employed on the Costa Rica railway works, resisting an attempt made to force them to work during a fog, are fired upon by the military at night, and six killed.

22.—In the course of the inquiry regarding the Claimant's witness Luie at Bow Street today, a certificate signed by Mr. Whalley and Mr. Onslow is read, certifying on their part "and on the part of all who have known Jean Luie in relation to the Tichborne case, that he has shown himself to be a man of thorough honesty and great intelligence, and that he has borne himself through all his life as a man entitled to confidence and respect. He has been exposed to great difficulties, harassment, and temptation through this affair, and has remained staunch and true, and rendered very great service to Sir Roger Tichborne."

23.—Married, at the Winter Palace, St. Petersburg, the Duke of Edinburgh and the Grand Duchess Marie Alexandrovna. The Orthodox ceremony was performed by Greek ecclesiastics, and the Anglican by Dean Stanley.

— The first division of the Court of Session sit in the case of Padwick *v.* Stewart, an action raised to test the validity of the entail executed over the estates of Murthly and Grandtully. In 1871 an agreement was entered into between Mr. Padwick and Sir William Stewart, who was then proprietor of Murthly, to sell the estates at Sir William's death to Mr. Padwick for the sum of 350,000*l.* Sir William died in April 1871, and Mr. Padwick brought this action to have it found that the agreement for the sale of the estates was an effectual one. Sir Archibald Douglas, Sir William's brother, who was the next heir of entail, maintained that the entail of the estates was a valid one, and barred any sale. The court decided against Mr. Padwick.

— Mr. Albert Grant intimates to the Metropolitan Board of Works his intention of presenting Leicester Square as a place of public recreation. "I further," he wrote, "intend to erect at the four corners granite pedestals, on which busts in marble of a suitable size will be placed of the following celebrated men, all known to have been locally connected with the traditions of Leicester Square:—These will be Hogarth and Sir Joshua Reynolds, both of whom lived and died in houses in the square; Dr. Samuel Johnson, the friend and constant visitor of Sir Joshua Reynolds; and Sir Isaac Newton, who lived in Leicester Place adjoining the square for many years after he became President of the Royal Society; men who, it will be admitted, are worthy of being illustrated by the sculptor's art, but who have not, that I am aware of, yet received any recognition of their greatness in that form in any public open space in London."

24.—To the surprise of all except a few familiar with the determination come to at a Cabinet meeting held yesterday, Mr. Gladstone announces the dissolution of Parliament in a long address to the electors of Greenwich. "That authority," he said, "which was in 1868 amply confided by the nation to the Liberal party and its leaders, if it has now sunk below the point necessary for the due defence and prosecution of the public interests, can in no way be so legitimately and effectually restored as by an appeal to the people, who, by their reply to such an appeal, may place beyond all challenge two great questions—the first, what they think of the manner in which the commission granted in 1868 has been executed; the second, what further commission they now think fit to give to their representatives, and to what hands its fulfilment and the administration of the Government are to be entrusted." On the Education Act, Mr. Gladstone did not doubt with regard to "one or two points, calculated to create an amount of uneasiness out of proportion to their real importance or difficulty," that "the wisdom of the renovated legislature will discover the means of their accommodation." Expressing his satisfaction at the rise of wages in the agricultural districts, which he regarded as "a new guarantee for the stability of the throne and institutions of the country," Mr. Gladstone passed to the consideration of the county franchise. "I have never concealed my opinion that those institutions will be further strengthened by granting to the counties generally that extended franchise which has been conceded with general satisfaction to the towns, and to the populations of a number of rural districts with a central village, which may perhaps be called peasant-boroughs." In estimating the revenue for the current year, the Prime Minister did not fear to anticipate as the probable balance a surplus exceeding rather than falling short of 5,000,000*l.*; and, with this sum in hand, he suggested the possibility of abolishing the income-tax. The proceeds of that tax, he said, for the present year "are expected to be between 5,000,000*l.* and 6,000,000*l.*, and at a sacrifice for the financial year of something less than 4,500,000*l.*, the country may enjoy the advantage and relief of its total repeal. I do not hesitate to affirm that an effort should now be made to attain this advantage, nor to declare that, according to my judgment, it is in present circumstances practicable."

- — Since the general election in 1868 the party losses and gains had been—Liberal seats lost 32, Conservative seats lost 9. The Liberal majority was thought to have fallen from 116 to about 70.

— News from Atchin announce the capture of Kraton by the Dutch, after a successful attack on its western side. When entered, the place was found to be abandoned. This result was considered as deciding the war against the Atchinese.

24.—Died, aged 90, Adam Black, publisher, Edinburgh, for which city he sat in Parliament from 1856 to 1865.

26.—Mr. Disraeli issues his address to the electors of Buckinghamshire. He did not think it necessary at present to consider whether Mr. Gladstone has advised the Queen to dissolve Parliament as a means of avoiding the humbling confession that he has, in a fresh violation of constitutional law, persisted in retaining for several months a seat to which he was no longer entitled, or to postpone or evade the day of reckoning for a war carried on without communication with Parliament, and the expenditure for which Parliament has not sanctioned. It is sufficient to point out that if under any circumstances the course—altogether unprecedented—of calling together Parliament by special summons for the dispatch of business, and then dissolving it before its meeting, could be justified, there is in the present case no reason whatever suggested why this was not done six weeks ago, and why the period of the year usually devoted to business before Easter, which must now be wasted, should not thus have been saved. The right hon. gentleman found in Mr. Gladstone's "prolix narrative," nothing definite as to the policy he would pursue except this—that, having the prospect of a large surplus, he will, if retained in power, devote that surplus to the remission of taxation, which would be the course of any party or any Ministry. "If returned to Parliament, I shall, whether in or out of office, continue the endeavour, to propose or support all measures calculated to improve the condition of the people of this kingdom. But I do not think this great end is advanced by incessant and harassing legislation. The English people are governed by their customs as much as by their laws, and there is nothing they more dislike than unnecessary restraint and meddling interference in their affairs. Generally speaking, I should say of the Administration of the last five years that it would have been better for us all if there had been a little more energy in our foreign policy and a little less in our domestic legislation. . . . By an act of folly or of ignorance rarely equalled, the present Ministry relinquished a treaty which secured us the freedom of the Straits of Malacca for our trade with China and Japan, and they at the same time entering on the West Coast of Africa, into those 'equivocal and entangling engagements' which the Prime Minister now deprecates, involved us in the Ashantee war. The Conservative party (he said) viewed the county franchise question without prejudice. They have proved that they are not afraid of popular rights. But the late Reform Act was a large measure, which, in conjunction with the Ballot, has scarcely been tested by experience, and they will hesitate before they sanction further legislation, which will inevitably involve, among other considerable changes, the disfranchisement of at least all boroughs in the kingdom comprising less than 40,000 inhabitants.

Writing of the proposed disestablishment of the Church and divorcing religion from the work of education, as solemn issues which the impending election must decide, "their solution (he went on) must be arrived at when Europe is more deeply stirred than at any period since the Reformation, and when the cause of civil liberty and religious freedom mainly depends upon the strength and stability of England. I ask you to return me to the House of Commons to resist every proposal which may impair that strength, and to support by every means her imperial sway."

26.—Proclamation issued for the dissolution of Parliament, writs for new elections to be returnable, 5th March.

— Grand parade of troops at St. Petersburg in honour of the visit of the Prince of Wales.

— Announcement made of the death of Dr. Livingstone, while journeying in the direction of Unyanyemba. He was born at Blantyre, near Glasgow, in 1817.

— Mr. Disraeli, writes Mr. Lowe to his constituents, tells us that he does not think the condition of the United Kingdom is improved by incessant and harassing legislation. "This means that it is best not to legislate at all, or, if you do legislate, to take care to offend no one. Compare the state of England with her state forty years ago. To what do we owe the change? To laws which harassed the owners of boroughs, the corrupt corporations, the protected trades and industries, and the universities — in short, all persons and institutions which held privileges adverse to the general welfare. The man who prefers custom to law announces a principle which would stereotype every abuse, and substitute the blind guesses of barbarism for the clear and well-considered conclusions of a civilized age." Mr. Lowe puts his trust in a university "which is itself a product of harassing legislation," and concluded with the remark, "The night comes upon all, but we will not draw the curtain while it is yet day."

— In the matter of the Taunton election petition, Mr. Justice Grove decides that the Attorney-General was duly elected, and that the cost of proceedings must be paid by petitioners.

— Fire at the British Embassy, Lisbon, Sir Charles and Lady Murray making a narrow escape from suffocation.

27.—Meeting in St. James's Hall to express sympathy with the German Emperor in his struggle with the Pope. Sir John Murray, Bart. (of Philiphaugh), presided, and the speakers were the Dean of Canterbury, Sir Robert Peel, Bart., Sir Thomas Chambers, Q.C., the Rev. Dr. Jobson (an ex-president of the Wesleyan Conference), Mr. Newdegate, Mr. J. Lowry Whittle, Colonel Macdonald, and Dr. Joseph P. Thompson, an American clergyman. A letter had been received from the Archbishop of York stating that while he declined to commit himself to the objects of the meeting, no one was more opposed to Ultramontanism than himself. A similar letter was received from the Archbishop of Canterbury.

27.—Accident at Manuel Junction on the North British line, the 6.35 London express from Edinburgh to Glasgow running into a mineral train shunting there, and killing fourteen passengers. The engine driver was wounded, and the stoker and another man killed. The collision was disastrous in the extreme, the carriages of the passenger train being piled up to a great height above the engine, and many of the passengers killed on the spot. A large number were injured, while others escaped almost miraculously, though buried in the *débris*. A staff of doctors and assistants was procured from Edinburgh.

— Nonconformist manifesto issued describing Mr. Gladstone's views on religious equality as vague and unsatisfactory. The Committee urged on the metropolitan constituencies the propriety of eliciting from candidates a promise to support those alterations in the Education Act, which, in the judgment of this Committee, are necessary—viz. the abolition of the 25th clause, the universal establishment of school boards, with a board school in each district, and compulsory attendance. "It is also desirable that the opinions of candidates should be ascertained on questions of religious equality. They recommend that, should the answers not be satisfactory, the advisability of securing candidates favourable to the principles of this Committee be carefully considered, and that the suddenness of the demand which has been made on the electors should not be allowed to interfere with the performance of this important and paramount duty." Another appeal to electors proceeded at this time from the Labour Representation League, asking working-class voters to vote for labour candidates, "that you may practically assert the principle of direct labour representation. We ask you also to vote for labour candidates that you may remove from yourselves the degrading stigma of class exclusion."

28.—Marshal Gablenz, formerly Austrian commander in the Sleswick-Holstein war commits suicide at Zurich.

— Mr. Gladstone addresses his Greenwich constituents at Blackheath. A large number gathered to welcome him, although the day was somewhat unfavourable. He defended the home and foreign policy of his government against the criticism of Mr. Disraeli, and undertook to show that the Dutch treaty regarding the Straits of Malacca had been carried through when that statesman was in office in 1858. On the subject of finance the Prime Minister was careful to have it understood that by repeal of the income-tax he meant its total and absolute repeal. His statement was received with loud and long-continued cheering. Any attempt (he said) to tamper with this or that schedule of the income-tax I am convinced would fail, and would likewise impair the general stability and credit of the finances of the country. Mr. Gladstone concluded by declaring—"I will not lead one section of the Liberal party—in what I think an unnatural and fratricidal war against some other section of it. I have too much respect for them all to enter upon such a course, and I am perfectly persuaded that there is plenty of work to be done upon which you are united and agreed, and for the doing of which you will give effect to your union of sentiment at this dissolution by a corresponding union of votes. If you do that—if again you march to the poll with one heart and with one soul, as you have done upon former occasions, in view of continued application and of further triumph of those principles to which you have so long and so energetically and so successfully been devoted—then I say with the utmost confidence that, in spite of Conservative reaction, and in spite of the seductions of foreign policy—aye, and in spite of the Straits of Malacca—once more, and not for the last time, victory will crown your cause."

29.—The Lord Chief Justice commences his summing up to the Jury on the Tichborne case, on the 169th day of trial.

— First members returned to the new Parliament, the elections in Cirencester, Harwich and Marlborough being made without opposition. Numerous nominations take place on this and following day.

30.—Died aged 92, Admiral Thomas Gill, who entered the navy in 1794, and was present at the capture of Port-au-Prince, St. Domingo.

31.—Election speeches made by Mr. Gladstone at Woolwich, Mr. Disraeli at Aylesbury, and Mr. Bright at Birmingham. In explanation of his position as Chancellor of the Exchequer the Prime Minister said, when he found that a question was raised as to his vacation of the seat, he obtained the best legal advice he could, and the present Master of the Rolls, the Lord Chief Justice of the Common Pleas, the Lord Chancellor, and the law officers of the Crown, had all advised him that he ought not to certify that his seat was vacant. He therefore reserved the question for the decision of the House of Commons. Mr. Gladstone afterwards urged upon the Liberal party the necessity for united action, and cautioned them to be moderate in their views, and not to strive after things which were, for the present at least, unattainable.— Mr. Disraeli amused his hearers by describing the Prime Minister's reason for dissolving— "as far as his meaning could be gathered from a document of remarkable length—that it was because the Government only enjoyed a majority of 66. Now, if the Conservative Government enjoyed a majority of 66 he believed it would be able to carry on the business of the country with satisfaction and benefit to the nation. He compared the position of the

country to that of a sick patient who really suffered nothing except from the nerves. Her Majesty's Government were evidently a nervous Ministry, for, in the midst of apparent prosperity and with a large majority in Parliament, they suddenly dissolved it." Concerning recent domestic legislation Mr. Disraeli reiterated his opinion that, for the last five years the policy of the Government had been to make everybody uncomfortable. Turning to foreign affairs, he urged that the consequences of inattention to these matters were costly wars, ignominious treaties, and sham arbitrations got up as a cloak in order to pay hush-money for blunders or insults committed. With regard to the Crimean war, he said—If we had declared that the moment the Russians crossed the Pruth hostilities would be declared, no war would ever have taken place; and if the country were indebted to any one more than another for the costly result of this indecision it was to Mr. Gladstone, the then Chancellor of the Exchequer. Mr. Gladstone evidently forgot now that foreign affairs were simply the affairs of this country in foreign parts; and, seeing that his policy had entailed on this country such an immense loss of treasure, it was the height of folly for him to pride himself on cutting down the dockyard establishments and paring the income of a few hard-worked clerks. Touching upon the Abyssinian war, he justified the conduct of the Conservatives for undertaking that war, and said that the cost exceeded the original estimate because it was found absolutely essential to conclude it at once without involving a second campaign. The appointment of Lord Napier of Magdala to the command of the army in Abyssinia was ridiculed by the Liberals because he was only an engineer officer, but so, indeed, was the appointment of Lord Mayo as Viceroy of India, the present Government going so far as to advise her Majesty to recall that noble lord from his post.—Mr. Bright remarked, "They say that we—that is the Liberal party—have disturbed classes and interests unnecessarily, that we have harassed almost all sorts of people, and have made ourselves very unpopular thereby. Why, if they had been in the wilderness, no doubt they would have condemned the ten commandments as a harassing piece of legislation." He pleaded guilty to the charge that they had disturbed a good many classes and a good many interests, and in doing so he offered as the justification the fact that in no single case had they injured a class or interest, and in every case they had greatly benefited the country.

— Died at Pau, whither he had gone for the benefit of his health, the Right Hon. Duncan McNeill, Lord Colonsay, aged 80 years.

— Sir John Byles takes his seat as a member of the Judicial Committee.

— Engagement at Amoaful between the troops under Sir Garnet Wolseley and the Ashantees. The latter fought desperately and suffered severely. The casualties on the British side were—Royal Engineers, Captain Buckle, killed; Major Home, wounded in two places; Lieutenant Hare, wounded in two places; two Sappers and thirty six labourers killed. The Naval Brigade, 145 strong, had three officers wounded — namely, Captain Grubbe, Lieutenant Mundy, and Lieutenant Rawson, and twenty-six men killed and wounded. The 23rd, about ninety strong, had one officer and five men wounded. The 42nd lost nine officers and 105 men in killed and wounded, including Major Macpherson wounded in two places. One bullet passed through his leg, but he led his men the whole way. Major Baird was badly wounded in both legs and in the chest, and carried to the rear unable to move, where he afterwards fell a victim to the fury of the natives. Operations commenced at 6 a.m. and continued with little intermission in the fighting till 3 p.m. The 42nd Regiment led the advance, and stormed the village of Amoaful. The Rifle Brigade, the Naval Brigade, and a company of the 23rd Regiment, with Wood's and Russell's native regiments, were all hotly engaged throughout the day. The Ashantees also besieged, without success, the village of Quarman, which had been occupied as a post, and attacked a convoy between Insarfu and Quarman.

February 1. — The Rev. Charles Waldegrave Sandford consecrated Bishop of Gibraltar, in the Cathedral at Christ Church, Oxford.

2. — Mr. Gladstone delivers a third address to the Greenwich electors at New Cross.

— Calcutta telegrams convey the welcome news that rain had at last begun to fall in various parts of Bengal. The maximum at Rungpore was reported to be three inches.

— Died, aged 85, Admiral Thomas Wren Carter, who had entered the navy when only eleven years of age, and been present at the battle of Copenhagen in 1801, in the Walcheren expedition, and at Flushing.

— Correspondence between the Duke of Argyll and Mr. Disraeli regarding an expression used by the latter, that the Liberal party had advised her Majesty to recall Lord Mayo from h's post. "Perhaps," wrote his grace, "you will allow me to ask you upon what authority or information you have gone in expressing this belief? and to inform you that it is altogether unfounded in fact." Mr. Disraeli replied that his authority was "a communication from Lord Mayo himself appealing to me to make some demonstration in the House of Commons, if possible, to prevent it. I consulted my friends at the time accordingly. I accept unequivocally your denial of the statement, but my own impression is that Lord Mayo died with the conviction that the step in question was contemplated by the Ministry." The Duke closed the correspondence by repeating his remark that no such advice was given to the Crown, nor was it even "contemplated" by the Government.

3.—The election returns up to this date show the Conservatives to have gained 29 seats and the Liberals 10. Mr. Gladstone was returned for Greenwich to-day second on the poll, Mr. Boord, Conservative, being at the top with 6,193 votes against 5,968 given to the Premier. At Cambridge two new Conservative members, Smollett and Marten, replaced two Liberals. At Wigan the Conservatives also gained two seats. Considerable disorder prevailed at Sheffield, Peterborough, Lincoln, and Dudley. Mr. Lowe, returned unopposed for London University, again criticized Mr. Disraeli as a most uncomfortable person to have as a governor of the country, having a harum-scarum, slap-dash, inconsiderate, careless way of dealing with things, and as possessing a slatternly, inaccurate mind.

— In the Italian Chamber of Deputies, Signor Visconti-Venosta, in reply to a question, declined on the part of the Ministry all responsibility for the publication of the dispatches printed in General Della Marmora's book. "The Government disapprove and deplore the publication of these documents, especially as it furnished a pretext for making against a friendly Power accusations which can only be based on a misunderstanding, inasmuch as they fall to the ground, when tested by the evidence of results."

— The election returns of Alsace-Lorraine show large majorities in favour of Ultramontane and French candidates.

— Archbishop Ledochowski arrested and conveyed under police escort to Frankfort-on-the-Oder.

4. — Addressing the electors at Newport Pagnell, Mr. Disraeli said Mr. Gladstone ought not to have involved us in entangling engagements as he admitted had been done. "If you employ a person in your business as a traveller, or if any of the farmers in this room sent a person to act for him in some distant market to buy stock, we will say in Scotland, and he came back and told you, 'I bought the stock, but I have bought it with equivocal and entangling engagements,' what would you say? 'This will never do;' and when you began to rate your agent for getting you into equivocal and entangling engagements, would it be any answer if he said, 'Oh, I am sorry for this, and it will be a lesson to me in the future; but I assure you I have been most economical in my personal expenses. I have always travelled by a second-class train, and as for any refreshments on the road, I have taken the temperance pledge.' Now, gentlemen, that is the economy of which Mr. Gladstone is so proud." Mr. Lowe was described as an ungrateful man, who would not likely have been in Parliament but for Mr. Disraeli. "Were it not for me the London University would not have had a member. Everybody was opposed to it. My colleagues did not much like it; the Conservative party did not much like it; but, more strange than anything else, the whole Liberal party were ready to oppose it. But I, with characteristic magnanimity said to myself, 'Unless I give a member to the London University Mr. Lowe cannot have a seat.' It was then impossible for him, and probably still is, to show himself upon any hustings with safety to his life. I said to myself, 'There is so much ability lost to England,' and I pique myself always on upholding and supporting ability in every party and wherever I meet it; and I also said to myself, 'One must have an eye to the main chance. If I keep Mr. Lowe in public life—and this is his only chance—I make sure that no Cabinet, even if it be brought into power by an overwhelming majority, can long endure and long flourish if he be a member of it; and, gentlemen, I think what took place perfectly justified my prescience."

5.—News published of the submission of King Koffee, and his consent to pay a ransom of 200,000*l*.

— Died, aged 83, Captain Tweedie, formerly of the Royal Artillery, and one of the few survivors of the Peninsular campaign.

— The first session of the newly-elected German Reichstag opened by Commission, Prince Bismarck reading the Imperial Speech. "The foreign relations of the empire," it was said, "strengthen our conviction that all foreign Governments, like our own, are resolved to use their endeavours to preserve the benefits of peace, and will not be diverted from this object or allow their mutual confidence to be affected by any party efforts to disturb peace. The repeated interviews of powerful, peace-loving, and personally intimate monarchs, and the cordial relations of Germany with peoples whose friendship with her is based upon historical tradition, render the Emperor firmly confident of the continuance of peace being assured."

— The vacant Jansenist archiepiscopal see of Utrecht filled by the election of Monsignor Cornelius Diependaal. This appointment was afterwards declined.

— The army under Sir Garnet Wolseley enters Coomassie after five days' hard fighting. The killed and wounded among his men were stated to be under 300. In the naval brigade seven officers were wounded, two men killed, and 36 wounded. In a general order issued to the soldiers, seamen, and marines of the expeditionary force, Sir Garnet thanked them in her Majesty's name for their gallantry and good conduct throughout all the operations. "In the first phase of this war the Ashantee army was driven back from the Fantee country into its own territory. Since then you have penetrated far through a dense forest, defended at many points with the greatest obstinacy. You have repeatedly defeated a very numerous and most courageous enemy, fighting on his own ground, in well selected positions. British pluck

and the discipline common to her Majesty's land and sea forces have enabled you thus to overcome all difficulties and to seize upon the enemy's capital, which now lies at our mercy. All the people, both European and native, unjustly held captive by the King of Ashantee, are now at liberty, and you have proved to this cruel and barbarous people that England is able to punish her enemies, no matter what their strength in numbers or position."

7.—The result of the elections up to this date put all doubt about a Conservative success beyond question. The administration of Mr. Gladstone, wrote the *Daily News*, was practically at an end, while the *Telegraph* observed that no one was needed to instruct the Prime Minister as to the course which his duty and dignity prescribed. The Conservatives had now gained 42 seats, and the Liberals only 27. In the city of London 3 Conservatives were returned in room of 3 Liberals, and Mr. Goschen only got in as "minority member." In the Tower Hamlets Mr. Ayrton was thrown out, and a Conservative headed the poll. They also gained 1 seat at Chelsea and Westminster, and 2 at Brighton and Nottingham. At Kilmarnock Mr. Bouverie was thrown out by a more advanced Liberal, and Renfrewshire was restored to that party by the unexpected victory of Colonel Mure over Colonel Campbell, who thus was never afforded an opportunity of taking his seat in the House.

— "Ten Days' Mission" services commence in London, the first preacher being the Bishop of the Diocese.

— Died, aged 96, John Christian Schetky, marine painter, a fellow pupil at Edinburgh High School with Scott, Brougham, and Horner.

— Sir Garnet Wolseley forwards a dispatch to the Colonial Office announcing that the main object of the expedition had been perfectly secured, and that the troops, now on their homeward march, would embark immediately at Cape Coast Castle for England. "The whole scheme," wrote Sir Garnet, "of Ashantee politics is so based upon treachery that the King does not either understand any other form of negotiation, or believe it possible that others can have honest intentions. Under these circumstances, my Lord, it became clear that a treaty would be as valueless to us as it was difficult to obtain. Nothing remained but to leave such a mark of our power to punish as should deter from future aggression a nation whom treaties do not bind. I had done all I could to avoid the necessity, but it was forced upon me. I gave orders for the destruction of the palace and the burning of the city. I had at one time also contemplated the destruction of the Bantoma, where the sacred ashes of former kings are entombed, but this would have involved a delay of some hours. Very heavy rain had fallen. I feared the streams might have risen in my rear sufficiently to seriously delay my march. I considered it better, therefore, not to risk further the health of the troops, the wet weather having already threatened seriously to affect it. The demolition of the place was complete. From all that I can gather I believe that the result will be such a diminution in the prestige and military power of the Ashantee monarch as may result in the break up of the kingdom altogether."

8.—Died, aged 67, Herman Merivale, C.B., Under-Secretary of State for India.

9.—Came on for trial in the Court of Queen's Bench, the case of Poles *v.* Goodlake, an action for libel against the publisher of the *Times*, in which newspaper the plaintiff, a Pole by birth, had been accused of obtaining by false representations certain papers from the house of M. Thiers when in the hands of the Commune, and endeavouring thereafter to extort money by threatening to publish the same. Plaintiff admitted in examination that he had along with Mr. Dallas obtained access to the house of M. Thiers, and saved certain writings and bronzes specially desired by the family, but the whole had been faithfully given up to their owners. On the 10th a verdict was returned for the plaintiff with 50*l.* damages.

— Died, aged 66, Dr. David Frederick Strauss, chief of the German Rational School, and author of "Leben Jesu."

— Died, aged 76, M. Michelet, French historian.

10.—Election returns show the Liberal gains at 27, and the Conservatives 78. In South Essex 2 seats were won by the latter, in West Gloucestershire 1, and in Edinburghshire 1.

— Addressing his constituents at Buckingham, Mr. Disraeli expressed sympathy with the difficulties experienced by Government in mitigating the distress in India. "There was nothing," he said, "in politics so difficult as for a Government to undertake to feed a people. Philosophers, indeed, who decide upon all subjects upon abstract principles, have laid it down that, under no circumstances, should such an office be undertaken by a Government. It is said that the moment a Government enters the market as a purchaser, with a view of feeding a nation, all private dealers disappear, because it is impossible for private dealers to compete with a purchaser who does not seek a profit. It is said, on the other hand, that if all private dealers retire, the Government has a monopoly, and, being the on'y purchaser, must necessarily obtain very great means ; but we must remember this, that the moment a Government undertakes to feed a people, although the Government may have no competitor in the market, the Government is obliged to give any price for food that is demanded. The Government has no option the moment it publicly undertakes that duty. Commerce is by no means an affair of gross purchase. It is an affair also of traditionary skill and of established connection, and the Government that

undertakes to feed a people by going into the market merely to purchase will often find that its resources are extremely limited, that with boundless capital it can only obtain, comparatively speaking, scanty supplies, and that in the distribution of them it will encounter difficulties unknown to the private trader." In concluding his address, Mr. Disraeli asked the electors of Bucks to repose their confidence in him for the tenth time. The county of Bucks had always been a political county, and he hoped would maintain its reputation in that respect. Since the accession of the House of Hanover there had been thirty Prime Ministers in England, and five of them had been supplied by the county of Buckingham. Surely then, he said, there must be something in the air of Buckinghamshire that was favourable to the growth of Prime Ministers.

12.—Despatch received at the Foreign Office making mention of the rumours at Zanzibar of the death of Dr. Livingstone in the interior, and the removal of his body in the direction of the coast.

— Died, aged 66, Sir Francis Pettit Smith, to whom was generally conceded the merit of first applying the screw for the propulsion of vessels.

— The Sioux Indians again rising against the United States troops, General Sherman instructs the officer in command :—"You will be justified in collecting the most effective force possible, even if you draw cavalry from Fort Riley by rail to Cheyenne, to march to the Red Cloud Agency, striking every party of Indians that opposes. Every Indian who has marauded south of the North Platte should be demanded and held as accomplices in the murder of Lieutenant Robinson. Their ponies must be very poor now, and the game must be scarce, so the occasion to give the Sioux a lesson long merited seems to me favourable. My own opinion is that the Sioux should never again have an agency away from the Missouri river."

13.—The Emperor of Austria arrives at St. Petersburg on a visit to the Czar.

— Treaty of Fommarah entered into with the King of Ashantee, providing for the payment of an indemnity, the renunciation of superiority over certain districts, and the keeping up of a road from Coomassie to the coast for purposes of trade.

— The Pantechnicon, in Motcomb Street, Belgrave Square, a large building occupying about two acres of ground, and used as a repository for furniture and all kinds of goods, destroyed by fire, together with its valuable contents. The fire broke out about 4.30 p.m., and spread so rapidly that in a very short time all hope was lost of saving any large portion of the property. The pictures of Sir Richard Wallace, M.P., deposited in the building, were supposed to be worth 150,000*l.* ; those of Mr. Winn Ellis, 200,000*l.* ; Sir Seymour Fitzgerald, M.P., 200,000*l.*, many being portraits painted by Sir Joshua Reynolds. Several well-known valuable paintings by Turner and other masters were among those destroyed. People flocked from all parts of London to the scene of the fire, and at one time it was thought as many as 100,000 were present in the surrounding streets. Touching the origin of the fire, nothing was ever exactly ascertained. All that the proprietors knew was that there was a strong smell of burning in the afternoon, traced to a warehouse on the second floor in the northern extremity of the building, where some goods were found to be on fire close to the wall. The foreman and the workpeople, twenty or thirty in number, at once got out their manual engine and tried to extinguish the flames; but they had difficulty in getting water, and were unable to make any visible effect. With the exception of the offices at the main entrance (uninjured), there was not a gaslight on the premises. The building was, as a rule, closed at dusk, and the only lights allowed afterwards were safety-lamps carried by the men, and lighted in a room set apart for that purpose alone. There was a water tank of great size on the roof, while there were smaller tanks on the various floors, and hose ready for use, and a manual fire-engine all kept on the premises.

14.—Mr. Bouverie writes to his old constituents that he had valued their confidence greatly, "and should have been proud to retain it, but I should never have been willing to purchase it, at the cost of my self-respect, by silence at priestly oppression, by subservience to an unscrupulous local faction, or by stimulated approbation in Parliament of acts and methods of administration which, in spite of the prevalence of Liberal opinions, have alienated the country, have disorganized the Liberal party, and have at last destroyed a once powerful Government."

15.—The Dutch troops make another successful attack on the Atchinese, and secure, it was thought, the submission of the district west of the Atchin river.

— In the course of a discussion in the German Parliament on the new Military Bill, Field-Marshal von Moltke pointed out how necessary it was for every great State, and especially for Germany, to have a numerous and powerful army. "What we acquired in the space of six months we shall have to protect by force of arms for half a century. France is imitating all the German army arrangements. How, then, can we give up what our opponents are adopting; it is her duty to act on the defensive." Count von Moltke proceeded to enumerate the measures taken by France for increasing her armament, notwithstanding the fact that the majority of the French people were convinced of the necessity of peace. He concluded by saying:—"We have become a powerful nation, but we remain a peaceable people. We require an army, but not for purposes of conquest." The bill was referred to a committee of twenty-eight members.

16.—The result of the elections placing the Government in a hopeless minority, a Cabinet Council was called to-day, and a resolution concurred in to resign at once without waiting for the meeting of Parliament.

— Sir Garnet Wolseley writes that King Koffee had sent a thousand ounces of gold to his camp as a first instalment of indemnity with a request for peace.

— Dr. Beke reports from the Gulf of Akaba that he has found the true Mount Sinai one day's journey north-east of Akaba. On the summit the traveller found the remains of sacrificed animals, and lower down some Sinaitic inscriptions, which he copied.

17.—Mr. Gladstone waits upon her Majesty at Windsor Castle, and tenders the resignation of himself and colleagues, which her Majesty was graciously pleased to accept. Mr. Disraeli left town soon after eleven o'clock this morning for Windsor Castle, in obedience to the Queen's commands received last evening. The right hon. gentleman arrived at Windsor at noon, and at once proceeded to the Castle. He was much cheered both on his arrival and departure.

— The London "Mission" closed by a thanksgiving service in St. Paul's.

— More favourable news received of a rainfall over various parts of the starving districts in Bengal.

— Advices from Havannah announce that a battle lasting seven hours had been fought at Narango, in the central department, between General Bascones, at the head of 3,000 Spanish troops, and 5,000 insurgents under the command of the Marquis Santalucia. The Cuban insurgents were defeated. The Spaniards lost 50 killed and 180 wounded.

— Information received by way of Calcutta that the Yarkund mission had been favourably received at Kashgar.

18.—The elections being over, parties were found to be divided thus:—England and Wales, 296 Conservatives, 193 Liberals; Scotland, 19 Conservatives, 41 Liberals; Ireland, 36 Conservatives, 68 Liberals (including a double return from Athlone, and counting all Home Rulers as Liberals). Total Conservative majority, 51. In the general contest they had won 98 seats against 38 by the Liberals. Election petitions were lodged in the case of 21 returns. Of the old members 215 failed to secure re-election. Among the Ministerial candidates recently rejected were Mr. Chichester Fortescue at Louth, and Lord Advocate Young at Wigtown, the latter by a mistake in reckoning up the votes. It was noticed that for the first time since 1829 no Roman Catholic was returned by any English or Scotch constituency. Assuming Louth and Galway as vacant, 49 of the 101

Irish seats were filled by Catholics, and 20 of these entered the House for the first time.

18.—The Emperor of Germany writes to Earl Russell :—"It is incumbent on me to be the leader of my people in a struggle maintained through centuries past by German emperors of earlier days, against a power the domination of which has in no country of the world been found compatible with the freedom and welfare of nations—a power which, if victorious in our days, would imperil, not in Germany alone, the blessings of the Reformation, liberty of conscience, and the authority of the law. I accept the battle thus imposed upon me in fulfilment of my kingly duties and in firm reliance on God, to whose help we look for victory, but also in the spirit of regard for the creed of others and of evangelical forbearance which has been stamped by my forefathers on the laws and administration of my States. . . . . I was sure, and I rejoice at the proof afforded me by your letter, that the sympathies of the people of England would not fail me in this struggle—the people of England, to whom my people and my Royal House are bound by the remembrance of many a past and honourable struggle maintained in common since the days of William of Orange."

— The Deputies from Alsace-Lorraine protest before the German Parliament against the annexation of that territory to Germany without consulting the inhabitants.

19.—At a Home Rule meeting in Dublin, Mr. Butt announces that 59 members pledged to that principle had been returned for Ireland, and 24 by England.

— Mr. Young, late Lord Advocate, announced to have accepted a Scotch judgeship in succession to Lord Cowan, retired.

20.—Mr. Disraeli submits his Cabinet to her Majesty, showing himself as First Lord of the Treasury, his colleagues (confined to twelve high officials) being—Lord Chancellor, Lord Cairns ; Lord President of the Council, Duke of Richmond ; Lord Privy Seal, Lord Malmesbury ; Foreign Affairs, Lord Derby ; India, Lord Salisbury ; the Colonies, Lord Carnarvon ; War, Mr. Gathorne Hardy ; Home, Mr. R. A. Cross; Admiralty, Mr. Ward Hunt ; Chancellor of the Exchequer, Sir S. Northcote ; Postmaster-General, Lord John Manners. The following appointments afterwards received the royal sanction :—Attorney-General, Sir John Karslake ; Solicitor-General, Sir Richard Baggallay ; Vice-President of the Council, Lord Sandon ; Lord-Lieutenant of Ireland, Duke of Abercorn ; Chief Secretary for Ireland, Sir Michael H. Beach ; Lord Advocate, Mr. E. S. Gordon ; Chancellor of the Duchy of Lancaster, Colonel Taylor ; First Commissioner of Works, Lord Henry Lennox ; President of Board of Trade, Sir Charles Adderley ; President of Local Government Board, Mr. Sclater-Booth ; Secretary of Local Government Board, Mr. Clare S. Read ; Judge-Advocate and Paymaster-General,

Mr. Cave ; Under-Secretary for Foreign Affairs, Hon. Robert Bourke ; Under Home Secretary, Sir H. Selwin-Ibbetson ; Under-Secretary, India Office, Lord George Hamilton ; Under-Secretary, Colonial Office, Mr. James Lowther ; Secretary of Admiralty, Hon. Algernon Egerton ; Civil Lord of the Admiralty, Sir Massey Lopes ; Secretaries to the Treasury, Mr. W. H. Smith and Mr. Hart Dyke. The Royal Household :—Mistress of the Robes, Duchess of Wellington ; Lord Chamberlain, Marquis of Bath ; Master of the Horse, Earl of Bradford.

— The French Minister of the Interior issues a circular designed to counteract the proceedings of Imperial partizans engaged in inviting friends to proceed to England to render homage to the Prince Imperial on coming of age. "Henceforth you will not permit any canvassing in public places to obtain adhesions to the proposed journey to England, or any passionate discussions which might result therefrom, and, perhaps, cause regrettable disorder. Our duty is to avert anything that might disturb the tranquillity so necessary to all interests, and, above all, those of the working classes in the present commercial and industrial crisis prevailing in the country."

20.—The Prussian House of Lords pass the Civil Marriage Bill by a majority of 89 to 51.

— Blockade on the northern coast of Spain suspended till 5th March.

— Died, aged 82, Sir Sydney Cotton, G.C.B., Governor of Chelsea Hospital, a survivor of the Mahratta war of 1817.

— Collision early this morning near Wigan between the Scotch limited mail and a broken-down coal train, causing the death of the engine-driver and fireman, and a severe shaking to many passengers.

21.—Legal proceedings instituted by the Prussian Government against the Moravian Bishop of Olmütz for transgressing the new ecclesiastical laws in the Silesian parishes belonging to his diocese.

— At a meeting of the London and North-Western Railway Company, the Chairman states that the directors had adopted the block system up to June 1872, on 266 miles of their main line, and up to December 1873, they had extended the block system to 732 miles of their main line, to 78 miles of junction lines, and 135 miles of branch lines ; and they could now boast of having altogether 1,200 miles of their railways worked on the block system. The company ran last year 600,000 passenger trains, and there were thirty-five accidents. This year they were running 700,000 passenger trains. Out of the thirty-five accidents, twenty-eight had been attributed to the negligence or mistakes of servants. The Chairman contended that on the whole people were safer travelling on the London and North-Western Railway system than they were travelling in their own carriages through the streets, walking through the streets, or staying in their own houses. At the Great Northern meeting the same day, intimation was made that the claims for personal injury, damages, and loss of goods during the year amounted to 24,905*l.*

— Severe fighting between the Carlists and Republicans on the heights of Sommorostro.

22. — Intelligence received of Sir Garnet Wolseley's entry into Coomassie, and the signing of a treaty of peace with the Ashantees. The European prisoners, it was also said, had been released and sent off to Cape Coast.

23. — Intimation given by circular that Parliament will meet for the election of Speaker and the swearing in of members on the 5th March.

— Died, aged 60, Shirley Brooks, editor of *Punch* since 1870, a popular novelist, and writer of many pleasing verses.

24. — The new Ministers officially gazetted. It was also announced that the Marquis of Westminster had been created Duke of Westminster. Other elevations at this time were Mr. Chichester Fortescue to be Lord Carlingford, Mr. Cardwell to be Lord Cardwell of Ellerbeck, and Sir John Pakington to be Lord Hampton.

— By a majority of 9 to 4 the First Division of the Court of Session affirm Lord Gifford's judgment in the Murthly succession case, finding that a marriage had been contracted between the prisoner, Miss Robertson, and the late Major Stewart.

— Died, aged 76, Rev. Thomas Binney, a popular Nonconformist divine, called to the congregation meeting in the King's Weighhouse, near the Monument, in 1829.

25. — The Mansion House Indian Famine Relief Fund stated to have reached 25,000*l.* Most of the other large towns in the kingdom also commence to forward money for the relief of the starving natives.

— Died, Major Charles Adams, Professor of Military History at the Staff College, Sandhurst.

— Decided in the Sheriff Court of Lanarkshire the case of Hopps *v.* Long, involving the question as to the relations now existing between alleged blasphemy and statute law. The defender, a Unitarian clergyman, had put forth a "Life of Jesus for Young Disciples," which he republished in its entirety with notes and comments at half the cost of the original. The defender alleged that the pursuer could not claim the protection of the law for the book, as it was blasphemous and heretical, denying, tacitly or expressly, the divinity of Christ. To this the pursuer replied that, apart from the fact that it was written by a Unitarian, and set forth the Unitarian view of the Saviour's life, a more unobjectionable book did not exist. Mr. Sheriff Buntine declared the interim interdict, which Hopps had obtained, perpetual, and ordered Long to pay

158

the costs. He held that the doctrine of Jesus Christ being the second person of the Trinity was statute law, yet the public were entitled to criticise and controvert any part of the statute law, provided they did it in such a way as not to endanger the public peace, safety, or morality.

26. — Dr. Beke writes to the *Times* that the mountain which he identified with the Sinai of the Pentateuch was Mount Bárghir, one of the principal masses of the chain of mountains bounding the valley of the Arabah on the East, which are marked on our maps as the Mountains of Shera, but of which the correct designation is the Mountains of Shafeh; those of Shera being a chain extending from that of Shafeh in a direction from north-west to south-east. "My astonishment and gratification may be better imagined than described when I learnt that this Mount Bárghir is the same as a mysterious Jebel-e'-Nur, or 'Mountain of Light,' of which I had heard vaguely in Egypt as being that whereon the Almighty spoke with Moses, and which, from its position and other circumstances, is without doubt the Sinai of Scripture; although, from its manifest physical character, it appears that my favourite hypothesis of Mount Sinai being a volcano must be abandoned as untenable."

27. — Lord Cairns sworn in as the new Lord Chancellor.

— Professor Huxley delivers his address as Lord Rector of Aberdeen University, selecting for his subject "University Education," and earnestly advocating the introduction of physical science in the University curriculum.

— The Court of Appeal at Paris give judgment in the case of Naundorff against the Comte de Chambord, the claimant in this case seeking to have it declared that her son was entitled to all the position and rights which belonged to his father and her husband the Dauphin, son of Louis XVI., generally believed to have died in the Temple, June 8th 1795, but now alleged to have escaped by a twofold substitution. Satisfied with the proof of death produced, the Court confirmed the judgment appealed against, and fined the Naundorff heir accordingly.

28. — End of the Tichborne trial, the Lord Chief Justice concluding his charge to the jury on this the 188th day of investigation. The law, said his lordship, required the unanimous verdict of twelve men before a verdict of guilty or not guilty is pronounced, and if a single juryman is satisfied, after having given every attention to the case that he cannot find the verdict of the rest, he does right to stand by his conviction. "Then we must recollect that it is his duty to give the case every possible consideration, and he may start with a fair presumption that one individual is more likely to be wrong than the eleven from whom he differs, and think of his own judgment with humility and diffidence." The jury retired at twelve o'clock, and after less than half an hour's absence, returned with a verdict of guilty. The main allegations against the defendant were—1. That he did falsely swear that he was Roger Charles Tichborne ; 2. That he did falsely swear that he had in July or August 1851, seduced Catherine Mary. Elizabeth Doughty, only daughter of Sir Edward Doughty, deceased ; 3. That he did falsely swear that he was not Arthur Orton, the son of George Orton, of Wapping, deceased. The jury found him guilty on all these three allegations. As a special finding, the jury further desired to "express their opinion that the charges of bribery, conspiracy, and undue influence brought against the prosecution in this case are entirely devoid of foundation, and they regret exceedingly the violent language and demeanour of the leading counsel for the defendant in his attacks upon the conduct of the prosecution and upon several of the witnesses produced in the case." The Lord Chief Justice thereupon sentenced the Claimant to fourteen years' penal servitude, and pending the charge of perjury against the witness Luie, authorised his removal in the meantime to Newgate.

March 1.—Bombardment of Bilbao by the Carlists, as many as 200 shells daily being now reported as thrown into the town.

2.—The Duke and Duchess of Edinburgh receive an enthusiastic reception at Berlin on their homeward journey from St. Petersburg to London.

— Boiler explosion at Alderman Thomson's Mills, Blackburn, causing the death of twelve workpeople, and serious injury to about twenty.

— Died, aged 86, Dr. Neil Arnott, F.R.S., Physician Extraordinary to the Queen, and inventor of the useful stove and ventilator bearing his name.

— Died, aged 86, Rev. J. W. Bellamy, B.D., Vicar of Sellinge, Hythe, formerly Head Master of Merchant Taylors' School.

3.—A proposal being made in the German Parliament to repeal the clause of the Alsace-Lorraine Administrative Law, giving the Governor power to institute a state of siege, Prince Bismarck said :—"We never expected that the Alsatians would greet our institutions with applause. People have to accustom themselves to foreign institutions, and when you have been with Germany for 200 years, the results of your comparisons will be in Germany's favour. From the acquaintance I have made of the gentlemen here, I believe I should seriously endanger my responsibility if I were to diminish the power of the Governor of the Imperial Province. In France there are twenty-eight Departments in a state of siege. Remember how we came to annex Alsace-Lorraine. What we required was a bulwark to defend our rights. The Alsatians are certainly not free from blame for what has occurred. They participated in the restlessness which led to the war that broke out against us."

3.—The Duke of Abercorn sworn in as Lord-Lieutenant of Ireland at Dublin Castle.

— Ex-Lord Advocate Young takes his seat in the Scotch Outer House, and formally hears two cases as Lord Probationer.

— Official announcement of the new peerages, Mr. Cardwell as Viscount Cardwell of Ellerbeck ; Mr. Chichester Fortescue as Baron Carlingford of Carlingford ; Sir T. Freemantle as Baron Cottesloe of Swanbourn ; and Mr. E. Hammond as Baron Hammond of Kirkella. Viscount Sydney was also advanced to the dignity of an Earl in recognition of his services as Lord Chamberlain of Her Majesty's Household.

— Died at Brighton, aged 64, Dr. Forbes Winslow, among the first authorities on brain disease, and for many years editor of the "Quarterly Journal of Psychological Medicine and Mental Pathology."

— The Dutch troops reported to have been so successful at Atchin as to lead most of the Sultan's allies to withdraw their aid.

4.—The "reception" of M. Ollivier said to be indefinitely postponed by the French Academy on the ground of the eulogistic tribute he intended offering to the memory of the late Emperor. "Had Lamartine," he wrote, "known him better, had he had experience of his great heart, of the charm and justness of his mind, of the gentleness of his character ; if he had become the confidant of his thoughts solely directed to the public good and to the relief of those who suffer ; if he had been witness to the loyalty with which he put in practice the freest institutions our country had yet known ; if he had beheld him modest in prosperity and august after misfortune, he would have done more than render him justice, he would have loved him."

— The steamer *Bothnia*, 4,500 tons burthen, the largest of the Cunard fleet, launched from the yard of Messrs. Thomson, at Dalmuir, on the Clyde.

— Under the signature "E.P.B.," the late member for the Kilmarnock burghs contributes to the *Times* a "Chapter of Contemporary History," in which a parallel or contrast was drawn between the recent Liberal defeat and the result of several former general elections. The writer thought there had been "no Liberal defeat like this since 1710, when Dr. Sacheverell was rashly impeached, at the instance of some angry Whig Ministers, and in spite of the prudent counsels of Lord Somers, and when the Tory Ministry, who then replaced them, unexpectedly dissolved the Parliament, in order to catch the ball of popularity at its bound. That election resulted in a decisive Tory victory." Having referred to the elections of 1784, 1841, and 1865, he proceeded to accuse Mr. Gladstone of having "at one blow (the dissolution) destroyed both his Administration and his party, and they are both wiped out of existence." He next endeavoured to account for the failure of the Government : "I say nothing of its minor delinquencies, of its failures in administration—these, though remarkable in men of conspicuous talent, do not tell very widely or deeply on general national opinion ; but I set down the failure to the wounds which it has inflicted on the great characteristic attributes of the English people —their pride, their jealous reverence for established institutions, their singular love of moderation." On this last head " E. P. B." wrote, "If in the daily conduct of ordinary public business a Prime Minister should fail to create confidence in his steady good sense and moderation by a constant exhibition of those gifts, the occasion will surely be seized by them, as it has been just now, to show that they no longer trust him, but that they wish for some other Minister, who can better appreciate their peculiar national instincts and represent their national character."

4.—Canon Gregory's motion to prohibit the London School Board from erecting new schools near denominational ones presently in existence rejected by 24 votes to 21.

5.—The new Parliament opened by Commission, and Mr. Brand unanimously elected Speaker on the motion of Mr. Chaplin, seconded by Lord George Cavendish. Mr. Gladstone was also present, and spoke strongly in favour of the nomination. Next day Mr. Brand presented himself in the House of Lords for formal acceptance by her Majesty, and in name of the Commons laid claim to the exercise of 'their undoubted rights and privileges. "I humbly," he said, "petition her Majesty that she will be graciously pleased to allow us freedom of speech in debate, freedom from arrest for our persons and servants, and, above all, freedom of access to her Majesty's royal person whenever occasion may require ; and that the best construction may be put upon all our proceedings. For myself, my lords, I desire that the m st favourable construction may be put upon my acts, and that whatever I may do in error may be attributed to myself alone, and not to her Majesty's faithful Commons." The Lord Chancellor rejoined : "Mr. Speaker, we have it further in command to inform you that her Majesty doth most readily confirm all the rights and privileges which have ever been granted to her Majesty's Commons by any of her Royal predecessors. With respect to yourself, sir, though her Majesty is sensible that you stand in no need of such assurance, her Majesty will ever put the most favourable construction on your words and actions." The Speaker retired, and the Lord Chancellor then took his seat on the woolsack. New members were thereafter sworn in, and writs authorized to be issued for vacancies occasioned by acceptance of office.

— The Claimant's witness Luie or Lundgren again examined at Bow Street, and committed on a charge of perjury extending over his entire evidence in the Tichborne case.

6.—The two Houses of Convocation of Canterbury attend Divine service in St. Paul's, and afterwards hold a brief sederunt for the transaction of business. In the Lower House, Archdeacon Bickersteth, re-elected Prolocutor for the fourth time, reviewed the work of Convocation during the last five years, and expressed satisfaction that the English Church condemned both the way in which the so-called Œcumenical Council was called together and the conclusions at which it arrived. The Athanasian Creed, by means of the Synodical Declaration, he regarded as set at rest for at least a generation, and he then passed on to speak of the great work set on foot at the last Convocation—the revision of the English version of the Holy Scriptures—and said that labour of deep anxiety and responsibility, unless the existence of this Convocation were cut prematurely short by some convulsion, would by it be presented to the critical judgment of Biblical students.

— Stewart's cotton mill, Musselburgh, destroyed by fire, with much valuable machinery.

7.—News received of the burning of Coomassie, and flight of King Koffee.

— The Duke and Duchess of Edinburgh arrive at Gravesend from Antwerp, and proceed to Windsor amid great manifestations of public enthusiasm.

— In a letter to the Emperor Francis Joseph, the Pope protests against the Church in Austria being handed over to dishonourable servitude, and his Catholic subjects visited with deep affliction. His Holiness in another letter condemned the new ecclesiastical laws as designed to bring the Church into most ruinous subjection to the arbitrary power of the State. He admitted that the Austrian laws appeared moderate as compared with those enacted by Prussia, but they were of the same spirit and character, and paved the way for the destruction of the Church in Austria as well as in Prussia. The Pope renewed his protest against the rupture of the Concordat, and described the assertion that a change was brought about in the Church by the promulgation of the dogma of Infallibility as a pernicious pretext.

9.—The French National Assembly, by a majority of 41 votes, agree to impose a tax of five per cent. on all goods conveyed by luggage trains.—M. Ledru-Rollin took his seat in the Assembly to-day.

— Henderson's jute-works, Dundee, destroyed by fire.

10.—The German Federal Council gives its sanction to the Ecclesiastical Bill proposed by Government providing for the punishment of refractory bishops.

— MM. de Lesseps and Baranowski submit to the Russian Government a definite scheme for the construction of a Russian and Central

Asian railway. They proposed that the line should go by Saratov and Kieff rather than by Orenburg and Katharinenburg.

10.—The Parliament of Victoria dissolved, the Ministry appealing to the colony on the one issue of constitutional reform. They desired, it was said, to bring both Chambers of the Legislature in harmony, and proposed the Norwegian plan—that on the rejection of bills by either House, both Houses should sit together to consider such bills.

11.—Died at Washington, aged 63, Charles Sumner, an eminent American politician.

— The *Record* announces (mistakenly) the intended resignation of the Archbishop of Canterbury.

— King Koffee's state umbrella, taken from the Royal Palace at Coomassie, presented to the Queen at Windsor by Lieutenant Wood, who had been commissioned by Sir Garnet Wolseley to bring the trophy to this country "as a humble tribute of the dutiful respect and affection borne to her Majesty by the military and naval forces engaged in the war."

12.—To modify various disquieting rumours regarding the leadership of the Liberal party, Mr. Gladstone writes to Earl Granville :—"For a variety of reasons personal to myself I could not contemplate any unlimited extension of active political service ; and I am anxious that it should be clearly understood by those friends with whom I have acted in the direction of affairs that at my age I must reserve my entire freedom to divest myself of all the responsibilities of leadership at no distant time. The need of rest will prevent me from giving more than occasional attendance in the House of Commons during the present session. I should be desirous, shortly before the commencement of the session of 1875, to consider whether there would be advantage in my placing my services for a time at the disposal of the Liberal party, or whether I should then claim exemption from the duties I have hitherto discharged. If, however, there should be reasonable ground for believing that, instead of the course which I have sketched, it would be preferable in the view of the party generally, for me to assume at once the place of an independent member, I should willingly adopt the latter alternative." Replying to an address from the Liberals of Tunstall, Mr. Gladstone wrote :— "I do not disguise from myself the importance of the verdict given at the late election, either as regards myself personally or in other and more important respects, but I neither can repent having confided in the people nor cease to confide in them similarly with reference to the contingencies of the future."

— The Queen, accompanied by the Duke and Duchess of Edinburgh and the Princess Beatrice, makes a state journey through London from Paddington to Buckingham Palace, by way of Edgware Road, Oxford and Regent Streets, Waterloo Place, Charing Cross, White-

hall, through the Horse Guards, and along the Mall. The decorations were abundant and elaborate, and the enthusiasm of the countless thousands through which the royal cortége passed apparently unchecked by the chilling frost or drifting snow showers. In the evening the City was brilliantly illuminated.

13.—Came on before Vice-Chancellor Malins the case of Dr. Hayman, of Rugby, in the form of a notice of motion that the Governing Body of the school might be restrained by an order of court for removing or dismissing the plaintiff from his office, and from electing any person in his place, or from taking any proceeding at law or otherwise for ejecting the plaintiff from his office and residence. That was demurred to, and it lay with the defendants to support their demurrer. The case continued before the court till the 21st.

— Soliciting the honour of re-election from his Buckinghamshire constituents, Mr. Disraeli writes from Downing Street, that in forming a new Administration he had recommended to the Queen "a body of gentlemen who will uphold the institutions of the country and defend the rights of every class of her Majesty's subjects. My acceptance of the office of First Lord of the Treasury vacates my seat ; but as I cannot believe that the favour of our Sovereign can be any bar to the renewed confidence of a constituency which I have served more than a quarter of a century, I again solicit the high and honourable trust of being your member in the House of Commons."

14.— James Brown, eating-house keeper, Shadwell, known in the Tichborne case as "Captain" Brown, examined by Sir T. Henry on the charge of perjury. He was afterwards committed for trial.

15.—Sunday demonstration in Hyde Park in favour of the release of Fenian prisoners, and resolutions passed calling upon Mr. Disraeli to use his influence with her Majesty for that purpose.

16.—Bonapartist demonstration at Chiselhurst on occasion of the Prince Imperial completing his eighteenth year, the age fixed by French law for his majority, and when he formally assumed the position of head and chief of his dynasty. The multitude which flocked out of London had its strength recruited from every department throughout France, and its members were furnished by no one special class of society, but from all ranks and orders in the social scale, from the working man in his blouse to the senator and officer of the Legion of Honour. For days past they had been coming across the Channel, undeterred by the inconvenience of the passage, and train after train, as it arrived at Charing Cross, had been loaded far beyond its powers by crowds of French visitors. Of eighty-seven Prefects under the Empire, sixty-five were described as present at the fête. The proceedings commenced with a service in the small church of

St. Marie, followed by the presentation of an address to the Prince Imperial, who replied to the same, and a reception of deputations, who in some instances had travelled from the extreme parts of France to offer their gifts and congratulations. The Prince was interrupted by loud acclamations when he spoke of the President of the French Republic as the "former companion of the glories and misfortunes of my father." Still louder cheers interrupted him when he claimed a plébiscite in order to settle the foundations of Government in France, and spoke of the plébiscite as at once the "safety" and the "right" of France. The audience again broke out into shouts when he declared that if the name of Napoleon should issue for the eighth time from the voting urns, he was ready to accept the responsibility imposed upon him by will of the nation.

16.—Several Government elections to-day, in all cases without opposition. At Oxford a Conservative candidate was carried in room of Viscount Cardwell, Mr. Hall polling 2,554 votes against 2,092 given to Mr. Lewis, Liberal.

— Carlist victory near Olot, Saballs capturing General Nouvilas with his column of 2,500 men, 104 guns, and 130 horses.

17.—The ship *Princess Tomawatty* run down and sunk in Gravesend Reach by the steamer *Indus*, from Southampton.

— Increasing distress reported from the famine-stricken districts of Bengal. At Tirhoot the number of persons applying at the relief works had risen from 20,000 to 100,000 in ten days.

— Died at Cannes, whither he had retired for the benefit of his health, John Candlish, a leading Nonconformist, and M.P. for Sunderland in the last Parliament.

19.—The Corporation of the City of London present an address of congratulation to the Duke and Duchess of Edinburgh. Numerous other addresses were received at this time by the Queen and their Royal Highnesses from Universities, Corporations, and other public bodies.

— Marshal Macmahon thanks the Duc de Broglie for a speech in the Assembly, in which he had so well described "the rights conferred and the duties imposed upon me by the confidence of the Assembly during the seven years." Following this letter the *Official Journal* reprinted the Marshal's speech to the Tribunal of Commerce :—"The Assembly on the 19th of January entrusted power to me for seven years. My first duty is to look to the execution of this sovereign decision. Be not uneasy, therefore.

During the seven years I shall be able to make the order of things legally established respected by all."

19.—Dr. Pusey writes to the *Times* in depreciation of the legislative action which he supposes is intended by the bishops against Ritualists. He defined his own position as that of "no Ritualist, although bound to many Ritualists by affection and by their labour for souls," and begged the bishops to be slow in entering upon a line of action which, once entered upon, would be irrevocable. "The Judicial Committee has included in its censures too many to be trodden out. As things are, they who would extirpate us would be obliged to leave their work undone. Endurance is stronger than infliction. There are too many, even for a summary process to sever from their flocks. Yet where there is one common offence, the judge who spares any condemns himself for not having spared all."

— Parliament opened by Commission, the Lord Chancellor reading a Royal Message having reference to the marriage of the Duke of Edinburgh, the termination of the war in Africa, and the steps taken for relieving the intensity of the famine in Bengal. Legislation was promised regarding the transfer of land, a re-arrangement of the judicature in Scotland and Ireland, improvement of the Master and Servants Act of 1871, (so far as the law of conspiracy was concerned), and the Act of last year regulating the sale of intoxicating drinks. In the Lords the Address was moved by Lord Lothian and seconded by Lord Cadogan, and in the Commons by Sir W. Stirling-Maxwell and Mr. R. Callender. Replying to an observation that the recent dissolution was an elaborate surprise—"a pit dug for the Conservatives into which the Liberals had fallen"—Mr. Gladstone said the justification of the dissolution was its result, showing a larger transfer of seats from one party to the other than had ever occurred since 1831. Though he could not but think the decision of the constituencies wrong, he admitted that it was emphatic. The present Government had acceded to power by the act of the country, and it had every title, therefore, to be fairly tried, without any factious opposition, and to have the opportunity of placing its policy and its principles before the country. —Mr. Disraeli replied, that although he thought Mr. Gladstone's reasons for not having called Parliament together before commencing the Ashantee expedition fallacious, he preferred not to enter into any captious controversy on a war which must be regarded as concluded, and in which the skill and energy of our commander and the admirable qualities of our soldiers had been so signally displayed. Neither did he think it incumbent on him to enter into Mr. Gladstone's defence of the dissolution. With its results Mr. Disraeli said he was quite satisfied.

INDEX.

INDEX.

THE END.